Mrs. Rowson

Reuben and Rachel

Or, tales of old times. A novel

Mrs. Rowson

Reuben and Rachel
Or, tales of old times. A novel

ISBN/EAN: 9783337148546

Printed in Europe, USA, Canada, Australia, Japan

Cover: Foto ©Andreas Hilbeck / pixelio.de

More available books at **www.hansebooks.com**

REUBEN AND RACHEL;

OR,

TALES OF OLD TIMES.

A NOVEL.

BY MRS. ROWSON,

AUTHOR OF CHARLOTTE, TRIALS OF THE HEART, FILLE DE CHAMBRE, &c. &c.

When oft, by pain or grief oppress'd,
Sweet Poesy, enchanting fair,
Has breath'd some heav'nly dulcet air,
And sooth'd my soul to rest.
But when her magic harp she strung,
And softly play'd and sweetly sung;
Bidding the tranced Fancy fly
O'er oceans vast from shore to shore;
Raising bright visions to the mental eye,
Of ages long since past, and days of yore;
List'ning enraptur'd to the strain,
Nor sickness, sorrow, care, or pain,
Was e'er remember'd more.

Published according to Act of Congress.

BOSTON:

Printed by MANNING & LORING,

For *DAVID WEST*, at Book-Store, No. 56, *Cornhill*.
Sold by him, and by the Author, in *Winter-Street*;
also by EBENEZER S. THOMAS, *Charleston*, *South-Carolina*, and by SOLOMON COTTON & Co. *Baltimore*.

1798.

PREFACE.

PREFACES in general are esteemed of so little consequence, that few persons take the trouble to read them. It is therefore an irksome task to be obliged to write, what will neither call up the attention, nor interest the feelings of those who may peruse the book; and yet, irksome as the task is, I find myself necessitated to perform it.

I am conscious that some apology ought to be made to the public, for the length of time that has intervened since I first awakened their curiosity by announcing my intention of publishing the present work. In excuse for this tardiness, I must allege several months of ill health, during which time I was incapable of pursuing my favourite amusement of writing; and since my health has been re-established, an avocation of a more serious nature has employed every hour, and almost absorbed every faculty of my mind.

When I first started the idea of writing " *Tales of Old Times*," it was with a fervent wish to awaken in the minds of my young readers, a curiosity that might lead them to the attentive perusal of history in general, but more especially the history of their native country. It has ever been my opinion, that when instruction is blended with amusement, the youthful mind receives and retains it almost involuntarily.

The first volume of the present work was written before I had entered on the arduous (though inexpressibly delightful) task of cultivating the minds and expanding the ideas of the female part of the rising generation. If I was before careful to avoid every expression or sentiment that might mislead the judgment, or corrupt the heart, what was then inclination became now an indispensable duty. And though none of my characters are so very faultless as to occasion the young reader to neglect imitating them at all, because they despair of attaining the same degree of perfection, yet they discover such an innate love of virtue, such

a thorough

a thorough contempt of vice, that the uncontaminated mind will contemplate with pleafure the beauty of the one, and fhrink with abhorrence from the deformity of the other.

As a novelift, I think it is more than probable that I have made my laft effay. Flattered and encouraged as I am in my prefent undertaking, in having the education of fo many young ladies entrufted to my care by their refpectable parents, it fhall henceforward be my ftudy confcientioufly to difcharge the truft repofed in me; and whilft I endeavour to cultivate their tafte, and improve their underftandings, implant, with the utmoft folicitude, in their innocent minds, a love for piety and virtue.

To this end, I fhall devote my leifure hours to preparing a fet of progreffive leffons in reading, for the youth of my own fex, from five years old to ten or twelve; after which period, there are a multiplicity of books, better calculated to forward the great defign of education than any my pen could produce.

It is obfervable, that the generality of books intended for children are written for boys: even Mrs. Barbauld's Leffons, which are the beft productions of the kind I ever met with, are addreffed to a boy. And as for the generality of little books which children are permitted to read, they are fuch a jumble of inconfiftencies, that though they may affift the child to learn to read with propriety, they do not convey one idea to the head that is worth retaining. Mrs. Trimmer, and fome few others, are exceptions to this remark, having laboured to correct this falfe idea, that it was neceffary to excite the young mind to the purfuit of learning by tales wonderful and indeed impoffible, and have difplayed to their view the real wonders and beauties of nature.

For my own fex only I prefume to write; and if hereafter one woman fhould think herfelf happier or wifer from the fruits of my endeavours, I fhall be overpaid for the time or pains beftowed in writing and arranging them.

REUBEN AND RACHEL;

OR,

TALES OF OLD TIMES.

CHAP. I.

An old fashioned Widow.

IT was about the middle of the fifteenth century that the lovely and amiable Isabelle found herself a widow, reduced from ease and affluence to a very confined income. Though her circumstances were altered; her mind elevated, her spirit noble and independent, was still the same. Isabelle was a native of Spain, of noble parentage, expanded heart, superior sense, and highly finished education. The beauty and elegance of her person, though striking, were but secondary objects of the esteem and admiration she was sure to excite wherever she was seen or known.

In the prime of life, having scarcely reached her 35th year, suddenly deprived of a valuable and beloved husband, she retired from a court of which she had been a principal ornament, to a castle romantically situated on the borders of Wales. Amongst her husband's vast possessions, this only had escaped the rapacious hand of his enemies. It was an antique castle which formerly had been designed for defence, as well as a habitation; but the fortress had been for many years totally neglected, and the castle itself, in many places, was fallen to decay. The ground belonging to it consisted of but a few acres, and those few were uncultivated and rude; a few clumps of old oaks were here and there scattered on the sides of the hill, on the summit of which the castle stood; and immediately surrounding it, was a small patch which once

B

had

had been used as a kitchen garden. The very trifling value annexed to this small demesne and its retired solitary situation, made it no object to the enemies of Arundel; and thither Isabelle, with her only child Columbia, retired.

An old female servant, a native of South-America, whose name was Cora, and Matthias, a veteran soldier who had grown old in the service of her husband's father, with a lively little girl particularly attached to Columbia, comprised the whole of her houshold.

Mina was the daughter of a peasant in the neighbourhood of London. The little Columbia, when quite a child, walking with her maid on the banks of the Thames, saw Mina gathering some dry sticks, which she carefully tied in a bundle, and, dropping a curtesy as Columbia passed, cried, " Blefs you, sweet little lady." Mina was just nine years of age, her complexion clear olive, a profusion of jetty hair waved in glossy ringlets over her neck, and partly shaded her expressive countenance; her full black eyes beamed unutterable softnefs, as taking up her bundle of sticks she gazed after Columbia, and cried, " Blefs you, my sweet little lady!" And " blefs you, my pretty girl," said Columbia; " why do you carry that heavy bundle?" " 'Tis wood to make a fire for mammy who is sick." " Where does your mammy live?" " There, in that little cottage by the road side." Columbia, though not eight years old, possessed a heart glowing with the strongest feelings of humanity; she darted forward, and in a moment was at the door of Mina's cottage. " You must not go in, Mifs," said the servant; " if the woman should be sick of any contagious diforder, and you should catch it, what would my lady say?" " What would she say (replied the child) if I passed by the house without inquiring what ailed the poor woman? I will go in, and then I can tell my mother, who will, I am sure, give me some money to bring to her to-morrow." Oppofition was useless; the benevolent child entered the cottage, and beheld a scene of misery, which, though she did not fully comprehend, she on her return home sufficiently explained to her mother, to obtain immedi-

ate

ate relief for the poor cottager ; and Mina was taken into the family and promoted to the honour of waiting entirely on her little benefactress.

When the lady Ifabelle retired to Auftenbury Caftle, Columbia was eleven years old. It was her mother's chief amufement to cultivate an underftanding naturally good, but where fometimes the fhoots of female vanity impeded the progrefs of thofe virtues, which nature with a liberal hand had implanted in her heart. Remarkably lovely in her perfon, fhe would frequently decorate her hair with field flowers, at the fame time placing garlands of them in fantaftic drapery about her drefs ; and then, having admired herfelf in the natural bafon, which ornamented their little garden, fly to her mother, and exclaim with tranfport, " Only fee how beautiful!" When Mina, who thought her young miftrefs almoft a divinity, would rapturoufly cry, " Don't fhe, my lady, look like an angel ?"

Ifabelle, though delighted to obferve the unbounded vivacity of her daughter, and the grateful affection of her little dependant, was fully fenfible of the neceffity there was for checking thofe ebullitions of vanity, which, if fuffered to pafs unnoticed, would effectually throw a fhade over the really valuable qualities of good fenfe, good nature, and benevolence, with which the foul of her daughter was amply ftored. Her reflections on this fubject were often painful in the extreme. Secluded from the world, fhe had no friend with whom fhe could advife. Severity (fhe would fay within herfelf) will but teach my child to confider me as a frigid monitrefs, her heart will contract and hide its thoughts from an eye that beams only with reproach ! No ; I muft watch the favourable moment, and effectually eradicate this error, by convincing her underftanding of its folly. I would be the guardian of my child's morals ; I would be her friend, and direct her in the way moft likely to fecure her prefent and future happinefs ; but for the univerfe I would not forfeit the exquifite pleafure of participating every thought, every wifh of her innocent heart.—No ; let me not, by ill timed harfhnefs, drive her guilelefs and unfufpecting nature to mean subterfuge and artifice; had she a thousand errors, she is still my child, and though it is my duty to correct, it is also my duty to conceal and palliate faults, which reflection tells me, are but the offspring of human nature.

It was ever the care of Isabelle to impress on the mind of her daughter a proper sense of a wife, benignant, overruling Power; to whom she was indebted for her being, and to whom she was accountable for her words and actions; but this was done more by example than precept. Calumny was a stranger to her lips; to perform every good work of peace and mercy was the delight of her heart. She worshipped her Creator with sincerity and fervor; no appointed hour, no set form of prayer; every blessing was received with thankfulness, every correction submitted to with patience. Amongst the most heinous offences she reckoned the misuse or neglect of time, and the total abuse or perversion of God's good gifts. Every hour of her life was usefully employed, and she dealt by every human being, as she wished them to deal by her.

It was a fine evening in the middle of September, when Columbia asked her mother to partake of some fruit in a neat arbour Matthias had dressed by the side of the pond: " You forget, my dear mother, (said she) that this is the day I always devote to joy and playfulness. This is the day on which you relieved poor Mina's mother, and brought that good girl home to live with me; and she has been so affectionate, so grateful, that to-day I am determined she shall be queen of the feast. You do not know how charming it will be! Matthias has got us some peaches, and Cora has provided cream, with baked apples and wheat cakes; and whilst you refresh yourself, Mina and I will sing and dance to divert you." Isabelle clasped the interesting child in her arms, and repaired to the appointed scene of infantile festivity.

After the collation was over, at which Mina was made to preside, Columbia told her mother, that she could never repay the pleasure her first acquaintance with that little girl had given her; " For," said she,
" before

"before I saw her diftrefs, and you, my beloved moth-er, gave me the means to relieve it, I had no idea of happinefs beyond myfelf; but that bleffed day taught me, that to confer happinefs on another, gave the mind fenfations a thoufand times more exquifite than any other enjoyment the world affords." She then, with the fwiftnefs and light bound of an antelope, fprang from her mother's embrace, and ran toward the caftle; but foon returned with Mina, decorated in all the finery they could put together. The jetty hair of Mina hung loofe and unadorned about her neck and fhoulders, whilft her little white jacket and petticoat were richly ornamented with orange lilies, poppies and blue iris.

The fine auburn treffes of Columbia were bound up with a garland of corn flowers, and autumnal daifies, whofe glowing tints vied with the colour, whilft the confcioufnefs of their becoming effect gave an addi-tional brilliancy to her eyes. Her drefs, which was compofed of light grey fatin, fhe had lightly and ele-gantly ornamented with feftoons of oak leaves, whofe dark native green was at this period of the year enliv-ened by the bright yellow, and glowing fcarlet hue, they had caught from the chilly breath of autumn. Light as the goffamer they bound over the turf, danc-ing to the notes of their own harmonious voices. The evening was ferene; the glowing fun juft touched with his broad difk the weftern ocean, whilft as he funk be-neath the fhades of night, the moon, emerging from her watry bed, reflected his departing beams, and tinged the cold eaftern fky with faffron hue, whilft here and there a fcattered cloud, dark in itfelf, caught her pale rays, and brightened by degrees to high-wrought filver.

Fatigued with the exercife of dancing, Columbia paufed upon the margin of the ftream; its furface was fmooth and even as the polifhed mirror;—her elegant form, becoming drefs, and angel countenance were re-flected in the water. She ftopped and gazed. A beam of exultation fhot from her eyes. It was the moment Ifabelle had fo long wifhed for.

	" And

"And what does my child fo intently gaze at?"
(faid fhe, approaching her daughter.)

Mina ftood at a little diftance; her own beauty was
to herfelf unknown, her whole foul was wrapt in admiring the beauty of her young lady. When the lady
Ifabelle fpoke, fhe drew near and liftened with attention. She loved her with grateful affection, and inftruction from her lips funk directly to her heart.

"And what does my child fo intently gaze at?"
faid Ifabelle, "is it the lovely form with which nature has bountifully endowed her; and which the un-
ruffled furface of the water fo beautifully reflects to her
admiring eyes? Alas, my child, if that is the object of
your admiration, how fragile is the pleafure you receive! What is it you contemplate? A fhadow; nay,
lefs than a fhadow; for beauty itfelf is but a fhadow,
fcarce feen before it is gone; and that fair femblance
you there behold is but the fhadow of a fhade. Behold, my child," continued fhe, throwing fomething
into the water, "fee that beauteous figure, how de-
formed, how difgufting; every trait of lovelinefs is
gone." Columbia turned from the ftream with an involuntary fhudder. Ifabelle continued—"Or fee, my
love, thefe flowers, with which but a few hours fince
you decorated your hair; they were then frefh-bloem-
ing and beautiful beyond defcription; behold them
now! their fweets are all exhaled, their vivid tints are
flown, and no longer valuable, you would throw them
from you with neglect and abhorrence. Even fo, my
dear Columbia, is it with the frail beauty which you
fo ardently admire. One breath from the creative
Power that gave you being, might level you with the
duft. Sicknefs, misfortune, poverty, might deprive
your eyes of their luftre, your fkin of its gloffy hue,
and fteal the luxuriant treffes from your head. Nay,
even at this moment, the cold hand of death might
fink you into nothing; and thofe who to-day looked at
you with admiration, would to-morrow turn from you
with difguft and terror. Like thefe poor flowers you
would be thrown upon the earth, be trod under foot
and forgotten."

Mina,

Mina, dropping her garland on the ground, feized her young lady by the arm, as though fhe would fave her from fo difgraceful an end. Columbia looked at her with affection, gently freed herfelf from her grafp, and, looking at the faded flowers, with eyes ftreaming with tears afked her mother, " Am I, then, of no more confequence than thefe flowers, and may I be as eafily deftroyed? Shall I be as foon reduced to nothing?" " No, my beloved girl, (faid Ifabelle) you are of a thoufand times more value than the faireft flower that ever bloomed, or the richeft gem that ever decked the brow of royalty. Look round, my love, behold this vaft, this glorious univerfe ; what beauty, what order ! How does the mind expand with wonder and delight as we contemplate the fields of ripened grain, the loaded fruit trees, verdant plains and majeftic mountains, whofe fummits feem to kifs the face of heaven. Obferve how grand, how ftrikingly fublime, appears the orb of day, juft finking in the weftern fky, which flames with crimfon, burnifhed gold and purple ; and fee, as he retires, the placid moon affumes her filent reign, whilft millions of ftars compofe her fplendid train, and glitter in the vaft expanfe of ether. Stupendous, great and wonderful as thefe appear, believe me, my child, one pure, virtuous human foul is of more value in the fight of the Creator, than all that you behold. They fhall fade away, fhall vanifh as a dream; and be no more remembered ; but the foul, ftudious to perform its duty, beneficent to its fellow creatures, and glowing with grateful, humble affection to the great Firft Caufe of all, fhall ftand fecure amid the general ruin, and rife triumphant from a finking world."

Thus did Ifabelle endeavour to infpire her daughter with a thorough contempt for all frivolous purfuits, and to give her a juft fenfe of the value of mental acquirements. From this time fhe fully comprehended of how much more confequence was the embellifhing of the mind, than the trifling decorations of the perfon. Befides, having been informed of the immortality of the foul, fhe was anxious in inqniry for the means by which fo invaluable a bleffing might be preferved ;

and

and to hint to her the danger of forfeiting fo great a privilege, was always fufficient to deter her from any thing that was wrong.

It cannot be imagined that a woman like Ifabelle could pafs at once from the court to the cottage, and be fuffered to glide unnoticed into obfcurity. Amongft the friends and intimates of her days of fplendor, were fome, tenderly attached to her from principle, and others, whom the united beauties of her mind and perfon had infpired with a wifh, to lead her again to the altar of Hymen. But Ifabelle had drank too deeply of the bitter cup of afflicten to fuffer love ever again to enter her bofom. Faithful to the memory of her regretted lord, her heart could receive no fecond impreffion. " Our love," fhe would fay, " was unfortunate, but he has left me an ineftimable pledge behind; fhall I give the daughter of my adored Arundel another father, or by extending my family duties have lefs time to beftow in rendering my child worthy of the name fhe bears? No; the fincereft proof I can give of my affection to her father, is to live a widow for her fake."

This refolve of Ifabelle being once known, and fhe ftill perfifting in fecluding herfelf from the world, fhe was foon forgotten, almoft as much as if fhe had been dead; for love cannot long exift without hope, and the gay and thoughtlefs foon forget thofe on whom the fun of profperity no longer fhines. She was left in peace to enjoy her retirement, and to cultivate un- molefted the mind of her lovely daughter.

CHAP. II.

The Dangers of Greatnefs.

AS Columbia increafed in years, her affection for her mother daily ftrengthened. It was an affection actuated by the enthufiaftic fervor of youth, yet fweetly tempered by a friendfhip which might have become maturer years. Ifabelle was to her daughter,

mother,

mother, sister, friend; every tender connexion combined in one. Never did child more love or fear a parent; yet her fear did not proceed from the apprehension of punishment or severe correction. But to see her mother frown, to be told she had offended her, and to be spoken to with coldness, gave her such inexpressible anguish, that the thought at any time was sufficient to fill her eyes with tears.

As she advanced towards womanhood, she could not but observe the extreme pensiveness of her mother's disposition; the pursuits and pleasures of childhood gradually lost their charms, she more frequently sought the society of Isabelle, and when sometimes she surprised her in tears, she would sink on her knees before her, and, folding her arms round her waist, cry, "Why, my beloved mother, will you confine your sorrows to your own breast, why not repose them in the bosom of your child? Let me share them, my mother, and in sharing soothe them." Isabelle would faintly smile at these effusions of her daughter's tenderness, and as she kissed the affectionate girl tell her, it was too early in life for her to be acquainted with sorrow, though she could feel it only from the tenderness of her nature, leading her to compassionate the sufferings of others.

"I am not so happy as I formerly was, my dear Mina," said Columbia to her attendant one evening as they were walking in the garden; "I see my mother daily sinking under the weight of afflictions I can neither comprehend or alleviate. Yesterday I tremblingly asked her, if I was the cause of her sorrow; she pressed me to her heart and said, in some measure I was. Alarmed, I inquired what I had done to offend her. Nothing, she replied; you are my only comfort, my greatest blessing, and I cannot but lament——Her tears at that moment impeded her words, and when she recovered her voice, she bade me leave her. I obeyed; but still I have a weight upon my heart, an anxious, restless wish to know, how without offending I can cause her so much affliction."

Mina could not satisfy her young lady's curiosity; she could only kiss her hands, and in a voice rendered
exquisitely

exquifitely foft by grateful affection, declare it was impoffible her dear little benefactrefs could offend any
one!

But though Mina was ignorant of the caufe of Ifabelle's tears, Cora, the Indian fervant, was not equally
fo.   She faw Columbia partook of her mother's depreffion, without underftanding the caufe; and the loquaci-
ty naturally prevalent in perfons of an advanced age,
made her eagerly watch for an opportunity to inform
the innocent girl of all fhe knew.   The moment long
fought at length arrived.   Columbia had frequently obferved her mother weeping over papers which fhe took
from a private drawer in an efcritoire which ftood in
her bed-chamber, and which in no other part was locked, except that which fhe moft wifhed to explore. One
day coming fuddenly into the room, fhe faw her gazing
at a portrait which fhe preffed to her lips, raifing her
eyes toward heaven with a fort of reverential awe.
" May I not, my dear mother," faid fhe, " behold the
object that feems at once to excite both grief and exultation."   Ifabelle turned the portrait towards her; it was
an Indian maid habited in the manner of her country;
but in habiliments that befpoke her of elevated rank.
Her jetty hair, which flowed in profufion round her
face and over her neck, was ornamented with a coronet
of pearl and gold; her thin white robe was clafped at
the bofom with ftuds of the fame valuable materials,
and her arms, which were naked to the fhoulders, were
in feveral places bound with bands of filver and coral.

" This," faid Ifabelle, as fhe prefented it to her daughter, " is the portrait of your grandmother; by birth a
queen, the only child of a monarch whofe wealth had
no bounds, and who, far from the haunts of thofe who
call themfelves civilized people, reigned unmolefted, till
the adventurous fpirit of your great anceftor Columbus
prompted him to feek in diftant feas for unknown worlds.
Oh, fublime and too daring fpirit," fhe continued, whilft
her raifed eyes gliftened with the tear of extorted remembrance, " why wert thou endowed with qualities,
which ferved but to ftir up in the breafts of thine enemies
the malignant fiend Envy.   Why! whilft thou wert labouring

bouring to benefit and enlighten posterity, wert thou
sealing thy own ruin!"

The portrait dropped from her hand, and her head
rested on the shoulder of her child. "Oh! my daughter," cried she enthusiastically, as her tears subsided,
"whilst I glory in the qualities with which it has pleased
Heaven to endow your mind and person, I cannot but
tremble for your future fate; for to possess superior
beauty, sense or genius, is but to excite the wonder of
the ignorant, and the envy of little minds, whilst those
who are wise, or great in their own conceit, will wound
your feelings with contempt or ridicule, which your
own good nature and sensibility will not permit you to
retaliate. I cannot proceed, my child; my powers
are not at present adequate to the task of recounting the
misfortunes of your family." Isabelle paused for a moment, then tenderly kissed Columbia, and leaving the
portrait in the hands of her child, passed from the apartment.

. Sinking upon the seat her mother had left unoccupi-
ed, one hand supporting her head as her elbow rested on
the escritoire, the other which held the portrait fell on
her knees, her eyes immoveably fixed on those of the
inanimate face she contemplated, Columbia sat im-
moveable as a statue, till roused by the voice of Cora.
"Look there," said she, putting the miniature towards
the aged servant; "see! my mother says it is the picture of my grandmother." "It is, it is," cried Cora,
dropping on her knees and kissing the picture with rapture; "it is the figure of my queen, my mistress, in the
dress she wore on the day she was espoused by Don
Ferdinando. Oh fatal day! unhappy hour! by that
union she sealed her own wretchedness, the ruin of her
father, the slavery of his people, and brought destruc-
tion on the heads of her adored husband and his respected parent! Ah! my sweet young mistress, I can no
longer forbear; I must tell you the fatal story of your
father's wrongs."

"Do so," said Isabelle, who at that moment returned
to her apartment; "do so, my good Cora; and let it be a
warning to my child how she quits the quiet paths of
retirement

retirement to enter on the gay or bufy fcenes of life. Here, take this key; what your memory cannot furnifh toward the recital, the papers you will find in that drawer will affift. Liften with attention, my dear child, and learn that content builds her dwelling in folitude, and peace fpreads her pinions over the cottage of the humble; whilft the paths of ambition are ftrewed with thorns, and the dwellings of the great are the habitations of mifery."

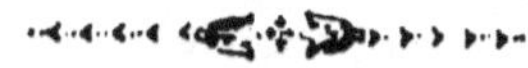

C H A P.   III.

An Old Woman's Tale interrupted.

"IT is many years ago," faid Cora, feating herfelf in an eafy chair, her right hand fpread out, as commanding attention, and every feature of her aged countenance beaming with the fatisfaction which the liberty of repeating tales of old times gave her; " it is a great many years ago, I was then fcarcely eight years old, when your great-grandfather Columbus arrived in our country; I never fhall forget it : for I can remember things which happened when I was a child much better than thofe which pafs now daily. Time fteals away our memory, but thofe things which either frightened, or furprifed us when we were young, are the laft which we forget. So as I was faying"——

"Stay, my good Cora," faid Columbia, "let us examine the papers; there may be letters which may ferve to elucidate your relation, and explain events which happened antecedent to the time of your remembrance."—— " I do not think you will find any worth reading," faid Cora, impatiently. "We will fee," replied Columbia, mildly, as fhe opened the drawer. "You may look," cried Cora fomewhat pettifhly, " but I am fure there is nothing worth attending to, till the time of Don Ferdinando's arrival in Peru and becoming enamoured of my royal miftrefs Orrabella." "Hufh, hufh, my kind friend," faid Columbia. " Here is a letter figned Columbus ;

there

there are several in the same hand writing; they must contain facts necessary for me to know, or they would not be thus carefully preserved. Be silent, and I will read them to you. Cora sat herself back in the easy chair, and shutting her eyes in token of attention, remained silent. Columbia opened the letter.

COLUMBUS TO BEATINA.

October, 1490.

I AM parted from you, my adored Beatina; but painful as the parting is, I feel it is for our future advantage. I am convinced, my beloved wife, that there are worlds beyond the narrow bounds which our natural philosophers at present prescribe. I have studied much, my lovely friend, and am almost certain, that were I supplied with vessels, men, provisions, and every thing necessary, I should make discoveries that would occasion my name to be revered in after ages; and those who blamed my lovely Beatina for giving herself to her Columbus, shall say, " You did right, Beatina; Columbus has an enterprising spirit that will carve out a fortune, even from a barren waste. For is not the ocean a barren waste? and yet even from that do I. mean to carve out for my soul's idol an empire, where she shall reign queen over all, as she does over my heart.

Why, why, my best beloved, are you not endowed with strength of frame, that your friendship might increase my fortitude in danger, and share the glorious triumph of unexpected success? Yet why should I wish you to lose the sweet feminine softness which first won, and still holds captive my heart? I know not what I wish, Beatina. You so entirely possess my thoughts, that whilst I search this vast globe for unknown worlds, to lay them at your feet when found, I would have the fame, the glory of the discovery all your own. And will it not be yours? Yes! surely yes; for you inspired the thought, prompted the search, and are the magic charm that actuates all my endeavours.

C   Tell

Tell our dear Ferdinando, that though I have by my marriage with his mother deprived him of his birthright as the only heir of an ancient and wealthy marquis, I will toil to recompenfe to him the facrifice his dear mother made to me. Sweet Beatina, do not grieve at this our long feparation ; when I return, I will return worthy of your love ; I will make my charmer worfhipped by thofe who now hold her in contempt. I am about to lay before the king of Portugal a plan for making thofe difcoveries, you have fo frequently heard me mention as more than probable. If he liftens to me, my fortune is certain ; if he treats my propofals as chimerical, the offspring of a difordered imagination, I will apply to fome other power. Dearell, have courage ; the perfevering fpirit muft in time conquer. Believe I but exift, whilft abfent from you, and think that exiftence fcarcely worth preferving but for your fake. Heaven blefs my Beatina.   C. COLUMBUS.

"That letter was written before my remembrance," faid Cora. "Very likely," replied Columbia, fcarcely noticing the date, in her eagernefs to open another.

COLUMBUS TO BEATINA.

January, 1491.

I HAVE been difappointed, my fweet friend, but be not you difheartened. Thanks be to Heaven, I left you and my darling boy in a fafe retreat, where, though not enjoying all the advantages your rank in life might demand, you have at leaft all the comforts neceffary to the real pleafures of life.

But think not, my beloved, my efteemed friend, I would wander forth in fearch of adventures, and leave the wife of my choice and the offspring of her affection to languifh out many years, ray, perhaps their whole lives, in obfcurity. No ! no ! Columbus labours not for his own advantage, but for the advantage of thofe fo nearly, fo dearly connected with him. I will leave you, my love, whenever I quit my native land, in a ftate of honour and opulence, or my fcheme fhall be totally abandoned.   If

If I fail, if in this (generally thought) romantic plan I lose my life, your father will no doubt be reconciled to you, nor slight the offspring of an only child, on account of his affinity to an unfortunate man, who, had he been monarch of the globe, would have laid his crown at Beatina's feet.

I leave my native land to-morrow, in order to solicit Ferdinand of Spain to grant me the vessels and supplies necessary for prosecuting my intended voyage. I am told the court of Spain is more enlightened than any other court in Europe.

I had, previous to my quitting you, found means to lay my plans before the British throne; but I fear they were treated as the project of a visionary; for though my brother undertook the charge, I have received no answer. Alas! Beatina, how hard it is to combat any received prejudice. The wise and learned men of past ages have held it impossible for mariners to find a passage, or proceed, without incurring immediate death, beyond certain boundaries which their confined knowledge has marked out. But I will not be withheld from the experiment. If I succeed, after ages will revere my name; if I fail, it will sink quietly into oblivion; or perhaps some future genius, enterprising and sanguine as myself, shall drop a tear to my memory, and as he laments my fate, tremble for his own. Adieu, my friend, my lovely comforter. I am more yours than my own.   C. COLUMBUS.

After this, several letters were perused by Columbia, which contained little more than a repetition of his attachment to Beatina, and accounts of his unsuccessful applications to Ferdinand, the then reigning king of Spain. At length the following called up all her attention.

COLUMBUS TO BEATINA.

May, 149:.

CONGRATULATE me, my lovely friend; I am at length successful! How have I counted the tedious months that kept me from my soul's idol; and how often have I feared that my perseverance would be of

no

no avail, and that I had facrificed ages of real happinefs (for hours are ages to the heart that loves as mine
does) to the vifionary hopes of future greatnefs.   But
I am fuccefsful.   I fhall explore thofe diftant feas, with
which my ftudies have fo well acquainted me, and in
fome unknown world feek out a kingdom of which my
Beatina fhall be queen.   Yes, you fhall be queen ; for
whatfoever world I find, be it the faireft, greateft, or the
beft the fun ever fhone on, no man fhould ever claim a
right to govern it.   For it is to a woman I owe the
means of making the great attempt.   I am fo overjoy-
ed I cannot proceed methodically ; yet I know you
languifh to learn every particular that concerns your
Columbus.

I have in former letters informed you of my hitherto
fruitlefs folicitations.   Wearied by attendance on min-
ifters and creatures, who hung about the king like bees
upon the fweet fcabious, draining it of its vital moifture
till its very root decayed, when they returned to their
hives laden with the precious ftore, regardlefs of the dying ftate of the flower from which they had extracted
both life and health ; difgufted with their unmeaning
profeffions, their hypocrify and ftupidity, I had nearly
relinquifhed the undertaking, when I one morning received an order to attend the queen's private drawing
room.   You may fuppofe I did not hefitate to obey the
fummons.   The royal Ifabelle received me with affability and encouraging fweetnefs ; fhe condefcended to
confer with me on my intended voyage, and on the
ftudies which led me to hope for fuccefs.   She liftened with attention to my reafons, and bade me attend
the levee next morning.   I went.   My royal patronefs
urged my fuit to the king with all the earneftnefs of
perfuafive eloquence.   He liftened ; but it was with
cold, almoft contemptuous filence.   Yet was fhe not
difmayed ; her fine features glowed with enthufiafm, as
fhe expreffed a prophetic affurance of fuccefs.   Her in-
terceffions were finifhed with this heroic declaration :—
" If your majefty," faid fhe, " conceives the plan too
wild, too eccentric to be countenanced, by ordering this
enterprifing man the neceffary fupplies from the public
                                        treafury ;

treafury ; and if your own private purfe will not at prefent allow of fo large a difburfement, fuffer me to raife the money on my own perfonal jewels. I befeech your majefty do not fay me nay. I want no ornaments to render me pleafing to my fovereign, and will cheerfully part with them, to benefit his fubjects, or add to his territories."

Struck with the magnanimity of the propofal, Ferdinand could no longer refufe ; he gave immediate orders for the equipment of a fleet, in which I am to proceed on my intended difcovery ; and a fum of money is to be paid to me from the treafury, to provide every neceffary for the voyage.

I fell at the feet of the royal Ifabelle, and kiffed, with grateful tranfports, the hem of her garment. She gracioufly raifed me, and with a fmile of heavenly benignity affured me, that you, my Beatina, and our darling Ferdinando, fhould be taken under her immediate protection. Haften then, my deareft, on the receipt of this ; haften to Spain, and let me introduce you to our auguft queen. I know you will partake my joy ; and if a tear does ftart at the thought of parting, I alfo know you will wipe it off unfeen, left it fhould unman the heart of your adoring.   COLUMBUS.

" Undaunted fpirit of my anceftor," cried Columbia, as fhe clofed the letter, " may you ever inhabit the bofoms of his defcendants." " But what is the next letter ?" faid Cora. She opened it, but it was only a farewel to Beatina, when he was ready to fail from Cadiz ; and by it Columbia difovered that lady and her fon were retained in the Spanifh court under the immediate protection of Ifabelle. The next was a large packet, and of fuch a nature as could not be haftily or flightly paffed over.

Isabelle, *queen of Spain, to* Beatina, *wife to* Columbus.

.Sbruary, 1493.

THOU bofom friend of the braveft man that ever lived, thy queen now claims thee as her friend and fifter. Ifabelle is in affliction, and calls on Beatina to

                    comfort.

comfort her.   Yet how can I afk comfort from you,
when I have none to offer in return?   I cannot fee
you, left you curfe the hand that fupplied the means
for this ill-ftarred voyage.   Our Columbus, the man
whofe name fhall be revered while time endures, is no
more!   He fleeps in the vaft ocean; but his memory
fhall live forever.

Did I fay I had no comfort to offer?   Alas! my
regrets for his lofs were fo great, I forgot that he triumphed ere he died.   He found the wondrous unknown world he fought; but his own words will beft
tell his fuccefs.   The inclofed was brought to our
court this morning by a fea captain, who, whilft yet
far from the Spanifh coaft, faw fomething floating on
the waves; and feeling an awakened curiofity prompt
him, went a little out of his courfe to take it up.   It
was a cafk painted white.   On opening it, they
found this fad teftimony of our fatal lofs, inclofed in a cake of wax, and furrounded by a quantity of
cork, in order, as is imagined, to facilitate its fwimming.   I am inadequate to the tafk of adding more;
only to fay, when you can fee me without diftrefs to
yourfelf, come to me, and let us mingle our tears together.   Bring Ferdinando with you; henceforth he
is my fon.   Farewel.   ISABELLE.

Inclofed in the foregoing.

COLUMBUS TO HIS ROYAL MISTRESS.

At fea, December, 1492.

Royal and revered Lady,

THE moft humble and grateful of your fervants
addreffes you at a moment, when he much fears he
fhall never again behold you.   I am, with my little
convoy, in a boifterous and almoft unknown fea, at a
feafon of the year when ftorms prevail, and the inclemency of the weather renders our fafety extremely
precarious.   The clouds hang low; the atmofphere is
thick; the hollow murmuring fea, and bleak wind
that whiftles through the rigging, portends an approaching ftorm.

I fhall

I shall not fulfil my duty to the most gracious of sovereigns, if I do not try some method to inform her, whatever may be my fate, her wishes are fulfilled. The new, the hitherto unexplored world, of which I fondly dreamed so many anxious years, is at length discovered! I shall annex to this the course by which I steered, the soundings as we approached the land, and every requisite direction for mariners to find the place where I have left a little colony of forty men.

Our voyage from Spain was tedious in the extreme, and those who had not the same internal assurances, which my intense study had given me, of our being in a right course, were almost tempted to mutiny, to confine me, and, taking command of the fleet, return to Spain; but to my inexpressible joy, when even my own spirits began to fail, nor could I longer have silenced the fears of the mariners, on the morning of the 12th of October, I discovered land. We made for the shore, and on the 13th landed and took possession of a beautiful fertile island, in the name of your august consort Ferdinand. I kissed the ground as I landed, and called it St. Salvadora, in honour of my gracious patroness; for her bounty relieved me when I was in utter despair of ever making the attempt of a discovery, and the sight of this island preserved me from the vengeance of a disappointed, terrified set of seamen, who thought I had foolishly dragged them from their friends and country to perish on the ocean. I found the inhabitants humane, social, and tractable; and left our little colony in a state of greater comfort than could have been expected. But the impossibility of obtaining proper provisions for the long voyage before us, and the very fragile state of our barques to combat seas unusually tempestuous at this season, renders me fearful I shall never again see Spain, or kneel at the feet of my royal mistress.

The island I have discovered yields plenty of gold dust; pearls are found in the rivers; and from what I could observe, diamonds and other precious stones are easily procured. For the natives not only wear them in their hair and about their necks, but decorate their
temples

temples with them, intermixed with gold and silver. These temples are in general dedicated to the *Sun*, which is their chief object of adoration. The sacred duties are performed by priestesses, who vow eternal virginity. Their men are tall and well proportioned; the women beautiful in the extreme.

Thus have I slightly touched on the many charms to entice my sovereign to make this territory her own. Oh may the wealth its mines contain, enrich her above all her cotemporaries; may the colony she plants increase and flourish; there may she found a new, a glorious world, that after ages shall at once admire and fear.

And now that life perhaps is near its close, will my benignant queen permit her servant to recommend once more to her protection, my wife and child? Ferdinando is now fifteen. When he attains the age of manhood, let him pursue the path I have marked out, and finish what his father but begun; and should his searches meet with the success my spirit prophesies, let the new world be called *Columbia*. It will unite the name of Beatina with Columbus, perpetuating her loved name with mine.

I would have wrote to my beloved wife, but what could I say? My heart bleeds for what she will suffer. You, my gracious mistress, will not forsake her. Comfort her, console her; tell her that Beatina will be the last sound that trembles on my lips. Pardon me, sovereign lady, my style grows familiar; but the grave levels all distinctions, and I am now standing on its brink. A few more hours, and I plunge into a vast eternity! If the storm increases, my vessel cannot much longer brave its fury; if mine cannot, what will become of the poor little caravels that accompany me? Their fate is certain! Royal Isabelle, farewel. While life lingers in this frail tenement, gratitude for thy munificence can never be extinct in the heart of thy servant,   COLUMBUS.

"Noble, brave commander," cried Columbia, giving way to a flood of tears; "and was this thy untimely end?"

end?" "No, no," said Cora interrupting her; "he made several voyages after that, or else how should he carry Don Ferdinando to Peru? He did not die till after the birth of Christopher and a sister of your mother, who was christened Isabelle, after the queen of Spain. He lived to a good old age, and was hearty and well till misfortune overtook him; then he moped and pined; nay, I have seen him weep like a baby, and he died at last broken hearted." "More shame for those who could wound a heart so noble," said Columbia, whilst resentment, as it crimsoned her cheek, dried up her tears; and she proceeded to the next letter. It contained an account of Columbus's safe return. After having encountered innumerable perils, he landed at Palos, in Spain, on the 15th of March, 1493. After which, several other letters announce another voyage, in which he was more successful than the first, returning laden with ingots of gold, with pearls, with diamonds, and immense plates of silver.

But his success and the homage the populace seemed inclined to pay him, awakened a spirit of envy in those who had at first opposed, or treated as the chimeras of a disordered fancy, his plans for the discovery of a distant continent. They had not time to bring their plots to ripen, before he again embarked for America, with a large company of volunteers, gentlemen of the first rank in Spain; amongst which was his own son, Don Ferdinando. A farewel letter from this young gentleman to his mother, was the first that awakened Cora's attention. It was dated in June, 1498. "That was the time," said she, "that was the very voyage, which I so well remember." "Were you eight years old then, Cora?" said Columbia. "Yes, I was indeed," replied Cora, "but I remember every circumstance, as well as if it had passed but yesterday!" "Then do tell me, dear Cora," said Columbia, "tell me all; for in listening to the recital of a person who was present whilst the events they relate happened, it seems as if you were transported to the very scene, and witness to the incidents recited."

CHAP.

CHAP. IV.

New Scenes, new Men, new Manners.

"IT was on the firſt of Auguſt," ſaid Cora, drawing herſelf forward, whilſt memory ſeemed upon the ſtretch to recal events ſo long paſt; "it was, as near as I can recollect, about the beginning of Auguſt, when my mother, who was chief attendant about the royal children of Orrozombo, king of Peru, was ordered to attend the queen and her children to a palace newly built on the ſea-coaſt, a great diſtance from the capital. I ſhall never forget it; it was as fine a morning as ever ſhone. The princeſs Orrabella was the oldeſt of five daughters; for my royal maſter never had a ſon, and ſhe was looked upon as our future queen. I was then, as I told you, but eight years old, quite delighted with our new habitation. I followed the princeſs, with whom I was a great favourite, from one apartment to another, till we reached the top. There, as we ſtood looking toward the ſea, we ſaw a monſtrous fiſh or bird, for it was impoſſible to tell which it was; its body was black, its wings white; it was coming quick toward the ſhore. The princeſs ſhrieked. The king and queen had, from a lower apartment, obſerved the ſame monſter haſtily approaching; and ordering forth the guards, bade them draw up on the beach, and as it drew near diſcharge their arrows at it. But, Oh terrible, if I was to live a thouſand years, I never ſhall forget how frightened every creature was, when the huge monſter, drawing quite near, ſtopped on a ſudden, and dropping all its wings, a burſt of fire and ſmoke iſſued from its ſide, with tremendous noiſe. Many fell to the earth with terror, as this dreadful phenomena was repeated three times. When our fears were in ſome meaſure abated, we plainly ſaw living creatures move upon it, and ſoon a ſmaller fiſh of the ſame kind, only without wings, came from its ſide, and ſeveral men were borne by it quite to the ſhore. The guards affrighted, dared not diſcharge their arrows, but let their bows fall, and gazed in ſilent wonder. The king, the queen, and all the

royal

royal children were ftanding on the fhore.　The princefs Orrabella was ever brave and undaunted ; fhe ftood
leaning on my mother's arm, the foremoft of them all.
I had hid my face in her robe ; but though afraid to look
long on the terrifying object, I now and then drew it
afide to peep at a creature fo wonderful.

"But, my good Cora," cried Columbia, rather impatient at the old woman's prolixity, "if you are thus
particular, you will never get to the end of your ftory.
This monfter, as you defcribe it, I fuppofe was the fhip
that bore the great Columbus to the Peruvian coaft ;
and the little fifh you mention was the boat in which he
landed."

"Well, I know that," replied Cora, angrily ; "but
I like to tell a ftory my own way.　If I am not allowed to tell all the particulars, I fhall never be able to
tell it at all."　Columbia fmiled and was filent.

Cora again began, but fhe fo often interrupted herfelf
telling the fame incidents feveral times over, and dwelling on each with a tirefome minutenefs, that Columbia,
though anxious, could fcarcely command her attention to the end of the ftory.　From it fhe gathered the
following circumftances.

Columbus, though he had made two voyages before,
one when he difcovered St. Salvadora, and another with
relief and fupplies for the colony he had left there, had
not difcovered the part of the American continent of
which Cora was a native, till his third voyage ; when
many noblemen and cavaliers from the court of Spain
accompanied him in his expedition, in hopes of fharing
at once the glory and emolument the difcoveries were
likely to produce.　Amongft the gallant group of gentlemen was Ferdinando, only fon of Columbus.　He
landed with his father, both richly habited and followed
by a train of cavaliers equally gay.　With white flags
waving, and their drawn fwords pointed towards the
earth, they advanced to the party defcribed by Cora to
be affembled on the fhore.　Orrabella, ftruck with the
majeftic yet conciliating mien of Columbus, perhaps
more with the perfonal beauty and elegant deportment
of Ferdinando, who advanced at his right hand, preffed
forward

forward to meet them; and with a countenance at once expreffive of wonder, admiration and timidity, her right arm extended feemed a barrier to prevent their approaching her parents and fifters, whilft laying her left hand on her breaft fhe knelt to the ground, raifing her fine eyes in token of fupplication. Ferdinando raifed her, laid his fword at her feet, and throwing a ftring of beads about her neck, told her, in the language of nature, which is alike underftood in all nations, that fhe had nothing to fear.

Orrozombo, affured of their friendly intentions, received them cordially, and fhewed them every mark of hofpitality. They refided on the continent many months, collecting ingots of pure gold, bars of filver, with pearls, diamonds and coral, forming the moft wealthy cargo ever borne into a Spanifh port.

During the time Columbus and his followers tarried at the Peruvian court, Ferdinando had numberlefs opportunities of improving the favourable impreffion his firft appearance made on the lovely Orrabella. He foon inftructed her in the Spanifh tongue; and with equal facility, became himfelf a proficient in her native language. He found her poffeffed of ftrong powers of mind, quick perception, ready wit; in fhort, an underftanding capable of the higheft improvement. The mutual paffion that fubfifted between them was early difcovered, and encouraged by their parents. Columbus looked forward to the union as a mean of infuring wealth and power to his pofterity, and Orrozombo imagined, by refigning his daughter to this young ftranger, he fecured to himfelf a powerful friend and ally in Columbus. For the Spaniards had taught his fubjects many of the ufeful arts; and Science, by their means, began to unfold her beauties to the delighted monarch and his court.

Upon their marriage, Orrozombo gave up part of his territories to Columbus, as a portion for his daughter; and a colony was begun, where every thing was regulated according to the Spanifh form of government.

This being fettled to the fatisfaction of all parties, the adventurers prepared to revifit their native land;

and

and the royal bride of Ferdinando determined to go with her hufband.   Several of her attendants were appointed to accompany her; amongft whom was the mother of Cora, who at the princefs's requeft took her daughter with her.   With many tears did Orrabella quit her parents and fifters; tears which feemed to forebode they would never meet again.   Alas! Avarice had difcovered this new world was an inexhauftible mine of wealth; and, not content to fhare its bleffings in common with the natives, came with rapine, war and devaftation in her train: And as fhe tore open the bowels of the earth to gratify her infatiate thirft for gold, her fteps were marked with blood.

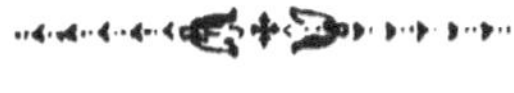

C H A P. V.

Ingratitude and Perfidy.

THE fhip in which Ferdinando and his bride embarked was deftined to proceed immediately to Spain; but Columbus himfelf, in a fmall caravel, determined to crofs over to Hifpaniola, and vifit a colony which now began to wear a very flourifhing appearance. Many families had emigrated from Spain, fome of confiderable diftinction; and Columbus had, previous to his embarkation, folicited the government of this colony for an indigent friend, hoping he might in the new world retrieve his ruined fortunes.   It was partly a wifh to fee how his intention fucceeded, that prompted him to vifit Hifpaniola at this time.   The reception he met with, and the manner of his return to Spain, Columbia found in the following letter.

COLUMBUS *to his Son* FERDINANDO.

Cadiz Harbour, 1499.

THY father is returned, my dear fon, returned to his native land.   But how? Not as an enterprifing fpirit whofe plans had proved fuccefsful, fhould return; but as a traitor to his king, loaded with ignomin-

D

ious

ious chains. Oh! my brave boy, I fee thy noble fpirit fire at the intelligence. But beware; conceal the workings of thy honeft foul. To profper in this ungrateful world, you muft wear the mafk of hypoc-rify; wear the femblance of humility, honefty, patriotifm, till you have obtained fome favourite point, then throw them afide as ufelefs, and glory in the fuc-cefs of your ftratagems.

Pardon me, my fon, I write from the impulfe of a broken heart. I know you would fcorn fuch advice if ferioufly given, even from a father; but I have fuffer-ed fo much from ingratitude and duplicity, and have feen thofe who practife them moft, feem to fucceed the beft, that I would willingly fhut my eyes on the light of day, and fink into eternal reft. My dear Ferdinan-do, your father has received a wound no time can heal. Surely we muft hope, that in the bleft abodes of immor-tality, the foul retains no remembrance of what paffed in this fublunary ftate; elfe certain I am, that the de-lights of paradife itfelf would be alloyed by the retrof-pect of the ignominy I have endured, and the chains I have worn.

And what will that treafure of my foul, thy adored mother, fay? How will my Beatina bear the degrada-tion of her Columbus? Will not her father, (but lately reconciled to his child) again fpurn her from him? And will not her haughty brothers and fifters pour their infolent reproaches on the wife of a difgraced, a ruined favourite? Your lovely Orrabella too! Alas! I greatly fear, whilft we were hofpitably entertained at her father's court, we were ungratefully paving the way for the introduction of war, rapine and deftruc-tion. Yet witnefs, ye immortal Powers, I am inno-cent. I fought not new worlds for conqueft, or for power; I felt, forcibly felt, the bleffings of Chriftian-ity, the comforts refulting from a commercial inter-courfe with other nations. I vainly thought thofe blef-fings through my means might be extended, and ear-neftly wifhed them participated by the whole world. But I am venting the forrows of my agonized foul, and forget you are a ftranger to what has caufed
them.

them. Oh! ever, ever, may you remain a ftranger to fuch anguifh. May my fon never experience how far beyond all other miferies which malice can inflict, or human nature fuffer, is the torture occafioned by the poifoned fting of ingratitude. But to my fad tale.

Light pleafant gales, and a fmooth fea quickly bore the caravel in which I embarked to Hifpaniola. A certain emblem of the viciffitudes of human life; for how often does the fun of profperity gild the horizon, and its delightful airs play around and fafcinate the fenfes, whilft the ftorms of adverfity hang, unobferved, ready to burft on our devoted heads.

Roldan (whom you muft remember was appointed through my interceffion to the government of this colo-ony) received me with the greateft marks of refpeft, and a profufion of compliments. I ought to have been upon my guard and fufpected his exceffive adula-tion. His profeffions of gratitude and attachment pained me; but as I knew the prefent affluent ftate of himfelf and family originated from my friendfhip, I attributed all to the nobleft motives, nor once fufpected, that as 1 held him to my bofom I was enfolding a fer-pent that waited but an opportunity to fting me to the heart.

The morning after my arrival the natives thronged in crowds to fee me, and in the moft tumultuous. man-ner expreffed their joy at my return. Roldan, with an infidious fmile, warned me to beware of giving them too much encouragement. "They are," faid he, "an encroaching fet of wretches, and will torment you with complaints, which, as they exift only in their own imaginations, it is not in your power to redrefs. You had better fpeak to them a little fternly, and dif-mifs them to their homes."

"How?" faid I, rather furprifed, "I do not rightly underftand you. What privilege can thefe people fo-licit from you or me, which they have not a right to demand? Is not this continent theirs by right of na-ture? and is not the privilege of living here unmoleft-ed enjoyed by us through their unfufpecting good na-ture, and the confidence they place in our honeft intentions?

tentions? and fhall we abufe this confidence, repay their hofpitality by infringing their natural rights? Heaven forbid! If they have complaints to make, it is our duty to hear, and to the utmoft of our power redrefs them."

As I fpoke with fervor, I obferved the countenance of Roldan change. A livid palenefs overfpread his face; his eyes gleamed, his lips trembled, and every feature exprefled a rage which he in vain attempted to conceal by a haggard fmile.

"All is not as it fhould be," faid I mentally; "I will inquire into the nature of the complaints he feems fo anxious to evade. If Roldan has made an unjuft ufe of his power, it is not our paft friendfhip fhall fcreen him from my reproach, or lead me to continue him in a ftation he appears inadequate to fill."

Full of thefe thoughts, I immediately fet an inquiry on foot concerning the general conduct of Roldan and his officers. I found they had grofsly abufed the power intrufted to them; that they had diftrefled and treated the natives in many cafes with the utmoft barbarity! and that this arbitrary governor had fupported the Spaniards in every act of injuftice or enormity they chofe to commit.

Having traced thefe grievances to their fource, I requefted a council might be called; and then, in the moft forcible language I could think of, yet with temper and mildnefs, I reprefented to them all the iniquity of their proceedings, conjured them to redrefs the injuries they had committed, and to reform the government. Some few feemed pleafed with my remonftrance, but the greater part heard me in fullen filence.

Roldan thanked me with a farcaftic fmile for my advice; but at the fame time told me he held his office by a commiffion from the royal Ferdinand, and to him only was accountable for his actions. I was thunderftruck by his fpeech and manner, and left the council room in a perturbation of mind not eafily defcribed.

Amongft the officers under the command of Roldan in this fettlement, was a young man of diffo-

lute

lute manners, named Diego.   He was younger fon to
a noble family ; but having diffipated a confiderable
fortune, and from being at firft only weak and foolifh,
having become vicious, his friends thought proper to
folicit employment for him in the new fettlement, and
he was accordingly appointed third in command.
This man I found the bofom confidant and privy
counfellor of Roldan.   His rapacity knew no bounds;
his paffions were his only mafter ; and hurried by
them to dreadful exceffes, he committed crimes at
which humanity at once blufhed and trembled.
Though the very little knowledge I had of Diego had
by no means prejudiced me in his favour, I could not
have fuppofed he would have perpetrated crimes of
the blackeft die without compunction, or that Roldan
would have openly dared to fanction his licentioufnefs ;
but I was at length fatally convinced, that when vice
and folly are leagued together, there is no wickednefs,
however horrible, at which they will hefitate.

Bruna was the only child of a venerable Indian,
whofe poffeffions were extenfive and valuable.   I had
cultivated a friendfhip with the father of Bruna, when
firft the fettlement was formed ;   and both myfelf and
followers experienced from him the kindnefs and attention which nature, when unadulterated by art, is ever
ready to offer to the friendlefs, or the ftranger.   His
dwelling was at our fervice ; he fupplied us plentifully
with goat's milk, the flefh of deer, dried maize, and
other comforts of life, which, to men who had experienced a tedious and wearifome voyage, were real
luxuries.

Bruna at this time was a lovely child of about
twelve years old ; fhe was wild and untutored ; but
there was fomething fo engaging in her manner, fo
fafcinating in her vivacity, that I could not fee her
daily without becoming infenfibly attached to her.
Her curiofity was unbounded ; and the fureft way to
become a favorite with her, was by gratifying a pro-
penfity which in general was directed to laudable objects.   I was charmed with her artlefs thirft for knowledge, and employed my leifure moments in inftructing

her.   But though eager to learn, that very eagerness counteracted her wishes.   She was too hasty and impetuous to allow herself sufficient time to become a proficient in any thing; therefore all my attention could do, was to give her a trifling knowledge of the Spanish language.   For when I spoke to her of the customs and manners of the European world, she would laugh, and declare her own country manners were best; for she could not possibly think any duty obliged us to conceal our thoughts, or that any custom whatever could make it laudable to speak one thing and think another.   I give you this slight sketch of her character, that you might not be surprised at what I have to relate concerning this Indian heroine.

It was about ten days after my arrival, as I was walking a few miles from the plantation, and remarking the improvement agriculture had made on the face of this beautiful fertile continent, when in a low-built hovel I saw an ancient Indian seated on the ground; his elbows rested on his knees, his hands clasped his forehead, as his head reclined upon them.   I stopped for a moment to contemplate a figure so striking; and as I paused, the sighs that broke from his agitated bosom, went to my very heart.   The noise I undesignedly made as I moved nearer the hovel, occasioned him to raise his head.   I was amazed; it was the father of Bruna!   He gazed for a moment eagerly upon me; then springing forward, fell on his knees, kissed my hands, my feet, the very hem of my garments.   In vain I attempted to raise him; he prostrated himself on the earth, and laid my hand upon his head, in token of owning me for his master.

Pray rise, my worthy friend, said I, and tell me what is the meaning of this humiliation? who has caused the change I perceive to have taken place in your circumstances?

"Christians! Christians!" replied he with vehemence, gnashing his teeth as he spoke, "they have plundered me of my wealth, torn my child from my arms; but you are come, and I shall be revenged."

The

The confidence this poor Indian seemed to have in my integrity, filled my eyes with tears.

"Yes," said I, "tell me who has treated you thus barbarously ; and if I have the power, you shall have ample restitution."   "Alas!" cried the old man, "of what avail will be the restitution of my wealth, unless you can restore my child, my darling to my arms pure and unspotted ?"

He then informed me that soon after the arrival of Roldan at the settlement, an entire change took place in the government; vice was tolerated, private property not in the least regarded, but every thing subjected to the lawless power of the new governor and his favourite.

Diego saw Bruna ; her beauty kindled in his bosom an unholy flame; he solicited her love and was rejected. He dared attempt her chastity, and was repulsed with scorn.   That moment sealed the ruin of her father. Diego complained to Roldan, that the father of Bruna refused to submit to the Spanish laws, and had even treated him with contempt and derision, who had endeavoured to enforce them.   Roldan, glad of an opportunity to gratify his ruling passion, which was avarice, gave ear to the complaint of his favourite ; and driving the unoffending Indian from a home he had inherited from his ancestors, seized on all his valuable property, ostensibly in the name of the Spanish King, but in reality to enrich his own private coffers.

Bruna, unknowing to what danger she exposed herself, and thinking this piece of injustice was entirely the act of Diego, flew to the governor for redress. Her tears, her innocent supplications, had no effect on the obdurate heart of Roldan ! he inhumanly rejected her suit, detained her person, and gave her into the power of Diego.   This horrid scene was acted but the day before my arrival.

"You shall have justice, old man," said I ; "come with me."   He followed me to the house of the governor. At sight of him, Roldan started and turned pale ; but soon recovering himself, he asked him, in a stern voice, what he did there.   "He comes for justice,"

faid

said I, " he comes to demand reftitution of his property, of which he has been robbed, and his daughter,
who is unjuftly detained from him." " The artful
wretch has impofed on you," faid Roldan fiercely,
" but go, flave," turning to the Indian, get from my
fight, and be thankful your infolence does not coft you
your life. I was preparing to reply in a proper
manner to this inhuman tyrant, when Bruna rufhed
into the apartment, her hair difhevelled her garments
difordered, and her eyes wild with terror. She threw
herfelf into her father's arms, and gave way to a violent gufh of tears ; but the tendernefs that feemed to
overcome her was but momentary. She recovered
herfelf, and raifing her head, looked round with a
kind of fullen dignity. Her eyes met mine. Perceiving fhe knew me, I offered her my hand, and was
proceeding to comfort her ; but with a rejecting motion, fhe put back my proffered hand, and covering
her face with both her own, turned from me. I inftantly comprehended the extent of the injury fhe had
fuftained, and my foul fhuddered within me.

Roldan's agitation was too great to efcape notice ;
he attempted twice to fpeak, but words were denied
him. His pale countenance betrayed his guilty heart.

At length he hefitatingly told Bruna, if that was
her father, and fhe had forcibly been detained from
him, fhe was now at liberty to return home. The
poor girl ftood for a moment the image of mute defpair ; then raifing her hands and eyes to heaven, cried,
" Home ! No ! never ! Bruna is the daughter of the
chafte Lilah, and was inftructed by the wife precepts
of her father, to prize her honour above her life. Their
manfion was the dwelling of innocence, piety, and virtue; and never will their wretched daughter carry pollu-
tion thither." Then turning toward her father, fhe
made as though fhe would have embraced him ; but
with a kind of involuntary fhudder, fhrunk again from
him, and drawing a dagger fhe had concealed in her
bofom, plunged it in her heart.

This fudden, unexpected event threw the governor
and all his attendants into the utmoft confufion.
The fervants, terrified, opened the doors ; and a
concourfe

concourfe of people, Spaniards as well as natives, rufhed in.   The bleeding form of the lovely Bruna, the agonizing forrow of her father, acted like a talifman on the minds of the people ; and in a few hours the whole fettlement was in a ftate of infurrection.   Juftice ! juftice ! was the cry : Deliver up Diego to our power, or we will extirpate the race of Chriftians from amongft us.   Roldan in this exigence applied to me to quiet the enraged multitude.   I fpoke to them ; I promifed they fhould have ample juftice! I foothed them by fpeaking of the virtues of Bruna, and execrating the author of her ruin, and confequent death ; and at length perfuaded them to depart quietly to their homes; affuring them that Diego was in confinement, and fhould be made to fuffer, to the extent of the law, the punifhment due to his crimes.

After a day of fuch unufual agitation, I retired to my apartment.   Fatigued in body, and diftreffed in mind, fleep was a ftranger to my eyes, and I was ruminating on the beft means to appeafe the irritated natives, when a band of Roldan's guards entered my chamber, and arrefted me as a traitor to my king, accufed me of being difaffected to his government, and inflaming the minds of his fubjects in Hifpaniola to rebellion.   Refiftance or remonftrance was vain; they were the tools of arbitrary power, and I fubmitted in filence. They manacled my hands and feet, and putting a gag in my mouth, conveyed me on board a veffel lying in the harbour.   Yes, Ferdinando, your father was chained, and fent to his native country as a traitor.

As foon as I was on board, and the guard departed, I found, by the motion of the veffel, we were under way ; the wind was fair, and fhe left the fhores of Hifpaniola with rapidity.

About two hours after daylight, the captain entered the cabin where I was, and entreated my pardon for having been obliged to act contrary to his inclinations. "I am but a fervant," faid he, "and muft obey thofe whom the king has fet over me.   I am ordered to keep you a clofe prifoner till our arrival in Spain ; but here I fhall dare to tranfgrefs my orders fo far as to releafe you from your chains." He then advanced to take off the infulting badges of my difgrace, but I forbid him. "No, Don Sancho," faid I, "if I am guilty, I will fuffer the fentence my fovereign may think proper to pafs on me with refignation. If I have been unjuftly accufed, to him do I look for redrefs; into his prefence will I go, loaded with thefe ignominious bonds, and when my innocence is proved, from his hands only will I accept of liberty."

Haften then, my dear fon, on the immediate receipt of this, to my royal miftrefs and patronefs; deliver to her own hand the inclofed few lines; and fhould fhe condefcend to requeft it, lay the contents of this letter before her. Comfort and confole your angel mother ere you leave her. Embrace your charming wife for me. Whilft I live, you fhare my heart amongft you. The ftrong fenfe I have of my prefent injuries, is only for your fakes? for of what confequence would the fmiles or frowns of princes be to me, were not my wife and children to be involved in my difgrace, or exalted by my fuccefs and honour. Haften, my fon, after you have fulfilled this commiffion, to the arms of your father; come, my brave boy, and by a filial tear heal the anguifh, which at prefent corrodes the heart of

COLUMBUS.

CHAP. VI.

Retribution.

COLUMBIA could only paufe for a moment to wipe off the tears which, fpite of her endeavours to fupprefs them, would rufh to her eyes. She then proceeded to the next letter.

FERDINANDO TO HIS MOTHER.

HAD I a conveyance, fwift as my own impatience, to forward to my revered mother the joyful tidings of my father's triumph over his enemies, the wings of

the

the wind would be too tardy to bear this to your hands.
Yes, my dear mother, Columbus, the great, the enterprizing Columbus, is reftored to all his former dignity,
and even frefh honours are heaped upon him.   But I
know you wifh me to be particular ;   and how can I
be more pleafingly employed than in recounting the
noble conduct of a father, and obeying the commands
of the beft of mothers ?

When in obedience to my father's mandate I repaired to court, and requefted an audience with the
royal Iflabelle, I was, within a few hours after the re-
requeft was made, admitted.   An unufual gloom, almoft approaching to feverity, was caft over a countenance, which heretofore had only on me beamed fmiles
of benevolence.   It chilled me to the heart.   I approached with extreme agitation; and, bending one knee
to the ground, prefented the fealed paper which was
inclofed in my father's letter.   The queen paufed for a
moment, feemingly irrefolute whether or not to break
the feal.   My agitation increafed, my knees trembled,
my heart beat violently.   My diforder did not pafs
unnoticed.   " Calm your fears, Ferdinando," faid If-
fabelle, as fhe at length opened the letter ; " your father has, it is true, powerful enemies ; but if his innocence is apparent, he will ever find in me a fteady,
powerful friend."   I bowed in grateful acknowledge-
ment of her goodnefs, and fhe in filence perufed the
letter.   A crimfon glow overfpread her face as fhe read ;
it feemed the glow of refentment, as folding the paper
fhe unlocked a fmall cabinet, and depofited it amongft
fome other writings.

" You have a letter from Columbus," faid fhe,
" permit me to fee it."   I prefented it.   " Go," faid
fhe, taking it from me, " retire in peace ; the fuccefs of
my hero has awakened the envy of thofe who had not
courage to follow his example, he has been traduced
to the king ; but Ifabelle will not fuffer a man, whofe
merit fhe efteems and whofe caufe fhe efpoufes, to be
injured with impunity."

Charmed by thefe condefcending expreffions, I bowed and retired.   In about two hours, I received a mandate

date figned by the queen's hand, ordering me to repair immediately to the port, and conduct my injured father to her prefence. "Take off his chains," were the words, "and let him come to his fovereign, attended with all the refpect and honour a man deferves, who, whilft he was adding new territories to our crown, whilft he had it in his power to heap up mines of wealth for his own coffers, forgot not the caufe of humanity, and rather than countenance one act of tyranny, hazarded the difpleafure of his king, the lofs of his fortune, nay even life itfelf. But his fovereign fhall reward him."

Her majefty's own fervants and mules attended my commands ; and quick as it was poffible, I purfued my journey, and flew to the arms of my father. Our meeting was beyond defcription. The agitation of his mind had affected his health ; his countenance was pale and dejected ; his perfon neglected. I offered to take off his fetters, fhewed him the queen's mandate, but in vain. " I will go to my royal miftrefs," faid he, " but I will go as I am." When he faw the fervants that attended to conduct him—" Poor pageantry, "faid he, " pitiful recompenfe for the injuries I have received ! No ! no ! I will have no attendants. I am a difgraced man, and will enter the metropolis with as little noife as poffible ; obfcurity and filence fuits beft with difhonour. But mark me, my fon, as my difgrace has been public, fo fhall be my juftification." There was fuch majefty in his manner, fuch fixed refolution in his looks, I dared not oppofe him. I difmiffed the retinue that attended ; and with only my own fervant, accompanied my father, by the moft unfrequented roads, to the court of Ferdinand and Ifabelle.

It was about twelve o'clock when we arrived, and orders were given for our immediate admiffion. Never fhall I forget the countenance of the royal Ifabelle, when fhe beheld her hero enter thus encumbered with the teftimonies of his difgrace. The king and queen were feated at the upper end of the prefence chamber, attended by many noblemen and cavaliers, tried friends of my father, and fome whom I knew to be his enemies. Columbus entered the door a few fteps, then

making

making a full ſtop, bent his knee to the ground, and raiſing his manacled hands, attempted to ſpeak; but pride, reſentment, wounded honour, ſwelled his brave heart nearly to burſting; and, ſpite of his endeavours to ſuppreſs them, the ſcalding tears rolled down his pale face. It was a reproach more poignant than words could have conveyed.

Iſabelle roſe from her ſeat, her own eyes gliſtening with the dew of ſenſibility; and advancing to my father, raiſed him. " Riſe, my brave admiral," ſaid ſhe, " and let thy queen take off theſe fetters, of which ſhe has more cauſe to be aſhamed than you have." Then leading him to the king, " Royal Sir," ſaid ſhe, " how ſhall we recompenſe this worthy man for the undeſerved humiliation he has received?" " Colum-bus," ſaid Ferdinand, " I bluſh for the indignities of-fered you in the perſon of my repreſentative; but you ſhall have ample revenge. Go to your wife and friends, indulge awhile in eaſe, and recruit your ſtrength and ſpirits; in the mean time, I will give or-ders for the preparation of a fleet ſuperior to any you have yet commanded; in it you ſhall return to our new colonies, of the whole of which I from this moment create you viceroy, giving you unlimited power to create or diſplace officers, and diſtribute rewards and puniſh-ments at pleaſure. I know it is a power you will not abuſe. Go, valiant chief, and reign over a people, whom you have conquered by practiſing humanity, not the arts of war. But take thoſe fetters from my ſight," continued he; " that Columbus ever wore them, will caſt a laſting ſhade on my memory; and ages yet unborn, when they ſhall hear the tale rela-ted, will accuſe Ferdinand of ingratitude."

" Pardon me, gracious ſire," ſaid my father, pla-cing his foot on the chains as one of the guards at-tempted to remove them; "theſe fetters are mine. I purchaſed them with fatigue and danger, went through many perils by ſea and land to obtain them, nor will I lightly part with them. Wherever I go, they ſhall go with me; I will contemplate them every day, leſt proſperity ſhould make me forget, on what a frail ten-

E   ure

ure I hold my happinefs. I will look at them ; and
whilft I recollect the anguifh I felt when they were impofed on me, learn to be cautious how I attempt to inflict the fame mifery on a fellow creature.   When I
am unhappy, I will cheer my heart by the remembrance, that the moment when my royal miftrefs took
thefe fetters off my hands, was the moft tranfporting moment of my life ; for it reinftated me in the good opinion of my fovereign, gave my friends caufe for exultation, and covered my enemies with confufion."

Ferdinand was filent.   Ifabelle fmiled ; it was a
fmile of triumph. "You muft do as you pleafe," faid
fhe.   Then turning to the guard, " convey them to
wherever Columbus orders ; his intrepid fpirit can
convert even fetters into badges of diftinction."

Their majefties then left the chamber followed by
the court, and in a moment I was locked in the arms
of my father, and mingled with him fome of the moft
delicious tears I ever fhed.   Tell my lovely Orrabella,
in a few hours after fhe receives this, I fhall be at her
feet.   Yes, my revered mother, I fhall behold once
more all the deareft objects of my affections united in
one family circle.   I fhall fee your dear countenance
beam with heartfelt fatisfaction ; fee my father happy
in the bofom of his family ; and in the fmiles of my
Orrabella and her fweet infant, enjoy every felicity of
which human nature is capable.   Farewel till we
meet.   FERDINANDO.

The next paper Columbia opened had the appearance more of a manufcript than a letter.   It confifted
of feveral fheets of paper wrote on all fides ; it was
from the wife of Columbus, addreffed to her grand-
daughter Ifabelle.

BEATINA TO ISABELLE.

Valladolid, 1520.

AS the perufal of the inclofed letters and papers
will no doubt awaken in the bofom of my dear Ifabelle,
a curiofity to learn the events that followed this triumph of Columbus over his enemies : and as I think
it

it neceſſary to inform her, not only of her deſcent from the native kings of Peru, but alſo of the fate of her parents, who now, alas! are no more, I have taken up my pen to trace every circumſtance that may tend to prove your right to the ſovereignty of Quito, and the ſurrounding territories, if hereafter you ſhould think it worth contending for. But as I leave you, my dear child, in the protection of my own family; and am fully ſenſible that my nephew, the marquis Gǎidova, will take ſuch care of your fortune, (now ample) that by the time you are of age to peruſe theſe papers, you will be one of the richeſt heireſſes in Spain; I fondly hope you will not ſuffer the vain ambition of bearing the empty title of queen to influence your conduct, or tempt you to throw away the real bleſſings of life in purſuit of ſhadows and toys.

I am old, my dear Iſabelle, and have lived to bury all my deareſt affections in the ſilent grave, except the kindly lambent flame that warms my languid heart when I behold your innocent ſmiles, and liſten to your lively prattle. You are now ſcarcely five years old; I cannot therefore expect to live to ſee you enter on the buſy ſtage of life. Let me entreat you then (and think, as you peruſe this, your grandmother ſpeaks to you from the grave) let me entreat you to pay the ſtricteſt attention to the advice of your uncle and his amiable wife. Certain I am, they will never impoſe harſh commands; and to them I leave the full power of controlling and directing you during the dangerous period of youth.

One thing I think it proper you ſhould know, in the choice of a partner for life, (though I would wiſh you to conſult thoſe dear friends,) you are entirely your own miſtreſs. At the age of 21, your fortune will be put in your own power; but, Iſabelle, remember the royal race from whence you ſprang, and do not diſgrace it by an ignoble alliance. It is not wealth, it is not titles, I would have you ſeek! no, my child; ſeek courage, honour, good ſenſe, and poliſhed manners. Theſe conſtitute true nobility; it was theſe ſo eminently
diſtinguiſhed

diftinguifhed the great Columbus; made him the delight of our fex, the envy of his own.

I fay you are your own miftrefs; in every point but one you are fo. I charge you, Ifabelle, as you value your eternal peace, unite not your fate with that of a heretic. Should you unhappily feel a growing inclination for one of thofe impious innovators on the rights and ceremonies of our holy mother church, repel it with your utmoft power; for in that cafe your guardian has my authority peremptorily to refufe his fanction to your union. And fhould you form fuch a connexion in defiance of his abfolute commands, your fortune, on the inftant of your marriage, becomes forfeit, and will go to the marquis's eldeft fon. My wifhes to fee you not only temporally but eternally happy, have led me to make this point indifputable; but I truft it is a needlefs caution, fince you will be brought up in the true religion, in the religion of your anceftors; and will feel a juft abhorrence for thofe licentious wretches, who arrogantly ftyle themfelves reformers. Of all the European courts, none are fo infefted with this fect as the Englifh. Beware, then; and when you behold a gay, accomplifhed Englifhman, and many fuch vifit the court of Spain, before you venture too nearly to contemplate his feeming virtues and graces, fay within yourfelf, May not this man be tinctured with the principles I am cautioned to avoid? Think thus, avoid him, and be happy.

⋖⋖⋖⋖⋐✦⋑⋗⋗⋗⋗⋗

C H A P. VII.

Return to the new World.

" ALAS," faid Columbia, laying down the paper, " I now fee the fource from whence fprang all my dear mother's forrow. She was bred in the Catholic perfuafion, and my father tempted her to difobey the rigid commands of her guardian, forfeit her fortune, embrace his faith, and, leaving all her connex-

ions

ions in Spain, follow him to England. Poor, bigot-.
ed Beatina, little did you think, when making your
will, that you figned the mandate for your grandchild's
mifery. For what might not avarice tempt the fon
of the marquis Guidova to do? Might not he wink
at a marriage that was to inveft him with all the vaft
wealth of the unfortunate Ifabelle? But perhaps I
injure him; he may be innocent of fuch an intention;
my mifguided parents themfelves may be alone to
blame. Yet knowing and adoring them as I do, how
can I believe that poffible?" Thus was Columbia
bewildered with conjecture. At length, thinking the
manufcript might fatisfy her curiofity, and remove
her doubts, fhe again addreffed herfelf to the perufal
of it.

"It was the beginning of the year 1500,
that the great Columbus embarked on board
the fleet which Ferdinand had ordered to be equipped
for his fervice, (with all the attendance, ceremonies,
&c. cuftomary on fuch occafions,) as viceroy of the
new-difcovered continent. Ferdinando was appointed
governor of the fettlements in Peru. Myfelf, the
princefs Orrabella, and her fon Chriftopher, embarked
with them. The king, queen, and all the court attended us to the water fide; a vaft concourfe of people crowded the fhore, wearying Heaven with prayers
for our happinefs whilft abfent, and our fafe return.
At parting from his auguft patronefs, Columbus knelt
to kifs her hand. She raifed him, and throwing a
gold chain over his neck, by which her own portrait
was fufpended, "Go, my invincible hero," faid
fhe, "go, and enjoy the reward of your labours.
And if we never meet again on this fide eternity, let
my memory ever be dear to you; for whilft you live,
Columbus, you will never find a truer friend than you
have found in Ifabelle." As fhe finifhed fpeaking,
fhe inclined her head towards him; he refpectfully
faluted her cheek. "Heaven ever blefs and defend
my royal miftrefs and her auguft confort," faid Columbus. "And protect my hero," added the queen.
Then turning haftily to hide her tears, fhe rufhed into

E 2

the

the midſt of her attendants, and retired. Yes, my
child, the good, the noble-hearted, royal Iſabelle retired; and we ſaw her no more. Before we returned,
ſhe ſlept in peace; but her name ſhall be revered to
after ages. The brave and worthy will remember it
with gratitude; and the pious tears of millions yet
unborn, ſhall ſanctify her memory to all eternity.

"It was determined at our departure, that the
whole fleet ſhould accompany Ferdinando and Orrabella to her native coaſt; and having ſeen him ſafely
ſettled in his government, proceed to Hiſpaniola, and
ſend Roldan and his licentious aſſociates home in the
ſame diſgraceful circumſtances in which he had before
ungratefully involved Columbus. A fine ſeaſon favoured our voyage; and in leſs than two months from
our embarkation, we ſaw the fertile ſhores of Peru riſe
upon our ſight. The joy of Orrabella as ſhe beheld
her native land was beyond all bounds. "I ſhall ſee my
father and mother," ſaid ſhe, " and embrace my dear
ſiſters; I ſhall ſit beſide them for hours, and relate to
them the wonders I have ſeen in your world; and only that they know my lips abhor falſehood, they would
think ſome of the ſtrange things I have to relate were
nothing more than fictions. Then careſſing her child,
ſhe would talk of the joy of her father's ſubjects when
they ſhould behold her offspring, whom ſhe fully believed was born to ſway the ſceptre of Peru.

" It was on the ſecond day after we had diſcovered
land, that we reached the deſired harbour. But as we
drew near no ſhouts of joy welcomed our approach;
no king, no guards, no exulting ſubjects appeared to
greet us. All was ſilent, all was deſolate. Our hearts
ſunk within us. " They are at Quito," ſaid Orrabella; but her pallid countenance and tremulous voice
betrayed that ſhe hardly dared hope what ſhe aſſerted.
" We will land, however," ſaid Columbus; accordingly
the boat was hoiſted out, and we proceeded to the ſhore.
When within a few yards of the beach, a party of armed men appeared. Their dreſs, their arms, beſpoke
them Spaniards. Our fleet bore the ſtandard of Spain,
we could not fear our countrymen as foes. Columbus
                                        addreſſed

addreffed them from the boat in terms of amity; they returned a haughty anfwer.   However, they permitted us to land.   But Oh! Ifabelle, what were our feelings, when we difcovered this beautiful continent had been invaded by a party of freebooters; its hofpitable inhabitants rifled of all their treafures, many of them maffacred, and the remainder driven in-to the interior parts of the country.   The palace of Orrozombo was converted into a den for thefe robbers, where riot and intemperance reigned without control.   The fettlers left by Columbus, ad-hering to the intereft of the king and natives, were driven with them to feek an afylum in the woods and mountains.

The chief of thefe banditti was named Garcias, fierce, cruel and vindi&tive.   He received Columbus with a gloomy haughtinefs of demeanor; and when queftioned as to his right in thefe dominions, he fcorn-fully replied, " By the right of conqueft; not by a ridiculous family compa&t with a favage."   Orrabella was prefent when Garcias thus infulted her family. " Infolent Spaniard," faid fhe, her eyes darting light-ning, her fine face and perfon uncommonly animated by the fire of refentment; " infolent Spaniard, the king my father, though you term him a favage, was your fuperior in every virtue! What though unpolifh-ed, he had but nature for his guide? that nature taught him humanity, honour, patience, fortitude, and Orro-zombo would have died rather than deceive a friend, or infult a fallen foe. Oh my father! my father!" continued fhe, burfting into an agony of tears, "where are you now? Where is my revered mother, my poor defencelefs fifters? Tell me, barbarian, have you entirely extirpated the race of the children of the fun, or do you hold the lawful king of this territory in bondage, whilft you ufurp his rights, and riot in the fpoils of his de-voted fubjects? If fo, Oh lead me to the dungeon where you have confined him, that I may weep in his arms, and die with grief to fee my king, my father, a flave to the nation he had vainly hoped to have held in eternal bonds of friendfhip, and gave his child as a

hoftage

hoftage of his faith towards them. Alas! what hoftage did he require to infure their faith to him? None; his noble heart harboured not deceit, nor could fufpect it in another."

From thefe pathetic remonftrances and lamentations of Orrabella, we perceived fhe fufpected Columbus and Ferdinando were knowing to the voyage and confequent invafion of Garcias and his lawlefs band; but in this fhe was foon undeceived. For Columbus, irritated by the infolence of Garcias, threatened him with fpeedy vengeance unlefs he informed him where Orrozombo and the royal family were. Garcias laughed at his menaces, but on being informed that Columbus was deputed viceroy of all the new-difcovered lands on that fide the globe, and being requefted to do homage to him as the reprefentative of his royal mafter Ferdinand, or expect the punifhment due to a pirate, a traitor and a robber, he became more humble, and many of his followers, underftanding the dangerous predicament in which they ftood, declared themfelves ready to fupport the new viceroy in the difcharge of his duty as the king's delegate, and as fuch fwore allegiance to him.

It was then we learnt that Garcias Du Ponty, a Caftilian by birth, young, diffolute and ambitious, having heard of the fuccefs of Columbus, and the vaft treafures himfelf and followers had brought from the new world, refolved to make an experiment himfelf; and having, by promifes of large future reward, and fome rich prefents artfully beftowed, won over an experienced mariner (who had been the laft voyage with your grandfather, and returned in the fhip with Orrabella) to undertake to navigate his veffel, and give directions to the pilots of the reft of the fleet how to follow him; Garcias prevailed on a number of young Caftilian noblemen and gentlemen to embark on the expedition. They applied for no letters of leave from Ferdinand; for had they, it is moft probable they would have been prevented purfuing this (in the end) ruinous voyage.

A large fleet collected from the different ports of Spain, met in the Mediterranean fea many other mariners

iners who wifhed to purfue their good fortune, and, not being content to wait till another fleet fhould be fent out by the king's orders, were eager to embark with thefe licentious noblemen, and direct their courfe to the land where they imagined they were to become petty princes, and revel in all the luxuries which nature could afford, or unbounded wealth fupply.

This fleet was on the ocean at the time Columbus returned from Hifpaniola. They had a more fpeedy voyage than their inhuman defigns deferved; but Heaven often permits the wicked for a while to profper, that the fuccefs of their lawlefs plans may become their punifhment, and the reverfe of fortune coming unexpected, may fall the heavier on them. And thus it proved with Garcias Du Ponty and his followers.

On their arrival on the coaft of Peru, they found the king with his family, as was their cuftom, fpending the fummer at their palace on the banks of a river that mingles its waters with the ocean. Garcias and his party landed. Orrozombo, and indeed the Spanifh fettlers, believed them to be a party fent by Columbus to bring fupplies to the colony, and received them with open arms and every mark of affection. But alas, they were too fatally undeceived, when thefe invaders of the rights of nature and the law of nations affumed the authority of mafters, exacting enormous fums as tribute from the king, and forcing his fubjects to labour in the mines, often rewarding thofe labours (when the produce of them was not equal to the inordinate avarice of their defires) with death.

Orrozombo, wearied by their repeated infolence, and terrified by their rapacity, entreated them to leave the continent, offering them immenfe treafures. But they were not thus to be fatisfied. They proceeded from one ftep to another, till neither age nor fex became a fafeguard from their cruelties. The chafte wife and the pure virgin were violated in the prefence of their parents and protectors, who, confined by thefe inhuman monfters, had not the power to refcue or avenge them.

Human

Human nature, however patient, could not tamely endure such enormities. The natives and the Span- iards united their forces to endeavour to expel the in- vaders; but it was too late. They had sent a part of their company to search the interior country for mines. These returned, boasting of the ravages they had committed, and displaying the spoils they had gleaned. They had plundered every village through which they passed, and then set fire to it. Thousands of innocent families, thus deprived of their homes and all means of support, fled into the mountains, where many perished through famine, and the rest dragged on a wretched life, living on wild fruit, and what game their bows and arrows produced, sleeping in caves or recesses of the rocks, and too often their miserable ex- istence was terminated by the fangs of the tyger or the lion. Flushed with success, the Castilians meditated on- ly how to make an entire conquest of the country.

Undisciplined in the arts of war, and though experi- encing its effect every hour, still unsuspecting of treach- ery,—the Peruvians were at this time, by the art of the Spaniards, induced to throw aside their arms, and agree to terms of peace with Garcias, who assumed a graver demeanor, and made some slight concessions to Orrozombo for the misconduct of his companions, who by a few weeks of quiet regular behaviour lulled him into security; then, when in full confidence of the faith of their enemies, the Peruvians, who had been celebra- ting the annual feast of the sun at which these strangers had been admitted to participate; then, when parting from them in amity they tranquilly sunk to rest; then did the blood-thirsty Garcias and his detested crew rush on the defenceless victims, and massacre them without mercy and without remorse.

Oh thou Power eternal, whose name is a tower of strength, and whose mercy is as infinite as thy wisdom! what shall we say, that these barbarians should call themselves thy servants, and bear the glorious appella- tion of Christians? Alas, mistaken men, the God you serve delighteth not in blood; his precept and example taught peace, mercy and good will to all mankind.

But

But the Peruvians were idolaters! cries the misguided enthusiast; and so was Garcias and his followers; their idols were avarice, ambition, luxury, and lawless passion; to them they bent the knee, and on their altars did they sacrifice millions of innocent people.——But I digress.

Du Ponty, though the wretch his actions proclaim him, was handsome in his person, gay, lively and gallant; his fair outside attracted the notice of Alzira, the youngest sister of Orrabella. Alzira was equally lovely as her sister, but she possessed not that greatness of soul, that intrepid firmness which characterized your mother. By nature soft, gentle and complying, when the subtle Castilian, who read her passion in her admiring eyes, sued for some token of her favour, she hesitated not to own her love, and confess, could her father be brought to approve it, to be the wife of Du Ponty would constitute her chief felicity.

But Garcias had not an idea of an honourable union; he meant to conquer her father's kingdom; and had it in contemplation to degrade the fair Alzira to the station of a slave, for the amusement of his looser hours. On the night of the horrid massacre, Garcias was purposely in the apartment of the princess, where he was frequently privately admitted after her parents were retired to rest. Alzira, who was listening to the adulating voice of her lover, did not at first attend to the confused murmur that ran through the palace on the entrance of the Spaniards; but a sudden shriek, that seemed to come from the apartment of her mother, roused her dormant senses. She started, and would have run to the assistance of her parents, whom she imagined were suddenly taken ill, but reiterated shrieks which now issued from every room in the palace, made her pause, and she became a motionless statue of horror.

" The palace is beset," cried Garcias, "let me bear you, lovely Alzira, to a place of safety; I will then return to the assistance of your father." " Oh no! now, now rescue him, or let me die with him," was all she could say, before Du Ponty bore her in his arms, out of the chamber, and down the stairs. At the foot of these stairs she saw (by the light of torches which were every where flaming round) her father dragged by the hair of his head; whilst an inhuman wretch, regardless of his grey hairs and defenceless state, plunged a poniard in his bosom. Alzira, driven almost to madness at the sight, sprang from the arms of Garcias, and threw herself into those of the dying monarch. He knew his child, pressed her to his bosom, faintly articulated a blessing on her, and expired.

Alzira's senses forsook her. In that state she was borne to the tent of her betrayer. The scene that followed is too horrid for repetition! Morning dawned, and the ill-fated princess awoke to a perfect sense of all the miseries of her situation. She wished for death, but all means of accelerating that period was removed from her. She once conceived the thought of refusing all food, but had not resolution to persist. Garcias was attentive and kind; pretended to mourn with her the fate of her parents: She, not fully acquainted with his treachery, listened to his soothings, was consoled, and endured life for his sake. But uninterrupted possession brought on satiety, and at length indifference and disgust. Du Ponty neglected and treated her harshly. She felt her situation, but she was now a mother, and more than ever attached to the father of her child; she dragged on a wretched existence, without joy, without hope, without even a dawn of comfort.

The natives of Peru who had escaped the swords of the Castilians on that memorable night, failed not to attribute their misfortunes to their unhappy sovereign Orrozombo; he had been slack in the observance of some of the ceremonious devotions directed to be paid to their deity, the Sun; he had even doubted whether their religion was the true religion; he had refused to dedicate one of his daughters to the service of their god; he had married the heiress of his crown and kingdom to a stranger, who absolutely denied the divinity of the power they worshipped, and called their rites and ceremonies, absurdities and superstitions; and had suffered this stranger to carry her with him to a distant land. These, in the eyes of the unenlightened

wned Peruvians, were heinous offences, and had drawn down the wrath of their deity upon them; and thus, for the crimes of an individual, did they foolishly imagine a whole nation was punished.

It was at this period our fleet arrived, but the name of Spaniard and of Christian had become hateful to the ears of the natives; not one therefore appeared to espouse the cause of Columbus, imagining no doubt that they should but expel one tyrant to make room for another. Some few ventured by stealth to come and see their princess; but their spirits were depressed, and their expressions of love and duty consequently cold and languid. When she presented her son to them as their rightful king, they would shake their heads, and cry emphatically, " He is a Christian and a Spaniard."

Whilst Columbus was ardently labouring to reduce the Spaniards to some degree of subjection and order, at the same time striving to draw the natives back to the duty and allegiance they owed the princess, the treacherous Du Ponty, who had for some time worn the mask of friendship in combination with some of the leaders of the banditti, had laid an infernal plot to burn our fleet, and then, having the few that might at the time be on shore entirely in their power, oblige them to submit to whatever terms they pleased to offer.

But this plot was providentially discovered by a young Peruvian maid, who, detained in the palace by Garcias to attend on Alzira, though too young to become a prey to any of his officers or associates, was yet old enough to detest their actions, weep over the ruin of her native country, and pray for some propitious hour to arrive, when its enemies might be punished. She had overheard Du Ponty discoursing with one of his comrades on their intended plan, on the very night before it was to be put in execution; and, waiting till all was wrapt in silence, she stole from her apartment, and came to our tent. Having disclosed what knowledge she had obtained of their designs, Orrabella told her she should stay with us, and become one of her attendants; but she laid her hand on her heart and cried, " No! I cannot;" then looking earnestly

F

nestly

neftly in the face of the princefs, fhe cried, "Poor Alzira! fhe is alive; fhe is miferable! I will live or
die with her." "Alive! my fifter alive!" faid Orrabella, ftarting from her feat; lead me to her; I will
deliver her, or fhare her fate."

The impatience of the princefs was only to be ftayed
by the remonftrance of her hufband and his father.
" Your precipitancy, my love," cried Ferdinando,
" may ruin all. Our enemies are now wrapt in fleep;
the time is favourable; we muft repay treachery with
treachery; fall upon them whilft they are unprepared,
and make them prifoners."

This refolution taken, Ferdinando took a fmall
boat, and, going to the fhips, ordered from them a
number of men, who were landed at different times,
in feveral boats. The officers were informed of Garcias's intended treachery; the private foldiers and
failors were not told of it, left the fpirit of revenge
might be more powerful than the refpect they bore
their commander, and tempt them in the firft moment
of paffion to commit outrages at which they would
have caufe to blufh hereafter. Columbus difpatched
parties to the dwellings of the principal officers; thefe
parties he took the command of himfelf. Ferdinando
was appointed with a ftrong guard to inveft the palace, which Du Ponty had made his own refidence
ever fince the night, when he put its unoffending inmates to the fword. Ferdinando knew every apartment, every fecret room in it; and the private entrance
by which the ill-fated Alzira ufed to admit her lover,
was pointed out by the Indian girl.

No perfuafions, however urgent, could prevail on
Orrabella not to accompany her hufband, who, anxious for her fafety, and more fo on account of her
fituation, (for fhe almoft daily expected to prefent
him with another pledge of mutual affection) earneftly
entreated her not to go, promifing to conduct her fifter in fafety to her—but in vain. Orrabella was not
eafily to be perfuaded from doing what fhe conceived
a duty. As I found her determined to go, I refolved to accompany her.

Through

Through a fmall gate, at the utmoft extent of the garden, we were all admitted, and about twenty yards from the houfe entered a door that appeared to be fixed in the fide of a green floping bank; this opened into an arched paffage, which led to the cellars of the palace, which we traverfed with no little perturbation; and, afcending a flight of ftairs, found ourfelves in a fpacious hall; when the young Indian, taking hold of Orrabella's hand, led her to the left, placing her finger on her mouth, in token of filence. I followed; and, entering a room in the midft of which glimmered a pale lamp, perceived by its feeble beams, an elegant female habited in the Peruvian drefs, kneeling on the floor befide a bed, on which lay a fleeping infant. Her long hair hung negligently over her neck and fhoulders; her arms were croffed on the bed, and her head refted between them. At the moment we entered, her forrows were lulled into forgetfulnefs. At the noife we made, (though it would have been fcarcely perceptible to another ear, yet mifery is wakeful, and ftarts at every found) fhe raifed her languid head, gazed carneftly at Orrabella, who funk on her knees befide her. "Sifter! fifter!" faid fhe; and, throwing herfelf into her arms, fainted on her bofom.

Whilft we were bufied with Alzira, Ferdinando and his followers made good ufe of their time. The inhabitants of the caftle were in a deep fleep, partly the effects of intemperance; fo profound were their flumbers, that many of them felt the chains on their hands and feet, before they could recover fenfe fufficient to know who had put them on. Some few made a faint refiftance; but thefe were foon intimidated into filence; and in fuch quiet did every party proceed, that before the dawn of day all the leaders, and a great number of their followers, were in confinement, and at the mercy of Columbus.

In the morning, the incidents of the night fpread terror and confternation through all the Caftilian party; and thofe who were ftill at liberty, readily vowed fubmiffion to the viceroy, in hopes by fo doing to fecure their lives and fortunes, as they imagined Du

Ponty

Ponty and his officers would be immediately executed, and their treasures seized on as public property. But in this they were mistaken; Columbus wished to secure his own and followers lives and properties, but he did not arrogate to himself the right of plunging a multitude of human beings into eternity, because they opposed his plans, or had been blindly led by an unprincipled commander to perpetrate actions their better reason would have shuddered at.

During the remainder of this eventful night, Alzira informed her sister of the circumstances I have already related to you. Orrabella's soul was in a flame at the thought of her sister's dishonour. She finished her melancholy recital in these words; " When I heard of your arrival, my dear sister, a gleam of joy shot through my bosom ; but reflection told me I had little reason to rejoice, for I was dishonoured, stained ! and could I hope to be pressed to the chaste bosom of Orrabella ? Oh no! I knew I had forfeited all right to your affection, and I resolved sedulously to seclude myself from your sight, suffering you to believe I had been sacrificed on the same night with my parents and sisters." " Would to Heaven you had," said Orrabella, fervently ; "for it is a thousand times more afflicting to my heart to see you thus, dragging on a miserable life, with public loss of honour, than to see you covered with wounds, and breathing out your soul in agony. Oh ! my poor ruined Alzira, where was the spirit that was wont to animate the children of the sun when the wretch first disclosed his impious proposal ? Why had not my sister raised her arm, and struck the monster dead ?" " Alas !" replied the weeping princess, " I loved him with such enthusiastic fervour, that I would have given my own life to preserve his. And pity me, Orrabella ; for cruel as he has been to me and mine, I still do love him almost to madness. I struggle with my passion, I strive to teach my heart obedience to the dictates of reason ; but in vain." " Weak, unhappy girl," cried Orrabella, with a stern look, " if your heart is so refractory, enforce its obedience with this ;" presenting her with a dagger, which she always wore in her girdle.
" Rath

" Rafh woman," faid I, fnatching the dagger from her, juft as the trembling Alzira had extended her hand to receive it; " rafh woman, what is it you do? Have you forgot that the precepts of the Chriftian religion forbid felf-deftruction?" " So, (fhe replied haughtily) does it forbid murder, rapine, fraud, perjury, and oppreffion. Du Ponty, I think, profeffes Chriftianity. Oh! madam! madam! the profeffors of your religion muft practife themfelves what they would teach others, before you can hope to make fincere converts." The argument was unanfwerable, and I remained filent.

Tranquillity was now in a great meafure reftored; it was refolved the leaders of this lawlefs expedition fhould be fent immediately home to Spain. Thofe of their followers, who chofe to fubmit to the laws put in force by the viceroy and governor, were to be permitted to ftay; and when all was eftablifhed with fome degree of permanency, your grandfather was to depart for Hifpaniola. But whilft we were laying thefe plans, it pleafed Heaven, by an awful and unexpected vifitation, to break our meafures, and haften our departure from a coaft, where, from our firft landing, we had been furrounded only by terror, vexation and difappointment.

CHAP. VIII.

Beatina's Narrative continued.

WHILST preparations were making for two of the fleet to return to Europe, that Garcias and his followers might, from the juftice of a regular court of judicature, receive their fentence, your mother prefented Ferdinando with a daughter, who (by promife given to the queen of Spain on our leaving that kingdom) was chriftened Ifabelle. It received the baptifmal benediction when but four days old; for the diftrefs of mind under which your mother

had

had laboured, had affected the health of the infant, and its life was very doubtful.

It was nearly a fortnight from the birth of this daughter, when as Alzira, your father, and myself, were fitting in the apartment of Orrabella, an unusual drowsiness seemed to affect us all. The atmosphere had been for some days heavy and oppressive, which at this time had increased to such a degree as to occasion something like a sense of suffocation; the heat too was intense, though in general the climate is temperate and pleasant. A torpor seized our senses, and we sat gazing at each other, without power to speak, and with scarce the faculty of thinking. From this stupor we were aroused by a tremendous noise, like the howling of a mighty wind, the rushing of waters, and the crash of thunder. In a moment the palace shook to its foundation, and in less than ten minutes all was again profound silence. "One shock is past," cried Alzira, in breathless agony; "another, and all is lost. Oh Garcias! beloved Garcias! let me save you whilst I can." She caught up her child, who was playing on the floor, and rushed toward the wing of the palace where Du Ponty was confined. Ferdinando, who had learnt from his wife the nature of these convulsions of the earth, caught her in his arms; and bidding me haste and follow him, bore her with precipitation from the palace. The two children, Christopher and Isabelle, were in an adjoining apartment with their attendants. I ran to the door in hopes to snatch them from impending death, when the house again began to totter. I saw the apartment fall that held the precious babes, and heard their cries as they were crushed beneath the ruins. At that moment, my son, who had borne his wife to an open field, returned, and carried me through the falling fabric, which nodded horror on every side, to the same place of comparative safety.

Two hours of such tremendous threatenings from gleaming meteors, bursts of thunder, and contortions of the earth, as could hardly be supported by human nature, we passed sitting on the ground, expecting ev-

ery

ery moment it would open and fwallow us, when at
length nature became more compofed ; the dark mifts
which had obfcured the face of heaven began to diffipate, and the fetting fun darted his watery beams acrofs
the harbour. What then were our fenfations, when,
added to our terror at feeing the whole face of the
country a univerfal wreck, we beheld the harbour
empty, not one veffel to be feen ? Columbus had gone
on board that afternoon, to give fome orders prepara-
tory to our departure for Hifpaniola, and we imagined
that the hurricane, attendant on the earthquake, had
buried him and his companions in the waves. We
caft our eyes towards the place where lately ftood the
tents and dwellings of our friends and affociates ; nor
tent nor dwelling appeared ; all was filence, all was
defolation. A vaft cavity was feen where once the
dwellings were, through which impetuoufly rufhed a
foaming torrent ; which, as it roared along, bore on
its furface trees, fhrubs, ruins, and bodies of wild
beafts which had perifhed in the tempeft.

Oh ! what a night of agony we paft. Yet this rude
fhock had not affected univerfal nature. The dews
fell as kindly, the zephyrs blowed as refrefhing, and the
fun arofe with as much fplendor, as though the night
had paffed in its ufual tranquillity. And why not ?
The whole world is but an atom floating in infinite
fpace, and we who crawl on its furface but as emmets,
thoufands of which might be accidentally crufhed
beneath the foot of the paffenger, without deranging,
in the leaft, the beauty, order and fymmetry of
the univerfal whole.

When we beheld the defolation which fpread far
and wide on every fide, defpair had nearly feized our
minds ; but as the morning advanced, we defcried
four of our veffels coming with a gentle breeze into
the harbour. Columbus landed, and our meeting was
fpeechlefs ecftacy.

From the devaftation of the night, about forty fouls
had efcaped, and thefe entreated to be allowed to embark and quit the coaft immediately. Columbus
having affented to their requeft, and had us conveyed
on board his own fhip, put immediately to fea. He
.   then

then informed us, that hearing the hurricane roar before it came upon him, he cut the cables of his ship, and ordering the sails to be loofed, prepared to put before it, whichever way it should drive, as the only hope of faving his veffel. Several others followed his example; and providentially the tempeft bore directly out of the harbour. Thofe who caught the firft moment to put to fea, were faved; three fhips remained in port, and were fwallowed in the general ruin.

Garcias and his whole party were in this dreadful night hurried out of time into eternity. Of all the princefs Orrabella's attendants, only Cora and her mother were faved. Poor Alzira, with the virtuous Peruvian maid who faved us from the vile fchemes of the Caftilians, were buried in the ruins of the palace.

On our arrival in Hifpaniola, Columbus fhewed his commiffion and authority to difplace Roldan and his officers, and to take upon himfelf the reins of government. The natives, and indeed the inhabitants in general, received him with acclamations of joy, and followed the degraded Roldan to the water fide when he embarked, with curfes, fhouts and hiffes.

Two years from this period paffed on in the utmoft tranquillity. The only alloy to our happinefs at this period, was the ill health of your mother, whofe delicate frame had received a fhock almoft beyond her ftrength to fupport. But time by degrees weakened the remembrance of her fevere loffes; and as her fpirits began to regain their wonted tone, health faintly tinged her cheeks, and enlivened her grief-fwoln eyes.

It was at the clofe of the year 1504, that we received the afflicting intelligence of the death of Ifabelle of Spain. When Columbus was informed of an event fo diftreffing to us all, but to him in particular, he preffed her portrait (which he ever wore about his neck) to his lips; "Oh! my royal miftrefs," faid he, "in the grave, with thy virtues, lies buried the fame, the honour, the happinefs of Columbus." He fpoke prophetically; for within fix months from the death of the queen, your grandfather was recalled; and Davilla, a crea-

ture

ture of the king's, and an intimate of Roldan's, was appointed to fucceed him as viceroy. Your father, offended at the indignity offered his parent, refigned all his offices, and we returned to Spain together. Columbus never vifited the court; but immediately on landing retired to an eftate he poffeffed in Valladolid. Ferdinando attended the levee of the king feveral times, but he was either entirely overlooked, or addreffed in fuch terms of chilling coldnefs, that his high fpirit could not brook it, and he followed his father into retirement.

Perhaps your inexperienced mind will wonder how Roldan, but a few years fince poor, and dependent on the friendfhip and bounty of Columbus, could have intereft fufficient to difplace that valiant commander, and place a favorite of his own in his office. But, my dear girl, the neglected Roldan was poor, the returning governor was rich. And they who in the former fituation treated him with contemptuous neglect, or at beft with cold, fupercilious civility, now received him with open arms, applauded every word he fpoke, and, like fummer flies round a veffel which contains honey, fwarmed with a fond, officious, greedy hum, in hopes to fhare the fweets that it contains.

Roldan was a man of the world; he heard them, received their careffes, fmiled internally at their duplicity, made them fubfervient to his purpofes, and then retaliated on them the contumely and fcorn which he well remembered once to have received. Added to this, Ifabelle was dead; and Ferdinand, who never cordially loved Columbus, eagerly caught at any opportunity, however frivolous, to difgrace a man whofe unexpected fucceffes were a conftant reproach to him.

Poffeffed of a princely fortune, beloved by his friends, and (even fallen as he was from power) ftill feared by his enemies, furrounded by a loving and beloved family, Columbus might have been expected to enjoy many years of uninterrupted tranquillity. But, alas! his noble heart was wounded paft cure. It was not power he had coveted from the firft; wealth he defpifed; titles were beneath his notice; it was honour, untarnifhed

nifhed and unfullied fame, he fought. The one had
been twice involved in fufpicion, and the other was
threatened to be wrefted from him ; for many of the
creatures that infefted the court of Ferdinand, pretended that the difcovery of the vaft continent now
called America, was nothing extraordinary ; and that
many had fpoken of it as a thing more than poffible
long before Columbus attempted it. Befides this, a
report was fpread that the continent had been formerly difcovered by fome mariners who were fhipwrecked
on its coaft, and providentially returned to their native
country ; that the chief of thefe mariners, being entertained at the houfe of Columbus's father whilft he
was yet a boy, he had liftened attentively to the de-
fcriptions he gave of its fituation, latitude, and com-
puted diftance from Europe ; that he had treafured
this in his memory, and the old mariner dying foon
after, Columbus had impofed the difcovery on the
world as his own, the fruit of indefatigable applica-
tion, and intenfe ftudy.

These reports, which were malicioufly circulated by
his enemies, preyed on his fpirits. His health daily
declined ; his appetite forfook him, and reft was a ftranger to his pillow. He fhunned the fociety even of his
neareft connexions ; he would fpend whole days in his
clofet, where he had carefully preferved his chains, and
I have often furprifed him weeping over them like an
infant. Life became a burthen to him, grievous to
fupport, and it pleafed Heaven to releafe him from it
on the 20th of May, 1506.

What my fufferings were, thus deprived of my firft
and deareft friend and companion, it is impoffible to
give you any idea of. For many months, I fhut myfelf from the fight of all ; even the prefence of your
father and mother were painful to me. Their affliction was fcarcely lefs poignant than mine, and the moft
luxurious moments any of us knew, were when we were
recounting the virtues, and weeping over the memory
of our departed hero. But from thefe tender indulgencies we were aroufed by a furious war breaking
out between Spain and the Ottoman Empire. Numbers

bers of volunteers, gentlemen of the firſt rank, prepared to repel theſe invading Moors.

Ferdinando inherited the ſpirit of his father; his
country required his aid, and unaſked, he offered it.
During a war of ſeven years, your mother and myſelf
(who remained retired in Valladolid) ſaw him but
three times. His viſits were always ſhort, and our
fears for his ſafety were ſo great and multiplied, that
the pain of parting more than counterbalanced the
pleaſures of meeting. His laſt receſs from arms was
four months, during the winter of 1514. At parting,
he tenderly embraced me. On taking leave of his
wife, who after ſo many years again gave him hopes
of becoming a father, he entreated her, ſhould he not
return before the birth of his child, and it ſhould prove
a girl, that ſhe would have it chriſtened *Iſabelle*. " It
was the wiſh of our late royal miſtreſs," ſaid he, " that
one of our children ſhould bear her name. She is
now no more ; but the ſmalleſt wiſh of the patroneſs
of my departed father will ever be a command to me."
" And to me," ſaid Orrabella ; " if my child is a female, lſabelle ſhall be her name." Your father again
embraced us, bleſſed us, and departed.

The war continued with unabated fury on both
ſides. Ferdinando was in conſtant and dangerous
ſervice. Six months paſſed, and no hopes of his return ; at the expiration of that period, you, my dear
child, were born ; and in ten days after, you were baptized by the name of Iſabelle.

Your mother had not left her apartment, when one
day as we were ſitting by the window, we perceived a
courier riding full ſpeed up the avenue that led to the
houſe. I left the room to take the expreſs, my heart
foreboding fatal tidings, and wiſhing to conceal
them as long as poſſible from your mother. But as
I went down the front ſtairs, a ſervant, who had received the packet from the meſſenger, ran up the
back way, and delivered it into the hands of the unfortunate Orrabella. She opened it, ſhe read. Ferdinando was no more, and I returned to the apartment juſt time enough to ſave her from falling to the
floor.

floor.   Violent convulsions succeeded each other ; and before morning, my poor little Isabelle was an orphan. How I supported myself through such accumulated misery, Heaven (who no doubt assisted me) alone can tell.

It was many days before I could summon resolution to examine the fatal packet particularly.   When I did, I found my brave son had fallen gloriously in single combat with the heir to the Ottoman sceptre ; that he saw his antagonist fall, and died triumphing in the excellency of his own religion, and exhorting all around him to persevere to the end.   I wept at the loss of my child, but I gloried in his faith, valour and constancy in the Christian cause.

From that time, my life has been a continued blank. I have seen but little company.   My nephew, the marquis Guidova, son to a brother of mine, the offspring of a marriage that my father contracted after my union with your grandfather, with two amiable young women his sisters, and a charming creature whom he had made his wife, were the only society that afforded me any satisfaction.   I endure ceremonious visits, it is true ; but I always feel them insupportably tedious, and impatiently look for the moment when the departure of my guests would release me, and I might either unbend my mind in observing your innocent sports, or in deep solitude, by reflection and hope, be again united to those departed objects of my affections, Columbus, Ferdinando and Orrabella.

In less than a twelvemonth after the death of your parents, I made my will.   For the contents and meaning of that *will*, I refer you to the beginning of this long epistle, which, at hours when my strength and spirits would permit the employment, I have been nearly three months in writing.   And now, my dear Isabelle, I bid you adieu.   May you possess all the virtues of your father and grandfather, all the beauty and fortitude of your mother, and be ever exempt from the sorrows that have lacerated the heart of

BEATINA.

Your

Your chief attendant was your mother's favourite Indian fervant, Cora. Should fhe live till you
reach the years of maturity, be to her a firm friend ;
her attachment to your parents, and affection for
yourfelf, has been unbounded ; let your gratitude be
the fame.

Columbia had read, and paufed, and wept, and
read again, till, in her anxiety for the fate of Orrabella, fhe had forgot what fhe fo earneftly had wifhed
to know, concerning the marriage of her mother.
The conclufion of the manufcript, however, brought it
frefh to her memory. She turned the paper on all
fides ; no farther intelligence was to be gleaned from
that. But Cora, Cora had been particularly mentioned, as ftrongly attached to the lady Ifabelle. No
doubt fhe could inform her of all fhe wifhed to know.
She had no fooner conceived the idea, than, folding
the papers which fhe replaced in the efcritoire, fhe
locked the drawer, and haftily fought the apartment
of her aged fervant.

C H A P.   IX.

Supplication, Rejection, Compliance.

" I HAVE read all the papers," faid Columbia, feating herfelf befide Cora, who was taking her evening's repaft ; " I have read them all, but they do not
give me any account of my father, or how he became
acquainted with the lady Ifabelle." " I did not fuppofe they would," replied Cora, fipping with affected
unconcern fome milk which ftood before her, and then
breaking into it the remainder of a flice of brown
bread, which lay befide it.

" Well, but dear Cora," faid Columbia, laying her
right arm over her old fervant's fhoulder, and looking
with fmiling earneftnefs in her face ; " but dear Cora,
I dare fay you could tell me all about it." " Oh !

G

not

not I," she replied, putting from her with a rejecting motion the lovely arm that encircled her neck ; " not I, indeed. I tell a story so badly, and make so many repetitions, and am so tedious and minute, you would have no patience to listen ; so you and Mina may go and walk, and I'll go to bed, and then, you know, we shall both be satisfied."

" Nay but, dear, dear Cora, now don't be angry. Pray forgive me if I was a naughty girl, and impatiently would not give you leave to tell the story your own way. Only inform me how my mother became acquainted with, and afterwards married to, an Englishman, and a Protestant, and I will promise not to interrupt you from the beginning of your story to the end."

" Aye, to be sure," said Cora, " we are mighty condescending now. O my conscience, there is nothing like curiosity to make a young lady gentle and complying. This morning it was, Be quiet, Cora, and pray hold your tongue. Hold my tongue indeed ; why I warrant I could have told you every thing that happened, as well as those letters. But you liked reading the letters best then, and so mayhap you may find some more to-morrow that will tell you every thing you wish to know."

" 'Tis well," said Columbia, somewhat haughtily, " I will go to my mother. She referred me to you ; but since you do not choose to comply with her desires, I will from her mouth request a recital of events, which, however the recollection of them may make her own heart bleed afresh, she will, I am sure, recount, to gratify the laudable curiosity of her child. You, Cora, may go to bed and rest ; your lady, the daughter of the princess Orrabella, and her unfortunate offspring, will pass the night in sorrow. She in tears of bitter remembrance, and I in lamenting afflictions I cannot but feel, though I have not the power to alleviate."

This was attacking Cora in the most vulnerable part. " Stay," said she, catching hold of Columbia's robe, " stay, my dear young lady, but a few mo-

ments,

ments, and I will tell you all." " That's my good Cora," said she, kissing her cheek with affection ; " I will now go and take leave of my mother for the night. You shall go to bed, Mina, and I will come and sit beside you. We will put out the candle. For you know the moon shines full into your chamber, and I always think a story doubly interesting when it is told by moonlight.

This arrangement made, Columbia went to the apartment of her mother, and partook of a flight repast. But little conversation passed between them. Isabelle was buried in reflection, and the mind of her daughter fully occupied by the events she had been so lately made acquainted with, mixed with a restless impatience to repair to the chamber of Cora. Supper finished, she requested leave to retire ; and Mina, being dismissed from her attendance on the lady Isabelle, they seated themselves on the side of Cora's bed, who eagerly began the promised recital.

" The old lady Beatina died when your mother was not seven years old, and so the Marquis Guidova thought it best only to leave a few people just to take care of the house and pleasure grounds in Valladolid ; and discharging the rest of the servants, take my young lady with him to Madrid, where he for the most part lived. He was a good gentleman, and his lady, Heaven bless her, was as kind a gentlewoman as ever breathed. They were as fond of your mother as though she had been their own child ; but who could help loving her ? She was so condescending, so benevolent, so good-natured, and more than that, so beautiful. So there was masters hired to teach her every thing, that ladies of quality generally learn, and they used to say they had no trouble in teaching her ; for she understood every thing they told her in a minute, and never forgot what she had once learnt.

" Many cavaliers and gentlemen sought her for their bride before she was fifteen. Not a family in the Court of Spain but would have thought it a high honour to have had her for a daughter-in-law. The young King of Spain used to call her a star of the first
magnitude ;

magnitude; a gem fit for the crown of a prince, and many other such pretty names. But she, sweet lady, was never made proud or conceited by these praises, but was always the same humble, affable creature as ever. Then she was so pious! Ah, when shall I see her equal? Her behaviour was an example, admired by all, but I am afraid followed by very few.

"Well, as I was saying, many noble gentlemen sought to win her love, but she was indifferent to them all; and at the age of eighteen, was still unmarried. At that time, Sir Thomas Arundel arrived at the Spanish Court. He was travelling to finish his education, and came with a design of passing a few months in Madrid. Ah! he was a brave gentleman."

"Yes," said Columbia exultingly, "my father was a brave man, a worthy man, an honour to human nature."

"Aye, but," replied Cora, "he was much handsomer then, so tall and graceful, such fine blue eyes, and such a complexion, so fair and ruddy, and his beautiful dark brown hair fell in such becoming ringlets round his face and shoulders, that he looked like something more than mortal."

"Why, Cora," said Mina, laughing, "you describe his person with such rapture, that I do believe you fell in love with him yourself." "Heaven help me!" cried the old woman, "that would have been a fine story truly! No, no, I knew my station better. Besides, I was old enough to be his mother. I could not shut my eyes, you know, and I hope there was no harm in admiring what I saw."

"No, to be sure," said Columbia, "and I dare say my dear mother admired him as much as you did."

"Indeed she did," replied Cora; "he was introduced to the Marquis by the Duke de Medina, and invited by him to a splendid entertainment which he gave to all the foreigners of distinction at that time resident at the Court of Spain. Oh! how beautiful did my dear lady Isabelle look on that day; her dress was always plain, but it was always becoming, and more than usually so at that time. No wonder the

young

young Englishman was captivated at first fight. I
could have gazed at her for the whole day without
being tired; what then must he feel, who had never
before feen a woman fo charming? For to excel her,
I am fure would be impoffible. A ball was given in
the evening; Arundel danced with your mother.
Every eye was turned upon them as they gracefully
and lightly followed the mufic. Every tongue murmured their praife.

"When the lady Ifabelle retired for the night, fhe
afked me if I had feen the accomplifhed cavalier
Arundel, and whether I did not think him very handfome. "I have been deaf to all my lovers as yet," faid
fhe, fmiling; "but I believe, Cora, if Arundel fhould
afk my hand, I fhould not long withhold it." The
next morning, as fhe was rifing, the whole of her dif-
courfe was on the gallant Englifhman; and fhe could
not help wifhing to fee him again, and wondering
whether he thought of her as much as fhe did of him.
Whilft fhe was prattling on in her lively innocent
manner, the Marchionefs Guidova entered the apartment.

"Ifabelle, my love," faid fhe, "I have fome papers
in my poffeffion, which I blame myfelf for not having
earlier entrufted to your perufal. Here are fome confidential letters which paffed between your father and
his parents; and here is a packet addreffed to you, my
love. It was written by your grandmother during
the laft years of her life. It will inform you of fome
particulars in her will, which it is neceffary for you
to know. You are there ftrictly forbid to unite yourfelf
to a man who profeffes the reformed religion.

"The Marquis and myfelf could not but obferve laft
night the pointed attentions, and undifguifed admiration, with which Sir Thomas Arundel addreffed you;
and I think it is not unlikely but he may requeft you in
marriage. Now, my dear Ifabelle, Arundel is a ftrict
Proteftant. This, you are fenfible, will place an in-
furmountable barrier between you. And fearful that
my dear girl might let her heart be allured by an
agreeable perfon and infinuating addrefs before fhe

knew

knew the fatal confequences that muft refult from fuch an indulgence, I would no longer delay requeft-ing you to give a few hours ferious attention to the papers I here leave with you, particularly that writ-ten by your grandmother."

"When the Marchionefs had thus fpoke, fhe em-braced the lady Ifabelle, who had not once attempted an anfwer; and laying the papers on the table, left the apartment.

"While the Marchionefs was fpeaking, I had retir-ed, out of refpect, to a window at the moft diftant part of the room; but I now approached my young lady, and found her pale, trembling, and her eyes brimfull of tears. "My fate, I fear, is fixed, Cora," faid fhe. "My heart has hitherto been infenfible to the admiration and love I heard numbers daily pro-fefs for me; but though fo lately acquainted with him, I had, almoft unknown to myfelf, fuffered a wifh to rife, that Arundel might be the man defigned to be my hufband. It is true, I never faw him till yefter-day; but to his character I am no ftranger. Fame fpeaks highly of his honour, integrity and wifdom. But I am told our fates can never be united. If fo, a convent fhall be my choice, and I will fhut myfelf from a world that will, I greatly fear, contain no charms for me, when deprived of the hope of fharing the fate of Arundel."

" She then haftily finifhed dreffing, and difmiffed me; nor did I fee the dear lady again, till noon. Oh! how her fweet countenance was altered fince the morning. She was bathing her eyes in water, in hopes to take off the rednefs; but it was in vain. The traces of her tears ftill remained upon her cheeks, and her eyes were funk and heavy. The papers lay open on the table before her; fhe fpoke but little to me; and though when fhe did fpeak, fhe forced a fmile, I could fee her poor heart was almoft breaking.

" The Marquis had rightly judged, that Arundel was enamoured of my lady; for on the very next day, he took an opportunity to call, when he knew the Marquis was at the levee, and going into the gar-den,

den, as he faid to amufe himfelf till the Marquis's return, he fent one of the fervants to defire I would
grant him a few minutes' converfation.   I went, you
may be fure; for I guefled his errand, and thought
it no harm to pity him, and hear what he had to fay
on the fubject.   So as I was faying, I went, and he
afked me a thoufand queftions about the lady Ifabelle;
as whether fhe was engaged, whether fhe had ever
mentioned him, and whether it was with diflike or
approbation.   Oh! Mifs Columbia, he was a fine
fpoken man; it would have done your heart good to
have heard him.

"Your lady is an angel, Cora," faid he; "and I fhould
think myfelf but too happy to be permitted to wear
out my life in her fervice.   I mean to afk her of her
guardian; but as I would firft be affured, that by fo
doing I offer no violence to her heart, I have written
to her.   Take this letter, then, my good Cora, and
deliver it into the hands of your divine miftrefs.   To-
morrow I will expect an anfwer, and my future conduct fhall be regulated by her commands.   Be not
alarmed, (for I drew back as he offered me the letter)
be not alarmed; I fwear to you, I have nothing but
honour in my thoughts."   He then forced the letter
into my hand, and with it his purfe, containing about
twenty ducats; and at that moment hearing the Marquis's voice in the garden inquiring for Arundel, I
could neither return his prefent, nor tell him of how
little effect his letter would be; fince my lady was
reftricted from marrying a Proteftant.   But the exact
terms of the reftriction I did not then know.   So, as
I faid, hearing the Marquis coming, I was glad to
avoid meeting him; fo turned into another walk, and
made the beft of my way to the houfe.

"When I gave your dear mother the letter, fhe chid
me for bringing it, fhe hefitated for fome time; but
when I told her he promifed to be guided by her commands, fhe opened and read it.   Then bidding me
bring her pen and ink, fhe wrote an anfwer, frequently
ftopping to wipe off the tears that gufhed into her
eyes.

"From

" From this time for above a fortnight, letters paffed. between them every day. My poor lady grew penfive, languid, and avoided company ; fpent great part of every night in writing ; and in the day time, every moment when fhe thought nobody obferved her, fhe would read over the letters of Arundel.

" At length fhe told me one evening, that fhe had promifed to give him an interview. " He fups here to-night," faid fhe, " and after fupper will retire to the alcove on the eaft fide of the garden, and thither I have promifed to go to meet him ; and you, Cora, muft go with me."

" I felt as though it would be right to perfuade her not to go, but did not know how to begin ; nor could I rightly comprehend how (as they both worfhipped. the fame God) the differing in a few trifling forms and ceremonies could make it fuch a crime for them to marry.. I thought perhaps the Marquis and his lady might be angry at firft, but that they loved her fo well they would foon be. reconciled. After this interview, the whole of which I did not hear, and what I did hear I did not fully underftand, only this I know, that Sir Thomas Arundel fpoke fo finely, that he made me cry more than once ; the lady Ifabelle told him, that by marrying a Proteftant fhe fhould forfeit her whole fortune. " And what of that, my lovely Ifabelle," faid he, " I have fortune enough for us both, it is your invaluable felf I adore ; you flatter me ; I am not indifferent to your generous heart ; why then does my charmer hefitate ? Let me call this dear hand mine ; and my wealth, which is more than enough for all the comforts, nay, even the elegancies of life, will be happily employed, if it can procure a moment's fatisfaction for the idol of my foul."

" Take me not thus by furprife," replied your mother ; " give me a few days to reflect ferioufly, and your generous propofal fhall have an ingenuous and candid anfwer. Believe me, Arundel, I will examine my heart with the minuteft fcrutiny ; and if I find its attachment to you unconquerable, I will not infult the majefty of Heaven by making profeffions with my lips
which

which my foul would refufe to ratify. I will then openly, in the face of the world, avow my choice ; and if I do fo, we will not have different interefts in fo ferious a concern as our everlafting peace in futurity.. No, Arundel, if I become your wife, I embrace your religion. Your faith fhall be my faith, your God my God."

"She then fuffered him to kifs her hand, and leaning on my arm, returned to her apartment.

" I fay, after this interview, my lady became more compofed ; in fome meafure regained her wonted cheerfulnefs, and the Marquis was pleafed to perceive a fadnefs wearing off, the fource of which he had been. afraid to inquire into.

" It was about ten days from this time, that my lady afked me if I would go with her to England. " For I am refolved, Cora," faid fhe, " to fhare the fate of Arundel. This day I mean to avow my defigns to my guardian, and relinquifh my eftates to my coufin. Will you, then, follow the ruined fortunes of your poor miftrefs ?"

" Will I ?" faid I, throwing my arms round her ; " can any thing but death ever feparate me from you ?"

" It was towards the evening of this day, that the lady Ifabelle fent me to requeft the Marquis, his lady, and their eldeft fon, would grant her half an hour's converfation. They returned for anfwer, that they were perfectly at liberty, and awaited her prefence in. the faloon. She then bade me go into the garden, where fhe knew Arundel was waiting, and bid him come to. her. He obeyed the fummons, and they entered the faloon together. It was then your noble mother declared to her guardian and his family the refolution fhe had taken. " Had you entrufted me," faid fhe, " earlier with the contents of my grandmother's will, I might have been upon my guard ; but my heart was irrevocably gone before I knew it was a crime to love a Proteftant. Having made my election, I do not fcru ple to confefs, that, deprived of Arundel, I would never unite with any other man. Seclufion from the world would have been my next choice ; but reafon

and

and religion told me, that a heart throbbing with all the anxieties of a difappointed paffion, is not a fit facrifice to be offered to a Being of infinite purity.   My fortune I refign to my coufin, and with him as much happinefs in the enjoyment of it as I feel in relinquifhing it.   My perfonal ornaments I imagine are my own.   To-morrow I fhall beftow them and myfelf on Arundel; and in becoming his wife, I embrace the Proteftant perfuafion."

" When my lady had finifhed fpeaking, fhe gave her hand to your father, who fpoke fomething very handfome, though I can't remember what.   But I know the old Marquis raved, his fon looked quite happy, the Marchionefs cried.   One moment embracing lady Ifabelle, and entreating her to remember her grandmother's laft injunctions, and not forfeit her eternal peace by quitting the bofom of the holy mother church; then fhe would entreat her fon not to enforce the will to its full extent, but to be content to divide the fortune with his coufin.   Oh! dearee me, it was a terrible night; for what with the rage of the one and the tears of the other, my poor lady was almoft diftracted.

" Well, fure enough the next morning fhe was married, and in a few days they fet off for England.   On our arrival in London, fhe publickly abjured the Romifh religion, and would have had me do the fame; but I thought changing my religion once in my life was enough.   I was taught by the good lady Beatina, to worfhip one God, and to look for eternal falvation through the merits of a Redeemer; to be humane and charitable to all mankind; and to the extent of my weak power, I have endeavoured to practife what fhe taught.   And I hope I fhall, when I die, go to heaven as well as if I had changed my religion twenty times."

" You cannot change for the better, my good Cora," faid Columbia; " yet you muft not blame my mother."

" Blame," cried Cora, haftily; " no indeed; the lady Ifabelle never did any thing that deferved blame.
She

She had sense and education to understand what she was doing; but I was weak and ignorant, and feared by renouncing one error, I might perhaps fall into a greater."

"Well but, Cora, what was the cause of my father's ruin? He was a man of family and fortune, and though I perfectly remember him, and recollect that I had not seen him for some months before, I lost him forever. I shall never forget the day on which I was told he died. My dear mother, who had been absent some days, was brought home in a state almost bordering on distraction. She embraced me, called me her dear orphan girl, wept, wrung her hands, and then clasping them, cried, Oh! my Arundel, you are lost to me, but I trust you are reaping the heavenly reward of your faith, constancy and fidelity. She then sent me from her, and a few weeks after we came to this old Castle. I did not half like it, Cora, nor am I quite reconciled to it now. Those old ruins at the west end, the long gallery that leads to it, the great arched gate-way that looks ready to fall down, and the nasty moat full of green water, fill me with terror and disgust; and if it was not for the little garden that Matthias has done up so cleverly, and the pond where we go to fish, I should be ready to die with melancholy."

"And so should I," said Mina, "and with fear too; for they people about here."

"Now do be quiet, Mina," said Columbia, "for it grows late, and I want Cora to finish telling about my father."

Mina was silent, and Cora continued. "Ah! my dear Miss, those were sad times indeed; it was then your dear mother was plunged into poverty; for you know your father was a Protestant. Well, he was a favourite with our young King Edward the VIth. and greatly beloved by the Protector Duke of Somerset. They favoured the reformers very much. And there was that wicked Bishop Gardiner, who was for burning and hanging every body that did not say their prayers just as he did. He hated your father; and so he, and several others as wicked as himself, laid a plan to take away the life of the good Duke of Somerset. They said he had laid a plan to murder the young King, and accused my worthy master, Sir Thomas Arundel, of being an accomplice; and they threw them into prison, and a great many more good men were confined. And then Gardiner, and the Duke of Northumberland, and others of his enemies, pretended to have a regular trial. But what sort of a trial was that, when the men that accused them were the judges? So they condemned them all to suffer death, and all their substance was forfeit to the crown, as they called it; but I warrant these righteous judges had pretty pickings out of them. So your dear father was beheaded on Tower Hill, and all his estates seized on by these robbers. For I am sure they deserve no better name; for Northumberland only took away the life of the good Duke of Somerset, that he might supply his place about the person of the King, and lay a plan for his own advantage. For he persuaded the King to make a will, and appoint the lady Jane Grey, daughter to the Marchioness of Dorset, his successor; and this he pretended to do out of love to the reformed religion; but it was only because she was married to his son, the Lord Guilford Dudley. But Heaven punished him for his wickedness, in the ruin and death of those beloved and charming children.

"Oh! what a heavenly creature lady Jane was; your mother loved her dearly. She, sweet soul, did not wish to be a queen; and when, on the death of King Edward, they offered her the crown, "I pray you pardon me, my friends," said she, "and suffer me to decline this honour; it is too much for me, frail mortal that I am. I would seek an eternal, not a temporal crown; and much I fear the cares and anxieties attendant on the one, will prove a hindrance to my doing my duty necessary for the obtaining of the other;" and when urged to comply, she bowed her head in token of assent. She said to those who knelt to do her homage, "Pray rise, my friends, this is mockery. You think I am ascending a throne; but I see clearer, and perceive it is a scaffold. Heaven pardon me this
usurpation,

ufurpation, for I feel I have no right to thefe honours, and fhall be ready, when called upon, to refign them to my rightful queen."

When Northumberland told her it was for the good of the Proteftant caufe that fhe fhould affume the reins of government, fhe replied, " The God of the Proteftants is all-fufficient for their protection ; he will not fuffer them to be punifhed or perfecuted, unlefs it be for his own wife purpofes, to prove their faith, and bring home more to the fold. He needs not the af-fiftance of my feeble arm. However, my good lord Duke, if you think you are in the way of your duty in heaping thefe unrequired honours upon me, I fubmit ; and Heaven forgive us both."

" I have heard Matthias, who was in London at the time, repeat her words fo often, that I cannot be miftaken in repeating them again. So the fweet, good lady was proclaimed queen, and nine days after, fhe was feized, with her hufband and her father-in-law, and fent to the tower, and foon after they were all be-headed. And fo I have no doubt but the wicked Duke repented, before he died, of his malice to the good lord Protector and your dear father ; and when he came to lay his own head upon the block, I dare fay he wifhed he never had been the means of bringing fo many innocent people there. The lady Jane left one fon by lord Dudley ; he was chriftened Henry ; but he bears neither the title, nor inherits the fortune of his father, more fhame for them that have wronged him of it."

Here Cora ceafed fpeaking ; but Columbia was un-able to thank her, or articulate a fingle word. The unmerited accufation and ignominious death of her father, the untimely fate of the lovely and pious lady Jane, had fo oppreffed her heart, that it was only by the indulgence of tears fhe could fave herfelf from fainting. At length fhe recovered fome degree of compofure, kiffed Cora, bade her good night, and ta-king Mina's hand, retired to her own apartment.

H   CHAP.

An Adventure.

IT was now near midnight. The moon, which had shone so bright on the beginning of the evening, was now enveloped in black clouds. The wind whist-led hollow through the branches of the half-naked trees, and the turrets of the old Castle echoed its mel-ancholy notes. A cold rain beat against the case-ments, that shook in their frames from the violence of the rising tempest, and every thing wore a dreary, sombre appearance.

"I declare," said Columbia, shuddering, "my spir-its are depressed, and the apartment looks so gloo-my. I wish I had not put out the candle."

"And I'm sure so do I," said Mina, "for I can't get these stories out of my head, that the people, who live round about, tell of this old Castle; for I do assure you they wonder how we can live in it, and often ask if we never hear or see any thing."

"What should we hear or see." said Columbia, "more than our own family?" But she shuddered involuntarily, and drew nearer to Mina, casting a fear-ful glance round the room.

"Nay, I don't know," replied Mina, "I never give much ear to such stories; but they do say the Castle is haunted; and that a great Baron, who owned it a good many years ago, killed his brother here, that he might win the love of his lady, whom he afterwards seduced, and then sent her beyond sea, where she was never more heard of. And they say the young Bar-on's ghost often is seen about the western ruins; and that he walks round the garden, and even sometimes through the long gallery and up the winding stair-case that leads to the turret that joins this range of apartments."

"I dare say it is all fancy," said Columbia, getting into bed, and covering her face with the bed-clothes."

"Very

"Very likely," said Mina; "for you know we never saw or heard any thing."

"No, nor, I will answer for it, never shall," replied her young lady, "so good night, Mina, for I'm sleepy."

Mina began to say, "Good night;" but stopping short, was seized with a universal shivering; her heart beat violently, and she trembled so that the bed shook under her.

"Oh heavens," said Columbia, "what's the matter?"

"Hush," replied Mina, "listen." In trembling silence they both raised their heads from the pillow, and distinctly heard human steps ascend the stairs, which led to the turret, and which winded on the side of their apartment immediately against the head of the bed.

"Perhaps Matthias is not gone to bed," said Columbia. "Oh! but I'm sure he is," replied Mina, "I saw him take the candle and go into his own room. Besides, what should he do up in the old turret at this hour, on such a dismal stormy night?"

"Well, I do believe," said Columbia, "it was only imagination." Just as she spoke, they heard the same noise repeated, but it was the sound of a person descending; and presently a man's voice was heard, but not loud enough to distinguish what he said.

At the same instant they both sprang out of bed, and rushed into Cora's apartment; there, as they stood trembling and trying to awake her, they discerned through a window, that looked towards the entrance that led to the long gallery, two figures come from the door; and by the pale glimmer of the moon perceived that one, by his beaver which appeared ornamented with feathers, was a gentleman of rank, the other seemed habited like a servant.

"There, there," said Mina, "do you see?" "Yes," said Columbia; "but there are two figures." "Aye, to be sure," replied Mina; "I dare say that was his faithful servant, who was killed endeavouring to preserve his master."

Columbia,

Columbia, terrified as she was, could scarcely help smiling at the readiness of her young attendant in thus explaining every thing according to her own fancy. They followed the two figures with their eyes, till they seemed to vanish amongst the western ruins; and then waking the old servant, and creeping into her bed, one on one side and one on the other, related the wonderful appearance they had seen, and the sounds they had heard.

Cora was strongly tinctured with the superstition so prevalent at that period in almost every rank. She fully believed that they had seen supernatural beings, and related, as she lay trembling between them, so many horrible stories, that the terrified girls were afraid to open their eyes, left some ghastly spectre should meet their view.

At length the clock in the great hall chimed three; and Cora, believing that at that hour spirits of every kind returned to their graves, composed herself to sleep, as did her young companions.

But the spirits of Columbia had been so harassed, that her sleep was disturbed by frightful visions, and she awoke before the sun had cheered the face of day. Glad to behold returning light, she arose, dejected and unrefreshed; and throwing a mantle over her shoulders, walked into the garden, in hopes the morning air would revive her, and take off the appearance of languor which the want of rest had given her, and which she was sure would alarm her mother. There, as she wandered through a walk of filbert trees which had been planted by Matthias near the margin of the pond, she endeavoured to persuade herself, that the terrors they had experienced in the night, were merely the effects of an imagination previously weakened by melancholy recitals, and tinctured by the gloominess of the weather. The storm was now past; the sun was above the horizon; the sky was serene; the air just sharp enough to brace the nerves, and give elasticity to the spirits. Columbia, enlivened by its vivifying power, had nearly assumed her usual cheerfulness and serenity, when turning out of the walk towards the house, from an arch-way in the ruins she saw, advancing

ing towards her, the same figures she had faintly perceived cross the court yard in the night.   She shrieked, drew her mantle over her face, and fell fainting to the earth.

When she recovered, she found herself supported in her mother's arms, the stranger standing beside her. The alarming mystery was now soon dissolved.   This phantom, who had so alarmed Columbia and her attendant, was a material substance, Sir Egbert Gorges by name; who, with his servant, flying from the persecution of Mary (that cruel oppressor and tyrant of her Protestant subjects) to the coast of Wales, in hopes to seek in some foreign land that liberty of conscience denied him in his own, was benighted, and had lost his way.

Sir Egbert, thus weary and disconsolate, wandering over the dreary heath, drenched by the storm, fatigued, cold and hungry, made up to Amesbury Castle, which he perceived at a small distance.   The ruinous appearance of the western wing, which, being next the path he had taken, he first entered, gave him little hope to find inhabitants in it.   He made his way through the mouldering apartments into the court yard, which he crossed; and in the hope of finding some room more habitable than any through which he had passed, he ascended the stairs which lead to the turret.   But disappointed in his wishes, he said to his servant as he came down, "This is certainly a desolated ruin, and we had better return to the most comfortable place we can find on the other side the court yard.   For this old turret is more dismal and shattered than any thing we have yet seen."   These were the footsteps and voices that had so alarmed Columbia.   And according to this resolution, they were returning to the western wing, when the terrified lady and her servant saw them from the window.

Sir Egbert, and his man Rawlins, having led their horses into a place of comparative shelter, sought for a room that might be best calculated to guard themselves from the damp nocturnal air.   Finding one less shattered by the hand of time than the rest, they stretched

                                themselves

themselves on the floor, and resting their heads on their saddles, composed themselves to rest. Hard as the bed was, Sir Egbert, worn out with fatigue and anxiety, soon dropped into a profound slumber; nor was Rawlins long in following his master's example. From this state of insensibility they did not awake till day light stared them in the face, and the all-cheering sun darted his beams through the high-arched windows.

Having seen that their horses were safe, they were preparing to explore the whole of the Castle, which they now perceived contained some apartments which wore a face of comfort, and seemed as though lately repaired; when as they came from the ruin, the first object that met their eyes was Columbia. Surprise riveted them to the spot. But her terror on beholding them, her shriek, and consequent fall, made them hurry to her assistance; when just as they had raised her from the ground, Matthias appeared at the further end of the garden. He hastened towards them, helped to support his dear young lady, and by his loud cries soon alarmed Mina and Cora. The fainting Columbia was borne into the hall, and the lady Isabelle, hurrying to her assistance, had just taken her in her maternal arms, when she recovered sense and recollection. The confusion of this scene had been too great to allow of any explanations on one side, or questions on the other; but Sir Egbert seeing the young lady now free from alarm, related, in as concise a manner as possible, the foregoing circumstances, entreating leave to rest for a few days in the Castle, whilst he sent Rawlins to the nearest sea-port to inquire for a vessel bound for Holland or Germany.

To this Isabelle assented; and in the course of the day Columbia, half ashamed of her terrors, related to her mother and her guest the adventures of the night. Cheerful and unrestrained conversation begets confidence; and before the hour of rest arrived, Sir Egbert had informed his fair hostess of the real cause of his hasty flight from London, and his resolution to quit the kingdom. Isabelle was astonished at the account he

gave

gave of the dreadful persecutions under which the Proteſtants ſuffered, from the bigotry and cruelty of Mary, and thoſe tools of her power, Gardiner and Bonner. Secluded as ſhe was from the world, though ſhe knew they had great difficulties to ſtruggle with, yet ſhe had no idea to what height they carried their barbarity, and that burning, ſtarving, hanging, and ſometimes drawing the victims of their miſguided zeal in quarters, was the method taken to bring back the heretics (as they were called) to the ceremonies and ſuperſtitions of the church of Rome.

"Ah! my dear child," ſaid ſhe to Columbia, "how much gratitude ought we to feel toward the divine Diſpoſer of all events, that it has pleaſed him, with a correcting hand, to lead us into this happy obſcurity, where we can enjoy that liberty of conſcience which calms and fortifies the ſoul, and ſits it for all events. Alas! Columbia, had your dear father lived to this day, we might all have ſuffered at the ſtake together. Then let us be humble and ſubmiſſive to the judgments of our Creator, ſince followed by the invaluable bleſſings of peace, life, and the liberty of worſhipping him in ſecurity, according to the dictates of our conſciences."

Sir Egbert was charmed with the poliſhed manners and unaffected piety of the lady Iſabelle. But the youth, beauty, innocence and vivacity of Columbia had faſcinated his ſenſes. The harmonious trio parted for the night, mutually pleaſed with each other; Iſabelle reflecting, in pious gratitude, on her preſent happy ſecluſion from a court which ſeemed a ſcene of murder, and where, perhaps, the morals and principles of her darling child might have been tainted by the bigotry and ſuperſtition of the times, Sir Egbert to ruminate on the intereſting figure, and ſweet ſimplicity of manner that characterized Columbia, and Columbia herſelf to chat with Mina about the handſome Sir Egbert Gorges.

CHAP.

CHAP. XI.

Girlish Chat, Maternal Advice, Departure of a Lover.

"DO you not think our visitor very handsome?"
said Columbia. "Yes, indeed I do," said
Mina; "and his man is a clever kind of body."
"And you think him very handsome too, Mina?"
"No, not very handsome; but he has a great deal to
say; and Cora says he must have travelled, for he
knows all about her country as well as if he had been
there." "But that may be from reading, Mina; for
my mother told me to-day, that her father, Ferdinando Columbus, wrote a full account of her grandfather's voyages, during the two years they lived retired at Valladolid. And that at the time my father's
papers were seized by his enemies, the manuscript was
found, and it has since been printed."

"And so, madam, this fine stranger, this Sir Egbert,
is going away to live amongst the Dutch people, Rawlins tells me. I'm sure, if I was as him, I would stay
where I was." "But that would be improper, Mina;
my mother could not possibly entertain a strange knight
here above a day or two, as she has neither husband
or son to bear him company."

"Well, if she has no son or husband, she has a
daughter; and I warrant Sir Egbert would excuse the
deficiency of the one for the sake of the other."
"How wildly you talk, Mina; I shall be angry with
you presently." "What, madam, for supposing the
handsome young knight is pleased with you; nay, now,
I dont think you would be very much out of humour
if a storm was to detain him at the Castle a week or
so; for then you know there would be some excuse
for his staying." "Pho! you talk like a simpleton,
Mina; I wish you would go to sleep."

"Well, I wonder how some folks can be so insensible;
for my part, as soon as I saw him this morning, and
found he was real flesh and blood, I said to myself,
Well, he is a charming cavalier, and if he would but

fall

fall in love with my lady Columbia, and she with him, we should have a wedding, and there is always rare doings at a wedding; and then we should go away from this old Castle. And now, if you won't be angry, I'll tell you the truth. I never do say my prayers, but what I pray that we may soon go away from this shocking old place. Why the arch, at the entrance of the great gate, looks as if it would fall whenever the gate is opened; but to be sure that a'nt very often, we are not much troubled with horsemen, except when Matthias comes from market, with the old blind crippled creature that brings home our provisions. And then one never sees a young man. I declare, I blessed my eye-sight when I saw Mr. Rawlins: for what with Matthias's stories about the wars, and Cora's earthquakes, and shipwrecks, and storms, and so forth, I am heart sick."

"And I'm sure, so am I, Mina, to hear you talk such a parcel of nonsense. However, if you are tired of staying in the Castle, you are at liberty to leave it whenever you please."

"Me leave it, madam? No indeed, madam; if it was ten times more frightful than it is, I would not leave it without you, and my dear lady your mother, for the whole world. No; I meant that if you were married to this handsome Sir Egbert, we should go to London again, and have fine dressing and balls and feasting."

"You don't know what you wish for, Mina. London is no place for Protestants. London is now the seat of every enormity which is practised under the mask of religion. Queen Mary is determined that every one of her subjects shall think as she thinks, and those who hesitate to obey her, are burnt at the stake."

"And pray, madam, why don't the people burn her? She is but one, and she has multitudes of subjects."

"She is their queen, Mina, and they dare not lift the hand against her."

"Queen indeed! Well, I am but an ignorant girl, to be sure; but I can't see why a queen should com-

mit

mit murder without being punished for it, any more than other people."

"But it is. not called murder, when a person is executed for acting contrary to a queen's commands."

"They may call it what they please ; but if a person is innocent of any real crime, and is only accused of not thinking as the queen does, or perhaps they don't preach and pray just as she would have them ; I do say, and will stand to it, if she orders them to be hanged or burnt, it is murder.   Aye, and I fancy her cruel queenship will find that out, when she dies."

"You are a strange girl, Mina, and are now talking on a subject we neither of us are competent to speak upon ; therefore let me beg you to say no more. Let us say our prayers, and be thankful we are, by our seclusion from society, and our distance from the metropolis, secure from any fear of her power.   And so, Mina, good night."

Columbia spoke this in so reserved a tone, that Mina did not dare to proceed, though she never felt less inclined to sleep.   Yet she endeavoured to obey her young lady, said her prayers, and addressed herself to sleep.

The next morning, Rawlins was dispatched to the nearest sea-port, to inquire for a vessel, and from some unforeseen accidents, he was detained nearly a week.

During this interval, the daily, nay, almost hourly opportunities Sir Egbert had of conversing with Columbia, and observing her mildness, modesty, and understanding, which had been highly cultivated by the tender and careful hand of maternal affection, inspired him with a passion ardent as it was sincere ; and he could not repel the rising wishes of his heart, that this lovely creature might be ordained his partner, to smooth the rugged path of life.

Columbia had not been insensible to the many virtues and graces of Sir Egbert ; but she had not learnt to disguise her thoughts from her best and only friend. She considered it no crime to love a worthy and accomplished man, and her mother became the confi-

dant

dant of her paffion almoft as foon as fhe difcovered it herfelf.

"I cannot blame you, my child," faid this indulgent parent, "for the admiration and efteem you feel for Sir Egbert Gorges; but I would wifh my dear Columbia had feen a little more of the world, before fhe felected a partner for life. You are yet fcarcely eighteen, and Sir Egbert is almoft the firft man you have feen above the rank of a clown. It is to be hoped, my love, we fhall not always be fecluded in this folitary Caftle. I underftand from Sir Egbert, that queen Mary's health is in a declining ftate. Should fhe die without iffue, her fifter Elizabeth is next heir to the throne. Elizabeth is herfelf a Proteftant, and will no doubt encourage all the profeffors of that religion. I fhall in that cafe, for your fake, my child, repair to court, and petition for a reftitution of your father's lands. I have alfo another duty to fulfil. A dear friend of mine, who fuffered death a few years after your father, in her laft moments recommended her infant fon to my care. Should fo fortunate an event take place as the princefs Elizabeth's acceffion to the throne, I fhall to her protecting care recommend this laft branch of an unfortunate family, the innocent part of which have been the fufferers for the guilty ambition of the reft."

"I apprehend madam," faid Columbia, "that you mean the offspring of the Lord Guilford Dudley and lady Jane. Cora informed me of their unfortunate exaltation and confequent death; and I have no doubt but the royal Elizabeth will, fhould fhe ever have the power, reftore to him his rank and the fortunes of his anceftors."

"Heaven grant that I may fee the day," faid Ifabelle. "And now, my dear child, though I would not put any reftraint on your inclinations, I could wifh you to decline a union with Sir Egbert Gorges, till quieter and more profperous times. Enter into no ferious engagements with him, which hereafter may caufe you much uneafinefs. Mix firft with the world. The heart is apt to be deceived in its firft emotions, when little knowledge of the world, and feclufion from

fociety,

society, prevents a free election; and the object who, when the only one, appeared to have every attraction, to possess every virtue, when compared with others of more shining talents, loses the charm that had at first engaged the affections. The disappointment then becomes intolerable, and the unfortunate victim of inexperience passes a life of unceasing regret and fruitless repining. I will confess to you, that Sir Egbert has spoken to me on this subject, and I then advised him, as I now advise you; and I hope my dear child will not find a difficulty in following advice, that can have no other end in view than her happiness."

"I cannot hesitate a moment, my dear mother," said Columbia, "to promise that your wishes, which to me are commands, will ever be observed as laws. Think not, beloved parent, that your child was so weary of your society, as to renounce it for that of a stranger, whom she had scarcely known a week. Oh no! however partial my heart may be, I could wish to be better assured of the merits of the object, before I gave my future happiness into his keeping. Let Sir Egbert pursue his intended voyage; if at some future period he should return still constant to me, I think I can answer for the stability of my affections."

"Make no rash promises, my dear child," said Isabelle. Columbia bowed her head assentingly, and remained silent.

Rawlins now returned, with intelligence that a vessel for Amsterdam would be ready to sail in the course of three days. On the morning of the second day, therefore, Sir Egbert, and his faithful Rawlins, departed; the former having, with many thanks for her hospitality, taken leave of his fair hostess, and entreated her permission for Columbia to accept a small diamond ring in remembrance of him; which, as it was of trifling value, she allowed, at the same time presenting him with a plain gold one from her own finger, saying, "I know you will condescend to accept this in token of amity, for trifles become valuable when we esteem the giver."

Mira

Mina had, at parting from Rawlins, received from him a small silver coin, on which with his knife he had marked the initials of his name, and over the letters were two hearts. A puncture was made near the extremity, and a string being passed through it, Mina suspended this pledge of affection round her neck.

But Mina, though she fancied herself in love past cure, and that she should be constant through long absence and trials of every kind, was a stranger to her own heart. She was by nature a coquette, fond of admiration, and pleased with those who gave it. She loved Rawlins, because he had professed to love her. But, alas! poor Mina, when she used daily pathetically to lament the absence of her lover, had she but searched her heart thoroughly, she would have discovered that it was the flattery she missed; and that food of female vanity, artfully administered by any other person, would soon have effectually banished the remembrance of Rawlins, and dried up her tears for his departure.

Far differently affected was the heart of Columbia. Her partiality to Sir Egbert was sanctioned by the voice of reason. She felt that, was she his wife, she could brave every hardship with him without repining. For his sake she would then have faced persecution, poverty, famine, nay, death itself. But at the same time she forcibly felt, that to descend in the smallest degree from the respect she owed herself, from that necessary pride and dignity of manner which is the safeguard of female honour, would be no longer to deserve him. When engaged in studies that enriched her mind and expanded her understanding, she thought such employment would render her a more pleasing companion to Sir Egbert. He was seldom from her thoughts in her waking hours, and frequently visited her dreams; and in her daily devotions were mingled constant prayers for his safety.

Yet Columbia was not totally divested of that vanity, which in her childish years had formed so striking a trait in her character; but it had been so judiciously repelled and corrected by her mother, that no

I

more

more of it remained than served as a foil to her virtues. She knew she was handsome, and she studied to set off that beauty by humility, benevolence, simplicity and candour.

C H A P.   XII.

Confusion, Distress, unexpected Journey.

ABOVE eighteen months after the departure of Sir Egbert passed in the usual way, in which time Rawlins had twice been to Austenbury Castle with letters from his master. But the enemies of Gorges, encouraged by Mary, pursued him with such unrelenting fury, that he dared not himself venture to England.

It was in the summer of 1558, that an event took place which had nearly put a period to the life of lady Isabelle, and involved her daughter in accumulated misery. A report had been circulated, that the child of lady Jane and lord Guilford Dudley was in existence, and in the protection of a Protestant family.

The furious zeal of Mary inspired her with the idea, that by getting this infant into her power, and having him educated in the Catholic religion, she should render Heaven an acceptable piece of service, and entirely atone to the child for the death of his parents, the signing of whose death-warrant sometimes lay heavy on her conscience; and in those fits of gloomy remorse, she always had recourse to her ghostly confessor for spiritual advice and comfort, who upon these occasions did not fail to inflame her mind, and render her bigotry more obstinate.

This man, who was in the confidence of Gardiner, bishop of Winchester, encouraged the queen in her desire to get young Dudley into her power; and accordingly, diligent inquiry was made after the place of his seclusion. At length, accident discovered what they had begun to despair of. Sir James Howard, a

younger

younger branch of the houfe of Norfolk, (a family re-nowned for their attachment to the Catholic perfua-fion,) a man in high favour with the queen, and in habits of ftrict jntimacy with Gardiner, Bonner, and the reft of the perfecuting party, having received an invitation to fpend the decline of the fummer in Wales, at the feat of Sir Owen Langwylling, and partake of the diverfions of hunting and fhooting, in the begin-ning of Auguft, repaired to the antique manfion of his friend.

Sir Owen was young, gay, and fond of diffipation and expenfive pleafures, which the fmallnefs of his pa-ternal inheritance would not permit him to enjoy to the extent he wifhed.   Howard was rich in money, as well as in court favour ; and Sir Owen invited him into Wales, in hopes the youth and beauty of his only fifter, Winifreda, might catch his affections, and at once fecure an honourable alliance for herfelf, and a powerful friend for him.

It was during this vifit, that Howard, tired one evening with the rude and turbulent mirth of his hoft and his Welfh affociates, left them to finifh their ufual libations to Bacchus; and mounting his horfe, on whofe neck he fuffered the reins to reft, giving a loofe to reflection, and intending only to efcape from dif-gufting fociety, and enjoy the pleafures of retirement and contemplation, he permitted the animal to take what courfe he pleafed.   Nor was his attention aroufed as to the time he had been abfent, till, coming fud-denly out of a wood into a wide-extended heath, he perceived the fun was drawing near the weftern hori-zon ; and turning his horfe with a defign to meafure back the path he had trod, on the fummit of a hill, he faw Auftenbury Caftle. The parting beams of the fun fhone full on the venerable ruin, and his rays gave an uncommon richnefs to the furrounding profpect. Curiofity urged him on, and once more turning his fteed, he proceeded at a good pace up the hill.

It has been obferved, that the moft ruinous part of this Caftle was that which fronted the heath ; and Howard, having led his horfe over a broken draw-bridge,

bridge, which appeared as though it had not been raised for more than a century past, fastened his bridle to
a ring which had formerly supported a swing gate, or
private entrance to the fortified part of the Castle, and
proceeded through an aperture in the wall immediately
into the garden, the neatness and cultivation of which
convinced him there were inhabitants in the Castle.
He went forward, and at the extremity of the garden,
in the arbour before mentioned as the scene of Columbia's childish sports and festivity, he saw a female, ty-
ing up a bunch of reeds in the form of a wheat sheaf,
and a boy standing beside her, apparently about five
years of age.   As he approached nearer, the beauty of
Mina struck him with surprise.   For it was she who
had been walking with young Dudley, who was now
become an inmate at the Castle, and who wanted to
go into the water after the reeds, that he might play
at reaping.   She had gathered a few to divert him,
and was employed in binding them up, when Howard approached them.   He spoke before she saw him.
She started from her seat, and the blood mounted to
her cheeks.   But Howard was young, handsome, and
addressed her with such an air of gallantry, that she
soon recovered herself, and felt more inclined to be
pleased than alarmed at his intrusion.

Night was now rapidly approaching, and our knight
was chagrined at it.   He wished to have entertained
the pretty, blushing Mina with expressions of his admiration and wonder, to see so much loveliness thus
buried in solitude; but time would not permit.   He
asked, however, a few trifling questions, ventured to
take her hand and kiss it, caressed the child, and presenting Mina with a jewel which he took from his
beaver, and which he had observed she eyed with attention, requested her to meet him there again early
the next morning.

"But be sure, pretty creature," said he, "you do
not mention having seen me to your father and mother."   "I have no father and mother, Sir," said Mina.

"Well, then, to your uncle, or aunt, or grandmother."   "La! Sir," said Mina, with simple earnestness,
"I have

" I have no relations; I am only poor Mina, and live
here in the old Caſtle with my lady."   "And who is
your lady?"   "The lady Iſabelle Arundel."

" Well, you need not tell her, or any body, that you
have ſeen me; I have a particular reaſon for it.   I
will be here by ſix o'clock to-morrow morning."

. Mina promiſed ſilence, and dropping a curteſy, wiſhed him a good night.

The thoughts of this ſimple girl were agitated and
confuſed, as ſhe proceeded towards the houſe.   She
was reſolved not to mention the ſtranger; but then
Henry, he might tell the lady Iſabelle.   But to prevent
this, immediately on her entering the Caſtle, ſhe put
the child to bed, and then repairing to her lady, gave
as a reaſon for having done ſo, that he was tired with
his walk.

The uſual avocations of the evening ſo entirely occupied Mina, that ſhe had no time to think, till the
hour of retirement.   No ſooner was ſhe in her own
apartment, than, drawing the jewel from her pocket,
ſhe compared it with the ſilver token of Rawlins' hon-
eſt love.   " It is much finer," ſaid ſhe, delighted with
its luſtre; " but then what will poor Rawlins ſay, if I
ſhould prove falſe-hearted?"   A deep ſigh, as this reflection paſſed through her mind, ſeemed to tell. her,
the aſſignation ſhe had made with the gallant ſtranger
was improper.   But Mina poſſeſſed that unfortunate
flexibility of diſpoſition, that unfits its poſſeſſor for oppoſition of any kind.   Her inclination to keep her
appointment was ſtrong, and the courtly manner,
handſome perſon, and rich preſent of Howard, had
ſuch an effect upon her deluded ſenſes, as to lead her
to imagine ſhe had never loved Rawlins half ſo well,
as ſhe found ſhe was inclined to love him.

Had the lady Columbia been preſent, ſhe would no
doubt, notwithſtanding her promiſe to the contrary,
have confided to her the intruſion of the ſtranger, and
her promiſe to ſee him again in the morning.   Indeed,
full of her own praiſes which ſhe had heard from his
lips, and occupied entirely in reflecting on his fine
perſon and rich dreſs, ſhe wiſhed for nothing more ar-

dently than an opportunity to repeat it all to her young lady. But Columbia now flept in an apartment by herfelf, and the young Dudley partook of Mina's bed; fo the fecret was of neceffity confined to her own bofom. Its importance in her ideas, was fufficient to banifh fleep from her eyes; and fhe impatiently counted the clock till it ftruck four. "Well, two hours will be foon paft," faid fhe, and immediately began to drefs herfelf. But quick as her impatient wifhes led her to imagine they might pafs, when fhe was anxioufly counting every minute, fhe thought the period an eternity.

Having dreffed herfclf, fhe defcended to the great hall, and thought to be fure it muft be near five; but poor Mina was deceived in her calculation, and found it but a quarter paft four. She liftened, fhe watched the hand, fhe could fcarcely perceive it move; it had certainly ftopped; her lady would be up, fhe fhould be prevented meeting the ftranger. Impelled by this idea, fhe had walked more than a dozen times from the hall to the arbour and back again, and ftill it was fcarcely half-paft five.

At length the long expected ftranger was feen approaching; for he had been impelled by a curiofity, as reftlefs as the new born paffion of Mina, to repair early to the place of affignation.

As he had leifurely walked his horfe homeward the evening before, he had reflected on the name of Mina's lady. Arundel! It was furely the widow of Sir Thomas Arundel; if fo, the intimate friend of lady Jane Grey. Might not that boy be the long-fought offpring of Dudley? If fo, how would it elevate him in the queen's favour, to inform her where the boy might be found! Let no one blame Howard; he thought it right to endeavour to fnatch the child from the dangers of what he termed an heretical education; he acted from principle; and it were well for every one, who courts the favour of the great, if they could lay their hands on their hearts, and with truth affert the fame.

In

In his conversation with the artless and infatuated Mina, he drew from her every circumstance he wished to know. Her inexperienced heart, fascinated with his flattery, and thinking him all that was amiable on earth, could not imagine him a Catholic. She thought he professed the same religion with her lady and herself. He perceived her error, and suffered it to continue, till he made himself acquainted with every particular within the knowledge of Mina; and in the end triumphed in the spoils of her innocence.

For three weeks, an illicit intercourse was carried on between them; during which period Howard had sent intelligence to his friend Gardiner, that the object of their hitherto fruitless search was now within their reach. At the name of Arundel, Gardiner felt all his hatred revive towards the widow and child of his departed enemy; and, glad of an opportunity to wreak on them the vengeance which the blood of the husband and father had not sated, eagerly flew to the queen, and obtained from her an order to oblige the lady Isabelle, and her daughter Columbia, with their young charge Henry Dudley, to repair immediately to London; and in case of hesitation and reluctance, to bring them away by force.

It was morning; breakfast had been removed; Isabelle and Columbia were employed at their needles. Mina was reading (as was the custom of that lady to make either her daughter or her attendant do every morning) some extracts from a book of devotion. A violent knocking at the gate alarmed them. Matthias, with all the haste his advanced age would permit, went to open it. In a moment the court was filled with horsemen, soldiers and friars, and at their head was Sir James Howard, who was appointed to command the party, and conduct the prisoners to London. Mina's heart leaped within her. She thought her lover was come with this noble train, to claim her as his bride, (as he had frequently promised he would) and take her with him to London. Lady Isabelle turned pale. Lost! ruined! undone! were all the words she could

could articulate, and she sunk almost lifeless on the nearest seat.

The little Dudley was playing in the hall, when Howard and Sir Owen entered. Unused to danger, unacquainted with fear, he ran to the brave gentlemen, as he called them, admired their waving plumes and laced doublets; and hanging on the hilt of Howard's sword, told him he remembered when he came through the broken wall into the garden. This circumstance, which a variety of other childish amusements had contributed to efface, had lain dormant in his youthful mind, till the appearance of Howard; who happening to wear the same dress then, as when the child first saw him, brought it fresh to his memory.

Howard took the child in his arms; and, followed by Sir Owen and a number of other gentlemen, entered the apartment of lady Isabelle. Though nearly overcome by her fears, the widow of Arundel had still a dignity of manner, a chaste severity of countenance, that awed even the most ferocious. Sir Owen Langwylling, a man neither celebrated for his politeness or sensibility, was a proof of this. He met the glances of her penetrating eyes, and sunk abashed behind Howard, mingling in the thickest of the crowd, his beaver off, and his eyes bent to the earth.

Isabelle arose from her seat at their entrance, and bowing gracefully, requested to be informed of the cause of their visit. Howard was confused; he hesitated as he attempted to speak, and at that moment catching the eye of Mina, who stood trembling behind Columbia, he bowed low, to conceal the agitation that prevented his articulating a single sentence. At length recovering, and obstinately fixing his eyes in such a manner as not to be able to catch a glimpse of Mina, he thus addressed the lady Isabelle.

"Our august sovereign Mary, queen of England, hearing that Henry Dudley, son and heir to the lord Guilford Dudley, (who suffered with his unfortunate lady for their attempt upon the British crown) is under your ladyship's protection, and wishing to compensate to the child for the enforced rigour with which she

was

was obliged to treat his parents, has commiffioned me, James Howard, in conjunction with thefe noblemen and ecclefiaftics, to bring the boy to her court, that fhe may reftore to him the title and eftates of his father, and have him educated in the principles of that holy religion, which alone leads to falvation."

The full conviction of the imprudence fhe had been guilty of, and the duplicity Howard had practifed, now flafhed on the mind of Mina. She gave a faint fcream, and funk lifelefs to the floor.

Cora, whom the general confufion had brought to the apartment, affifted to raife her, and fhe was borne into the open air. It was not till fhe was quite out of the room, that the lovely form of Columbia attracted the notice of Howard. He beheld her following, with looks of the tendereft fenfibility, the apparently lifelefs form of her fervant, and in a moment every other object was obliterated from his mind. He feemed attentive to the lady Ifabelle as fhe fpoke, but his ears drank not one word of what fhe uttered; nor was he awakened from his trance of admiration, till fhe ceafed fpeaking, and prepared to lead her daughter from the room. He then endeavoured to recollect himfelf, and afked, " If fhe would not accompany her young charge to London ?"

" I thought I had expreffed my intention fo to do," replied Ifabelle, with a look of furprife; " if you, Sir James, did not underftand me, I here repeat that I will go with him. Not to refign my precious charge to the queen, but to affert my prior right, the right of friendfhip, fealed by a moft folemn vow, that Henry Dudley fhould be educated in the religion of his parents. I know you will tell me there are tortures to enforce obedience to the queen's will; but I have learnt to defpife them. Happinefs and I have long been feparated, nor do I hope ever to tafte it more, till, in the realms of blifs, I am again united to my martyred friends and hufband. Think not, then, the threats of death can terrify me. Death is the only period I can look forward to with calmnefs, hope and comfort."

She

She then slightly bowed her head, and taking young Dudley in her right hand, and leaning on her daughter with her left, she passed into an inner apartment.

In half an hour's time, she sent a message, intimating that she would be ready to attend their orders by four o'clock the ensuing morning. In the mean time, she requested they would make themselves welcome to whatever her poor habitation afforded.

It was late in the day before Mina was sufficiently recovered to be able to quit her apartment. The weather had been sultry, the anxiety of her mind had contributed to enervate her frame; and as she attempted to walk, the universal debility and weakness which she experienced alarmed her. She thought the air might refresh her. Passing from her chamber through the hall into the garden, the first object that met her view as she descended the steps, was Rawlins. She trembled, she gasped for breath; but she recalled her fleeting senses, and hastily gliding down the steps, catching his hand, in silence hurried him to an obscure part of the garden. There, as soon as the tumultuous throbbings of her heart would permit her to speak, in a few words she unfolded to him the unhappy situation of her lady and family; but shame prevented her revealing the unfortunate part she had unintentionally had in their ruin.

"If you have any letters," said she, "give them me quick, and then fly and conceal yourself in the western ruins till I can bring you answers, which you must with all speed convey to your master."

Rawlins gave her the letters, and would have embraced her; but conscious guilt made her shrink from him, and covering her face with her hand, she waved him toward the place of concealment, and returned to the house. She passed unobserved to the apartment of her lady, and delivered the packet to the hands of Columbia.

Fortunately Rawlins had not been seen by any of Howard's party; and Isabelle, having assured herself of this, determined by his means to send Henry Dudley

ley into Holland, to Sir Egbert Gorges. She even urged Columbia to fly with the child from the perfecution that awaited them. But that heroic girl refused to defert her mother in the hour of diftrefs. " Befides," faid fhe, " the fafety of Henry will be more certain, when Rawlins has no woman with him, with her fears and her weaknefs, to impede his journey."

Ifabelle, anxious to put her plan in execution, at night-fall fent a meffage to Howard and his followers, craving their excufe, that the preparations for the morning's journey would not permit her to fee them again that night ; but that fhe hoped they would not fpare her poor provifions, and as early in the morning as they pleafed, fhe would commence her journey.

Mina, who delivered this meffage to them as they were taking their repaft in the great hall, led young Dudley by the hand round to bid them all good-night ; then through an apartment, which by a private door communicated with the weftern wing, fhe conveyed him immediately to Rawlins, who waited till midnight ; and then mounting his horfe, with the child before him, proceeded with all poffible fpeed to the neareft fea-port, where the bark he had come over in laying ready, he went immediately on board, and prevailed on the mafter, by promifes of a large reward, to put directly to fea.

The fortitude Mina had been obliged to exert in the execution of this plan was almoft too much for her frame to fupport. The facing the perjured Howard, and delivering to him a meffage from her lady, the taking what fhe firmly believed to be a laft farewel of Rawlins, were excruciating trials. But fhe thought the fevereft fufferings were too little to atone for the mifchief fhe had brought on the houfe of Arundel ; and the confolatory reflection that fhe had been the means of faving one innocent victim from the power of Mary, having fhed a temporary calm over her foul, fhe enjoyed a few hours repofe, which in fome degree enabled her to fupport the confufion of the enfuing day.

By

By three o'clock, Howard and his followers were in motion. Isabelle heard them, and awaking Columbia and Mina, who that night both slept in her chamber, they equipped themselves for their journey. Their clothes had been previously packed the night before, and sent down stairs.

As the clock struck four, the widow of Arundel, with her daughter and attendant, descended the great stair-case into the hall. Howard received them at the foot of the stairs; but not perceiving the child, eagerly inquired for him. "He is gone," said Isabelle, with a dignified composure; "but that he has escaped is not your fault. I have sent him out of the reach of bigotry and cruelty, and am now ready to go and answer to the queen for my crime. It is I, I only, that am guilty, if guilt it can be termed. And I do entreat you, Sir James Howard, and you, holy fathers, whose profession is peace and mercy, suffer not these children to be insulted or punished for my faults. To you, Sir James, I solemnly commit the safety of my daughter; that young woman is her attendant. Attached to her from almost infancy, I do beseech you let them not be separated. Your family is noble, you wear the badge of a soldier; I should hope you would neither disgrace the one or the other by injuring unprotected women, whom ill fortune only has thrown into your power. Now I am ready to set forward, and Heaven be my support."

The majesty of her manner as she spoke, awed them into silence. Sir James Howard, confounded by the pointed rebuke she had innocently given him, when she recommended her daughter to his protection, had not power to answer; nor was it till they had proceeded a considerable way on their journey, that they began to consider the very foolish appearance they should make at the court of Mary without Henry Dudley, who had been the chief object of their excursion.

During the journey, which the badness of the roads and the heat of the weather rendered fatiguing and tedious in the extreme, Howard let no opportunity
pass

paſs in which he thought he could effectually pay his
court to Columbia.   But the confeſſion of Mina (who
on the firſt night after their departure from Auſten-
bury Caſtle, had on her knees to her aſtoniſhed ladies
revealed the whole of her imprudence, and Howard's
feductive arts) would have effectually ſteeled her heart
againſt him, had there been no other motive for her
rejection.   But with ſuch a woman as Columbia, the
levity and unmeaning gallantry of Sir James Howard
could make no impreſſion on her heart; eſpecially
when it is remembered ſhe had been previouſly awakened to ſenſibility by the intrinſic merit of Sir Egbert
Gorges.

Iſabelle and her daughter bore the journey better
than could have been expected, and on the tenth day
from the commencement of it, they arrived in London.   Mina had drooped from the beginning, and was
on their arrival ſo ill, from fatigue and grief, that
there ſeemed but little hopes of her recovery.

The old ſervants, Cora and Matthias, were left in
the Caſtle, heart-broken for the departure of their kind
and beloved miſtreſs.   Their ſolitary days were paſſed in enumerating her virtues, and in offering up prayers for her ſafe and ſpeedy return.

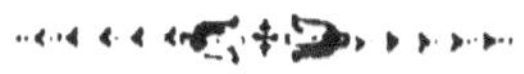

CHAP.   XIII.

Revolution—Tranquillity reſtored.

ON the arrival of Iſabelle and her daughter in
London, they were committed to cloſe confinement; though by the care of Howard, whoſe power
kept the eccleſiaſtics at a diſtance, they were treated
with reſpect.

The enſuing morning Iſabelle was ordered to attend
the queen.   With a moſt threatening aſpect did Mary
interrogate her on the ſubject of Henry Dudley's eſcape, and demanded to know where ſhe had ſent him.
The widow of Arundel was inflexible.   She only re-

K

plied,

plied, that she had sent him to a place of safety; that in so doing she only conceived she had performed her duty, since, being herself convinced of the errors of the Catholic persuasion, she had given by letter a solemn promise to his dying mother, that whilst she lived, Henry should be carefully instructed in the tenets of the reformed religion.

Irritated beyond expression by the noble firmness, which she termed obstinacy, of the lady Isabelle, Mary commanded her from her presence; at the same time giving orders for her to be put to the torture, to force a confession from her. But Gardiner, who was present, and conceived this would be an impolitic measure of the queen's, humbly entreated a few days might be allowed for reflection. "Perhaps, most gracious sovereign," said the designing prelate, "your royal clemency may have a more powerful effect on the generous mind of lady Arundel, than rigour; and the power of gratitude may draw from her a secret, which the most cruel tortures might not effect.

Isabelle was preparing to speak again, but Howard, who feared she might too far irritate the queen, and trembling for the fate of Columbia, hurried her out of the presence. Having committed her to the guards, who waited to re-conduct her to prison, he returned to the queen, and informed her of his passion for the daughter of the haughty Isabelle. "She is young, royal madam," said he, "and if I can judge of her disposition by her countenance, might be easily converted to the true religion; for she appears all compliance, affability and gentleness. Permit me to try to bring her over to our party. When once convinced of the errors of the faith she now professes, it will become a point of conscience with her to retrieve young Dudley from his present lost state."

"I suppose this girl is handsome?" said Mary. "I should call her superlatively so, had I never seen your majesty," replied Howard, bowing profoundly.

Mary, though at this period past her fortieth year, naturally plain in her person, and now more than ever so from the ravages of a disease which daily gained

ground

ground and began to give some very alarming symptoms, was still open to the voice of flattery. The compliment of Howard had an instantaneous effect on her temper. She smiled, and told him she would see this paragon. " I will converse with her myself," said she, " and endeavour to draw her by persuasive arguments to the true faith. But if I fail, let her and her proud mother beware. Her beauty shall not save them; they shall submit to the punishment appointed for obstinate heretics."

Columbia had suffered almost a martyrdom in the absence of her mother; a thousand fears had distracted her. Sometimes she imagined she should never see her again; that the furious queen, provoked by her refusal to discover the retreat of Henry Dudley, would doom her immediately to the stake; then would she wring her hands, and utter the most piercing lamentation, in which she was joined by Mina, whose distress was the more poignant, as it was mingled with self-accusation. At length she beheld her return, and her joy was for a few moments as wild as had been her sorrow.

Isabelle was convinced within her own mind, that the hour drew near in which she would be called upon to seal her faith with her blood, and endeavoured to arm herself with patience and fortitude for the expected trial. Every hasty step she heard, every unusual noise that issued from the street, she imagined was the messenger of her fate. But she carefully concealed these thoughts from her daughter, thinking to save her the misery of hourly expecting an event that would leave her an unprotected orphan, and which, however she might lament, she had no power either to prevent or retard.

They partook but sparingly of a repast that was brought them, when Isabelle endeavoured to divert her own and Columbia's melancholy by conversation; at the same time selecting those subjects which might tend to strengthen and fortify their minds against impending misfortune.

The

The afternoon was not more than half worn, when Howard arrived with the queen's mandate for Columbia to repair forthwith to the palace. It was then the tender mother had need of all her fortitude. In vain she pleaded to be permitted to go with her child; it was contrary to the commands of Mary.

Finding entreaty fruitlefs, fhe embraced her with tendernefs, and faid, " Remember, my child, thy mother's happinefs depends on thee. Oh beware ! Suffer no temptation, however great, to draw thee from thy duty to thy Creator. No, Columbia, not even to fave the life of thy mother, let thy faith be fhaken. If I muft fuffer, let me at leaft have the confolation of reflecting, in my laft hours, that my child preferred mifery to apoftacy."

" Fear me not, beloved parent," replied Columbia, returning her embrace, " I can never forget the noble examples of firmnefs and refolution fet me by my anceftors; and if the remembrance of thofe fhould fail to animate me, I will think that my failure in fo important a point would call a blufh into the face of my mother; and that would give me ftrength to withftand all temptation, however alluring, and defy all threats, all tortures, however terrible to human nature. Pray for me, my mother, pray for your poor child." She fell on her mother's neck, and fobbed aloud. Howard re-affured them, by pledging his folemn word, that no evil was intended; and taking her reluctant hand, led her from her mother into the prefence of the queen.

Columbia, though endowed with all the rigid virtues that fo eminently adorned her mother, yet had an appearance of more foftnefs; and the awe a young perfon, totally unacquainted with the forms of courts, as well as of the world in general, might be fuppofed to feel on finding herfelf in the prefence of her fovereign, and that fovereign incenfed againft her, gave her an air of timidity and humility highly gratifying to the pride of Mary.

The queen queftioned her concerning the departure of young Dudley. " He went away with a fervant
belonging

belonging to a particular friend of my mother's," said she, "who wifhed me to have gone too, but my love for the beft of parents, and my confcience, which told me I fhould be wanting in filial duty, prevented my embracing the propofal."

"Confcience?" faid Mary, fiercely, "the confcience of a heretic cannot be fuppofed very tender; tell me, are you not a heretic?"

"I do not underftand the meaning of the appellation," replied Columbia mildly.

"I will endeavour to explain it to you," faid the queen; "come, child, be not alarmed. I will talk with you a little on religious matters. Your ignorance is really pitiable, but it is more your misfortune than your fault."

"I humbly pray your majefty to pardon me," replied Columbia; "I am a weak girl, and totally inadequate to the tafk of fpeaking on fo reverend a fubject, efpecially before a perfon of your majefty's fuperior underftanding and extenfive erudition. I have hitherto lived a peaceful, happy life, unknowing and unknown; where, to the extent of my abilities, I have endeavoured, ftrengthened as I was by the example of a refpectable mother, to difcharge my duty both to my Creator and my fellow creatures. I befeech your majefty, fuffer me to return to that calm retirement, where the remainder of my days may glide on in obfcurity, and my name pafs quietly into oblivion."

"I fear," faid Mary, " you entertain erroneous ideas of your duties, both moral and religious. Your faith and mine are different." Columbia was filent. "I will appoint fome holy men to vifit your mother in her retirement," continued the queen, " and they fhall alfo inftruct you in the tenets of our holy church. Are you willing to be inftructed and converted?"

"I am willing to be inftructed by wife and good perfons," replied Columbia; "I will liften to them with patience; and if my reafon is convinced——"

"It muft, it will be convinced," faid the queen, eagerly, "unlefs you wilfully fhut your eyes and ears."

K 2

"And

"And that I hope I never shall do," said Columbia, fervently, "againſt the light of truth."

Mary was ſatisfied, and diſmiſſed her, and ſhe was conveyed by the guards to the arms of her impatient and anxious mother.

Both Howard and the queen from this interview entertained ſanguine hopes of converting Columbia. They did not perceive that all her anſwers were ambiguous, and might have been explained in a very different ſenſe than the one they took them in.

Howard ſeized the favourable moment of the queen's good humour, to requeſt the charge of the priſoners might devolve on him. "I have a houſe, moſt gracious ſovereign," ſaid he, " not far from London ; ſome of the apartments have heretofore been uſed as a ſtate priſon. Suffer me to convey the widow of Arundel and her daughter thither ; I will anſwer for their being kept in ſafe cuſtody, with my life. In the mean time, my confeſſor, with whatever other eccleſiaſtic your majeſty may pleaſe to appoint, can viſit them every day."

" I ſee," ſaid the queen with a half ſmile, " you wiſh to have an opportunity of proſecuting your ſuit to the fair daughter of Arundel without interruption. Well, be it as you deſire ; into your charge I commit them, and at the hazard of your head," continued ſhe, ſternly, " be they forth coming whenever I demand them. For by the crown of my anceſtors I ſwear, they ſhall not eſcape my vengeance, unleſs they renounce their heretical opinions, and give up young Dudley to my power."

Howard, pleaſed that by this manœuvre he had got the perſon of Columbia entirely in his power, thanked the queen for her condeſcenſion, reiterated promiſes of not permitting them to eſcape, and haſtened to the place of their confinement, where he informed the lady Iſabelle and her daughter, that he had prevailed on the queen to let him remove them to a manſion of his own, not far from London. " You will there," ſaid he, " have the benefit of the air, and the indulgence of ſometimes exerciſing yourſelf in the garden. But I

have

have obtained this favour at the hazard of your difpleafure ; for I have promifed the queen that you will
daily converfe with ecclefiaftics of the Catholic perfuafion.   Your patience one moment, dear lady," feeing
Ifabelle was about to reply, "it is what you muft
fubmit to if you remain here.   Let me on my knees-
entreat you, then, to fuffer me to convey you, and
this angel your daughter, out of the reach of the tyranny of Mary.   Whilft you remain fecluded in her
palace, the inftruments of her power may, in the dead
of night, rufh in and facrifice you to her vengeance ;
but under my roof you will at leaft be fecure from.
fudden infult and furprife, and fhould fhe menace your
precious lives, I will preferve them at the hazard of
my own."

"Howard," faid Ifabelle, "I would fain believe
your profeffions are fincere ; but when I remember who
betrayed us into the power of the queen, how can I ?"

This was the firft moment Howard had fufpected
that Mina had difcovered his frequent vifits at Auftenbury Caftle.   He had ftrove feveral times, during
their journey, to draw her apart from her ladies, but
in vain.   She had always carefully avoided him.   But
this he thought proceeded from her fears of awakening
fufpicion ; nor did he once imagine fhe would confide
an intercourfe, that would appear fo much to her difadvantage, to the ear of a woman fo rigidly virtuous
as Ifabelle.   It is true, Ifabelle was rigid in her own
practice ; but fhe always made a juft diftinction between the errors incident to human nature, and pre-
meditated guilt.   For the folly of Mina, fhe found an
excufe in her fimplicity, and ignorance of the world ;
but for the art and feduction practifed by Howard,
fhe felt only contempt and horror.

"What reliance," continued fhe, ftedfaftly fixing
her eyes on his face, "what reliance can I place on
the word of a man, who by flattering promifes drew
an artlefs, innocent girl to her ruin, whilft from the opennefs of her unfufpecting nature, he learnt fecrets, the
divulging of which has plunged her only friends and
benefactors in unavoidable deftruction ?"

The

The cheek of Howard glowed with the crimson tint of shame. The penetrating eye, the forcible voice of Isabelle, sunk to his heart.

"I have been to blame," said he, in accents scarcely audible, "but do not too haftily condemn me. Allow something to the impetuofity of youthful paffion; and if, betrayed by an enthusiaftic partiality to the religion in which I was educated, I haftened to inform my sovereign where she might find the offspring of Dudley and lady Jane, let it be some expiation of my error, that I am severely punished in having unintentionally involved two ladies in misfortune, who, to every grace that can excite admiration, unite every virtue that should command efteem. Let not, I befeech you, the difcovery of my errors blind you to what is abfolutely neceffary to your own intereft and fafety, nor, by obftinately refufing the afylum I offer, heap frefh guilt upon me, by making me in a manner acceffory to your death, and that of your lovely daughter. The beauty and innocence of the fair Columbia have already awakened in the breaft of Mary a malignant fpirit, which fhe will be glad to gratify by facrificing her to her pretended zeal; for your daughter has already expreffed her attachment to the reformed religion, in terms too pointed to be overlooked. Another interview with the queen, and fhe will be loft beyond recovery."

Howard paufed for an anfwer. The mind of Ifabelle was in a ftate of agony. Her own life would have been nothing; fhe would have defpifed the protection of Howard, and imdauntedly braved the power of the queen; but her child, her darling Columbia, her fate, perhaps, hung on her anfwer. She was within the reach of the bigotted queen, Howard might protect, might fave her. What mother, in fuch a cafe, could hefitate?

Ifabelle bowed her head, and, in a voice tremulous through fear and ftifled indignation, affented to his propofal. A fhort time fufficed for preparation, and that very night they flept in the houfe of Howard, at Hamftead, if fleep it could be called, when to their

other

other anxiety was added the difappearance of Mina. She came with them to the houfe, retired after they had taken fome refrefhment, and when the hour of reft arrived, was not to be found. Howard was fufpected by Ifabelle, but Howard had departed with the fetting fun, and could not be queftioned.

At the firft appearance of day, Columbia arofe ; and for the firft time, eagerly counted the hours that would moft probably intervene before fhe could hope to fee Howard. The morning wore heavily away; Ifabelle was dejected and uneafy ; her daughter endeavoured to hide her own painful fenfations, that fhe might divert the anxiety of her mother.

About noon, their attention was aroufed by the entrance of two ecclefiaftics, who were appointed by the queen to vifit, exhort, and endeavour to convert the two prifoners. Ifabelle heard them in filence. Columbia was feveral times on the point of replying ; but a reproving look from her mother repreffed her thoughts before her lips could give them utterance.

At the conclufion of the conference, the widow of Arundel ventured to inquire of thefe religious men if they had any knowledge of the fate of Mina ; but fhe received from them a ftern reproof, and was bid to think more of eternal and lefs of temporal things, as her deftiny was as yet undetermined, and it remained folely with herfelf whether a few days would reinftate her in her late hufband's forfeited eftates and property, or fign the mandate for her death.

When the priefts left her, the fortitude of Ifabelle feemed entirely to forfake her. She threw her arms round the neck of her daughter, and gave way to an involuntary gufh of tears. Columbia, unprotected, dependent on the bounty, and liable to be enfnared by the artifice of Howard, was pictured to her imagination in colours fo ftrong, that fhe could not fupport the idea.

Thus miferably did day after day wear on, diverfified only by the tedious exhortations of the monks, and the agonizing feelings of fufpenfe and apprehenfion. A fortnight was now paft, and they had not

once

once seen Howard. They were attended with re-spectful assiduity; they had but to name a wish, and it was instantly complied with. And only that they were not permitted to pass the boundaries of the gar-den wall, their situation might have been thought en-viable.

The charms of autumn were now beginning to fade, and winter was rapidly approaching, when one even-ing, after a chilly walk to the extremity of the ave-nue of ancient elms that fronted the house, as Isabelle and her daughter were sitting down to their repast, experiencing some small degree of comfort, in the neatness of their apartment, and the cheerful blaze of a wood fire that glowed on the hearth, they were startled by a loud knocking at the gate, and in less than two minutes Howard stood before them. Spite of the reasons they had for disliking him, yet their long seclusion from all society, (except the persecut-ing zealots who daily visited and tormented them) the many comforts they had through his means enjoyed, and the earnest wish they had to inquire after the fate of Mina, gave to their countenances an air of pleasure that was not altogether foreign to their hearts. Isa-belle arose from her seat as he entered; Columbia ad-vanced two or three steps towards him, and half ex-tended her hand to welcome him. These tokens of joy at his appearance, thrilled to the enraptured heart of Howard. He eagerly sprang forward, caught the half-reluctant hand, and, dropping on one knee, im-printed on it a fervent kiss. The action recalled their momentarily forgotten dignity; the features of Isabelle assumed their usual frigidity. Columbia blushed scar-let deep, and putting him from her with a rejecting motion, " Rise, Sir," said she, " nor, by affected hu-mility, insult your prisoners."

Howard now hastened to inform them, that, anx-ious only for their safety, he had been assiduous in his court to the queen, and, bribing the priests to conceal the ill success of their endeavours, he had persuaded Mary that there was more than probable hopes of their conversion. " But I fear," continued he, " I shall fhall not long be able to elude her fufpicious vigilance. She this afternoon hinted fomething of recalling you to London, examining you herfelf, and accordingly as fhe found you inclined, either receive you into the bofom of the church, or give orders for your immedi- ate execution."

"Then our fate is inevitable," faid Ifabelle, with as much firmnefs as fhe could affume. Columbia caft a look of unutterable tendernefs at her mother, and, gafping to fupprefs the anguifh of her heart, cried, "Yes, my mother, we will die together."

"Not fo," faid Howard, ftruck with the magna- nimity of the two charming women; "not fo. My employment at court, which places me almoft imme- diately about the perfon of the queen, gives me an opportunity of knowing her defigns almoft as foon as fhe conceives them. I will attentively watch her; not a command fhall be iffued forth of which I will not learn the motive and intent; and fhould I find her aim at the lives of my lovely, my efteemed prifon- ers, I will deliver them from her power, or die in their defence."

Ifabelle ejaculated an expreffion of gratitude, and Columbia, in tremulous accents, ventured to inquire after Mina. But Howard, with a look of furprife, protefted his entire ignorance of her abfence in terms fo pofitive, that it appeared impoffible any longer to doubt his veracity.

The remainder of the evening was fpent in focial converfe. He inquired if they had all the accommo- dations they wifhed, and if their commands had been readily obeyed by their attendants? On taking leave, he requefted them to be conftantly ready for a remov- al, as he fhould take care to give them early notice of impending danger, and provide them with horfes and attendants to facilitate their efcape.

After this vifit, their time was paffed in the ufual way, till the morning of the feventh of November; when, juft before day, Howard arrived, attended by a numerous retinue, and, hurrying Ifabelle and Colum- bia from their beds, told them the moment fo long

dreaded

dreaded was at hand, and nothing but immediate flight could save them. They arose with precipitation, and mounting the horses that stood ready for them, proceeded, with all the expedition their strength would permit, to the borders of the kingdom next the sea on the coast of Suffolk, where, in a mutilated fortress, (a very small part of which was habitable) Howard requested them to repose, till, as he said, a vessel should arrive, the master of which had orders to meet them there, to convey them in safety to Holland, Germany, or some place of security.

Fatigued, dispirited, and ill, Isabelle attended but little to the desolate appearance of their habitation, or the few accommodations they were likely to meet with in this solitary place. A numerous assemblage of male domestics had attended them on their journey; but they saw only one female throughout the whole dreary mansion, and she was almost insensible through age and infirmity, being quite deaf and nearly blind. However, she performed the most menial offices, and Isabelle was too intent on the miseries of her situation, and the danger to which Columbia would be exposed, should they be discovered and forced back to the court of Mary, to feel any of those inconveniencies, which in her more prosperous days would have appeared intolerable.

All hope of a departure from England during the winter season soon vanished; the weather became uncommonly tempestuous, the snow fell in great quantities, and the frost was intense. Howard was the constant inmate of their gloomy mansion; for, under pretence that his life was in danger on account of his having aided their escape, he secluded himself with them, and declared his intention to accompany them, whenever the weather would permit them to depart.

During the dreary months of December and January, he endeavoured, by amusing conversation, and a display of the various accomplishments of which he was master, at once to divert the melancholy of the lady Isabelle, and awaken the attention of Columbia. But he presently perceived his endeavours were ineffectual;

effectual; the defpondency of the mother daily increafed, till it almoft bordered on defpair, and every
tender emotion of the daughter's heart was excited by
hope, fear, and conftant anxiety for the fate of the abfent Sir Egbert Gorges.

This difcovery once made, it became the bufinefs of
Howard to undermine a paffion which militated fo
powerfully againft his fuccefs. To this end, he frequently pretended to receive private news from London, and amongft other incidents, related one day, in
a feemingly carelefs manner, that a number of heretics
had been executed, naming feveral, and at laft Sir
Egbert.

Columbia was prefent; he eyed her attentively.
She did not fhriek, fhe did not faint; but the blood
forfook her lips and cheeks, her heart beat violently,
fhe raifed her fweet eyes mournfully to his face, and
attempted to afk a confirmation of the fatal tidings.
But the words died upon her tongue; fhe ftruggled in
vain to give them utterance; her voice was inarticulate. She clafped her hands, leaned her head on her
mother's fhoulder, and large tears rolled in flow and
filent fucceffion down her cold cheeks. Such mute
grief, fuch figns of real anguifh, moved the heart of
Howard. He attempted to comfort her; but Ifabelle
waved him from the apartment; when taking her
daughter tenderly in her arms, fhe foothed, confoled,
and fympathized with her, till her tears flowed more
free'y; and by degrees fhe became compofed.

Howard had always been open in his declaration of
love for Columbia; it was therefore not furprifing that
he continued his fuit, or that, being thus conftantly in
her fociety, he fhould plead his paffion with more than
common fervour. She in general heard him in filence; but if preffed to anfwer, her reply was always
that her heart was dead to affection.

He applied to Ifabelle; fhe urged the difference of
their religions, even was Columbia inclined to favour
him. He promifed fhe fhould never be difturbed in
the free exercife of her religious duties, according to
what fhe thought right; and Ifabelle, worn out by

L

conftant

conftant anxiety, feeling her health daily decline, firmly believing Sir **Egbert Gorges** dead, and wishing to fecure for her child a noble and powerful protector, at length feemed inclined to liften to him, and to plead his caufe with Columbia.

The advice and reafonings of her mother ever had due weight with this amiable girl ; and though whenever her parent mentioned, that in all human probability, a few months would put a period to her exiftence, fhe would mentally offer up a prayer, that her own life might terminate in the very fame moment with that of her maternal friend. Yet as fhe faw her mother fecretly wifhed to fee her united to Howard, fhe endeavoured to difpofe her mind for fuch a union, tacitly confented to liften to his fuit, and at the commencement of the enfuing fummer, to give him her hand.

With flow and tardy fteps winter receded ; and fpring began to fhow her fmiling face, and wreath her modeft brows with fnow-drops, crocufes, and primrofes. All nature feemed to wear a cheerful afpect ; but the heart of Columbia partook not of the hilarity the vernal feafon was ever wont to infpire. If at any time fhe feemed to enjoy a gleam of fatisfaction, it was when fhe was wandering through the woods, remarking the daily increafe of the foliage, or feated on a rock by the fea-fhore, liftening to the fullen murmur of the waves, or watching them as they conftantly fucceeded each other, dafhing againft the rude crags that hung frowning over their fource.

It was about the middle of May ; the lady Ifabelle had declined walking, though the evening was remarkably fine. Howard had been abfent from the Caftle two days ; his abfence was a relief to the dejected fpirits of Columbia. She took her folitary ramble through the wood. The fragrance of the evening air, the ferenity of the fky, the melody of the feathered race who were chanting their vefper fong of thankfulnefs, awakened in her bofom fomething like cheerfulnefs. She ftrayed to her ufual feat by the fea fide, and indulged in the pleafurable fenfations the furrounding

rounding profpect infpired. Pleafure had long been a ftranger to her heart, and fhe welcomed her return, though in fo flight a degree, with an emanation of gratitude to the benignant Power, who had ordained that time fhould weaken and meliorate the fevereft affliction.

Entirely occupied by her own reflections, fhe did not obferve any perfon near her till a young woman addreffed her, and inquired the way to the Caftle. "I want to fee our mafter," faid fhe, "for the young lady he put to live with mother be very fick, and mother fays fhe do think fhe will die."

"I am going to the Caftle," faid Columbia, rifing, "and will fhew you the way."

"Where does your mother live?" continued fhe; "and how does it happen, that as you call Sir James Howard your mafter, you do not know the way to his dwelling?"

"Why daify me," replied the young woman, "nobody never lived in that there old place fince I can remember, till mafter cum'd here laft winter; and to be fure, mother faid, feeing as how Sir James was a fingle man, and wildifh or fo, it was beft for brother to go when the lady wanted to fend for him; but brother never went only into the kitching, and fo never knowed whether there was any ladies there; but mayhap you be cum'd here lately."

"How far from the Caftle do you live, my dear?" faid Columbia, planning in her mind a vifit to the fick lady.

"About two miles," replied her companion, "down in a valley near the fea; it be but a poor place, full of rocks, and nobody lives there but fifhermen. But father was afear'd to ftay in town, caufe as how queen Mary had ordered all the heretics to be burnt; and father and mother be both heretics, and fo we cum'd and lived here; and we had like to a gotten into trouble there. For Sir James be one of Mary's folks; but that's no matter now, feeing that fhe be dead, and I hope fhe repented of all her cruelty before fhe died."

"Before

"Before who died?" said Columbia; "who are you talking about, my good girl?"

"Why about queen Mary, madam."

"Is queen Mary dead?"

"Laws daily, yes; she died last November; and then we should have gone home, only father was took sick and died, an so mother——"

The girl might have run on for an hour. Columbia would not have interrupted her. Mary dead—dead so long, and Howard still detaining her mother and self in that solitary place, gave her an idea that his designs were not laudable or honourable; and then a ray of hope darted into her mind, that he had deceived her in reporting the death of Gorges. She quickened her steps; she longed to cheer her mother with this new-born hope. Besides, if Mary was dead, no doubt her sister Elizabeth filled the throne. She asked the question, and was answered in the affirmative. Her heart bounded at the tidings; she scarcely touched the ground, so light and swiftly did she pass over it. She left her young companion below with the old servant, and flying to her mother, imparted to her all she had heard, all she suspected, and all she fondly hoped.

CHAP. XIV.

Change of Scene, Weddings, Burials, and Christenings.

ISABELLE joined her daughter in severely censuring the conduct of Howard, by comparing the time of their departure from Hamstead with that of the late queen's death. They found they were removed on the morning following the night she died.

"We are, I fear, in the power of a villain," said Isabelle, "but we must exert ourselves to shake off this bondage in which he, contrary to the laws of his country, detains us. I will seek the protection of my sovereign, nor longer persuade my child to give her

hand

hand oppofed againft her heart.   Howard is ftill abfent, nor do I think he will return to-night.   We will leave his dreary prifon, and, conducted by the young woman you mention, feek an afylum amongft the poor fifhermen ; they may perhaps procure us a conveyance to fome neighbouring town from whence we may get to London."

"Alas ! my dear mother," faid Columbia, " you forget that we have no money."

" I have a trifle, my child," fhe replied, " and we muft fummon all our fortitude to brave even hardfhip and danger without fhrinking.   We are women, it is true, and ought never to forget the delicacy of our fex ; but real delicacy confifts in purity of thought, and chaftity of words and actions ; not in fhuddering at an accidental blaft of wind, or increafing the unavoidable evils of life by affected weaknefs and timidity.   How many of our fex are obliged by hard and daily labour, to procure for themfelves and children the bare means of exiftence ! How many brave the feverities of the moft inclement feafons, with hardly covering fufficient to keep them from perifhing ! I allow that you and I, my beloved child, have been accuftomed to tenderer ufage ; but we are particularly called upon at this time, to exert the ftrength and faculties of both mind and body, with which nature has bountifully endowed us."

" Oh ! my adored mother," faid Columbia, " taught by your bright precept and example, I feel myfelf equal to almoft any trial.   But ill as you are, to undertake fo long, fo fatiguing a journey, without the means of procuring either comforts or conveniencies, if you fhould fink under it, who then would advife, confole and direct your orphan Columbia ?"

" Courage, my love," replied Ifabelle ; " I am not fo ill as your tender anxiety leads you to think I am. Believe me. the agitation of the mind weakens and enervates the whole fyftem. The heart, eafed of a load of anguifh, beats lighter, gives a freer play to the lungs, and a fwifter circulation to the blood. What is more conducive to health than change of air

and

and exercife? Befides, I have now fome object in view, which will give conftant employment to my thoughts. Employment naturally begets cheerfulnefs. Nothing is more pernicious to the health of mind or body, than indolence and inaction. The faculties become torpid; even the chords of fenfibility lofe their fine tone, and the heart itfelf grows cold and inanimate as marble. Keep the hands employed, and the mind occupied in fome laudable purfuit, and a fweet ferenity will diffufe itfelf over the foul. The day paffes without our noticing the hours, the night brings peaceful and refrefhing flumbers, and by throwing the golden chain of induftry over the wings of pleafure, we take the little fleeting phantom prifoner, and make it our own forever."

Columbia felt the full force of her mother's argument; for, being bufied in putting a few neceffaries together for their journey, fhe was fo wholly occupied by the pleafures of anticipation, that every obftacle feemed to vanifh. "Heaven in its mercy guard and fupport my dear mother," faid fhe mentally, "and for myfelf I have no feais."

The young woman, whofe name was Cicely, undertook to conduct them to the cottage of her mother. For the lady Ifabelle faid, as Sir James was not at home, fhe would herfelf vifit the fick lady, and adminifter fuch confolation as fhe might find needful. The laft tints of day were fading in the weftern fky, and the moon, in full majeftic fplendour, tipped with her filver beams the lofty and antique trees that furrounded the manfion of Howard, when thefe two interefting women, accompanied by Cicely, entered the wood through which they were obliged to pafs in their way to her mother's habitation.

In filence they purfued their way. Columbia and her mother could converfe but on one fubject, and on that one, prudence forbade them to fpeak in the prefence of a third perfon; and Cicely, though fo communicative to the daughter, was awed by the prefence of the mother.

At

At length they reached the cottage; it was small and meanly furnished, but withal so clean and neat, that it seemed the habitation of comfort and content. A middle aged woman, decently clad in home-spun stuff, met them at the door, and looking at the strangers with an air of surprise, eagerly asked for Sir James. Isabelle did not give her little guide time to reply, but answered for her, that Sir James being from home, and she being his particular friend and guest, had come to visit the sick lady, and see if any thing could be done to help her.

"Alack a day, my lady," said the woman, "I believe she be past help; I did not think she would have lived till now; but walk into the next room, I believe she is quite sensible yet, and seems to have something heavy on her mind. I do think the poor soul would die easier, if she could tell somebody her troubles."

As the loquacious landlady finished speaking, she opened the door of the adjoining apartment, and Columbia, with trembling impatience, approached the bed, and softly put back the curtain. The light, which stood on the table by the beside, shed its rays full on the face of the invalid, and discovered the features of Mina. A momentary slumber had lulled her in forgetfulness. Beside her lay an infant, to all appearance but a few hours old.

"My heart foreboded this," said Isabelle. Columbia's eyes streamed as she hung over the pale form of her beloved Mina; she sobbed aloud, but was unable to speak. The dying sufferer unclosed her eyes, she saw, and instantly recollected her lady and dear benefactress.

"Then my prayers are heard," said she, faintly; "I shall leave my child, the wretched offspring of shame and folly, to the care of an angel."

"Oh! my poor Mina," cried Columbia, sinking on her knees by the bedside, and endeavouring to stifle her grief. "Unfortunate creature," said the lady Isabelle, taking the cold, damp hand of her servant; "severely hast thou suffered for thy deviation from the path of rectitude; but do not despond, my child. Your

Your prefent weak ftate, and the depreffion naturally attendant on your fituation, makes you think yourfelf near your end ; but we will hope——"

"Hope!" faid Mina, raifing her languid eyes ; "yes, I do hope that my fufferings are nearly at an end, and that they have in part made atonement for my errors. I did not, believe me, I did not leave your protection voluntarily. I was forced away and brought to this place ; I was taught to believe that you had left England. I have fometimes, fince my feclufion here, feen the auther of my ruin ; but could not learn from him, that he knew aught concerning you. I was particularly anxious to fee him to-night ; for fure I am, my dear lady, I fhall never again view the light of day. And I wifhed to have with my own hands committed his child to his care ; but I can with more confidence leave it to your protection."

Here a fudden faintnefs made her paufe. A few drops adminiftered, fome what revived her, and fhe proceeded :—"A few ftruggles more, and I fhall be at peace. My heart, my heart is broken. Yet truft me, it is not my own fufferings, the flights of the man for whom I facrificed all, or the fcorn of a contemning world under which I have funk. No! it was the confcioufnefs of loft innocence ; it was the reflection that my lapfe from virtue had involved my kindeft, beft friends in ruin, which penetrated deep into my foul. Sleeping or waking, you were prefent to my thoughts, and I have died a thoufand deaths, in daily anticipating yours."

The lady Ifabelle endeavoured to foothe and compofe the affectionate, penitent Mina ; affured her that what was in her power fhe would cheerfully promife to perform ; that fhe would look on her child as an infant given to her protection by the immediate agency of Heaven ; and though fhe fhould think it a duty to endeavour to awaken in the breaft of Howard the feelings of a father towards the helplefs innocent, yet it would be her care to fee that his health and morals were in no ways neglected.

"Yes,

" Yes, my dear Mina," said Columbia, " he shall be my charge. Come, compose yourself; endeavour to rest. When you are better, we will nurse the little rogue together, and I warrant I shall prove the better nurse."

" Blessed—blessed—" said Mina, grasping the hand of Columbia (which from her first awaking, she had held in her's). Her eyes were ardently turned upward; they gradually closed; her fingers relaxed their hold, and her head sunk upon the pillow.

" She is dropped asleep," said Columbia, " I hope it will refresh her." " It will," replied her mother, drawing her from the bed-side; she will awake relieved from all her pain."

" Do you think so indeed ! my dear mother."

" Yes, my child, most assuredly; for in this world she will awake no more."

The feelings of such a heart as Columbia's, on such an occasion, cannot be described. The soul alive to sensibility, can easily conceive them; and to the unfeeling, a repetition of her complaints and sorrows. would be tedious and uninteresting. She took the poor motherless infant in her arms, and sitting down in one corner of the room, baptized it with her tears.

The scene became too painful for the lady Isabelle; and whilst the landlady and her daughter, assisted by a servant, prepared the body of the departed Mina for her last resting place, she walked in a little garden before the door, seeking, from the cool evening air, a relief from that oppression on the heart, which the recent scene had occasioned.

The air in a slight degree had the desired effect. She returned to the house, and approached the door that led to the apartment of death. The lifeless body was now stretched upon the bed, on the side of which sat Columbia still weeping, and clasping the infant to her bosom. Her sorrow was too sacred, the lesson was too important, for her mother to interrupt her. The sound of footsteps called the attention of Isabelle from her daughter. She turned to see from whence

the

the found proceeded, and beheld juft entering the houfe, Howard.

"The lady Ifabelle," faid he, with a look of aftonifhment, "by what miracle do I fee you here ? and where is my charming Columbia ?"

"She is here alfo," replied Ifabelle, with a folemn voice. "Follow me ; I will lead you to her."

They entered the apartment together. Columbia raifed not her eyes. The heart of Howard beat quick, as, leading him toward the bed, Ifabelle drew the covering from the death-ftamped face of Mina, and pointing to her, faid emphatically, "Behold the works of thy hands, Howard ! Here contemplate the fruits of feduction !"

At the name of Howard, Columbia ftarted ; fhe read the emotions of his foul in his expreffive countenance. Rifing from her feat, fhe prefented the infant to him, and laying her right hand on his arm, called his attention from the pale corfe of her lamented fervant. "Gaze not there, Howard," faid fhe ; "the injuries of the mother are paft redrefs ; but behold your child, make reparation here !"

Howard, the gay, the thoughtlefs, diffipated Howard was ftruck to the heart. He faw the once lovely, blooming, cheerful Mina, an inanimate mafs. Thofe fparkling eyes, that firft awakened the licentious paffion, were clofed in death ; that heart, that had but too much fenfibility, too much fincerity for its own peace, was cold and ftill. His feductive powers had hurried an amiable creature out of the world, and introduced into it a helplefs being, who, fhould he live, through life would blufh for the frailty of his mother, and execrate the licentioufnefs of his father. He took the infant from the arms of Columbia, preffed the hand which fhe had laid on his arm, attempted to fpeak, but his voice died away in inarticulate founds. The bitter tears of felf-accufation rufhed down his cheeks ; he returned the child to her ; and throwing himfelf befide the lifelefs Mina, gave a loofe to the anguifh of his heart.

Ifabelle·

Isabelle led her daughter from the room; but during the whole night Howard never left it for a moment, and small was the portion of repose which any of the inhabitants of the cottage tasted.

By the dawn of day, Isabelle wished to begin her journey towards London. She sent in a request to Howard, that he would grant her a few moments audience. He complied. When he entered the apartment, she thus addressed him. "I sent for you not, Sir James, to irritate your sensibility by unseasonable reproaches, nor to inquire what injury I had ever done you, that you have thus wantonly heaped misery on me and mine. I wish but to tell you, that I am fully sensible how unjustly and on what false pretences you have detained me here; and that, knowing myself perfectly free, and safe in the protection of my queen, and the laws of my country, I may travel without molestation whithersoever I please. I shall immediately proceed towards London. I also wish to inform you, that the poor departed victim, in her dying moments, recommended her infant to my care, and died in the full confidence of my protection and tenderness being extended towards it during its years of helpless infancy. I am sensible of your prior right; the right of nature is incontrovertible; and I have still so good an opinion of your heart (when left to the dictates of reason and religion) as to think you will discharge the duty of a parent with conscientious strictness. But I have to request, you will suffer me to be informed where the child may be placed, that in case of indisposition. I may have it in my power to visit and see that he is properly nursed and attended."

Howard was for a moment silent. His proud spirit was humbled to the dust. But Howard, when convinced of an error, knew how to make atonement without descending from the dignity of man.

"Noble lady," said he, "I have been highly culpable. My heart tells me at this moment, I have forfeited all right to the protecting power of an Omnipotent, by abusing his good gifts, and debasing the noblest work of his hands. But I am not so far lost to virtue,

virtue, as to perſiſt in error againſt the conviction of reaſon. I have injured you, lady Arundel, I have wounded the heart of your lovely daughter, by a falſe tale of the death of her lover; but, thank Heaven, reparation here is not beyond my power. My ſervants ſhall attend you; my horſes are at your command; depart when you pleaſe. You ſhall have ſafe conduct to the court of the royal Elizabeth, where you will meet Sir Egbert Gorges, rich in every virtue as well as in the favour of his ſovereign. Your requeſt in regard to the hapleſs offspring of indiſcretion, ſhall gladly be complied with; his infant wants I will take care ſhall be amply ſupplied; I will endeavour, by tenderneſs toward him, to atone for the injuries I have done his mother. But your friendſhip and attention, in directing my cares to a proper channel, will be a valuable acquiſition to him, and an act of condeſcenſion toward me. I will ſee the loſt Mina repoſe on her laſt bed, and then conduct my child and his nurſe to London, where, making ample proviſion for his ſupport through life, I will leave him to your protection, and ſeek, in the claſh of arms and the purſuit of glory, to loſe the remembrance of circumſtances which tend at once to my diſhonour and diſquiet."

Early in the day, Iſabelle and her daughter commenced their journey toward the metropolis. Though the ſpirits of Columbia had received a ſevere ſhock from the death of her favourite Mina, yet the bright proſpects that opened to her, in her recovered liberty and the certainty of Sir Egbert's life and ſafety, contributed in a great degree to diſſipate her melancholy; and as they drew near the concluſion of their journey, her heart vibrated with the moſt pleaſurable ſenſations. A ſudden thunder ſhower, which obliged them to ſtop when within a few hours ride of London, impeded their journey, and they were neceſſitated unwillingly to ſleep another night on the road. After an early repaſt, they retired to their apartment, when juſt as Columbia was going into bed, ſhe miſſed her ring from off her finger. "Oh! madam," ſaid ſhe, "I have loſt my ring; and yet I am ſure I ſaw it on my fin-

ger

ger juft before we went to fupper." Every part of the bed-chamber was now fearched, every article of her attire carefully fhaken, her pockets turned infide out, but all in vain.

"Perhaps," faid Ifabelle, "you may have dropped it in the room below." The hoftefs was fummoned, and requefted to look for it, whilft Columbia, too anxious to think of refting, had (almoft unknown to herfelf) again put on her clothes. The hoftefs returned. "I have been very fortunate," faid fhe ; "a gentleman who has been feeking game in the neighbouring foreft, being overtaken by night fooner than he expected, entered the houfe juft as you came up ftairs, and being fhewn into the apartment you had left, has found the ring, and here it is."

Columbia eagerly extended her hand to receive it ; but overcome with joy and aftonifhment, fhe gave a fudden exclamation of pleafure, and fpringing toward the door, was inftantly folded in the arms of Sir Egbert Gorges.

It was he, who with Rawlins had been in purfuit of game in the adjacent woods. Entering the apartment Columbia had juft left, he faw fomething glitter on the floor, and ftooping, picked up the identical ring which he had placed on her finger at partirg. His furprife was exceffive ; he had heard that the lady Ifabelle and her daughter had been in the power of Mary, and it was univerfally believed they had, through Howard's means, efcaped ; that they were at that moment under the fame roof with him, he had not the moft diftant idea ; but the perfon who dropped the ring might probably give him fome information concerning her. He was gazing at it, loft in conjecture, his bofom throbbing with anxiety to learn her fate, when the hoftefs entered the room.

"I beg pardon," faid fhe, "but I come to look for a ring which a lady thinks fhe has dropped here ; I hope if you have feen it, gentlemen, you will reftore it ; for indeed the poor young lady feems in a fad taking about it."

"A young lady ?" faid Sir Egbert.

M

"Aye,

"Aye, a young lady," replied our loquacious hoftefs; "and as fweet a young lady as eye ever looked on. I warrant it is fome love token. Oh! if you had but feen her earneftnefs, when fhe entreated me to come and look for it."

"I have found the ring," faid Sir Egbert, his heart throbbing fo violently as to render refpiration difficult; "here, take it to the young lady, and as you give it her, fuffer me to fee her; leave the door partly open as you go in." A golden argument, with which Sir Egbert enforced his requeft, prevented objections, and taking the plain gold ring from his own finger, he fent it to Columbia.

It may eafily be fuppofed, that fo happy, fo unexpected a meeting, banifhed fleep effectually from the eyes of all. Ifabelle and her daughter returned to the parlour, where inquiry, recital, and unreferved confidence on both fides, occupied the remainder of the night. They learnt that young Dudley was fafe in the protection of Elizabeth, who had reftored to him the title and eftates of his father, and promifed to be his friend and patronefs.

Nor was Mina forgot; Rawlins feized the firft paufe in their interefting converfation to inquire after the object of his fincere affection.

Ifabelle hefitated; fhe read his tendernefs in the emotions of his countenance. At length the fatal truth was difclofed, and the piece of filver which Columbia had taken from around her neck after her deceafe, was reftored to him.

He took it; he gazed on it in filence. His manly features were tinged with the pale hue of death. He raifed his eyes to the face of Columbia. The look was expreffive; it feemed to fay, "You loved her lady; do you not lament her?" Columbia breathed a figh of commiferation. His heartftrings, which were drawn almoft to breaking, were foftened by its balmy influence. He paffed his hand acrofs his eyes to diffipate the tear, the mournful cataftrophe of his beloved Mina had extorted, and putting the piece of filver into his bofom, haftily left the apartment.

The

The ruddy morn peeped through the eastern gates, before this happy trio thought of separating. Isabelle and Columbia at length retired to their chamber; but Morpheus was flown beyond recall. Unfeeling deity! he makes his longest visits to the ignorant and insensible. The peasant, whilst he labours amongst the corn he sows, strews the somnific poppy; and in return, the leaden-winged power collects its sweets, and sheds them on his pillow. From the couch bedewed with tears he takes his flight, and when ecstatic joy has strung each nerve, and the exhilarated spirits mount toward heaven, he stands aloof and shakes his heavy wings, nor for one moment will impede the tide of bliss, though courted earnestly by weary nature, who languishes for rest from each extreme, whether of grief or pleasure.

Presented at the court of Elizabeth, Columbia shone conspicuous. Her beauty struck the admiring eye; her affability, good sense and virtue captivated the heart. Her delighted, happy mother bestowed her hand on Sir Egbert Gorges with unfeigned satisfaction; and remaining in the capital till Columbia was mother to a son christened Ferdinando, and a daughter named Elizabeth, she retired to Austenbury Castle.

Her old servant Cora was no more. Matthias was in his second childhood; but he experienced all the pleasure of which human nature in its last stage is capable, in the return of his revered lady. The autumn following, he slept in peace; and before the ensuing spring had called forth the primrose, or decked the almond tree in blushing sweets, the lady Isabelle, the descendant of the great Columbus, the daughter of the Peruvian princess *Orrabella*, gently declined into the vale of years, and rested in the house appointed for all living.

Columbia on this occasion visited the scene of her juvenile pleasures. Her feelings on the departure of her mother were indescribable. Her tears again consecrated the memory of the unfortunate Mina; and having given orders that the court yard, the filbert walk, the tower and eastern wing of the Castle should

be

be kept in constant repair, she returned to London, where she continued for many years to shine eminently in the characters of wife, mother, and mistress of a family.

She died in the fiftieth year of her age, after having given birth to five children; Ferdinando, heir to his father's title and estate; Elizabeth, who was married to lord Henry Dudley; Jane, who died in her infancy; Edward, who, embracing the service of his country in a nautical profession, and in the year 1585 embarking with the brave and enterprizing Sir Francis Drake, perished in the attack against St. Domingo; and Beatina, who married into the ancient and respectable family of the Penns.

Sir Egbert Gorges himself lived to a good old age; and dying, bequeathed his title and estates to a son, who thought hereditary honour of little value to the possessor, unless supported by humanity, justice and mercy.

Sir Ferdinando Gorges regarded the honour of ancestry in no other light than as a stimulus to 'praiseworthy actions. "My father," said he, "was beloved and esteemed for his virtue, honour and integrity; I will not sully the name I bear, by any action derogatory to the character of a MAN and a CHRISTIAN."

Sir Ferdinando Gorges was a gentleman of the old world; should the character appear unnatural to any of the present time, let them remember that they are reading a "tale of old times," and exculpate the author from the charge of romance and improbability.

A certain modern author, a noble author too, (if inheriting a title constitutes nobility) has been at infinite trouble to explain the requisites necessary to form the character of a fine gentleman; unfortunately, he forgot humanity, truth and religion. Sir Ferdinando Gorges imagined, that to love and worship his Creator, to scorn to assert a falsehood, and to do as he would be done by in the most minute particular, was to deserve the distinguished rank he inherited from

his

his anceſtors; and it is a moral certainty, that Sir Ferdinando was perfectly right in his ideas of the character of a real gentleman.

CHAP. XV.

A Century when paſt is but as a Moment.

SIR Ferdinando Gorges took but a ſmall ſhare in the active ſcenes of life, till the unfortunate Earl of Eſſex, favourite to Eliſabeth, incurred the cenſure of his ſovereign by neglecting her commands, and hurried by the impetuoſity of his paſſion, inſtigated the populace (ever eager for novelty) to arm in his ſupport and defence, which called forth the aid of the loyal ſubject in behalf of the queen's diſputed power. It was then Sir Ferdinando ſtarted into notice; he aſſerted the prerogative of royalty, and enforced the commands of his ſovereign, not as the will of a deſpotic tyrant, but as the laws of a well-regulated government, neceſſary to be ſupported, for the peace, intereſt and ſecurity of millions who lived under their protection.

He was a man remarkable for public ſpirit; it was the main ſpring that actuated all his purſuits. Every wiſh of his heart, every undertaking in which he engaged, was deſigned to promote the general welfare.

About the year 1624, a number of perſons having formed themſelves into a company for planting and ſettling a colony in New England, North-America, Sir Ferdinando was appointed by royal authority one of the directors, and expended great part of his paternal inheritance in promoting the deſign. The ſpirit of his great and enterpriſing anceſtor ſeemed to revive in him, and nothing but his advanced age prevented him from croſſing the Atlantic himſelf, in ſearch of diſcoveries that might enrich or enlighten the riſing generation.

His

Sir Ferdinando had married, at an early age, a lady of family and fortune; but she lived only to give birth to a daughter; and Sir Ferdinando was so firmly attached to her whilst living, and so sincerely regretted her untimely departure, that he thought no other woman could supply her place. His sister Elizabeth was nearly at the same period left a widow, with only one child, a boy about five years old. To whom could Sir Ferdinando apply to take the charge of his infant daughter, so well as to lady Dudley? And where could the young, the lovely widow find herself so safe, so secure from reproach, as in the family and under the protection of her brother?

As the children grew up, Henry regarded his little cousin Isabelle with more than fraternal affection; but the tenets of the reformed religion forbidding a union between two persons so nearly related by the ties of blood, neither Sir Ferdinando nor lady Dudley encouraged an affection, which in their ideas was a crime; and with a design to prevent its progress, at the age of nineteen, Henry was sent to travel, and finish his education by gaining a competent knowledge of foreign courts and manners.

Though Isabelle Gorges, at the departure of her cousin for the continent, was scarcely fourteen years old, yet Henry was fully sensible of the nature of the emotions he felt in her favour; whilst she, the pure child of simplicity, had no idea but that she might love him beyond all other terrestrial beings, and confess it with impunity. She hung upon his neck at taking leave, besought him not to forget her, and spent the whole day in tears. Every ensuing day seemed still to make his absence more intolerable. She thought of him incessantly, spoke of him often, and when a letter arrived, would hang over her father's shoulder with delighted attention whilst he read the contents.

Henry Dudley was a man exactly calculated to do honour to the noble race from whence he sprang; the letters of his governor to his mother were filled with his praises. To a brave, undaunted spirit he united a

soul

foul alive to all the finer feelings of humanity. With an ardent thirst for knowledge, he possessed an understanding that directed his studies and researches to the most useful, laudable objects ; from the gentleness of his nature liable to error, but open to conviction, and ever ready to make atonement.

" He has but one fault," said his governor in one of his letters, " and that is an impetuosity of disposition when in pursuit of any favourite object ; his affections are ardent in the extreme, and his passions, or rather his excessive sensibility, hurry him often beyond the bounds of reason and discretion. But this error is like a spot on the sun, which may be discernible whilst his beams are weakened by the mists of the morning, but when he shines in full meridian splendour will become imperceptible."

" Dear, beloved Henry !" exclaimed Isabelle, as she listened to her aunt whilst she read the passage. " Oh! why is he not my brother ? I am sure though, if he were my brother, I could not love him better than I do now ; and you, my charming aunt," she continued, throwing her arms round the neck of lady Dudley, " I think I could not love you more than I do now, but yet I should like to call you mother. 'I never knew my own mother ; you have amply supplied her place. Let me call you mother, dear ! dear ! mother. Oh ! there is something so delightful in the word, that my heart overflows with tender transports as I utter it. What a happy girl I should be if I could say, My father, my mother, and my brother Henry."

The lady Dudley perceived that the innocence of Isabelle was equal to her tenderness, and that in wishing to call her mother, she meant no more, than that by her being so, Henry would become her brother.

Henry continued his travels till he had reached his twenty-third year ; it was then thought necessary to call him home ; and as in his letters he had never mentioned Isabelle only as a relation, Sir Ferdinando hoped absence, and a variety of scenes, had totally eradicated the youthful predilection he had conceived

in

in her favour. But in this he was miftaken ; the paffion which began in childhood had increafed with his
years ; and though during his travels various other
purfuits had contributed to keep it dormant, it ftill remained in his.heart, and waited only for a re-union
with Ifabelle, to blaze anew with more than its former
ardency.

During his refidence at the court of France, Henry
Dudley formed an acquaintance with Howard Fitz-
Howard, grandfon to the unfortunate Mina.

Sir James Howard had confcientioufly performed
his promife, in providing fplendidly for the education
of his fon, whom he had chriftened James Fitz-Howard ; but as he left him in charge with an ecclefiaftic
of the Romifh religion, in order to his being brought
up in that faith, the lady Arundel could do no more
than fometimes vifit him during his infancy. His
father died abroad before he was fifteen. Leaving
him a very large fhare of his eftates, foon after this
event his governor removed him to Paris ; and from
that period, the family of Sir Egbert Gorges were totally unacquainted with his welfare or purfuits.

The prieft to whofe care he had been entrufted,
was a man of ftrict probity ; he paid the utmoft attention
to his education, and, uniting the friend and companion with the inftructor, made him love virtue for its
own fake ; for, beholding its effects in the converfation and manners of his refpected tutor, he grew em-
ulous to copy what appeared fo amiable. His father
had been well-known to fome of the moft noble families in France, and Fitz-Howard, at an early age,
found himfelf in a very elevated circle, careffed and
efteemed by all. He married the daughter of a rich
farmer-general, and Howard Fitz-Howard was the
only furviving fruit of the union.

This young man was a character compofed of con-
trarieties, at once verfatile as the wind, and boifterous
as the waves. With fcarcely a trait of his father's
virtues, he inherited the vices of his grandfather, with
all that imbecility of mind, that heedlefs credulity,
which had been the caufe of the ruin of his grandmother.

mother. Eager in the pursuit of pleasure, a passionate admirer of female beauty, and master of an affluent fortune, uncontrolled by any, he lavished it with a profuse hand on those who flattered his follies, careless whether they were deserving favour or contempt.

It may be thought strange, that a young man like Henry Dudley could form an intimacy with such a character. But youth is ever unsuspecting, and the generous nature of Dudley could not imagine the gaiety and vivacity of Fitz-Howard was almost the only recommendation he possessed.

At the time Henry was recalled home, Fitz-Howard expressed a wish to accompany him to England. Madame Fitz-Howard had never, from his infancy, ventured to contradict any wish of her darling ; and, unwilling as she was to part with him, she at length consented to his going, on condition that the visit was limited to six months. Accordingly the two friends, attended by their respective governors, arrived in England about the middle of November, and with all the speed the mode of travelling then in use would allow, proceeded immediately to London. The last rays of daylight glimmered in the west as they crossed the Thames, and before they reached the mansion of Sir Ferdinando Gorges, the family were quietly settled to the employments of the evening.

Sir Ferdinando was reading to his wife and daughter, who were employed in embroidering a dress, in which Isabelle was to be presented at the court of James the First, who now filled the throne of the deceased Elizabeth ; uniting, by his accession to the British crown, the two kingdoms of England and Scotland in one. (This monarch was son to the unfortunate Mary, queen of Scots, who was beheaded at Fotheringay Castle during the reign of Elizabeth, after having been detained a prisoner there upwards of fifteen years.)

Isabelle Gorges was now eighteen. Her features were regular, but not at first view strikingly handsome. The radiance of her mild blue eyes did not dart at once upon the heart, taking the astonished senses captive ;

tive; but through the softening shade of long, dark, silken lashes, stole imperceptibly on the soul, and made it all her own. Her stature was above the middle size, yet not so tall as to render her person masculine. Her limbs were round, and finely proportioned. A chaste dignity, tempered by the most winning softness, informed her manners, and rendered her irresistibly charming.

It must be remembered, that Dudley had not seen her for above four years. Imagine, then, what must be his feelings, when he saw the lively, affectionate girl, transformed into the elegant, dignified woman!

Isabelle had been hourly expecting her cousin, and was too much occupied in anticipating the pleasures of their meeting, to be very attentive to her father's reading; nay, even the work in which she was engaged, though it continued to employ her fingers, did not for a moment occupy her thoughts. Every noise in the court yard, every quick step ascending the stairs, made her heart beat quick, and her eyes would glance eagerly toward the door.

A confused murmur in the great hall had made Sir Ferdinando pause. "He is come," said Isabelle, dropping her work and starting from her feat. The door opened, and Dudley was in a moment at the feet of his mother. Released from the maternal embrace, he turned toward his lovely cousin, and received a welcome, which filled the breast of Fitz-Howard with envy. Recovered from the momentary delirium that ever pervades the too sensible system upon a re-union with beloved friends, Dudley presented his new friend, who was received with cordiality, and immediately invited to take an apartment in the house of Sir Ferdinando, during his residence in London.

A very few days served to convince the father of Isabelle, that the absence Henry had been obliged to submit to, from his cousin, had acted in the same manner as a small quantity of water does when thrown on a fierce fire, gave a momentary damp to its progress, only that it might burst forth with double violence,

lence, deftroying every object that attempted to oppofe its fury.

Ifabelle, modeft, timid, and tremblingly alive to feel the fmalleft infringement on the delicacy of her fex, was yet fufceptible of a pure, ardent paffion for her coufin. Fitz-Howard, an inmate in their family, read the workings in the minds of all; for each ftrove to hide from the other their real fentiments. The lady Dudley, and her brother Sir Ferdinando, faw with concern the paffion which confumed their children; but they endeavoured to conceal that knowledge even from each other, ftill labouring, by various fchemes, to divert the attention of Ifabelle and Henry different ways.

Henry, when converfing with Fitz-Howard, would fpeak with rapturous eloquence in praife of his coufin; but if his friend at any time accufed him of being too partial, he would fay, " Is it not natural for brothers to be partial to their fifters?" " Surely," replied Fitz Howard, " but do you love Ifabelle Gorges no more than you would love a fifter?" " No more, on my honour," Dudley would reply, and immediately change the converfation.

Lady Dudley, thinking to fathom the fentiments of Ifabelle in regard to her fon, would fpeak of him in her prefence. At the fmalleft encomium beftowed on Henry by his mother, the eyes of Ifabelle would beam with pleafure; a brighter glow would ornament her cheeks; and her coral lips, half unclofed by the fmile of innate fatisfaction, difplaying her pearly teeth, would give that chafte animation to her whole countenance, as rendered it fcarcely a degree below angelic. When on the contrary, fhould fhe hear a fyllable of difapprobation efcape her aunt, her lips would tremble, her cheek lofe its carnation hue; and her eyes half filled with tears, her brow contracted by the oppreffion of her heart, would feem to fay, " Do not fpeak harfhly of him, I am certain he does not deferve it." And when lady Dudley has remarked that Henry was an uncommon favourite, fhe would reply, " Certainly he is, and can you blame me? Is he not your

fon?

son? Surely I may love him for your sake, and you will not contemn me."

Thus every person that composed the family of Sir Ferdinando, endeavoured to conceal their real feelings; but Fitz-Howard read them all. From his first introduction, he had felt his heart strongly drawn toward Isabelle. At first, he imagined an insuperable objection would arise from the passion of Dudley; but when from various circumstances he learnt that the parents of neither party approved that passion, he conceived the idea of ingratiating himself with lady Dudley, and leading her, by imperceptible degrees, to approve his own pretensions. He foresaw that the difference of religion would prove an almost insurmountable obstacle; but Fitz-Howard had not been educated in a manner, that would lead him to think either religion or morality was of any very great consequence, when opposed against his own inclinations.

In order to accomplish this desired end, he in turn made himself the friend and confidant of all. He listened attentively to Sir Ferdinando's account of new discoveries, and approved all the plans he had formed for the extending of the blessings of navigation and commerce over the whole habitable globe. With Dudley, he joined in extolling the beauty, virtue and accomplishments of Isabelle, and without pretending to perceive the extent of his attachment, encouraged the affection he seemed to disapprove.

To the lady Isabelle he was another character; talked of the different opinions that were adopted by the people of England in regard to religious matters; mentioned his own faith, not as opposing it to the faith of the pious, enthusiastic lady Elizabeth; but appearing to wish instruction in the right way, as desiring to have his own errors corrected. Nor was this conduct entirely the result of art; it was chiefly the effect of nature. For Fitz-Howard could never maintain his own opinion against strong argument. Indeed, he could hardly be said to have an opinion of his own; and had he conversed four successive days with persons of four different religions, he would, at

the

the end of that period, have been perfuaded that he with whom he converfed laft, was certainly moft right. Thus verfatile by nature, it cannot be wondered at, that, finding this verfatility likely to forward his moft favourite views, he took no pains to correct it, but gave free indulgence to a difpofition, which, whilft it rendered him agreeable to every feparate branch of the family, promifed him ample gratification in the favour of the aunt of Ifabelle.

To Ifabelle herfelf he was tender, affiduous; in fhort, all that love could infpire, or friendfhip wifh. She rode, fhe walked, fhe danced and chatted with Fitz-Howard without reftraint; though at the fame time fhe would have preferred the company of Dudley. But if his company gave her moft pleafure, it was a pleafure fo mixed with anxiety, fuch fear of offending, fuch trembling apprehenfion and embarraff-ment, that it became no longer defirable, and fhe evidently avoided giving him any opportunities of entertaining her, except in the prefence of her father and lady Dudley.

Fitz-Howard poffeffed but little penetration, but a very competent fhare of vanity fupplied its place. He imagined that the apparent preference Ifabelle fhewed him, was the effect of real liking, and that fhe was captivated by his perfon, manners and fortune. Buoy-ed up by thefe ideas, he made propofals to her father, offered to become a profelyte to the reformed religion, and in every other refpect his alliance was unexcep-tionable.

Sir Ferdinando, flattering himfelf that Ifabelle was not altogether averfe to the union, referred Fitz-How-ard to his fifter for a final anfwer; and lady Dudley, prepoffeffed in his favour by his fpecious manners, ea-ger to confirm him a convert to the Proteftant caufe, and willing to put an end at once to the hopes of her fon, approved his fuit; and that very evening, as they were fitting converfing together in an unconftrained, confidential manner, declared to her niece the appro-bation fhe had given to the propofals of Fitz-Howard, and advifed her ferioufly to think of him as the man deftined to become her hufband.

N

Aftonifhment

Aſtoniſhment for ſome moments kept her ſilent; at length ſhe told her aunt, that ſhe was by no means partial to the man ſhe ſo warmly recommended, nor did ſhe wiſh to alter her ſtate; ſhe was perfectly contented with her preſent condition. Happy in the affection of her father and lady Dudley, ſhe wiſhed not to quit their protection for that of a ſtranger, and begged leave to decline the propoſed union.

"I am much afraid, Iſabelle," ſaid that lady, "that you nouriſh improper, nay, criminal wiſhes. I fear you indulge chimerical hopes of a future union with Henry Dudley. But do not deceive yourſelf, my child; whilſt I live, thoſe hopes can never be realized, without incurring the ſevereſt malediction of an offended parent."

"If I know my own heart, madam," ſaid Iſabelle, ſomewhat piqued by her aunt's peremptory prohibition, "it never yet has indulged improper hopes or criminal wiſhes. Its every emotion has been regulated by your precepts, and I truſt it will never diſhonour its noble inſtructreſs. But if to love and prefer your ſon above all other human beings conſtitutes guilt, I am in ſome meaſure guilty. I am ſenſible of the barrier cuſtom, and perhaps you will ſay, religion, has placed between us; I have no wiſh to break through that barrier; but whilſt I am ſatisfied with loving him only as a brother, I ſee no reaſon why I ſhould be compelled to become the wife of another."

"Nor ſhall you be compelled, my deareſt couſin," ſaid Dudley, who being in the adjoining apartment (the door of which had been accidentally left ajar) had overheard the whole converſation; "no divine ordinance forbids our union; then why ſhould ſuperſtition impoſe ſuch ſhackles on us? Have we not reaſon to direct us? Why then ſhould we ſubmit blindly and implicitly to the opinions of others? Madam, look not thus angry on me," continued he, turning toward his mother. "You have heard from her own lips the preference with which my charming couſin honours me; then give her to me freely, and with her beſtow your maternal benediction. For here, in
                                                    the

the fight of Heaven, I vow folemnly to have no wife but her, to live but for her fake, and may that moment put a period to my exiftence, in which fhe is feparated from me."

It was in vain lady Dudley attempted to interrupt him before the folemn vow had paffed his lips; in vain fhe entreated him to recal it. He repeated it with a vehemence that made her tremble; and turning from him in difpleafure, fhe took the hand of the affrighted Ifabelle, and led her from the apartment. Difguife had now become ufelefs to all parties. Ifabelle, daily tormented by the affiduities of Fitz-Howard, admonifhed by her aunt and threatened by her father, felt exiftence a burthen. The time fhe was obliged to pafs in company fhe laboured under the moft cruel conftraint, and her hours of retirement were fpent in fighs, tears, and unavailing complaints.

Dudley no longer made one of the family. He had removed to a houfe of his own, where he had folicited his mother to prefide; but her affection for her brother had prompted her at firft to decline the propofal, and the reafon may eafily be conceived, why Henry now ceafed to urge his requeft. Fitz-Howard too had quitted the houfe of Sir Ferdinando, for apartments where, being himfelf mafter, his actions were not fo ftrictly fcrutinized as they were liable to be in the family of a man virtuous from principle, and fincerely pious, without being either a bigot or an enthufiaft.

Though Dudley was no longer an inmate in the family, he was a daily vifitant at the houfe of his uncle, and found fufficient opportunities to forward his fuit with Ifabelle; perfecuted on one fide, and earneftly folicited on the other, where is the wonder that fhe fhould liften to the fyren voice of honourable love, and, beftowing her hand on him who had long poffeffed her heart, become the wife of Dudley? Secretly, and by his own chaplain, was the ceremony performed. They waited a favourable moment to fupplicate a paternal bleffing, and, fearful of a premature difcovery, became more circumfpect in their behaviour towards each other; their interviews were conducted
with

with the utmost caution, and suspicion was again lulled asleep. But Fitz-Howard still persisted in his addresses, though treated with the most contemptuous coldness by the object of his adoration.

The spring was now rapidly advancing, and the lady Dudley removed with her niece to an elegant seat she possessed near Windsor. Sir Ferdinando, fully occupied in the laudable design of extending the blessings himself enjoyed, to distant, unenlightened nations, seldom quitted the capital, except for an hour or two, to breathe the fresh air, and enjoy the pleasure of beholding his beloved child.

In this retirement, Dudley often visited his wife; and unfortunately, Fitz-Howard, who had taken up his summer residence at Windsor, saw him come from the garden of lady Dudley one morning at four o'clock. That a son should be seen coming from the dwelling of his mother, was in itself nothing surprising; but Fitz-Howard knew there was a coolness between them, and shrewdly suspected to whom these early visits were paid. His chief knowledge of the sex being formed from his acquaintance among the most unworthy part, he had always affirmed that every woman may be won, however seemingly virtuous. Impressed with this idea, he imagined Isabelle had forgot the respect due to herself, and, whilst his breast swelled with envy at the supposed good fortune of Dudley, he resolved to share her favours with him.

To this end he became more assiduous in his visits; and one evening having followed her into the garden, informing her first with his knowledge of Henry's visits, he addressed her in terms that made the chaste soul of Isabelle congeal to an icicle. Swelling resentment for a moment kept her silent, and when her words found vent, that laudable resentment added keenness to her reproof. Her pointed rebukes, which should have effectually repulsed his passion, served but to inflame it; he caught her in his arms; she shrieked; her voice caught the ear of her husband, who had just entered the garden by a private door, to keep an appointment he had made with her the preceding day. Again

the

fhe fhrieked ; he redoubled his fpeed, and entering the arbour, ftruck the affailer of his honour to the earth, before his ftep had been heard approaching.

Ifabelle was a woman poffeffed of ftrong fortitude ; but terror, joy, apprehenfion at once affailed her, and fhe funk fainting upon the earth. Her hufband ftooped to raife her, and the cowardly Fitz-Howard, meditating only revenge, recovered from the blow which had for a moment ftunned his faculties, fnatched a ftiletto from his fide, where he conftantly wore it, and plunged it into the bofom of Dudley.

The cries of Ifabelle had reached the ear of her aunt, and fhe had fent out fervants in queft of her. They approached the arbour with torches, at the very moment this bloody deed was perpetrated, and in the confufion that enfued, Fitz-Howard efcaped. The apparently lifelefs bodies were raifed, and borne into the houfe. Ifabelle in a few moments recovered, but the foul of Dudley was fled forever.

The defpair of his mother was great, yet was it not to be compared with the anguifh of heart under which the unfortunate Ifabelle fuffered ; for to the lofs of the being fhe prized moft on earth, was added the reproaches of her aunt, and the refentment of her father. In the firft moments of her forrow fhe difclofed the fecret of their marriage, and lady Dudley, far from blaming herfelf as the author of the fatal cataftrophe, told the heart-broken Ifabelle, it was a juft punifhment (no doubt fent from Heaven) for her difobedience and unlawful love.

Sir Ferdinando forbade her his prefence, and fhe was driven from the houfe of her aunt by repeated taunts and upbraidings. As the widow of Dudley, fhe was in affluent circumftances ; but of what value is wealth to the poffeffor,

> " When each fond affection is fled,
> " And each fenfe of pleafure lies cold."

She could not be faid to live ; it was barely exiftence ; exiftence not worth preferving, yet obliged to be endured.

N 2

At

At length she became a mother, and the tenderness, the cares and pleasures naturally attendant on the maternal character, awakened her dormant sensibility. Her feelings were not dead, only benumbed ; as the limpid stream, arrested in its course by the chilly hand of winter, becomes stagnant, nay, almost an impenetrable mass, till the infant spring, with genial warmth, gradually dissolves the frigid spell ; when it again proceeds in its usual meanders, beautifying and fertilizing every meadow through which it passes. So the mind of Isabelle, awakened from its torpid state by her infant son, expanded to receive the new-born pleasure of rearing and instructing him. Every fond affection of her soul centered in him, and if she studied to improve her mind, it was ever with the delightful hope of transmitting that improvement to the mind of her child.

From the day of Henry's death, the lady Dudley had declined, and she died without forgiving Isabelle.

Sir Ferdinando's resentment had been powerful, but his affection towards his daughter was greater ; and when there was no longer any one to keep the former awake, it gradually died away, and the latter revived with all its primitive fervor. He sent for his daughter, was reconciled to her, and breaking up his own houshold, became an inmate in her mansion. His grandson amused his solitary hours, and made the chords of sensibility vibrate in delicious harmony ; whilst Isabelle, with cheerful, unaffected, filial piety, softened the pillow of declining age, and strewed the path that leads but to the grave, with flowers so sweet, its rude descent was scarce perceptible ; nor did one thorn or briar appear, to impede the journey or to wound the foot, that must per force pass over it.

Young Dudley was christened Edward ; " For alas!" said his mother, " Henry was an unfortunate name. Caressed, almost idolized by his grandfather, and educated immediately under his own eye, Edward almost imperceptibly imbibed the enterprizing spirit that had characterized his ancestors.

He

He delighted in converfing with Otooa, a native
of North-America, who was a fervant to Sir Ferdinando.   His little heart would bound with tranfport
at the defcription of vaft oceans, immeafurable conti-
nents, and climes as yet unexplored by Europeans;
and, feized with an irrefiftible defire to vifit the new
world in America, in the year 1632, embarked for
New-England.   His inquiring nature found ample
gratification, in obferving in this novel fcene, the various flowers, plants, fhrubs, infects, birds and animals,
to which the European world were ftrangers.   Simple
in his manners, rational in his opinions, and truly fincere in his profeffions of piety, Edward Dudley became
a favourite in the colony.   And when the death of
his grandfather called him home, he was parted with
unwillingly, and with fincere regret.

He married in the year 1644 the lady Arrabella
Ruthven; and the troubles in England foon after increafing, on account of the perfecution of diffenters,
whofe religious tenets Dudley favoured, he fold his
eftates; and, purchafing a veffel, which he loaded
with provifions, farming utenfils, and fome merchandize, himfelf and lady, (who from that time was ftyl-
ed dame Arrabella) with an extenfive houfehold, embarked for New-Hampfhire, and landed, after a fatiguing voyage, in October, 1645, in tolerable health, and
moft excellent fpirits.

∗ ∗ ∗ ∗ ∗ ✦ ✦ ∗ ∗ ∗ ∗ ∗

C H A P.   XVI.

Bidding the tranced fancy fly
O'er oceans vaft from fhore to fhore.

DUDLEY and his fair companion having tranf-
ported over, in the veffel with themfelves, the
frame, and every material neceffary to form a complete habitation, immediately on landing, employed
workmen to fet it up; but the cold coming on more
rapidly than they expected, but little progrefs could
be

be made that winter, and Arrabella suffered much inconvenience from the want of thofe indulgencies to which, from her birth, fhe had been accuftomed. But fhe was not a woman to complain for trifles, or, having once embarked in a caufe, eafily to be frighted from purfuing it.

The inclemency of the winter was accordingly paffed over with patience, and as foon as the enlivening fun relaxed the fprings and called the tender herbage forth, two apartments in their new houfe being rendered habitable, fhe exerted her utmoft endeavours to add a degree of neatnefs and elegance to what was abfolutely neceffary for comfort. All the accomplifhments fhe poffeffed, were at her leifure hours exerted to embellifh and render their dwelling pleafant. It was fituated above ten miles from the fea.

Dudley had, on his firft arrival, purchafed a large tract of uncultivated land. Having got a fmall portion of it clear, immediately furrounding his habitation, Arrabella, both by her tafte, and knowledge in agriculture, affifted in rendering it at once pleafant and ferviceable. Part of it was converted into a kitchen garden, to the cultivation of which Arrabella was particularly attentive. With her own hands would fhe weed, water, or tranfplant the young vegetables; and having fown a few flower feeds which fhe had brought with her from Europe, the watching a plant as it advanced in growth, or a bud as it gradually difclofed the opening flower, afforded her the moft innocent fatisfaction; and from this conftant attention to her garden, fhe gleaned at once employment, health and amufement.

But Arrabella did not neglect her needle; and when the enfuing year produced them a fmall quantity of flax from their own land, with what exulting pride did fhe purchafe a wheel, and fet about manufacturing it into linen for her family ufe!

Delightful age of primitive fimplicity, when the mother of a numerous family did not blufh (though furrounded by affluence) to fet the example of induftry to her daughters; when fhe would prefide amongft
them,

them, whilst they were converting the produce of their father's flocks and fields into clothing for the family. And with what a laudable pride did she look round on her husband, her children and servants, and say, "That cloth, that linen, those gowns, are all of our own manufacturing."

Their wants were few, and those few were amply supplied; plenty presided at their board, and cheerfulness was a constant inmate in their dwellings. But indolence introduced luxury with her innumerable train of artificial wants. Though at first repulsed, still would the sorceress return, varying her shape to gain her favourite point; to pride, she took the form of necessity; to the voluptuous, she wore the semblance of indulgence; to each she appeared in some seductive form, and none but the truly industrious hand and contented heart could bid defiance to her arts. Alas! the number was but small that escaped the contagion she spread through all ranks of people, till at length the fascination became universal. By her magic power she threw a mist over the discerning optics of even the most rational; they saw not the deformity she concealed under her gorgeous robe, but blindly worshipped, whilst she led them to the very brink of ruin.

A few years rendered the habitation of Dudley and Arrabella extremely delightful, and, added to other numerous comforts and blessings which they enjoyed, was a rising family of beautiful children. How did this family at once increase the pleasures and the cares of their respectable mother! Anxious not only for their present but future happiness, she laboured to cultivate their understandings, and point out to them sources of mental pleasure, that would delightfully fill up every moment when employment paused.

The morning walk, the evening ramble, still afforded something to instruct and improve. Nor was the winter evening sterile or unprofitable. Edifying conversation, books and needle-work, charmingly diversified the scene, blending the useful with the agreeable.

It was in the summer of 1661, the eldest child of Dudley, a son named William, who was about fifteen

years old, and his youngeſt, a daughter called Rachel,
ſcarcely two, when ſome diſagreements having fallen
out between the native Indians and the Engliſh ſettlers,
the former frequently made inroads on the latter, plundering and burning their habitations, and either maſ-
ſacreing the inhabitants, or taking them priſoners and
carrying them up the country, where they often exer-
ciſed on them the moſt wanton barbarity; ſcalping,
maiming and disfiguring them, if at laſt they ſuffered
them to eſcape with life. But what could be expected from the untaught ſavage, whoſe territories had
been invaded by ſtrangers, and who perhaps had ſuffered, from the cruelty of the invaders, in the perſon
of a father, brother, ſon, or ſome near connexion.
Revenge is a principle inherent in human nature, and
it is only the ſublime and heavenly doctrine of Chriſ-
tianity that teaches us to repel the impulſe, and return
good for evil.

The morning was fine. Cheerful had Arrabella
aroſe, and, ſurrounded by her little family, joined with
their father in their morning adorations to the Giver
of all good. This indiſpenſable duty performed, Dudley went to ſuperintend his mowers; and his wife,
calling her girls, to the number of five, together, began
the uſual taſk of inſtruction. But the little Rachel
was not inclined to be quiet; ſhe was more inclined
for play than ſitting ſtill. She climbed up in her
mother's lap, kiſſed her, and in childiſh ſport threw
the book on the floor.

"It is impoſſible to attend ſeriouſly to any thing,"
ſaid her mother, "whilſt this little mad-cap is here.
Do, William, take her into the garden. William
obeyed, and from the garden ſtrayed into an adjoining
wood, where, intent on a book which his father had
deſired him to peruſe with attention, he ſuffered the
little prattler to play round, pluck flowers, and catch
graſshoppers.

Arrabella was purſuing her employment, with all
the delight a fond mother can feel, who marks the
daily improvement of her children, and ſees them eagerly ſtriving who ſhould foremoſt reach the goal of
perfection,

perfection, when an old servant, the only male then about the house, rushed into the apartment, exclaiming, with looks of horror, "The natives! the natives!" Starting from her seat with precipitation, she turned towards the window, and saw a band of savages crossing through a field of corn, not very far from the house. "Fly! fly! my children," she cried, taking the two youngest by the hand; and followed by the eldest, they rushed out of a door that led a contrary way to the road the savages were coming.

There was in the very wood where William had wandered with his infant sister, a cavern formed by the cunning hand of nature, the recesses of which Arrabella had in days of happiness frequently explored. Her presence of mind in this terrifying exigence did not forsake her. With hasty, yet trembling steps, she led her children thither; nor was it till resting on the ground in its remotest winding, when she felt her five children hanging about her, that she recollected William and Rachel.

"Oh! my children! my children!" exclaimed she, suddenly starting up. "We are all here, mother," they answered with united voices.

"But where! Oh where!" cried she franticly, "is your brother William, and your sister Rachel?" "Oh! my poor brother, my dear, sweet little sister," said the children severally; "let us go back, mother, let us go back and look for them."

"No, my darlings, no!" she replied, sinking again on the ground, and drawing them closer towards her; "that would indeed be to suffer you to run into the very claws of the destroyer. The great God of heaven and earth inspired me with the thought of bringing you here for safety; he will, I trust, protect us; and his power to protect and save, even from the jaws of death, is equal throughout this wide-extended universe. He can guard all your brothers, your sister, and your father too. Let us kneel, my children, and implore his mercy."

At the mention of their father, and the recollection of their brothers, Charles, James and Christopher, who

were

were in the field with him, the girls wept aloud. Arrabella poured forth her foul in fervent prayer, and the kneeling innocents, in broken accents, fobbed *amen*.

The female fervants, terrified at the approach of the favages, in their eagernefs to elude them ran directly into their power, and inftantly became victims to their fury. They difpatched them with their tomahawks, and, ftripping off their fcalps, kept them as proofs of their endeavours to extirpate the Englifh from amongft them. The man who had alarmed his miftrefs ran out of the houfe by the fame way fhe had taken; but thinking it would be right to alarm his mafter, inftead of following her, made the beft of his way to the field where the mowers were at work.

The favages having rifled the houfe of provifions, wearing apparel, and every thing which they conceived would be any ways ferviceable to themfelves, fet fire to it, and then departed, with horrid yells of exultation at having done all the mifchief in their power to an Englifh family. William was, at the moment the flames burft forth, juft returning with his little fifter. His father's houfe on fire, and a band of Indians in frantic rage haftening towards them, was a fight that filled with the moft horrid prefages the breaft of William. He faw there would be no way to efcape them; fo, clafping the infant Rachel in his arms, he knelt on the ground, fear almoft fufpending every faculty.

One of the foremoft of the favage troop had raifed his tomahawk to difpatch the boy; but the child, with one arm clinging to her brother's neck, extended the other little innocent hand as if to ward off the blow, and fcreaming, cried, "Don'tee, don'tee." At that moment a fquaw, who held a papoufe at her breaft, threw herfelf before the fuppliant children, and faid in their own language, "You fhall not kill the infant."

The attempt feemed to have been the impulfe of the moment, for it required but little perfuafion to turn the Indian from his purpofe; he dropped the inftrument of death; William ftarted from the ground, ran to the kind hearted woman, kiffed her hands, bathed

them

them with his tears, and pointing to the fky, gave her to underftand, that the Power who dwelt above that azure firmament would reward her. Her own infant being returned to her back, (the mode in which the Indian women in general carry their children) fhe took Rachel in her arms; and William being made to affift in carrying their plunder, they proceeded on their march; a weary march it was to the poor little captives.

Otawee, for that was the name of their protectrefs, did all fhe could to make little Rachel eafy, but fhe continued at intervals to cry for her mother; and William, his feet lacerated by the fharp flints and thorns he encountered in the rugged paths through which he was obliged to pafs, his heart bleeding for what he thought muft have been the fate of his beloved parents, brothers and fifters, proceeded as well as he could till towards the evening of the fecond day, when, overcome with fatigue, grief and long fafting, (for he could not eat the food they offered him) he fell fainting to the earth. ' Fortunately they were now near the end of their march, or it is more than probable the unfortunate boy would have been left to perifh in the woods. As it was, two young Indians bore him between them to the water-fide, put him in a canoe, and Otawee fitting down befide him, threw water on his face, raifed his head on her knee, and forcing him to fwallow a little fpirits, he by degrees recovered.

This party of plunderers were natives of Narhaganfet. Two or three unprincipled and licentious Europeans having made incurfions amongft them, plundering their little fettlements, burning their wigwams, and practifing other enormities, as muft certainly awaken a fpirit of revenge in the bofom of perfons better regulated than thofe of untutored favages; feveral families who had beed particularly injured, formed themfelves into a party, and embarking in their canoes, proceeded up Connecticut river, landing wherever they thought there was no fear of oppofition,

O

and

and wreaking their vengeance on the unguarded and innocent inhabitants.

Dudley had, from his firſt ſettlement, been a man of *peace;* happy in his family, fully employed in cultivating and improving his little domain, he ſtepped not out of his own domeſtic concerns, except it was to aſſiſt a neighbour, (for any European family, ſettled within twenty miles, was at that early period termed a neighbour) or to inſtruct a new ſettler in the beſt mode of clearing his lands ; to which inſtructions he ever readily added any help his ſervants, horſes, oxen, or even himſelf could give.

Such a man could hardly be ſuppoſed an object of enmity to any ; but his habitation had been marked by an Indian who had ſtrayed from his companions. Its lonely ſituation, its flouriſhing appearance, which promiſed plenty of plunder without fear of oppoſition, determined them to attack it ; but when they had committed this outrage on a quiet, inoffenſive family, they well knew it would not be long before they were purſued. They accordingly made all the haſte they could to the place where they had left their canoes, and embarking with the plunder they had obtained, proceeded immediately home. On their way thither, meeting with a party who came from the more eaſtern parts ; and, fearful that the young captives they had, might, if ſeen, betray them to the Engliſh, they ſold them, and William and Rachel were carried to a greater diſtance than it could hardly be believed poſſible for the Indians to proceed in their little birch canoes. When being landed on a very wild and totally uncultivated place, they were marched three days journey from the ſea-ſhore, and preſented to the ſquaw of their ſachem for ſervants.

Otooganoo was a man naturally gentle, fond of peace, and eager in his endeavours to promote the welfare of his people. He had ever recommended to them to treat the ſtrangers who were come to ſettle amongſt them with hoſpitality ; but it was not in his power to reſtrain the impetuoſity of youth, or to curb the licentious hand of the rapacious. When the

young

young captives were brought to his wigwam, he rebuked thofe who brought them, and bade William to banifh all his fears; for he would be a father to him, and, if ever opportunity offered, reftore him to his natural parent. His wife was particularly pleafed with little Rachel, and the kindnefs of thefe two good Indians rendered the lives of tho brother and fifter as comfortable as the nature of their fituation would admit of.

C H A P.   XVII.

Real Afflictions.

AT the alarm given by the fervant mentioned in the preceding chapter, Mr. Dudley, accompanied by his labourers and little fons, made all poffible hafte to the houfe; but who can defcribe his feelings, when he beheld the manfion where he had taken his morning's repaft in all the fecurity of confcious innocence of heart, and in which he had left thofe treafures of his foul, his wife and feven children, a heap of fmoaking ruins? When he beheld, ftretched on the earth, the mangled bodies of his female fervants, the fortitude of the man was loft in the anguifh of the hufband and father. He raifed his hands and eyes in agony towards heaven, his heart was too much oppreffed to allow even the relief of tears, and he fell lifelefs to the ground. His three fons endeavoured to raife him, they called repeatedly on his name, and finding he remained totally infenfible, wrung their hands, and wept with convulfive violence.

At length nature, which had been only ftunned by the fuddennefs and greatnefs of the affliction, in fome meafure revived. He raifed his eyes, he caft them on his weeping boys, and as if, at the fight of them, recollecting that it was a fignal mercy that they were faved from the general wreck, he endeavoured to repel the fenfibility that had overpowered him, and fummon refolution to fearch round the garden, fields and out houfes, out-houfes, fome of which had efcaped the fury of the Indians.

But in vain he fought, in vain he repeatedly called on Arrabella and her children; not a veftige of them could he find. That they efcaped out of the houfe before the favages entered, the fervant had informed him; but their weaknefs from age and fex, he imagined, would prevent their going far. They might be overtaken in their flight. They might be carried into captivity. A thoufand conjectures prefented themfelves to his diftracted thoughts, but none of them glanced towards the right. At length, weary and heart-broken, he was perfuaded by his fervants to go, with the remains of his family, to the neareft European fettlement. Accordingly, they put the children in a cart, and Mr. Dudley mounting a horfe, the labourers followed in the beft manner they were able, and late at night they arrived at Plymouth; where the relation of the fad events of the day filled the whole fettlement with alarm. Every one was ready to fympathize with the refpected Dudley, and their fympathy was doubly cordial, as in pitying him, each father of a family felt it might have been his own cafe.

But to return to the afflicted mother and her daughters. Never was a day and a night paffed in more agony, never did day and night appear fo tedious; the mother, trembling for the fate of her children, and in her own mind certain that her hufband and their father had fallen victims to their favage foe, fhuddered at every blaft of wind that howled through the dreary cavern, thinking it was the yell of the Indians. And if, during the long, long night, weary nature paufed in momentary forgetfulnefs, fhe would ftart with redoubled terror, and call on her children feverally, fearing, whilft fhe had ceafed to watch, they might have been fnatched from her.

Several times did fhe venture almoft to the mouth of the recefs; but the ruftling of the trees, the found of animals' feet, which fhe miftook for human, would make her run back; and nothing but the moft preffing

calls

calls of hunger, which her children began to exprefs by loud and impatient cries, could have driven her at laft from her retreat.

She ventured at laft entirely to quit it, and with fee-ble fteps led her almoft famifhed little group towards the place where their manfion had ftood; but alas! no manfion was there. Faint and difpirited, fhe fat down on a rock, and gave free vent to the agony of her foul.

"Do not cry fo, mother," faid the eldeft girl, her own voice almoft choked with fobs. "I am very hungry," faid a younger one.

"Oh! my children! my children!" cried the dif-tracted mother, "we muft all perifh together. Your father is no more; your mother has neither bread to give you, or where to fhelter you from the inclemency of the weather, unlefs we return to the cavern, and I fear we are too much exhaufted to reach even that afy-lum again to-night.

"There is the corn-barn, mother," faid one of them, "let us go there." Arrabella confented; they enter-ed it, and fome few grains of Indian corn being fcat-tered here and there, the children gathered them up, and ate them with avidity. But it was a kind of food, however faint and exhaufted, their mother could not fwallow. From the ruins of the houfe they brought part of an earthen pan; this they took to the fpring, wafhed it clean, and took it full of water to her. She drank, and was in fome fmall degree re-frefhed.

Arrabella had it in contemplation to go to Plym-outh; but her own increafing weaknefs, and the ex-treme youth of two of her girls, made her reject the idea as impracticable; added to which, in the after-noon was a heavy tempeft of thunder, lightning, rain and wind, which would have made fuch a journey almoft impoffible, even in the beft circumftances.

During the whole night, the tempeft continued; and in the morning this unfortunate mother was fo re-duced by anguifh of heart and continued fafting, added to the damp of the floor on which fhe lay, which had

given

given her a violent cold and ftiffened all her limbs, as to find herfelf totally unable to rife. She firmly believed her laft hour was at hand, and recommending her children to the protection of the Almighty, fhe lay in filent and uncomplaining expectation of terminating a life, in which fhe had enjoyed a very large fhare of happinefs, and which, deprived of its chief comfort in the chofen friend and partner of her heart, had now no longer any charms for her.

The elder girls, by fearching abroad, had procured fome little fuftenance from the fields and hedges; and this they would have gladly fhared with their fifters; but alas! poor innocents, they were too far exhaufted to be revived by the participation. They lay on the floor befide their mother, and a faint moan, expreffive of their fufferings, was the only fign they gave of exiftence.

The third morning dawned from the time of the enemy's invafion, and ftill no hope of relief prefented itfelf to the mind of Arrabella; and indeed to fuch a ftate was fhe reduced, that hope, fear, every lively fentiment was extinct, and a torpid defpair had taken entire poffeffion of her foul.

Dudley, from exceffive anxiety, was fo very ill as to be unable to leave his bed. The three boys were ftationary in his chamber; they hung over him, they adminiftered every nourifhment or medicine the doctor prefcribed. Whilft he flept, they waited in trembling filence, and when he awoke, eagerly ftrove who fhould receive his firft requeft, and fly to comply with it.

But the old fervant and one of the labourers, after talking the matter over one evening, refolved upon vifiting the fcene of defolation the enfuing morning, to fee if any thing worth prefervation could be found amongft the ruins. It need hardly be mentioned, that in thofe early days, fuperftition, (the natural attendant on ignorant minds and contracted educations) pervaded the underftandings of almoft every clafs of people.

During

During the walk of old Philip and his companion, from Plymouth to the domain of Dudley, their converfation had turned chiefly on fpirits, haunted houfes, and fupernatural appearances of every kind. Philip affirmed, that it was his belief, innocent blood was never fpilt, but that the fpirit of the departed, nightly vifited the fpot where it had been driven from its earthly tabernacle, and called for vengeance on the murderer; nor would it be at peace till that vengeance was executed. "And for my part," continued he with great earneftnefs, his aftonifhed auditor (who not knowing how to read and write his own name, looked upon Philip, who could, as a wonder of learning) liftening with aftonifhment, "for my part, I would no more go to thefe ruins after funfet, than I would put my hand into a burning fire; for I have no doubt but my poor miftrefs and her dear little ones—" And here he paufed to give vent to a gufh of tears, and then, as if thinking fuch weaknefs in a man required an excufe, he added, "She was a good miftrefs; we all loved her like a mother."

"Yes, that we did," replied his companion; "I fhall never fee the likes of her."

"Don't fay that," replied Philip; "I hope there be many as good; but I am morally certain it be an unpoffibility to find a better. But as I was faying, I dares to fay, fhe do walk over the ruins every night, and with her dear little girls. Oh! mercy on me, what's that? Only that it be noon-day, or I fhould think——"

"As I am a finner," faid the other, "I do fee fummat as like little Eliza."

They ftopped, they gazed upon what at the moment they believed a vifion; it was the eldeft daughter of Dudley, who, having ftrayed toward the road in the hope of feeing fome human being, of whom fhe might folicit help for her dying mother and fifters, fhe faw Philip approaching, and inftantly knew him. The excefs of her joy had nearly proved fatal to her, and fhe funk down amongft fome bufhes, which inftantaneoufly

ftantaneoufly conceealing her, the fimple clowns imagined fhe had vanifhed.

"Well, could not you have fworn you faw her?"
faid Philip.

"Yes, indeed," replied the other, "I would take.
my bible oath of it."

They had now got nearly oppofite the fhrubs which
concealed her.   The poor child had not entirely fainted ; but her languid frame, overcome by the fudden
flood of tranfport that rufhed on her heart at the fight
of a human creature, and one fhe knew, had occafioned a momentary fufpenfion of her faculties.   She heard
their fteps as they approached nearer, and raifing herfelf on her knees, cried, "Philip, dear, good Philip!"
at the fame time extending her hand towards him.

Philip trembled, ftood aghaft, and ftruggled for
breath.   His companion covered his face with his hat,
and fell on his knees.   But Eliza foon diffipated their
fears, by coming feebly towards them, again repeating, "Philip, dear Philip!"   Then earneftly clafping
her hands, fhe added, "Come, come, and fave my
mother."

Fearful conjecture was now loft in joyful certainty.
"It is Eliza herfelf," cried Philip, catching her up in
his arms.   "She is alive!   Oh! thank God! thank
God!   And my miftrefs too.   How did you efcape
the Indians?   Oh! this will cure my mafter ; this
will make him forget his other loffes ; they are nothing.   A man may build another houfe, but where
could he find another wife like my worthy madam Dudley ?"

They now, directed by Eliza, had reached the place
where, fcarcely exifting, lay the defpairing Arrabella.
One child lay on her left arm, its head refting on her
bofom ; another lay at her feet, to all appearance inanimate ; a third was feated at a little diftance, fup-
porting in her feeble arms a younger fifter.

"Oh merciful!" faid Philip ; "good father, what's
here ? My miftrefs and my fweet little ladies all dying.
Go run," turning to the labourer, "run back to town,
tell them to fend a cart, to fend victuals and drink,
and

and a nurse and a doctor, with bed and a bedstead, and every thing.   Good Sirs, what shall I do? Why don't you run? What do you stand for?"

In this manner did Philip exclaim, walking backward and forward in wild disorder; one moment stopping to gaze at the pale and almost inanimate form of Arrabella, and the next running from one child to the other, sometimes weeping, sometimes bidding them to be hearty, and frequently searching his pockets, as though he could in them find something to satisfy their hunger.

Extreme sensibility is often not only painful to the possessor, but prejudicial to those whom we may wish to serve. Philip, with a soul exquisitely formed to dictate all the soft offices of humanity, was not so capable of rendering a real service to his distressed mistress, as was the labourer, who, simply comprehending the necessity of immediate relief being obtained, exerted his utmost speed to return to Plymouth, where, explaining the nature and urgency of his errand, a short time only elapsed before, with an easy conveyance, restorative cordials, and several women, he again reached the desolated mansion of Dudley.

The meeting between Arrabella, her husband and children, was too pathetic to admit of description. The joy such an unexpected meeting occasioned, would have been too exquisite for human nature to support, had it not been allayed by the certainty that William and Rachel were lost beyond hope of recovery. With hearts overflowing with transport, they blessed God that eight of their children were living; and though they acutely felt the loss of two, yet gratitude tempered affliction, and prevented their repining at the decrees of Him, whose judgments ever go hand in hand with his mercies.

When Dudley's health was in some measure restored, he began to think of preparing another habitation before the approach of winter; but no persuasion could prevail on him to suffer another house to be erected on the spot where he had formerly lived. He even took a dislike to the whole colony of New-Hampshire,

shire, and felling his lands, he joined a number of persons, at that time about to make a settlement at Casco-Bay.

It was in vain Arrabella reprefented to him the difficulty of clearing and cultivating a new fpot; his mind had never regained its firmnefs after the fhock it had received, and he perfifted in removing, from the bofom of his friends, to an uncultivated wildernefs. But Arrabella was no longer in her prime. The brilliant genius and induftrious hands which had contributed to improve and embellifh their former dwelling, debilitated by ficknefs and forrow, had funk into inanity.

For fifteen years, Dudley and his wife fuffered almoft every fpecies of affliction which human nature can endure and live. The throat-diftemper raged, and in ten days fwept off all their children; the cold Arrabella had contracted in the cavern, and fleeping on the damp floor of the corn-barn, had given her a rheumatic complaint, which often confined her eight months out of the twelve. Dudley fought, in the fociety of his neighbours, a relief from reflection; and his intellectual faculties were fo weakened, that he eafily became the dupe of the artful or avaricious, and his fixtieth birth-day beheld him poor in purfe, depreffed in fpirit, and devoid of health.

"And if virtue, piety and integrity are thus overwhelmed with mifery," (afks the man who profeffes infidelity) "who can believe in an over-ruling Power, who punifhes the evil doer, and rewards the good according to their works?"

"All muft, all do, who do not wilfully harden their hearts, and fhut their eyes againft the light of Heaven," replies the humbly hoping Chriftian; "for as the manfion of an earthly king is adorned by gold feven times tried, filver purified by fire, and precious ftones, which, ere they attain a proper brilliancy, muft fubmit to the knife, the faw, or chiffel of the artift; fo muft thofe fouls, deftined to fhine in the everlafting manfion of the King of kings, pafs through the

fiery

fiery ordeal of affliction, be purified, and polished by the correcting finger of the great Source and First Cause of all symmetry and beauty."

C H A P.   XVIII.

William and Rachel.

IN the year 1674, the war between the native Americans and the European settlers raged with uncommon fury. William Dudley, who had, with his little sister, been carried into captivity in 1661, had now become a personage of great consequence amongst them. Otooganoo, the sachem to whom he had been presented, possessing talents naturally good, and thirsting for knowledge, yet unable to attain it, soon learnt, from his conversations with William, that he could in some measure gratify this very laudable desire to be instructed. William, though young, had, by attention to the documents of his father and the milder instructions of his mother, obtained a very decent knowledge of reading, writing, arithmetic, geography and history.

Otooganoo no sooner made this discovery, than William became to him the most valuable thing he possessed. " I will certainly restore him to his European friends," said he, " but he shall first teach me all he knows. In the mean time, I will be kind to him, nor shall his little sister ever want a friend or protector ; as soon as he has imparted to me his stock of knowledge, I will certainly send him to his friends."

Thus argued Otooganoo. But, alas! human nature will be human nature ; and when the period arrived that he had gleaned all the knowledge poor William had to impart, his heart was so attached to him, his society had afforded him so many days, months, years of real felicity, that he made to his own conscience daily fresh excuses for not sending him from him.

William

William himfelf, though he frequently fpoke of them, and expreffed a wifh to fee his parents, no longer felt that ardent defire to return to them, which he experienced in the early days of his captivity. He had become infenfibly attached to Otooganoo; and as, from the effects of his inftructions, his protector had made rapid advances towards civilization, had entirely loft his natural ferocity, and attained fuch a degree of rational information as made him a pleafant companion, William felt that attachment daily increafe.

Otooganoo had a daughter. Oberea was full five years younger than William; fhe was tall, ftraight, and finely formed. She was, at the time of his arrival amongft them, a lively girl of ten years old, wild as the rein-deer, that with fleet fteps bounds over the frozen plains of Lapland, and untutored as it is poffible for a human being to be. Her looks, her words, her actions, were the genuine impulfes of nature.

As the little Rachel increafed in years, it was the employment of her brother's leifure hours, to inftruct her in the Englifh language in the beft manner poffible. The book he had with him, on the morning of his capture, was of infinite affiftance to him, as by looking at that, he was enabled to form a very tolerable alphabet upon bark, ufing fome of their ftrong dye inftead of ink; and this alphabet ferved alike, Otooganoo, Rachel and Oberea, who delighted in partaking their leffons, and profited daily by his inftructions.

Educated under the immediate eye of a woman like Arrabella, it may naturally be fuppofed, William, though young, had imbibed very ftrong and juft ideas of female delicacy and decorum, and thefe ideas he laboured inceffantly to imprefs on the mind of his fifter. Oberea liftened attentively, and treafured every fentence he uttered in her heart. She had heard him tell his fifter, that his country-women were the moft charming women in the world, and Oberea early formed the wifh of being thought charming in the eyes of William. This wifh was a powerful talifman to correct the bad effects of habit, and at the age of feventeen,

teen, she was so much superior in manner to her un-
civilized associates, that William, without being aware
of it, adored the lovely statue his art had animated.

He was not sensible of the excess of his tenderness
for the charming Indian, till an accident, by nearly
depriving him of her, convinced him at once how necessary she was to his happiness. Some Indians, who
dwelt in the town with them, having by traffic with
the Europeans, who inhabited the sea-coasts, procured two or three musquets, one was brought and presented to Otooganoo, who being mightily pleased with
the present, loaded it, with a design of going out in
pursuit of game ; but not putting his design in immediate execution, it was left standing in one corner of
the wigwam. A young savage, particularly attached
to Oberea, took it up to examine it, and not understanding how to handle it properly, touched the trig-
ger. It went off, and the contents were lodged in
the right side of Oberea.

William heard the report, and the instant cries of
his sister ; he flew to them, and entering, saw both his
sister and her he now found he loved equal with her,
lying on the ground, which was covered with blood.
The young man, frantic at what had happened, told
what he had done, and that he feared he had killed
both the girls ; but Rachel's fall was the effect of sudden surprise, and it was soon discovered she was not
in the least hurt. But Oberea wounded, to all appearance dying, was an object distracting to William.
He raised her in his arms, called aloud for help, and
having assisted his sister and an old squaw, to staunch
the blood, and bind up the wounds, which were chiefly in the fleshy part of the arm, and having seen her
open her eyes, and sign to him that she knew him, he
walked backwards and forwards, watching her as she
dozed, sometimes applying a feather to her mouth to
be satisfied she still breathed, and often kneeling down
to kiss her hand, which lay motionless on the outside
of the bed.

Otooganoo, during the time she was thought in
danger, observed the extreme solicitude of William,

and

and when she was perfectly recovered, thus addressed him. "You have been to me, young Englishman, a friend, a companion, an instructor, now above eight years. I love you with sincerity, and I believe you love me."

"Do you doubt?" asked William eagerly.

"No, I do not for a moment doubt your sincerity. But I have also discovered that you love my daughter. Your counsels and instructions have rendered her unfit to match with any of her own countrymen; you are now almost become one of us; take her, then, to wife; and when age, infirmity or death shall occasion me to cease from the cares of life, supply my place, govern my people, direct them by your wisdom, teach them the real value of well-constructed laws, encourage them in studying the arts of war; yet lead them, by your example and forbearance, to cultivate a social and commercial intercourse, and to preserve peace with your countrymen, who are become their neighbours, as long as they can preserve it with honour."

William, weaned from his natural friends, tenderly attached to Oberea, perhaps not altogether insensible to the charms of power, and harbouring a fond hope, that by this union with the family of a sachem, he might promote the interests of his countrymen in general, and be the cement to bind them in bonds of lasting amity, listened with delighted attention, plighted his vows of love and constancy to Otooganoo, and in a few days ratified those vows, by binding himself, by the most sacred of all ties, to protect and love through life his charming Oberea.

Otooganoo lived to see his son-in-law equally beloved and respected with himself, to embrace a grandson whom William called Reuben: "For," said he, "I have been a bondman and a servant unto my wife's father, and this my first born shall pay my ransom."

As the old sachem felt his hour approaching, he called his chiefs, and the oldest men of his tribe, about him; and taking the little Reuben in his arms, whilst Oberea, William and Rachel stood on his right hand, thus addressed them:

"Warriors

" Warriors and Chiefs, Natives and undoubted Lords of this vaft country, liften to your departing father.   I have ruled over you now above forty years; I have ever found you obedient to my commands, and affectionate to my family.   But the great Spirit whofe throne is on the loftieft mountain, and whofe breath paffing over the great lake, can make it rage even as the wild tyger, when, fuddenly fpringing from his fecret hiding-place, he tears and mangles his defencelefs prey; or foftly moving over its broad furface, renders it fmooth, beautiful and enticing as is the fyren, who charms but to deftroy; this wondrous, incomprehenfible Spirit, who gave me life and motion, recals the precious gift, and in a fhort time I fhall be duft."

Otooganoo paufed; his whole foul was filled with the fublimity of the BEING of whom he had been fpeaking, and a moment was given to feelings beyond expreffion exquifite.   Recovering the firmnefs of his voice, he thus proceeded :

" Friends, Countrymen, Children, had I a fon, I well know your unanimous confent would nominate him my fucceffor.   Behold, then, the fon of my choice, the friend of my foul, the hufband of my daughter.   He is brave, he is wife, he is humane ! alike competent to profecute war with vigour, or preferve peace with honour.   He is, you will fay, a fon of our invaders, of our common enemy.   But confider them as enemies no longer.   Bury the war-hatchet twenty feet under ground, and fmoke the great pipe of peace, whofe fragrance may afcend even to the heaven of heavens.   Hail thefe Europeans as brethren, and follow henceforth their precept of doing as you would be done by."

" We will ! we will !" they all exclaimed; when Otooganoo thus continued :

" Chiefs, Elders and brother Warriors, in recommending to your choice this young man, I mean not to relinquifh the affection you have ever fhown my family.   No.   Behold this child, the fon of my daughter; in him you fee your rightful fachem.   But I am

paffing

paffing from this world to the land of fpirits, and this infant is incompetent to fupply my place. Who then fo able, who fo worthy as his father, to govern and direct you, and inftruct the young fachem how to guard your liberties, and preferve your love inviolate."

Otoogano ceafed, and an old warrior thus replied: "The offspring of Otooganoo, the fon of Oberea, will ever be honoured and refpected. We are content to receive, during his childhood, the Englifhman William, and to adopt the new faith thou haft lately taught and practifed. As the Europeans deal by us, fo deal we by them, and the great Spirit judge us both."

Otooganoo furvived this conference but a few days; he paffed (to ufe his own expreffion) to the land of fpirits, and William Dudley was chofen fachem in his ftead, by the unanimous voice of the whole tribe.

"As the Europeans deal by us, fo deal we by them, and the great Spirit judge us both." This was the oath they took, and moft religioufly did they keep it. But if the profeffors of Chriftianity practife not themfelves what they would teach to others, who can blame the favage, who (in feeking his own gratification, or promoting his own intereft, regards not the happinefs or intereft of a fellow creature) follows but the example fet him?

The new fettlers made daily encroachments on the native inhabitants, drove them from their lands, robbed them of their wives, and made their children prifoners. Was it in human nature to bear thefe injuries tamely? No; they refented them. And even William himfelf, though his heart bled at what muft be the confequence, could not attempt to repel the fpirit of juft vengeance that actuated the minds of all. War was declared on both fides, and purfued with unremitting fury.

Amongft the young warriors that lived under the government of William, was Yankoo. He was intrepid, bold, and daring. He hated the Europeans; yet, fpite of that hate which feemed inherent in his nature, his heart was fufceptible of tendernefs for one of the race. The beauty of Rachel had penetrated his foul.

He

He loved, revealed his love, and found it was returned.

The war continuing to rage, it became neceffary for the fachem in perfon to quit his home, and head his warriors. The undaunted Oberea would follow her hufband to the field, and Rachel, though naturally more timid, yet having her nerves new-ftrung by affection, accompanied her. They encamped near the fea-fhore. By the morning's dawn they expected the enemy.

Yankoo paffed a few hours the preceding evening in the wigwam of Oberea. "Oh! my friend," faid Rachel, as fhe was parting from him, "be careful of your own life for my fake; and if at any time your tomahawk fhould be raifed againft an ancient Englifhman, paufe for a moment, and think, perhaps it may be the father of Rachel, and let the idea difarm your rage."

"It would do fo," replied Yankoo, "did I not at the fame time remember, that every Englifhman is the enemy of my country."

"Would you not fpare my father then?" faid Rachel.

"No! not even my own father in fuch a caufe," anfwered the warrior, and broke from her embrace. Rachel retired to her bed, and paffed the night in tears.

C H A P.   XIX.

Long looked for come at laft—Reuben and Rachel born.

THE fituation or feelings of William Dudley were at this period by no means enviable. Ruler over a nation of favages, who by their attachment and fidelity had conciliated his affection, his principles would by no means fuffer him to defert their caufe in the hour of danger; yet remembering that his natural parents were Europeans, and the tendernefs he once

P 2

experienced

experienced for them not being extinct in his bosom, he felt his heart divided between two separate interests; and if at any time a skirmish took place, he would think that, perhaps, amongst the killed or wounded of the enemy, he might have to lament a father or a brother. And whilst he was publickly obliged to appear rejoiced at the success of the Indians, he would privately lament the defeat of his own countrymen.

The soul of Rachel was equally agitated. Alas! who can describe the feelings of a heart thus divided? She dared not pray, for to which party could she wish success? "Oh! save, protect and support my father," she would cry; then in a moment recollecting, she would wring her hands and cry, "Oh! poor Yankoo." It is anguish only to be felt, it is impossible to convey the smallest idea of its excruciating tortures, to any who have not experienced the agonizing effects of divided affection.

The English had been driven to the very borders of the sea; the Indians had pursued them with unremitting fury, ravaging the habitations, and, giving the unoffending inmates a quick passport to eternal rest with their tomahawks, nor command nor entreaty could restrain their impetuosity.

William had followed a party led by Yankoo, to a house situated in a deep wood. As they approached, a cry of terror issued from the dwelling. The heart of William throbbed with anxiety; he quickened his steps, and arrived at the door just as Yankoo had dragged forth by his venerable locks, a man, whom he no sooner beheld than he recognized the features of his father. The arm was raised that was meant to destroy him.

"Hold, monster! barbarian!" exclaimed William, and throwing himself on the body of his father, received the falling weapon on his own shoulder. It fell heavy, it sunk deep, and the blood issued in a torrent from the wound.

Yankoo recoiled with horror; he beheld his ruler, his friend, and more than those, the brother of Rachel, weltering in gore, wounded even unto death, and by

his

his hand. He knelt upon the ground, he took his hand. "Oh! brave warrior," said he, "why did you throw yourfelf in my way?" William raifed himfelf, and pointing to old Mr. Dudley, cried, "To fave a father."

The old gentleman, in fome meafure relieved from his fright, endeavoured to rife from the earth; but hearing the expreffion of father from the lips of one whom he fuppofed an Indian chief, the truth began to dawn upon his mind. He knelt befide the dying fachem, and taking his hand, looked earneftly in his face, and cried, "Is it indeed poffible? are you my fon?"

"Your own fon William," replied the bleeding warrior.

"But alas!" faid the old man, "you are, I fear, mortally wounded."

"And if I am," replied the heroic William, "it is a glorious wound; for I give my life to preferve the life of him from whom I received it."

As he finifhed thefe words, he fell back and his eyes clofed. The whole party were now affembled round their wounded chief; they raifed him from the earth, and bore him into his father's cottage, where, confined by infirmity, was the unfortunate patient Arrabella. She had heard the exclamations of her hufband; her heart had not yet become callous to mifery. The beholding her long-loft fon, was double agony, fince fhe but beheld his clofing fcene. He recovered a moment after they had laid him on the bed, gazed on the countenance of his mother, faintly articulated her name, and his laft breath paffed in imploring a bleffing on her.

The news of their fachem's death, and by whom, foon reached the tribe William had governed, and they repaired to the place of his deceafe, vowing revenge on his murderer; for in that light they looked upon Yankoo. But when they rufhed furioufly into the houfe, intending to wreak their vengeance on him, the mute forrow depicted on his face, as with his arms folded on his bofom he ftood contemplating the mangled

gled form of his departed friend, for a moment dif-
armed their rage.   He faw them enter, and advancing intrepidly towards them,

"Friends, Countrymen, and brother Warriors,"
faid he, with a firm voice, "that I have incurred your
hatred, that your rage is juftly excited, is a truth I
pretend not to evade or deny.   I have deferved death
at your hands, and behold, here I ftand prepared to
meet it.   Strike; I will not flinch; or lead me forth,
and let me experience the moft cruel tortures, I will
not complain; nor figh nor groan fhall efcape my lips.
Alas! if torture could wring them from me, how
loud would my lamentations now be!   The chief
whom we all loved, the man we all revered, is gone
to the land of fpirits; is gone to that Father, that
great Firft Caufe, of whom we have fo often heard
him fpeak.   He is paffed from us, and my hand gave
the paffport, figning it with his blood."

He paufed, and his untamed fpirit fwelled even to
his eyes; but he repelled the tokens of his fenfibility,
that were almoft burfting from the gliftening orbits,
and ftruggling for a moment to recover the firmnefs.
of his voice, proceeded:

"Thou art gone, brave chief! (turning as he fpoke
towards the body of his friend) thou art gone; and
where fhall thy equal be found to fupply thy place?
Thou wert bold and daring as the young lion, and like
him, generous and noble, exerted not thy power againft
the feeble and defencelefs.   Firm and unfhaken in af-
ferting the rights of innocence, as the mountain whofe
foundation is in the centre of the earth, and whofe top
reacheth unto the clouds; yet gentle as the fouth-weft
breeze on an evening in the bloffom feafon, and complying as the willow, that inclines its head as the
breeze paffes.   Thy voice was the voice of wifdom.
Thy words taught leffons, which thy example enforced.
But thou art gone! and where fhall thy equal be
found to fupply thy place?   Thou wert glorious as
the fun at his uprifing, mild and beautiful as the beams
of the moon, when it dances on the bofom of the lake
which the wind gently agitates.   In the chafe, fleet

as the young ftag, and the arrow from thy bow never
miffed its aim.   Thou didft fpeak, and none could refufe to believe ; thou didft command, and none but
were eager to obey.   The bad loved, whilft they feared thee ; the good adored, and endeavoured to imitate
thee.   Under thy wife government we refted in peace,
on matts made of ofiers ; our wigwams were improved, our bows better ftrung, our corn was multiplied
an hundred fold, and our fkins dried with more care.
In peace thou wert as the dew of the evening, refrefhing and invigorating all who lived beneath thy influence ; and in war terrible as the tempeft that breaks
the tall pine, roots up the ftubborn oak, and makes the
foreft tremble, as it rufhes with tremendous fury through
it.   Thy enemies beheld thee, and fear fhook their
fouls ; thou wert the father of thy people, Oh ! valiant fachem.   But thou art gone—by my hand gone !
and where fhall thy equal be found to fupply thy
place ?"

The numerous affecting images he had called together, whilft fpeaking the eulogium of the deceafed,
had now awakened feelings too powerful to be repreffed.   The afflictions of his heart burft forth in loud
lamentations.   The rage of his countrymen was totally fubdued.   They dropped their tomahawks, and
joined him in piercing cries and groans, repeating at
intervals, " Our chief, our warrior, our friend is gone,
and who can fupply his place ?"

Arrabella had not lived fo many years in the very
bofom of America, at different times obliged to have
fome kind of intercourfe with the natives, without attaining a confiderable knowledge of their language.
She liftened whilft Yankoo was fpeaking, and as he enu-
merated the virtues of her fon, fhe felt that, amongft the
tears of regret that fell for his death, were fome of
exultation that he had deferved fuch an eulogium, and
her heart was confoled.

But who can paint the anguifh, the diftrefs of Rachel, or the diftraction of Oberea ? When they heard
the fatal tidings, they fought the body of their Hufband, Brother, Chief.   But here nor tears, nor cries
declared

declared their sorrow. When the soul is too full, language is of little use. There are no words capable of expressing real affliction.

Oberea led her son Reuben (now nearly six years old) to the bed on which lay the corse of his father, and pointing to the body, pronounced in a tone deeply mournful, "Behold !"

"My father !" said the boy, and, terrified at his ghastly appearance, clasped his arms round his mother, and hid his face in her bosom. She seated herself on the side of the bed, folded her arms round her child, and resting her head on his shoulder, appeared the mute image of despair.

The feelings of Rachel would have been equally poignant, had they not been directed to another channel. She had, as she entered the apartment, faintly articulated the word *brother*. Arrabella caught the sound, and calling her daughter by name, Rachel was folded in a moment to her bosom, and in the embrace of a new found mother, felt a relief from her sorrows. Dudley kissed his daughter with tenderness, but the lively affection he had once experienced towards his children was now almost extinct. It had indeed for a moment revived when he heard the voice of William, but the icy finger of death had silenced that voice forever, and the heart of Dudley could no more vibrate with the exquisite delights springing from paternal love.

By the united efforts of Rachel and Arrabella, Oberea was at last aroused from that state of apparent insensibility into which she had fallen. Rachel released her arms from the neck of her child, and drew her gently towards her mother, who soothed, caressed, and called her her dear daughter, the relic of her beloved William.

At the name of William, she started. Arrabella perceived she had awakened her attention, and from her own son, made a quick transition to the son of Oberea. She begged her to call forth her fortitude, to exert the faculties of her mind, and as she loved
her

her hufband, for his fake, live, to protect and inftruct his fon.

"I am his mother," faid fhe; "have I not reafon to lament the lofs of a fon fo worthy? But that he was worthy is my comfort.. Had he not a thoufand virtues? and will you not ftrive to live, to teach his fon to emulate his father, to be as good, as great, as wife as he was?"

Oberea caft her eyes on her child, then fuddenly covering her face with part of her garments, fhe wept aloud. The defired end was now attained. Acute fenfibility being relieved by the effufion, Arrabella was filent, and leaving nature to its courfe, waited till the firft rude fhock was paft before fhe attempted, by reafoning, to convince her of the inutility of grieving. Alas! it was a leffon (hard as it was) which Arrabella had long fince learnt; but it is what the children of forrow all learn. Repeated difappointment firft blunts the keennefs of our feelings; corroding forrow, from overftraining, weakens the chords of fenfibility, and at length age and infirmity, creeping by chilling yet almoft imperceptible degrees through the whole fyftem, totally relaxes every fibre, whilft the heart becomes cold and impenetrable as the ice on the higheft fummit of the Andes.

The Indians mourned with fincerity for their departed fachem. The chiefs and elders affembled, declared that Reuben, when of a proper age, fhould fill the feat of government, till when they entreated Dudley to take the charge of his education. In the mean time, they prepared to inter the remains of their chief, with every mark of refpect and honour. But on the very day when the folemnity was to be performed, the Europeans made an unexpected fally on them, routed the main body, killed many, and took the remainder prifoners. Amongft thofe who fell was Yankoo. He fought, defending the houfe where lay the body of William, and died exhorting his companions to conquer or die.

Dudley, his wife and daughter, with Oberea and Reuben, were conducted to an Englifh fettlement,

where

A 4

where the former funk into a ftate of debility nearly
approaching fecond childhood, and in a few months
refted from all his forrows. When this event took place,
Arrabella determined to return to England, partly
from the hope of her native air acting as a reftorative to
her health, and partly in the wifh of fecuring to Reuben the eftates of his great-grandfather, Sir Ferdinando Gorges ; befides which, fhe knew that in Europe
fhe could procure him to be properly educated, which
the very imperfect ftate of literature in America, at
that early period, would not allow her to hope, fhould
fhe continue there. Rachel of confequence accompanied her mother ; and Oberea, attached to them by
every tender tie, would not be left behind. " The
mother and the fon of my William," faid fhe, " I will
follow to the furthermoft part of the earth."

It was early in the fpring of 1680, when the widow
Arrabella Dudley, her daughter, daughter-in-law and
grandfon arrived in England, from which fhe had been
abfent about thirty-four years. Internal feuds and
difcontents had driven herfelf and hufband at firft from
their native land, and thefe feuds in fome meafure
ftill continued.

Arrabella found it would be in vain to folicit for
any part of the property of Sir Ferdinando. Himfelf
and family in general had been attached to the royal
party, and during the years Dudley had been abfent
from England, the eftates had paffed through fo many
different hands, that it was almoft impoffible to trace
them ; or could fhe have done fo, fhe would have found
it difficult to make Reuben be received as the heir.
His dark complexion, the nature of his father's marriage with Oberea, which in law would have been
termed illegal, all militated againft fuccefs, fhould any
fuit be commenced againft the prefent poffeffors ; and
Arrabella wifely determined to confider them as inev-
itably loft.

She herfelf inherited, from the bequeft of an aunt,
a fmall eftate in Lancafhire, and thither fhe retired,
where, devoting one half of its produce to the education of Reuben, fhe made the other half ferve all the
purpofes

purposes of life; and this estate was worth but three hundred pounds per annum. Yet Arrabella was contented, and enjoyed not only the neceffaries, but the comforts of life. Her own appearance and that of her daughters was always neat, always refpectable; and their countenances ever ferene, if not cheerful. But their hands were conftantly employed, and indolence and luxury were alike ftrangers in their dwelling.

A return to her native climate, added to the tranquillity fhe enjoyed, in a great meafure reftored the health of the widow Arrabella.

Rachel, true to the firft impulfe of her heart, refufed to marry, though her beauty and fweetnefs had attracted many fuitors. "I may," fhe would fay, "find men more accomplifhed, who will talk with more eloquence, are more polifhed in their manners; but where fhall I find the equal to Yankoo for fincerity?" Rachel preferred a ftate of "fingle bleffednefs."

Oberea lived to fee her fon attain his twenty-third year, to fee him beloved and refpected by all who knew him; fhe then fell a victim to an autumnal fever. She had lived beloved, and died univerfally lamented.

About eighteen months after the deceafe of his mother, Reuben became acquainted with Cafliah Penn. Cafliah was tall, well fhaped, not fo fair as to be pale, nor dark enough to be termed brown; it was a beautiful mixture of the white rofe and carnation that glowed on her forehead, tinted her cheeks, and gave animation to her dark hazel eyes. Her face, which was elegantly ftriking, without being regularly beautiful, received much improvement from a few curls of bright chefnut hair, which efcaped, here and there, from the confinement of a pinched cap (for Cafliah was a Quaker.) Reuben faw and loved the fair maiden. An intimacy had taken place between their parents, and by converfation it was difcovered, that the father of Cafliah was a defcendant from Beatina Gorges, the youngeft daughter of Sir Egbert and Columbia. It was a kind of relationfhip that fanctified friendfhip in

the

the elder branches of the family, and encouraged the affection of the younger.

Reuben wooed, and was succefsful.   He threw afide the habit of vanity, and affumed the drefs and faith of his beloved.   Their hands were joined in the face of the church, and Arrabella, about three months after this event which gave her much pleafure, went to the manfions of the bleft.

Caffiah was young.   Reuben wifhed his aunt Rachel to ftay in the family and manage his houfehold. It was the very thing her heart wifhed for.   " My fifter," faid fhe, fmiling, " will have enough to do to nurfe and educate her children."   But, awelladay ! aunt Rachel was wrong in her predictions ; for Reuben was married above ten years before he had the leaft profpect of a young family.

At length his beloved Caffiah bid fair to make him a father.   Univerfal joy pervaded the whole family ; but, alas ! how tranfient ! The eagerly wifhed for, the long expected hour at length arrived.   Caffiah gave birth to two infants, a boy and a girl.   She heard fhe was a mother, bleffed her children, and recommended them ftrongly to the protection of their father, and the care of aunt Rachel.

" Will you name them, my love ?" faid her hufband, bending over the bed with affection.

" They fhall be called after the two beings I love moft," faid fhe, extending a hand to her aunt and hufband. " Call them Reuben and Rachel."   A fudden faintnefs feized her as fhe fpoke.   Gently, and without pain, her pure fpirit paffed from its earthly to its eternal manfion.

END OF THE FIRST VOLUME.

Reuben and Rachel;

or,

Tales of Old Times.

VOLUME SECOND.

REUBEN AND RACHEL;

O R,

TALES of OLD TIMES.

VOLUME SECOND.

C H A P. I.

*Tales by Comparison modern, by the same Rule ancient;
or, Tales of Old Times continued.*

TO lose the partner of the heart, and not feel
acutely, would be justly termed stupidity. To
attempt to delineate those feelings, might with equal
justice be called presumption. The first year of our
hero and heroine's existence must therefore be passed
over in silence. At the end of that period we behold
their father combating, by the efforts of reason and
constant employment, the barbed shafts of affliction.
The very attempt to repel them weakened their force;
by repeated resistance they became entirely harmless,
and fell, totally bereaved of point or power, to the
ground.

Reuben Dudley regained his serenity; his affections,
his hopes, his fondest wishes were now centred in his
children. Regret for the mother was swallowed up
in expectation of the children's future virtues and happiness. Aunt Rachel presided over the household,
and superintended the nursery.

Reuben and Rachel were by no means superior to
the generality of children of their age and condition.
Rachel was a lively brown girl, and both she and her
brother very soon discovered, that by crying vocife-
rously they could obtain almost any thing. Aunt

Q 2

Rachel

Rachel would not suffer the dear creatures to be crossed, and papa thought them, without exception, the
sweetest, most charming children in the univerfe. Alas!
cries affected wifdom, how foolish the fuppofition;
but reafon, unbiaffed by prejudice, declares it is only
nature, pure, undifguifed nature.

Nature! dear goddefs! how beautiful thou art,
when, chafte and unadorned, thou appeareft in the
veftments of fimplicity; when the undeviating features portray but the feelings of the heart; when the
tongue, uncontaminated by vice, unverfed in the practice of deception, gives utterance only to what thofe
feelings dictate; then, who can refift thy eloquence?
then, who can liften to thy voice, or behold thy beauties unmoved? The philofopher gazes at thee with
rapture; the ftoic cannot inveftigate thy charms and
retain his apathy; forgetting his affected infenfibility,
he beholds with wonder, admiration and love, thy in-
obtrufive excellence, and joins involuntarily in the exclamation of the enthufiaft, Oh Nature! dear goddefs! how beautiful thou art.

The children were neither ftrikingly beautiful, or
remarkably brilliant. Health, cheerfulnefs, and difpofitions naturally good, rendered them engaging;
but their minds, like the minds of moft infants, were
perfect blanks, on which the hand of education might
imprefs whatever characters the inftructor pleafed.
As they were educated in the ftricteft principles of
Quakerifm, neither trouble nor expenfe was beftowed
on the ornamental parts, though every thing ufeful
was attended to with the utmoft care.

As they advanced in years, their characters naturally developed themfelves. Reuben was open, generous, unfufpecting, and poffeffed a firmnefs of temper,
almoft approaching to obftinacy. Enthufiaftic in his
attachment to his fifter, from earlieft infancy his actions had declared, that to fee her contented and happy, made him fo.

Rachel was modeft, unaffuming, meek, timid and
affectionate. Poffeffed of a good underftanding, a
quick and clear perception, and a ftrong memory, the
tafk

talk of inftructing her was moft delightful. Daily,
nay, almoft hourly did her mind unfold fome new,
fome unexpected beauty. Her love of literature, and
the rapid progrefs fhe made in every ftudy in which
fhe engaged, at once charmed and aftonifhed her aunt
and father. But her extreme diffidence prevented her
excellencies from being univerfally known, and it was
only by a long and intimate acquaiptance her intrinfic worth could be difcovered. Yet Rachel was not
faultlefs. The meeknefs of her temper was fuch, that
refentment was a ftranger to her bofom. An injury
was no more remembered than as it had given pain to
her heart, and that heart, moulded by the hand of
pure innocence, was credulous in the extreme. Her
exceffive anxiety to fee others happy, made her inattentive to the means of promoting or preferving her
own happinefs ; and if any one profeffed to love her,
though but a moment before they had held a dagger
to her breaft, fhe would have forgot the intended injury, and never doubting their fincerity, admitted them
to her confidence and friendfhip. Her affection for her
brother was equal to his for her. To feparate them,
though but for an hour, was to give them the fevereft
uneafinefs. They were parted with tears, and met
again with fuperlative fatisfaction.   ·
     Such were Reuben and Rachel at ten years of age.
Their father doted on them with the tendereft affection, and aunt Rachel thought they were the moft fuperior beings in the whole univerfe. She would fometimes talk to them about America, defcribe the vaft
woods, boundlefs plains, majeftic rivers, and extenfive
lakes of that great continent. Reuben would liften
with rapture, and fay, " When I am a man, aunt, I
will go there." " I fhould like to go too," Rachel
would fay, " but I am fure I fhould be afraid to go to
fea."
     It was on a winter's evening, as their father was
overlooking fome papers, old deeds, &c. that had lain
mouldy in an old trunk for many years, (intending to
deftroy thofe that were ufelefs) that Reuben efpied a
fcarlet plume, or rather coronet of feathers, which had
                                        been

been thrown with some other rubbish in a heap, in order to be burned.   He seized it, examined it with attention, and at length, conceiving the purpose for which it had been made, tied it round his head, and marching up to his father, cried, " Look at me, Sir."

" Upon my word, Sir," replied his father, smiling, " why you look like a sachem indeed now."

" Why, father, did the sachems of the Indians wear such things on their heads ?" asked Reuben.

" Yes," replied his father, " that was your grandfather's coronet."

" My grandfather, Sir !"

" Yes, child ; he became a sachem by marrying the daughter of an Indian chief; but I thought your aunt had told you that long ago."

" No indeed, Sir ; will you tell us all about it, how it came to happen, now ?"

" No ; it is a long story, and I am busy."

Curiosity is perhaps the strongest impulse of the human mind.   In extreme youth its power is irresistible. The children felt theirs awakened, and softly opening the door of their father's study, they slipped out, and ran into the parlour to aunt Rachel.   Aunt Rachel was, it is true, an old maid.

> Full fifty winters, as they pass'd, had shed
> Their silver honours on her rev'rend head ;
> But still her heart its pristine warmth retain'd ;
> The days were past, but mem'ry still remain'd.
> Still the lov'd form of the lamented youth,
> His faith, his love, his constancy, his truth,
> Were treasur'd there.

The coronet that bound the brows of Reuben, recalled a thousand tender recollections.   Her dear brother William seemed to stand in miniature before her. The form of Yankoo arose to her remembrance.   Oberea too seemed present ; and when the boy asked her if she knew whose crown that was, her feelings were so powerful as for a moment to suspend her answer.

" It was my brother's," said she in a mournful tone, taking it from the child's head and laying it on her own knee ; " I have seen him wear it often."

He

"He was a great man in America, aunt," said Reuben.

"He was more than great, my love, he was good."

"Pray, aunt," said Rachel, "do you remember my grandmother?"

"Perfectly."

"Was she an Indian?"

"Yes."

"What, quite a wild savage?"

"No, my dear, she was what is in general erroneously termed so; but her heart was as gentle, as compassionate, as full of virtue and piety, as that of the most enlightened Christian."

"Was she black, aunt?"

"No; dark brown, or rather copper. But the complexion of her face was like that of her mind. Its charms and imperfections were discoverable at one glance, and it was ever beautiful, because invariable."

"But was my grandfather a sachem?"

"He was."

"What is a sachem?"

"It is a title given to a chief amongst the Indians, and is the same as governor with us."

"How came he to be a chief of the savages, aunt?"

"I will tell you," replied aunt Rachel.

It was a subject on which she delighted to expatiate. She stirred up the fire, folded up her work, and placing the attentive children on each side of her, began.— But my readers already know the whole story, and repetitions are ever tedious and uninteresting. Aunt Rachel was minute in her recital. At the account of her capture, Rachel wept; but Reuben started from his seat, his countenance glowing with resentment, and cried, "I wish I had been there."

"And what could you have done, my love?" said his aunt.

"Have rescued you, or died," replied our hero.

"Charming, undaunted spirit," exclaimed his aunt, and then continued her narrative.

When she recounted the death of Otooganoo, and the solemn manner in which he recommended their
father

father (then an infant) to the care of the chiefs, " Good old man," said Rachel, in the moſt expreſſive accent of affection, " what a pity he ſhould die."

" Then my father is a ſachem," said Reuben ; and the ſeeds of ambition which nature had implanted, but which till that moment had lain dormant in his boſom, ſtarted into life. At the account of their grandfather's death, the children both ſobbed audibly.

" I will ! I am determined I will ! go to America," said Reuben, firſt ſuppreſſing his emotions.

" What, without me, brother ?" aſked Rachel, in a mournful voice.

" No, no," he replied, " not without you, but when I am a man we will go together ; we will find out our grandfather's government, and diſcover ourſelves to his people ; I dare ſay they would be glad to ſee us, ſince they loved him ſo well."

" But what ſhould we go there for, brother ? I am ſure we are very happy here, and papa would not be willing to part with us, and aunt Rachel too would miſs us."

" Well, then, I will go, and leave you with them, and when I have ſettled myſelf in my government, I will ſend for you all. Oh ! what a fine houſe I will have, and then what a number of ſervants, and horſes, and coaches."

Aunt Rachel ſmiled, to hear how eagerly the fancy of youth catches at the hope of future greatneſs, and how readily they connect the ideas of grandeur, affluence, and numerous attendants, to the poſſeſſion of a title. She gazed for a moment with pleaſure on his intelligent countenance, which the emotions of his little ſwelling heart had lighted up with uncommon animation ; and pauſed, unwilling to throw a damp on thoſe delightful ſenſations he appeared to enjoy. At length, " What would you ſay," cried ſhe, " if I were to tell you that your grandfather had no attendants except a few warriors, who, from voluntary attachment to his perſon, followed to protect him from danger ; that he had neither horſe nor carriage ; that his palace was chiefly compoſed of the bark of trees ; that

his

his bed was the skins of wild beasts, and his seat of state the trunk of an old tree, hewn into something refembling a chair, covered with beaver and other skins, and its ornaments the teeth of tygers, polished shells and fish bones?"

"But he was good," said Rachel, "and consequently happy."

"And he was brave and wife," said Reuben exultingly, "and every body loved him."

"Sweet children," said aunt Rachel, "those are confequences which ought ever to follow goodnefs, bravery and wifdom. But, alas! they are not always certain.

"What, then, are not all good perfons happy?"

"Not always in their outward circumftances; but they enjoy internal peace."

"And are not the brave and the wife always efteemed?"

"By thofe who have fenfe and difcernment they in general are; but unfortunately, great and fhining qualifications, of either mind or perfon, excite in general more envy than love."

"What is envy, aunt?"

"A paffion, my dear Rachel, to which I hope you will ever remain a ftranger." With this wifh the good old lady kiffed the children, and difmiffed them to bed.

∙∘∙∘∙∘∙◄◄◄◄◆✦✧✦►►►►∙∘∙∘∙∘∙

CHAP. II.

Education may polifh the Manners, but Human Nature will be ftill the fame.

THOUGH the father of our hero and heroine was a man moderate in his wifhes, and of that reafonable caft of mind that preferred mediocrity to affluence; yet he conceived it an indifpenfable duty to endeavour to improve his fortune for the fake of his children. He had retained fome faint idea of the beauty and fertility of the American continent; he alfo

felt

felt an irrefiftible impulfe to vifit once more the place of his nativity; and a number of families, of his own perfuafion, about this period emigrating to the colony of Pennfylvania, amongft whom were fome of his wife's neareft relations, he collected together all the ready money he was mafter of, and turning it into fuch merchandize as was moft likely to be productive of emolument, embarked with a defign of purchafing land, building a houfe, and putting the whole in fuch a ftate of cultivation, as might render it at once a pleafant and profitable habitation for his children, when arrived to the age of maturity.

How naturally do we expect our children, or thofe in whofe welfare we are interefted, to adopt the fentiments moft congenial to our own feelings, without confidering that nature is as various in the formation of the minds of men, as of their faces; and thofe purfuits and acquirements, which to one will give the moft fuperlative delight, to another would bring only mifery. Thus the father of Rachel and Reuben, being himfelf a man of peace, fond of retirement and the ftudy of agriculture, thought he could not render them a more acceptable fervice, than to prepare them a habitation, where they might enjoy uninterrupted quiet; where plenty would prefide at the board, and the ftudy of nature, in all her varieties and beauties, enliven folitude.

He placed his fon at a public fchool to finifh his education, and making proper arrangements for the fupport of his family during his abfence (which he imagined would be about two years) he entrufted Rachel to the care of her aunt, with inftructions, that in cafe of death fhe fhould remove to the houfe, and fubmit to the direction of her maternal uncle, Hezekiah Penn.

Reuben and Rachel were in their thirteenth year when this feparation took place. Their tears fell at the idea of being parted from their father; but when the brother and fifter were informed that, during a period of two years, they muft not expect to meet on-

ly

ly at each returning Chriſtmas, their grief was beyond expreſſion.

When the carriage came to the door that was to convey Reuben from her, Rachel burſt into an agony of tears. "My brother! my dear, dear brother!" ſhe cried, hanging round his neck.

"God bleſs you, my charming ſiſter! my dear, amiable ſiſter!" cried he.

Aunt Rachel drew her niece from the door, from the parting embrace of her brother (who was led to the carriage by his father) and by degrees compoſed and conſoled her.

It cannot be ſuppoſed that their father was an unmoved ſpectator of this affecting ſcene. No! he felt and compaſſionated their ſufferings; but he knew that a maiden aunt and ſequeſtered manſion, would in no wiſe prepare his ſon for the active ſcenes of life in which (however contrary to his own wiſhes) he would moſt likely hereafter engage.

His family concerns being now ſettled to his ſatiſfaction, he embarked for Pennſylvania. His commercial plans were executed with great ſucceſs, his intended purchaſe made on very advantageous terms, and at the cloſe of the third year from his firſt arrival, he prepared again to viſit England. Mr. Dudley had taken from Europe with him a diſtant relation of his wife's, a young man, of whom, as he will make a conſiderable figure in the enſuing pages, it may not be thought an unneceſſary digreſſion to give ſome account.

The mother of Jacob Holmes was niece to the father of Caſſiah Penn. She had been left an orphan in early infancy; but the loſs of parents was amply ſupplied by her benevolent uncle and aunt. She was nearly of the ſame age with their own daughter, and, brought up with her, received the ſame benefit of education. When Caſſiah married the father of our hero and heroine, Mary Holmes continued with her aunt, and by tender aſſiduity endeavoured to prevent her feeling too acutely the privation of her daughter's ſociety. Mary was naturally ſincere and artleſs; but Mary was handſome, and loved to be told of her beau-

R   ty.

ty.   She poffeffed what is in general termed one of
the beft difpofitions in the world, becaufe fhe feldom
took the trouble to contradict any one.   Her eafinefs
might, without much exaggeration, have been termed
indolence ; and her extreme good-nature, folly and
want of feeling.   To praife her beauty, was to win
her heart ; and being often extolled for her fweetnefs
and evennefs of temper, fhe conceived, that to be perfectly paffive was to be perfectly amiable ; and Mary,
with a face extremely lovely, and a form captivating,
poffeffed neither expreffion of countenance, nor fenfibility of heart ; but like fome kinds of tropical fruits,
which, when ripe, are fo fweet as to be infipid, and,
though beautiful to the eye, have neither poignancy
or flavour to delight the tafte.   She had loved her
coufin Caffiah with as much tendernefs as her nature
was capable of ; fhe thought her the moft perfect of
human beings ; and whilft Caffiah was her conftant
companion, Mary was free from error.

In the neighbourhood of the dwelling of Obadiah
Penn, was the ancient feat of the family of the Fitz-
geralds.   Arthur Fitzgerald was an only child ; his
father had been dead many years ; his mother's indulgence had been unbounded ; and at the age of
twenty-five, Arthur had fcarcely ever known what it was
to be contradicted.   Heir at once to the eftates of his
father and the hereditary honours of his mother ; a
defcendant of the houfe of Aumerle, of which he was
the laft male branch, Arthur thought the chief end of
his exiftence was pleafure ; and though poffeffed of a
good underftanding, and a not naturally corrupt
heart, he often performed actions which did honour to
humanity ; yet unlimited indulgence and unclouded
profperity, by degrees rendered thofe divine impulfes
of nature, compaffion and benevolence, weaker and
weaker, till at length his heart ceafed to be influenced
by either.

His mother, lady Allida, chiefly refided at the Pinery, the name the feat had taken from its being furrounded by a deep wood of pine trees.   Mrs. Pinup
was lady Allida's chief attendant, and fuperintendant

of

of her houfehold in general. Though it might be fuppofed, that the vaft diftance pride places between the family of a woman of quality in actual poffeffion of eight thoufand pounds a year, and expectant of twice the fum, and that of a fimple country gentleman, whofe whole annual income did not exceed eight hundred, did not allow of any intercourfe between lady Allida Fitzgerald, and the wife of Obadiah Penn; but the fervants of thofe families fometimes met, and Mrs. Pinup, in the extreme condefcenfion of her heart, and likewife having her mind fixed on fome excellent rafpberry brandy (which the old lady kept as a wholefome ftomachic) fometimes paid a vifit to dame Prue, upper fervant in Mr. Penn's family.

In fome of thefe vifits, Mrs. Pinup had often feen both Caffiah and Mary; but there was always a modeft dignity in the manner of the former, that repelled any approach to familiarity from perfons whofe education, manners and ftation rendered them unfit companions; yet it was a dignity no ways tinctured with haughtinefs. She was ever gentle and affable, fo much fo as to be a univerfal favourite, from the higheft to the loweft.

But Mary would laugh with the maids; and though refpect for her as their mafter's niece, kept the menfervants in fome awe, fhe endured from them familiar praifes of her beauty, not only without refentment, but even with fuch an apparent degree of fatisfaction as encouraged, rather than repelled their freedom. Sometimes, when Mrs. Pinup was there, fhe would go down ftairs purpofely to chat with her, afk a thoufand queftions about lady Allida, the houfe, the pleafuregrounds, and other more infignificant fubjects, fuch as her drefs, the fafhion of it; for Mary Holmes was no Quaker in her heart, and would often pull off her clofe mob, and let her hair, which was very fine, fall loofely over her fhoulders. But if the more fedate Caffiah ever beheld any of thefe figns of vanity, fhe would mildly reprove them, and as Mary feared to offend her, fhe would ever reftrain them in her prefence.

Mrs.

Mrs. Pinup, ever communicative, and wonderfully eloquent in the praife of lady Allida, would expatiate for hours on her grandeur, her rich clothes, her houfe, her plate, and jewels ; nay, fhe often afked dame Prue to come and bring the young ladies to fee all thefe fine things. Caffiah uniformly refufed thefe invitations, but Mary, though fubmiffive to the fuperior wifdom of her coufin, fecretly wifhed to accept them.

On the marriage of Caffiah, her mother accompanied her home, and remained with her as a vifitor nearly a month. During this time, the heedlefs Mary, unable to combat her inclinations, though fhe knew they were wrong, yielded to the folicitations of dame Prue, and accompanied her to the Pinery. Lady Allida was abfent for the day. Mrs. Pinup led her guefts through the antique and fuperbly furnifhed apartments. The rich velvet canopies, the ftately beds, the maffy filver cups, large marble tables with burnifhed fupporters, China vafes, large looking-glaffes, and beautiful tapeftry, were gazed on by Mary with wonder and delight. Plenty, unreftrained by parfimony, prefided over every department of the houfehold economy of Obadiah Penn. His furniture was excellent in its kind, but it was plain.

The wardrobe was next difplayed. The rich tiffue, brocaded or velvet fuits were in turns the object of her admiration and defire. The fine lace pinners, the diamond earings, necklace, and other ornaments—Oh ! how fine ! how beautiful ! how elegant ! was repeated a hundred times.

" Well," faid Mary, " I wonder how I fhould look, dreffed in fome of this finery ?"

" Look ! why like an angel, I'm fure," faid Mrs. Pinup. " Oh ! there is nothing like drefs, to fet off a pretty face ; and if you look fo handfome in that brown padufoy gown and plain muflin cap, how do you think you would look in a full drefs fuit ?"

Mary was holding a rich blue filk robe in her hand at the moment ; fhe held it up againft her fide. The delicacy of the colour was exactly fuited to her complexion ; the effect it had gave an additional flufh to

her

her cheek. It was a loose robe, made with open sleeves, and fastened at the bosom with a diamond clasp. The ground was blue, but it was superbly embroidered with silver, and round the neck and sleeves was a net of silver thread.

"Put it on," said Mrs. Pinup.

The fashion of the dress was such as partly to expose the neck. The neck of Mary was covered with a fine cambrick handkerchief. Mrs. Pinup took it off; and then, slipping the robe over her other clothes, fastened it at the bosom, released her luxurious flaxen hair from the confinement of the cap, and turning her to the glass, said, "What do you think of yourself now?"

Dame Prue sat by, a silent spectatress of this scene. She was too good-natured to condemn, and too wise wholly to approve. Mary gazed and smiled, walked along the room to admire herself at full length in the glass, and said, in a tone expressive of mortification, "Well, I shall never like myself in my Quaker dress again."

"With this expression, she turned with a design of throwing off her borrowed plumes, when she beheld a young man, whose dress bespoke him of consequence, entering the apartment. He stopped for a moment; he looked unutterable admiration; then exclaimed, in an accent of wonder, "Angel! goddess! bright divinity!" Covered with confusion, Mary would have escaped through the opposite door; but he saw her design, and seizing her hand, besought her not to be alarmed. "Compose yourself, lovely creature," said he, "I meant not to frighten you."

"I did not know you were in the house, Sir," said Pinup, in evident confusion.

"I have not been in ten minutes," said he. "I intended to dress and join my mother at lord Aumerle's, but while Le Beau was settling my peruke, he informed me, if I would come up into my mother's dressing-room, I should see one of the prettiest Quakers in the world. But I see a celestial being. A Quaker! what! shall those lovely tresses be concealed, that enchanting

R 2form

form be disfigured by their puritanical, formal dreſs? Forbid it, all ye loves and graces."

Mary had neither ſenſibility nor diſcernment ſufficient to comprehend the inſult to which ſhe had expoſed herſelf, in thus aſſociating with the ſervants of a family, who, if her ſuperior in point of fortune, was not of a more elevated deſcent. But the feelings of Mary were never very troubleſome to her, and the Lethean draught of flattery her ears had drank, intoxicated her ſenſes and perverted her underſtanding. Inſtead of reſenting the freedom of Fitzgerald's addreſs, ſhe was ſilent, and her heart ſecretly exulted at having excited his admiration. Inſtead of inſiſting on going immediately home, ſhe threw aſide her ſumptuous and imprudently aſſumed ornaments, and in her own ſimple attire deſcended to the houſekeeper's apartment, where refreſhments were ſerved, of which Arthur partook.

The evening approached. Dame Prue aroſe to depart. "I will ſee you ſafe through the Pinery," ſaid Arthur. The moon was riſing in full, unclouded majeſty. The evening was calm, mild and inviting.

"My lady will not return till late," ſaid Pinup; "I think I will go a little way with them myſelf, and not trouble you, Sir."

"I thought you knew, Pinup," ſaid Arthur, "that I never do any thing that I conceive a trouble. You ſhall accompany the old gentlewoman, and I will offer my arm to the young divinity."

"How ſilver-ſweet ſound lovers' tongues by night,' ſays our immortal Shakeſpeare; and who ſo well underſtoód human nature, its weakneſs, its virtues, its paſſions; who ſo well delineate?"

The extent of the Pinery was a mile and a half; yet the meadow, the ſtream that watered it, and the hill on the ſide of which ſtood the manſion of Obadiah, appeared to view before they thought they had walked half way. For Arthur Fitzgerald talked of love, and Mary Holmes, though incapable of feeling a real paſſion, liſtened in delighted ſilence to the voice of adulation.

Dame

Dame Prue was confident Mrs. Dudley would not greatly approve her own visit to the Pinery, much more, that she should have taken her niece with her. She therefore desired Mary to be silent on the subject. Mary was not inclined to speak upon it to any one. Had Arthur taken no methods to see this weak girl again, in all probability, the transient liking she had conceived for him would have died away; but Arthur, unaccustomed to put any restraint on his passions, and being greatly charmed with the beauty of the fair Quaker, without once considering the consequence of seducing so young, so lovely a creature from the paths of rectitude, wrote to her in a style of submissive adoration, and implored her, if she wished to save him from despair, to meet him at the margin of the brook in the meadow. Mary complied; repeated interviews ensued, and she fell a victim, not to sensibility or passion—No; Mary Holmes was the victim of vanity and too great pliability of temper. Conscious of her deviation from virtue, the presence of her virtuous aunt became painful to her; yet did she not experience the laudable kind of uneasiness which leads to repentance and amendment.

Indifference is the lethargy of the soul; it is the grave of virtue and excellence. Indifference acts upon the mental faculties, as indolence does on the body; for as the man who indulges in inactivity can never expect to rise into notice, secure or amend his fortune, so the soul incrusted in indifference is incapable of inciting one great or glorious action. It conceives not the beauty of virtue, nor the real deformity of vice. Its affections are cold; its pleasures so languid, they scarce deserve the name. Its pains are few indeed. But then what satisfaction does the possessor lose! The beauties of creation are unfolded to him in vain; in vain the gorgeous canopy of heaven displays ten thousand thousand moving worlds, that, as they roll in the expanse of ether, contribute to embellish, cheer and warm the globe which we inhabit; in vain the teeming earth brings forth her fruit; nor field of ripened grain, nor opening flower, nor flock, nor herd, afford one joy for him.

him. He gazes at them all with stupid vacuity of thought, and wonders at the grateful tear that springs to the eye from the heart of sensibility.

The history of poor Mary is soon finished. She left the protection of her uncle, and accompanied Fitzgerald to London. Dissipation of every kind was rushed into with avidity. Her purse was liberally supplied by her seducer; her house was elegant; her equipage gay; her dress always splendid, and not seldom capriciously extravagant. But though beauty may fascinate the senses, prudence, virtue, and a good understanding, are necessary to make the charm powerful and lasting. Fitzgerald grew weary of her folly and profusion; he forsook her; yet not ungenerously. He settled sufficient on her to procure all the comforts and some of the elegancies of life. But, alas! Mary was still young, still lovely, and still indifferent. The opinion of the world was of little consequence to her; nor scarcely one individual in it was more regarded than another. Adulation she sought, and it was poured in upon her from every quarter. She regretted not the desertion of Fitzgerald; another and another spoiler came; and Mary Holmes sunk into the lowest abyss of guilt and shame.

CHAP. III.

" We all know what we are, but we know not what we may be."

THAT misery is ever the certain concomitant of guilt, is universally allowed an incontrovertible fact. Mary Holmes, with as little reflection or feeling as it is possible for a rational being to possess, was a proof of the truth of this assertion. Dissipation, whilst it had the charms of novelty, intoxicated her senses, and kept her mind in such continued employment, that her generous uncle Obadiah, her affectionate cousin Cassiah, home, the brook, the meadow, and the Pinery,

were

were all forgotten in the constant vortex of folly. But the same scene, however fascinating at first, by continual repetition loses its charms, and becomes insipid and disgusting. So Mary, often in the midst of noisy mirth and tumultuous pleasure, would cast a wishful, though transient thought, towards her uncle's quiet parlour, and the tranquil happiness that was ever her companion there.

Seven years had passed, and Mary was no longer followed, courted and admired. She had lost her most powerful charm. Her cheek was no longer suffused with the crimson of timidity, nor her manners attractive from that feminine bashfulness, which renders even a plain woman agreeable; and a beautiful woman on whose brow sits modest bashfulness, enthroned in native purity, ever is, ever will be, irresistible. But, alas! when virtue has forsaken the heart, the vermillion of chastity ceases to visit the cheek, and beauty without it, however exquisite, can catch even the eye but for a moment. Charmed with the most finished workmanship of nature, we look for the soul that should inform it. But we find it blotted! disgraced! lost! Admiration ceases; pity succeeds; and whilst we wish to reform, we cannot but despise.

Mary had arrived at this last stage. Forsaken by the men, her vanity was no longer gratified; and to enliven her home, where could she find, amongst the unhappy females with whom she had been accustomed to associate, one whose conversation could either amuse or instruct her. Unaccustomed, even in her happiest days, to seek amusement within herself, it cannot be supposed, when "sin and shame had laid all waste," she could find pleasure in reflection.

The life of Mary was a continued blank; unloving, unloved. Joyless passed her days; nor wish, nor hope, nor fear diversified it; all was inanimation.

At this period she found herself in the most interesting situation a female can experience. She was about to become a mother. If Mary ever was sensible of any thing like remorse, it was on this occasion. She wished she had not swerved from the path of rectitude; she wished her child had not been the offspring of shame.

It

It was about the middle of April. The meadows began to affume a cheerful appearance; the fruit trees, rich in blufhing fweets, fcented the air with perfume, more grateful to the fenfe than the moft coftly compound of art. Mary's health had been impaired, by midnight vigils, riot and intemperance. She fought, from the frefhnefs of the country air, a reinftatement of it, and a relief from that laffitude and inanity which weighed upon her fpirits; a neat cottage but a few miles from London became her refidence.

Late one evening, as fhe was preparing to retire to reft, the found of a carriage driving haftily by, attracted her attention. In a moment the noife of the wheels ceafed; a fudden fhriek was heard, and then all was filent.

" Why, as fure as can be, ma'am," faid the fervant who was helping her to undrefs, " the carriage is either broke down or overfet."

" I hope not, Dolly," fhe replied, going to the window to liften. Before fhe had time to unbar the fhutters and raife the fafh, a loud ring at the gate announced an unexpected vifitor. It was the perfon who drove the carriage; it had been overturned; a lady in it was hurt, and her hufband had fent him to requeft they might be permitted to repofe for the night in her houfe, as the carriage had been fo damaged as to render it impoffible for them to proceed on their journey.

Mary was not deficient in the knowledge, nor backward in the performance of the rites of hofpitality.

" The ftrangers fhall be welcome, " faid fhe, " to every accommodation my humble manfion affords."

The lady had fainted; for her arm was diflocated, and the pain had overcome her natural fortitude. A gentleman, affifted by his fervant, bore her into the houfe; their drefs ftruck on the heart of Mary. She went to the fofa on which the fair infenfible was laid, with a defign of adminiftering volatiles and a reftorative cordial. She raifed her head, which was reclined on her hufband's fhoulder, and beheld the features of Caffiah. Her hands trembled, her cheek turned pale.

" My

"My coufin!" faid fhe. Mr. Dudley looked at her with attention, and, though decorated in the habiliments of vanity, recognized the conntenance of Mary Holmes.

But little now remains to be told. The hurt Caffiah had received, confined her above a week, during which time Mary was delivered of a fon. The advice and admonitions of her friends determined her to abjure a way of life, into which fhe had been firft fedu. ced by want of refolution, and in which, want of refolution alone could have induced her to continue.

Bufinefs of importance had brought Dudley from the country ; and, prompted at once by affection for her hufband, and a wifh to fee the capital, Caffiah was induced to accompany him. The defired ends fully accomplifhed, they prepared to return.

"Come, Mary," faid Caffiah, "throw off thefe trappings of vanity ; they become not the penitent, Affume the drefs of fimplicity and purity, in which thou wert wont to appear. Return with a noble firmnefs, to the man who feduced thee, the wages of thy guilt, the piice of thy difhonour. I pray thee, Mary Holmes, return to the bofom of thy friends, to the paths of innocence and virtue. Albeit thy good uncle Obadiah is no more, yet I and my brother Hezekiah are his reprefentatives. Had he been living, and thou hadft returned repentant, he would have exceedingly rejoiced ; would have killed the fatted calf, and have bid his friends and neighbours to come and welcome thee. And fhall not we perform the will of our deceafed father ? Yea, verily will we, fince in fo doing we fhall alfo perform the will of our Father who is in heaven. Dear Mary, turn not a deaf ear to my prayer ; for the ways of truth are the ways of pleafantnefs, and where innocence dwells, dwells alfo peace forevermore.

'Mary muft have been infenfible indeed to have rejected the earneft folicitations of her amiable relation. Every feeling of the force and beauty of virtue was now powerfully awakened and called into action. She returned the fettlement fhe had received from Fitzgerald,

ald, and accompanied Dudley and Caffiah into Lancafhire, where a few years put a period to her exiftence. Mr. Dudley had from his birth adopted her fon Jacob Holmes; and when he embarked for America, Jacob accompanied him, was witnefs to every tranfaction on that fide the Atlantic, enjoyed his unlimited confidence, and when he propofed returning to Europe, Jacob was entrufted with a copy of his will, the title-deeds of the newly purchafed eftate, and left in poffeffion of it, with directions to fpare neither coft nor pains to improve, cultivate and beautify it.

C H A P.   IV.

Things as they were, as they are, and as they ever will be.

REUBEN and Rachel had, during the abfence of their father, increafed in ftature, and improved in mental acquirements. Their perfons were much altered for the better. Rachel was now approaching womanhood; tall, ftraight, and well-proportioned. An intelligent animation lighted up her countenance, which prepoffeffed the beholder, at firft fight, in her favour. It was that kind of honeft countenance in which you might read every emotion of the heart, and feemed to fay, " I cannot deceive you, if I would."

Reuben almoft idolized his fifter, and when the holidays permitted his annual vifit, never were three human beings more fuperlatively happy, than the brother, fifter, and aunt RacheL It was in one of thefe vifits, as they were focially feated round their fire, their family party enlivened by the company of a Mifs Oliver, who was paffing the winter with her grandmother, in the neighbourhood, when a letter was brought. " It is from your father," faid aunt Rachel; " take it, Reuben, and read it." Reuben broke the feal, and read as follows.

" IT

"IT is with fatisfaction of the pureft kind, that I take up my pen to inform my dear aunt Rachel and my beloved children, that the bufinefs which brought me to this place is at length finifhed, and the completion of it is equal to my moft fanguine expectations.

"The purchafe of the land, (which is delightfully fituated on the banks of the Schuylkill, within a pleafant ride of Philadelphia) the building of the houfe, barn, ftable, &c. in fuch a ftyle as might unite a degree of fimple elegance with convenience, the ftocking the farm, and other contingencies, have led me rather to exceed the fum I firft fat out with, though that was greatly augmented by trade; and I have been neceffitated to give bills on England for five hundred pounds; but they are at fuch a date as will enable me to reach home before they become due, or fhould I not, I have given my agent, Mr. Atkins, inftructions to fell part of the Lancafhire eftate, if he has not in his hands money fufficient to pay the bills without. You will, therefore, without hefitation, acquiefce in whatever arrangements he may make for that purpofe.

"I intend embarking for England about the end of October, and hope to fee you all before the new year commences.

"I fuppofe my darlings, Reuben and Rachel, are almoft grown out of knowledge. I would have anfwered their letters, but time preffes. I am pleafed with their evident improvement in writing and orthography. Tell Reuben here will be an ample field for his afpiring and inquifitive genius. Tell him, at the fame time, I wifh him ever to afpire to be eminently good; for that only can render him eminently great. Tell my deareft Rachel, that if fhe emulates the virtues and perfections of her fainted mother, fhe will be every thing that is amiable. Fare thee well. May the Creator and Preferver of the univerfe guard, protect, and keep you all.

R. DUDLEY.

"P. S. I fhall leave Jacob Holmes in care of my eftate here. I fhall alfo leave him a trifle to put him

S

in

in a little way of bufinefs, that by prudence and induftry he may render himfelf independent.   The man who depends for the neceffaries of life on a patron, can never affert that freedom of fpirit which is the natural prerogative of every human being.   Jacob is ferious, affiduous, and fcrupuloufly confcientious in all his dealings.   I have placed an unlimited confidence in him, and am firm in the belief that he will never abufe it.   Once more, God blefs you."

"So then," faid Reuben, his fine eyes beaming with pleafure, "fo then, my father intends that we fhall all go to America.   Well, I always earneftly wifhed to go, and I find I fhall be gratified."

"But brother," faid Rachel, "look at the date of my father's letter, and remember what he faid about failing in October; why, my dear brother, he will be home very foon."

"He may arrive in a few days," faid aunt Rachel.

"A few days!" cried Reuben eagerly, "why he may arrive this very night."

"Oh dear! dear Reuben, do you think fo?"

"Yes; and perhaps in fix weeks or two months time we may be all on the Atlantic ocean.   Blefs me! Mifs Oliver, are you not well?"

This queftion and exclamation, which Reuben addreffed to their fair vifitor, was extorted by fudden furprife.   He had cafually glanced his eye towards her as he was fpeaking, and beheld her interefting countenance pale as afhes.

"What is the matter, Jeffy Oliver?" faid Rachel, whofe attention was awakened by her brother's queftion; "is the room too warm?"

"No! no! my dear," faid Jeffy in tremulous accents; "only! only! indeed I don't know what ails me; but I was feized——

"With a fudden ficknefs at the mention of the Atlantic ocean," faid Hezekiah Penn, who had been fmoking his pipe in one corner of the room.

The dry manner in which he fpoke, the look he caft towards her, recalled the rofes to the cheeks of Jeffy.
She

She affected to laugh at the idea; but it was not the laugh of nature. Her heart was full, and her eyes had nearly betrayed its feelings. Reuben was at firft furprifed; but he looked on the confufed fair one, and an idea croffed his mind which gave birth to a fentiment which could not be extinguifhed but with life.

Jeffy Oliver was two years older than our hero and heroine; extremely lovely in her perfon, accomplifhed in her manners, and endowed with an underftanding far fuperior to the generality of her fex. She was fedate beyond her years; but that fedatenefs was the offspring of forrow, occafioned by the lofs of her mother when fhe was about twelve years old; foon after which, her father unthinkingly united himfelf with a young, volatile woman of quality, who, though fhe brought him a very ample fortune, yet by her extravagance, threatened him with ruin, and by her levity, with difhonour.

Jeffy had a brother, one year younger than herfelf. Archibald Oliver was claffmate with Reuben, and ha l twice invited him to his father's country-houfe, which was in Oxfordfhire, to pafs a few days in the midfummer vacation. This friendfhip between the young men naturally led to an intimacy with the fifter; and Jeffy, without a thought which fhe would blufh to own, was tenderly attached to Reuben.

Her fituation at home became difagreeable in the extreme. Fond of reading, drawing, needle-work, and every elegant domeftic employment; without affectation; delicate in her manners and converfation, and fincerely pious; it cannot be imagined that Jeffy could find pleafure in the fociety of a woman, ignorant, diffipated and irreligious.

To her maternal grandmother fhe wrote, in confidence, the miferies of her fituation, and received from her an invitation to pafs the winter with her in Lancafhire. Perhaps the vifit was not anticipated with lefs fatisfaction becaufe in the neighbourhood of the family of Reuben Dudley. Not that Jeffy was confcious of being too partial to him; but that fhe expected

pected

pected much pleasure from the society of his sister and aunt, of whom she had often heard him speak with enthusiasm.

She was charmed with the unaffected *naivette* of Rachel, and the more she knew of her the more she loved her; and though unperceived by herself, the friendship she conceived for the sister strengthened her partiality for the brother. Their persons were alike, as much so as it was possible for a face truly feminine, strikingly to resemble one whose features are more marked, more manly, more expressive of character.

Jessy looked at Rachel with admiration. "How much you are like your brother," she would say. Alas! poor Jessy; she was unconscious, that it was that resemblance which chiefly drew her heart, with irresistible power, towards her new friend. The mind of Jessy was as pure as the chaste dew which glitters in an April morn upon the bosom of a half-blown snowdrop; and when with undissembled joy she flew to meet him on his arrival in Lancashire, and presented her hand and smiling mouth to greet him, it was with the sensations of a seraph who welcomes a kindred spirit to the mansions of the blest.

Oh why! why! is this pure, this unimpassioned intercourse between the sexes, so rare, as to be almost incredible? Alas! it is a humiliating truth to own; but human nature is so weak, so liable to error, that its purest emotions may be construed into guilt, and, conscious of our own imbecility, we tremble for the firmness of another. Besides, wherever beauty, sense, or merit dwells, there envy hovers round, with haggard eye, and pale, distorted brow; the poison falling from her baleful tongue discolours every object, and casts on even innocence itself a sallow, doubtful hue. Oh! how happy, how superlatively happy, is the youthful, inexperienced, yet susceptible bosom!

<blockquote>
Charm'd with each object that it meets,
 Blythe as the vernal morn,
It from the rose inhales the sweets,
 Nor feels nor dreads the thorn;
When hope, unfetter'd, pure as light,
 Free as the passing wind,
</blockquote>

Bounds

Thus pure, thus ſuſceptible, thus fearleſs of evil, were the hearts of Reuben, Rachel, and their fair friend Jeſſy Oliver; when on the evening juſt mentioned, the reception of the letter, the eagerneſs Reuben expreſſed to embark for America, and the remark uncle Hezekiah made on the ſudden ſickneſs of Jeſſy, awakened new ideas in the breaſts of all.

Reuben had folded up his father's letter, returned it to his aunt, and ſeated himſelf beſide Jeſſy, took her paſſive hand, and ſeemed for a moment buſied in counting over and over again, the beautifully white and finely tapering fingers. Rachel ſeated herſelf on the other ſide, and aſked, with innocent earneſtneſs, "if ſhe was not better now."

"Yes," replied Jeſſy, almoſt unconſcious that ſhe ſpoke at all.

"I thought you were," ſaid Rachel, with the greateſt ſimplicity; "for the colour is returned to your lips and cheeks."

The remark did not make her paler. And when uncle Hezekiah, adjuſting his broad-brimmed beaver, and putting on his great coat, bade Reuben talk no more of the Atlantic ocean, America, and ſuch frightful things, the lily was entirely exchanged for the carnation.

Hezekiah went to the door, with a deſign to go home; his horſe had been previouſly brought out. But he opened the door, and ordering the poor beaſt back to the ſtable, returned to the parlour, and proteſted that it ſtormed tremendouſly.

"Does the wind blow very hard uncle?" ſaid Rachel.

"Yes," replied Hezekiah, deliberately ſeating himſelf, and filling another pipe.

"And does it blow on ſhore?" ſaid aunt Rachel, who, having experienced the dangers of the ſea herſelf, felt more ſenſibly the perils to which her nephew

might

might be expofed, fhould he be coming near the land on fuch a ftormy night.

"It blows ftrongly from the fea," faid Hezekiah, drawing in a vaft quantity of fmoke, and then fuffering it gradually to evaporate, as it efcaped in fmall curling clouds from his mouth.

As he fpoke, a fudden guft rufhed impetuoufly by the houfe, and fhook the apartment in which they were fitting.

"Does it fnow or rain, brother?" faid Rachel.

"It fnows," faid Hezekiah, not giving Reuben time to reply; "it fnows, and is very dark indeed."

At that moment, the difcharge of a diftant cannon was heard; and Hezekiah, dafhing his pipe on the hearth, ftarted from his feat, and exclaimed, "There is fome fhip in diftrefs." Before any one could reply, another and another gun was heard, and the fervant and carriage arriving for Mifs Oliver, they were informed that a fhip had been feen in the offing, before dark, as it was fuppofed, endeavouring to make the port of Liverpool; but that fhe appeared much difabled in her mafts, yards and rigging, and it was imagined fhe was now on fhore, or in imminent danger.

It was not the remonftrances or entreaties of his friends, that could now reftrain the impetuofity of Reuben. He was prepoffeffed with the idea that his father was in the veffel, and he would fet off immediately for Liverpool. He might be enabled to fend relief to the diftreffed mariners.

"Oh! my dear brother, it is impoffible," faid Rachel; "only hear how the wind roars."

"I do hear it," he replied mournfully, "and every blaft feems to fay, Reuben, thy father is perifhing."

A momentary filence now enfued, when Hezekiah propofed going with his nephew. "I do not think," faid he, "that we can render them any fervice; but fufpenfe is painful, and we may at leaft learn earlier intelligence of the fate of the veffel and her unfortunate crew; difcover from whence fhe came, and what paffengers were on board."

"Then

"Then promife you will not attempt to go off in a boat, my dear Reuben," faid Rachel.

"Oh heavens! he will not furely think of fuch a thing," exclaimed Mifs Oliver.

"Silly children," faid Hezekiah, "do not raife imaginary miferies to afflict yourfelves with. If he was fo mad as to wifh to do fo, he would not find any one mad enough to carry him."

The horfes were now at the door. Reuben handed Mifs Oliver to her carriage, and then, accompanied by Hezekiah, made all poffible fpeed to Liverpool; whilft aunt Rachel and her niece paffed the night in traverfing the apartment, liftening to the ftorm, and ejaculating fervent prayers for the prefervation of the unhappy failors, whofe perils (they were affured by the repeated difcharge of guns) ftill continued. Neither of them attempted to reft; they fpoke but little, but each in filence indulged her own melancholy thoughts.

Aunt Rachel had, added to the anxiety fhe felt for her nephew's fafety, a prefentiment that, fhould any thing happen to him, his children would be involved in very difagreeable circumftances. Mr. Dudley had not entrufted her with the exact fituation of his affairs previous to his leaving England. He had told her fhe might draw on his agent, Atkins, for two hundred pounds each year, and that Atkins had alfo orders to pay for Reuben's education, and defray all his expenfes; but fhe knew that the laft half year of Reuben's board remained unpaid, and fhe had herfelf received a letter, recommending prudence to her, and hinting, fhould Mr. Dudley extend his ftay abroad another fix months, he, Atkins, fhould not be able to fupply the money neceffary for houfe-keeping.

This had previoufly given birth to many uneafy reflections; and now that fhe found he had drawn for fo large a fum, and given Atkins unlimited power to fell or mortgage part of the Lancafhire eftate, fhe feared, fhould any fatal accident prevent his reaching England, Reuben and Rachel might be fevere fufferers, in more ways than the lofs of a father.

For

For herſelf, ſhe had no fears; and though the half of that eſtate conſtituted the whole of her worldly poſſeſſions, yet ſuch was the native philanthropy of her mind, ſo little was ſelf regarded, and with ſuch enthuſiaſm did ſhe regard the offspring of her lamented brother William, that to ſupply the ſmalleſt of their wants, ſhe would have cheerfully diveſted herſelf of even the common neceſſaries of life.

Aunt Rachel was now nearly approaching her ſixty-fifth year; but temperance, cheerfulneſs, and a decent competence, joined to a conſtitution firm by nature, had given even to this advanced period, ſtrength of intellect, hilarity of ſpirits, and uncommon perſonal vigour.

In reflections like thoſe juſt mentioned on her part, and earneſt prayers for her father's ſafety and her brother's return on the part of Rachel, was the weariſome night paſſed. Towards morning the ſtorm abated, and the ſun aroſe in a clear, unclouded horizon; but the ravages of the tempeſt were to be ſeen; ſeveral trees were lying on the ground, torn from their roots by the violence of the wind. A barn had been unroofed during the night, and the chimney of a neighbouring cottage blown down.

"I wonder my brother don't return," ſaid Rachel.

"I wiſh he may bring us good news when he does come," replied her aunt.

From the riſing of the ſun, till it paſſed the meridian, Rachel ſcarcely for a moment quitted the window that looked towards the road. At length, about three o'clock, ſhe ſaw her brother ſlowly winding down the hill.

"Ah! my dear aunt, here comes Reuben," cried ſhe.

"But he comes not like the meſſenger of joy," replied aunt Rachel.

"He is weary, aunt." The affectionate ſiſter ran to open the door, and receive her brother.

"What news, my dear Reuben?" ſaid ſhe eagerly, as he led her into the parlour.

"The veſſel is loſt!" he replied.

"And

" And the crew ?"

" All perifhed."

" Did you learn where fhe is fuppofed to be from ?" faid aunt Rachel.

" A pilot boat, that paffed her yefterday morning, brought intelligence fhe was from America, but not what particular port."

" Had they no pilot on board ?"

" Yes, and he has perifhed with them."

The tears ftarted into Reuben's eyes as he fpoke ; Rachel wept audibly. Their aunt took a hand from each.

" Weep not, my children," faid fhe, " but truft in God. If it has pleafed him to deprive you of your father, he is able to fupply his place. Look up to him, my children ; worfhip him, ferve him, obey him, in fincerity of heart. He may of his infinite wifdom afflict ; but remember, and let it fill your fouls with humble hope and comfort, that his chaftifements are but temporal, but his rewards to thofe who love him, eternal."

" Then you think we are orphans ?" faid Rachel.

" I think," replied her aunt, " that it is more than probable your father was in the fhip which was laft night loft."

Two days from this paffed, and no certain intelligence could be procured. Sometimes they encouraged a dawn of hope, and then again relapfed into defpair. Rachel was the earlieft rifer in the family ; fhe had been up above an hour when the newfpaper was brought, as it was cuftomary twice a week from Liverpool. She took it from the fervant, and as fhe held it to the fire to dry, the following paragraph met her eyes.——" We are at length certain, that the large fhip which was loft on Monday night laft, endeavouring to get into this harbour, was the Aurora, of London, from Philadelphia. Two men, who providentially efcaped, brought the melancholy intelligence of the captain, mate, ten hands and fourteen paffengers having perifhed ; amongft the latter was Mr. Reuben Dudley."

Rachel

Rachel read no more. The paper fell from her hands, and fenfe, feeling, almoft life itfelf, was for a while fufpended. She funk on the floor, her head refted on the elbow of her aunt's eafy chair, her eyes were open, but fhe was as devoid of fpeech and motion as a ftatue. In this fituation her brother found her. "My fifter! my dear Rachel!" he exclaimed, eagerly raifing her. His voice recalled her flecting fenfes. She threw her arms round his neck, faintly articulated, "Our father! our beloved father!" and nature relieved her burfting heart by a violent gufh of tears.

Aunt Rachel was prepared for the intelligence; her heart had prefaged it from the firft. She bore it with the fortitude of a Chriftian, though fhe felt it as acutely as her niece. But fhe had learnt to reprefs her feelings, and to bow with refignation to the will of an all-wife Providence.

⋅◄⋅◄⋅◄⋅◄⋅◄✦✦➤⋅ ➤⋅➤⋅➤⋅➤⋅

C H A P. V.

"Soft as the filver dews that reft
    On flow'rs that fcent the morning air;
So foft, fo fweet, to forrow's breaft,
    Is Friendfhip's fmile and Pity's tear."

IT may naturally be fuppofed, that when the heavy misfortune Reuben and Rachel had fuftained was univerfally known, condolements of form and fafhion poured in upon them, and fome few offered confolation with fincerity, and participated in their afflictions with feelings truly philanthropic. Amongft the latter clafs was Mifs Oliver. She was fo fenfibly affected by the lofs they had experienced in the death of their father, that nearly a week elapfed before fhe could fummon fortitude fufficient to enable her to pay them a vifit. At length, her wifh to adminifter comfort triumphed over the fear fhe had entertained of the anguifh fhe muft necefsarily encounter in the interview.
She

She arofe with a refolution of paffing the day with Rachel, took an early breakfaft, and by nine o'clock was at her habitation.

Anguifh of heart had fo enervated the mental faculties of our heroine, that fhe no longer arofe with the lark, fought employment with avidity, or purfued it with alacrity. "Why fhould I work?" fhe would fay; "I have no expectation now to cheer me; no fond hope of a returning father's fmiles and approbation rewarding my labours." Her mind occupied by reflections fuch as thefe, Rachel gave more hours to her pillow than was her ufual cuftom; not that fhe found there the reft fhe fought; but there fhe could weep unreftrained, there fhe could uninterruptedly indulge in contemplation. And if haply fleep for a few hours fteeped her fenfes in forgetfulnefs, fhe bleffed the fweet oblivion, and courted its return. She was feated at the breakfaft table when Mifs Oliver entered.

"Jeffy!" faid fhe mournfully, and half rifing to prefent her hand; but overcome by the fenfations which rufhed on her foul, fhe funk again on her feat.

Mifs Oliver took the proffered hand, preffed it tenderly, feated herfelf befide her, but was filent. Yet her fpeaking eye met the glance of Rachel's; its expreffion conveyed more than was in the power of words; it faid, in the moft intelligent language, Dear Rachel, I feel, I participate your forrows.

It was the confolation moft congenial to the foul it meant to addrefs. Rachel felt its fincerity, its energy, and was relieved. Oh! faid fhe mentally, how far preferable is this to the profufion of words, with which the unfeeling attempt to confole me. She returned the preffure of Jeffy's hand; a few tears efcaped from her eyes; Reuben kiffed them off, and feating himfelf oppofite the two charming young women, contemplated them till his own eyes were fuffufed; and the fuffufion did honour to his heart, to nature, to reafon, to manhood!

How long this filence might have continued, is uncertain; but it was abruptly interrupted by aunt Rachel, who entered the apartment, followed by a diminutive

minutive figure habited in a grey coat, black waistcoat and breeches, an immense and not very fashiona-
ble peruke, high boots, a very deep pair of ruffles, and
a long neckcloth twisted through the fourth button-
hole of his waistcoat.

This extraordinary personage appeared to be about
fifty years old.   His black eyes, which were not the
less penetrating for being extremely small, darted their
glances at the three interesting figures that presented
themselves in the persons of Reuben, Rachel, and Miss
Oliver.

He bowed profoundly on entering.   Rachel rose
from her seat.   Her sorrows seemed to retire within
her heart, and a dignified composure took possession of
her features, as she received and returned his compliments.

"This gentleman comes from Mr. Atkins," said
aunt Rachel, as pointing to the sofa on which Reuben
had sat, she motioned for him to be seated.   "His
name, I understand, is ——"

"Allibi, at your service," said he, bowing again,
and recovering himself with an air of consequence ; as
if he had said, I believe I am pretty universally known.
"Mr. Dudley, I presume," turning toward Reuben,
"and Miss Dudley, his charming sister, (bowing to
Rachel) if I may judge from your mourning habits.
Give me leave to condole with you on the unfortunate catastrophe of our mutual friend.   But man is
born to die ; so regret is useless.   Permit me, therefore, to congratulate you on your accession to his fortune."

The mention of her father had called forth the
smothered sensibility of Rachel ; but the conclusion
repelled it by rousing her indignation.

"Congratulate ?" said she, in a voice scarcely articulate.

"Congratulate ?" echoed Reuben, and his fine
countenance glowed, his eyes darted resentment.   "Sir,
we are the children of Mr. Dudley, his natural offspring, reared by his care, nurtured by his love, and

taught

taught by his wifdom. Who then fhall dare infult us ?" And he rofe from his feat, laid one hand on his breaft, and with the other motioned as though brandifhing a weapon. "Who fhall dare infult us by congratulation for his death? Oh! my father!"

"My dear, loft father!" repeated Rachel.

"My afflicted friends," faid Mifs Oliver, foftly.

It was a fcene fo new, the manners and fentiments of the young trio were fo elevated, as to be almoft unintelligible to Allibi. He figetted on his feat, hemmed at leaft half a dozen times, and at length he began with hefitation—

"I beg pardon. I proteft I did not mean—that is, I did not know. But as I was faying, young Mr. Reuben Dudley, and his fifter Mifs Rachel Dudley, being twin brother and fifter, and in the eye of the law joint heirs of the poffeffions and eftates, of what kind foever, that is to fay, of money, plate, jewels, landed property, houfes, merchandize, or what not, belonging or appertaining to their late father, Reuben Dudley, deceafed——"

"Oh heavens!" faid Rachel, folding her hands acrofs her breaft, as if to accelerate her breathing, which was evidently laboured.

"My dear creature!" faid Mifs Oliver, in the accent of commiferation.

"Good Sir, be expeditious in explaining the nature of your bufinefs," faid Reuben; and he walked to the other end of the room to conceal his own emotions.

Allibi with the fame *fang froid* proceeded.—"You being, as I have before faid, co-heirs, do thereby ftand anfwerable for all debts contracted by, or owing from the faid Reuben Dudley, deceafed."

"Granted," faid Reuben, haftily. "Pray come to your conclufion.

"The conclufion is," faid Allibi, deliberately drawing forth his pocket book, "that you muft of confequence pay this bill of five hundred pounds, which your father drew previous to his leaving America, on my client Andrew Atkins. Now he, Andrew Atkins, having no property whatever in his hands wherewith

T

to difcharge this demand, and being empowered by your father before the late fatal cataftrophe to fell, mortgage, or otherwife difpofe of the Lancafhire eftate, in order to liquidate this and other debts he had contracted, I am fent by him, my client, the faid Andrew Atkins, to inquire when it will be convenient for you to difcharge the bill ; or in cafe of non-ability on your part, I am empowered to take poffeffion of the faid eftates on the part of my client, the faid Andrew Atkins, in order that he may mortgage, fell, or otherwife difpofe of it, to enable him to anfwer this and other demands which may be made on him."

"I fuppofe," faid aunt Rachel, " you know that half the eftate is mine."

" Pardon me, madam," faid the man of law, " I know no fuch thing. The late Mr. Reuben Dudley inherited from his grandmother, the lady Arabella Ruthven, wife to Edward Dudley, who went to America in the year 1645 ; and as the faid Reuben was the only male defcendant of the faid Arrabella, and fhe dying inteftate——"

" Sir," faid Reuben haftily, " the eftate is half my aunt's; we wifh not to conteft it. It is, it muft be her's, by all the rules of juftice."

"I know nothing of juftice," faid Allibi ; " the law, the law, Sir, is my profeffion."

I thought, Sir, law and equity were fynonimous terms."

" You are a very young man, Mr. Dudley, very young, very inexperienced ; when you are older, you will be wifer."

Reuben could not anfwer ; a look of pointed contempt fully expreffed his fentiments. Allibi continued :

" And fo, Sir, yourfelf and fifter being minors, it is neceffary to throw the eftate into Chancery, when, after your father's debts are difcharged, the refidue will be paid to you when of age."

. " And in the mean time how are we to live," faid Rachel.

" Oh ! my dear young lady, you have friends, wealthy relations. You have alfo youth, beauty, and
may

may command a home in twenty different families, and in fo doing confer a favour. Well, Mr. Dudley, I prefume from your filence that you cannot pay thefe five hundred pounds ?"

Reuben bowed his head.

" I imagined it would be fo, and have brought down people to take poffeffion of the houfe, plate, ftock, farming utenfils, &c. and muft beg you will remove as foon as may be convenient. With your leave, (rifing and putting on his hat) I will take an inventory of the family plate which I faw in the beaufet in the next room."

He drew forth his pen, ink, and folded paper, and without waiting for the leave he had requefted, walked into the adjoining apartment.

" Alas! alas!" cried Rachel, " whither fhall we go? Who will receive us? Where fhall we find either home or fupport ?"

" Had I a home I could call my own," faid Jeffy Oliver, " you fhould not have occafion to repeat the queftion."

" And poor aunt Rachel too, what will become of her?" faid Rachel, tenderly taking her hand, which hung paffively over the arm of her chair, as loft in painful thought fhe leaned her head againft the fide of it.

" What will become of her?" faid Reuben with energy, " why I will labour to fupport you both. Yes," continued he, fervently clafping his hands, and dropping on his knees before them; " yes, here in the fight of Heaven, I vow to dedicate my life to her and you. I will cheerfully work to procure you fuftenance. Induftry fhall fupply our wants, innocence and content make our dwelling, however humble, the abode of pleafure; and I will protect you from the fcorn and infults of the world at the hazard of my life."

As Reuben arofe and folded his fifter in his arms, Hezekiah Penn entered the room. He was foon informed of their difagreeable fituation. But Hezekiah knew fo very little of the world and its concerns, that

he

he could not offer advice; all he could do was to bid them cheer up, and hope for better times.

"In truth, my dear kinsman, said he. "I do commiserate your sufferings much; but I know not how, young as you are, you can extricate yourselves from your present difficulty. Come, then, home to my house; abide there till we can fix on some feasible plan for your future well-doing. I am not overcharged with the good things of this world; but come and partake of such as I have, and take with it a hearty welcome. I pray thee, Rachel Dudley, be not down hearted, but come to my mansion; bring these children with thee, and He who feedeth the young ravens will provide the means of subsistence."

The heart of Hezekiah overflowed with the "milk of human kindness;" he meant all he said, and felt more, much more, than he could find words to express. His friendly offers, and the endearing kindness of Miss Oliver, healed the bleeding hearts of Reuben and Rachel, and even aunt Rachel was revived by their influence. That very night they removed from their own habitation to that of the benevolent Hezekiah, and left the loquacious Mr. Allibi in full possession of the premises, in behalf of his client Mr. Andrew Atkins.

C H A P. VI.

Death of an old Friend—Acquisition of a Lover—Formality personified.

SOON after this arrangement took place, Miss Oliver was recalled home. With many tears she took leave of our heroine, told her, if ever fortune should put it in her power to offer her an asylum, she might freely command her purse, her house, her unbounded friendship in every particular. When she had again embraced Rachel, she turned towards Reuben.

"Mr.

"Mr. Dudley," said she, "the friendship of a girl like me is an offering of so trifling a nature, I hardly know whether you will think it worth accepting. You are advised by your friends to visit America, to look after and secure the property your father possessed there. It will probably be many years before we meet again; and what changes may take place during this separation, it is impossible now to determine. Accept my most ardent wishes for your prosperity. I know you will often write to my brother; in those letters perhaps you will sometimes remember me."

"Oh! doubt it not, charming Miss Oliver," said he, pressing her hand to his lips; while she, fearful that she had said more than the exact line of propriety she had prescribed to herself rendered allowable, hurried to her carriage, to hide emotions she found it impossible to stifle.

Atkins having now taken the management of the estate entirely into his own hands, pretended to advance money himself for the liquidation of Mr. Dudley's debts, and at the end of three months laid before Hezekiah Penn, Reuben and aunt Rachel, a statement of accounts, which, to the minds of these three inexperienced, honest children of simplicity, made it appear as so involved, that it would be a long term of years before it could even clear itself. In the mean time, how were the orphans and their venerable relation to be supported?

Letters were written to Jacob Holmes, a proper time allowed, and no answer being returned, Hezekiah persuaded Reuben, who was now nearly eighteen, to visit that continent and make inquiry himself concerning his father's effects.

"Your sister," said Hezekiah, "shall stay with me till you return. She shall not want a home nor a father whilst I live."

A voyage to the western continent had ever been the primary wish of Reuben's heart; he hoped he knew not what, but that hope led him on; and even to part with his sister was thought of with more composure, since, if he amended his own fortune, she was

to be the partaker of it.   Jeffy Oliver too was foremoft
in the happy group his fanguine imagination portray-
ed as eagerly flying to welcome his return to England.
Nay, fancy would fo powerfully take poffeffion of his
mind, that fhe would fometimes carry him a fecond
time acrofs the Atlantic ocean, and place him tranquilly in the habitation his father had defcribed, fur-
round him with a blooming offspring, and give them
Jeffy Oliver for a mother, his fifter too heightening
by partaking their felicity ; and even provide a fnug
corner and eafy chair for aunt Rachel.

" Uncle Hezekiah," he would fay, " will not be perfuaded to quit Old England, or elfe what a charming
family party we fhould make."

Oh ! how delightful are thofe day-dreams of youth ;
like the fhadows of a magic lantern, that pafs before
the admiring eye in quick fucceffion, each one as it
comes forward more pleafing than the laft.   But forrow, difappointment, poverty, throw a damp upon the
fire of youth, which had given brightnefs to the picture ; the brilliant tints grow pale ; the figures are
fcarcely perceptible ; they pafs before us almoft unnoticed ; when age entirely extinguifhes the flame,
and all is darknefs, undiftinguifhable chaos.

Spurred on by the native impulfe of his mind, which
incited him to activity, and infpired him with the moft
fanguine prefentiments of future profperity, Reuben
took leave of his friends in Lancafhire, and embarked
for Philadelphia.

Previous to his departure, he had thrown off both the
habit and manners of a Quaker.   Hezekiah remonftrated, but Reuben would reply, " Nay, uncle, can
you believe it is of any confequence to our eternal
welfare, whether we wear a plain drab coat or a fcarlet one ? or do you not think I fhould commit more
fin in continuing the habit, when I cannot fubmit to
the tenets of the Friendly fyftem ? I admire their
primitive manners, and the fimplicity of their language ; but I am a young man, uncle, and have to
make my way through the world.   Befides, I feel that
within me that tells me, fhould my king or country require

quire my aſſiſtance, I ſhould readily draw a ſword in their defence. What, my dear uncle, if we were all men of peace, who would protect us from the encroachments of our enemies? No; you ſhall pray for peace, and if the haughty foe is not inclined to grant it, I will aſſiſt my brave countrymen to force them to it."

Perhaps Hezekiah did not ſay ſo much as he might have done, had he not recollected that Reuben's father had only become one of the ſect in compliance with the wiſh of his wife; and Hezekiah had charity enough to think that a man might be a very good Chriſtian, though he wore a button to his hat, and ruffles to his ſhirt.

From the time of Mr. Dudley's unfortunate death, aunt Rachel's ſpirits flagged. She was no longer the life of every ſociety in which ſhe mixed. The loſs of her little independence, the being obliged to the hand of charity for her daily bread, depreſſed her generous mind. The deſtitute ſituation too of her darlings, Reuben and Rachel, was a heavy affliction. Reſt and appetite forſook her. Reuben's departure for America was the finiſhing blow. The anxiety ſhe ſuffered for his ſafety brought on a ſlow nervous fever, and gradually undermined her conſtitution. Rachel watched over her with unremitting tenderneſs and attention; adminiſtered every medicine; read to her, prayed by her; endeavoured to cheer her by affected ſerenity when ſhe was awake, and wept over her with agony when ſhe ſlept.

But care, affection, prayers and tears were alike ineffectual. Aunt Rachel departed this life, and our heroine felt, as the laſt breath lingered on the lips of her maternal friend, that in loſing her ſhe ſhould become forlorn, unconnected, and be left to ſtruggle through a world with which ſhe was totally unacquainted, without a comforter, adviſer, or protector. Reuben ſtill lived, to be ſure, but Reuben was far, very far from her; and ſhould ſhe ſtand in need of advice or protection, ſhe might be loſt, and Reuben

not

not even hear of her diſtreſs till ſhe was paſt the reach
of relief or aſſiſtance.

Occupied by reflections ſuch as theſe, Rachel would
often ſtray into the rural church-yard, where, reſting
on the "lap of earth," lay the remains of her mother
and her lamented aunt.

It was midſummer. The days were extremely
long, and at half-paſt eight o'clock in the evening, juſt
enough of the twilight remained, as threw over the
face of nature that modeſt, duſky veil, ſo congenial
to the contemplative mind. Rachel ſeated herſelf on
the fragment of a broken tomb-ſtone, and caſting her
eyes upon a new-made grave, where that very afternoon a youth had been interred, the only ſon of a
farmer in the neighbourhood, ſhe, almoſt unknown to
herſelf, audibly repeated the following ſtanzas.

> Reſt, gentle youth, here reſt in peace,
>   Secure from vanity and noiſe;
> For here thy earthly ſorrows ceaſe,
>   From hence commence thy heavenly joys.
>
> Short was thy ſpan; 'tis paſt! 'tis gone!
>   Early thou'ſt reach'd the appointed goal;
> Freed from its clog, and upwards flown,
>   Angels receiv'd thy ſpotleſs ſoul.
>
> Here in thy quiet manſion reſt,
>   Safe from all anguiſh, pain or care;
> Light ſit the turf upon thy breaſt,
>   Nor weed nor briar flouriſh there.
>
> And when the chilling arms of death
>   Shall fold this fragile frame of mine,
> May my laſt ſigh of parting breath
>   Paſs tranquil and reſign'd as thine.

"My lovely moraliſt," ſaid a voice, as Rachel finiſhed the laſt ſentence, "if you ſit here much longer,
you will ſtand a chance of ſoon being as tranquil as
that poor youth. His diſorder was a cold, and you
are taking the right method to catch one."

Rachel roſe, turned her head, and beheld the apoth-
ecary of the village. Dr. Lenient was a man nearly
fifty

fifty years old, very humane, very learned, very skil-
ful in his profeffion ; but with regret it muft be added,
not very rich.   For if he attended a family whofe
wants were great and means fmall, when the journey-
man inquired if he fhould make out the bill, as was
cuftomary, at Chriftmas, he would fay, Pho, pho, tear
out the account and burn it ; if I fend it in, they can't
pay it.   It is only my own time loft ; and the few
drugs—what did they coft me ? Nothing worth talking of.   Oh ! burn it ! burn it !   If the poor man has
got a trifle beforehand, why he wants it, in this feafon
of hilarity, to provide a good large plumb-pudding
for his little ones.''

With fentiments fuch as thefe, though the Doctor's
practice daily increafed, yet it did not greatly augment
his revenue.   However, he fupported his family with
comfort and fomething more than decency.

Our heroine was a great favourite with the good
man.   Studious from her infancy, of an inquiring
genius, eager in the purfuit of knowledge, and attentive to the converfation of thofe who had the power
to impart it, Rachel at the age of twelve had prefer-
ed a converfation with the doctor, to a ride or a ramble
with her young companions.   Charmed by her ardent
thirft for inftruction, the old gentleman would anfwer
her queftions, correct her errors, direct her ftudies,
and labour to give her an unaffected turn for literature and the polite arts.

When Rachel painted or worked flowers, the Doctor
would affift her in arranging her fhades with propriety ; defcribing, as he fat befide her while fhe worked,
the natures, properties and ufe of every plant, fhrub
or flower.   If fhe read, he corrected her pronunciation,
and taught her how to convey the full fenfe of what
fhe read to her auditors, by a pleafing modulation of
voice.   If fhe wrote, he would point out the errors in
her ftyle, and often has been heard to fay, It was a
great pity fhe could not fpeak and read Latin.

" Come, my good girl," faid he, " you fhall go home
with me.   You are too melancholy of late, and indulge too much in folitary walks and gloomy contem-
plations.

plations. And let me tell you, my young friend, you are infenfibly falling into an error, which, if indulged, will increafe and grow upon you, till. it becomes guilt."

Rachel ftarted. "What mean you, Sir?" faid fhe.

"I mean," replied the Doctor, "that you are finking into torpor and inactivity; you are fuffering the functions of your foul to be entirely locked up by grief, and you are diftrufting the power of a Divine Providence, in giving way to immoderate affliction."

"Alas! my dear Sir," faid Rachel, "have I not caufe to be afflicted? am I not a moft unhappy creature? My parents dead, my brother at an immenfe diftance from me, my good uncle Hezekiah in a very infirm ftate, and the only fource from whence I could look for fupport entangled in the law!"

"All this is true, I muft allow," faid the Doctor gravely, "but yet, Mifs Dudley, you have a firm, unalterable friend, who has faid, (and his word is truth itfelf) "Though thy father and thy mother forfake thee, yet will not I forfake thee." And this friend, my dear, has endowed you with wonderful qualifications of both mind and perfon; he has given you good fenfe, genius, and the benefit of improving thofe qualities by education; and all he requires of you is, not ungratefully to bury the talent entrufted to your keeping, but exert yourfelf to improve it to the utmoft, depending on him to fecond your endeavours, and he will amply reward your faith, patience and induftry."

Cheered and comforted by converfation fuch as this, the melancholy cloud began to difperfe from the brow of Rachel. Her features affumed a fweet, an interefting compofure; and, arrived at the dwelling of the good Doctor, fhe confented to go in and partake of his fupper. For the houfe of Hezekiah Penn was within five minute's walk of the Doctor's, and a lad was difpatched to inform him that Rachel was fafe, but would fup out.

This little neceffary bufinefs was fettled in the garden that fronted the houfe, where the lad was bufied

in

in watering some pots of curious flowers ; and the Doctor then led his fair companion through the shop into a back parlour, where they usually sat.

"I have brought you a welcome visitor, sister," said he, as he opened the door. Mrs. Auberry rose from her seat, and taking the hand of Rachel, cried, "Welcome indeed." Then turning to an elegant young man in military uniform, she continued, "My dear Hamden, give me leave to present you to Miss Dudley. This, Miss Dudley, is my son Hamden Auberry, of whom you have often heard me speak."

The majestic figure, the soft, melancholy countenance of Rachel, rendered more striking by her deep mourning habit, (for Rachel was not Quaker enough to neglect that outward token of respect to the memory of departed friends) made her appear in the eyes of the young soldier almost divine. She bowed her head, and presented her hand with a grace peculiar to herself. There was something in the action *nouvelle*, and irresistibly charming in the eyes of Hamden. He took the snowy pledge of amity, and bowed low upon it ; and if his fingers did contract closer than the frigid rules of politeness render admissible, surprise and admiration must plead his excuse. Rachel was sensible of the pressure, and life's warm fluid, rushing impetuously to her heart, from thence sprang to her cheeks, and gave uncommon animation to her expressive countenance.

Dr. Lenient was an old bachelor. Himself and sister were nearly of an age. She had, in her youth, united herself to a young man, who, being a younger son though of the united families of Hamden and Auberry, had nothing but a commission and the interest of his father to depend on. Joanna Lenient was poor in every thing, save personal beauty and a good heart. Young Auberry saw her, loved her, and bidding defiance to every suggestion of prudence, in direct opposition to the will of his father, married her. His father renounced him, and he never rose above the rank of captain. He sought preferment in the field of action, fought bravely under the gallant Marlborough, and

and fell in the memorable battle on the plains of Bleinheim.

His wife had never been acknowledged by his family, and after his death she retired, with her infant son, then only fifteen months old, to the village where her brother resided. He had just entered upon the busy scenes of life, had a pleasant house, a considerable degree of employment; but no social companion to render the fireside cheerful, or preside at the temperate meal. He invited his sister to come and increase his comforts by sharing them. She complied, and his home from that hour became her's. Her pension was devoted to the education of young Hamden, and the supply of her own pocket expenses; and the Doctor found himself so happy in her sisterly affection, her economy in managing his family, her good humour, sincerity, and study to please, that every other woman of his acquaintance lost something in his opinion, when compared with his sister Auberry.

It happened that when Hamden was about seven years old, the maid-servant of Dr. Lenient requested leave to go to a neighbouring fair, and take little master with her. Hamden joined his solicitations with Susan's, and was permitted to go. The brother of Susan was the head-waiter of an inn, in the town to which they went, and thither the girl (after having paraded through the fair with some of her companions, and purchased for Master Auberry a gun and a drum) repaired, in order to procure some refreshment. Hamden, satiated with cakes, fruit and sugar-plumbs, left her to take her repast in quiet, whilst, taking his little musket on his shoulder, and slinging his drum before him, he paraded in the court before the front of the house, supporting his gun with his left hand, and beating the drum with his right.

Hamden was a remarkably handsome boy; his complexion at once fair and florid, his eyes large and expressive, of the finest sapphire hue, and his forehead shaded by innumerable ringlets of beautiful flaxen hair; tall of his age, and sufficiently robust to prevent an appearance of effeminacy. Such a boy so employ-

ed,

ed, could not fail to attract notice. A lady, who in passing to her country-seat had stopped to take dinner in this place, had observed his martial air and step, as he marched before the windows, and throwing up the sash, called him to her.

" So you have been to the fair, I see, my pretty boy," said she.

" Yes, ma'am, and Susan gave me this gun ; a'n't it a pretty one ? and the drum too ; only hear how loud I can beat it. She wanted to give me a fiddle and a coach, but I chose the gun, and next fair I will have a sword."

" You shall have a sword now, my sweet boy ; here is a shilling to buy one."

" No, thank you, ma'am," said Hamden ; " mamma gave me money enough, and she would be angry if I took any from strangers."

" You are a charming fellow ; will you go with me ?"

" If mamma pleases, and you will promise to make me a soldier."

" Why do you wish to be a soldier ?"

" Because papa was a soldier. He was killed at the battle of Bleinhem, and I should like to know how to fight, that I might kill the man that killed my father."

The lady felt her eyes fill with tears ; the undaunt-ed spirit of the boy delighted her.

" What is your name, my love ?" said she.

" Hamden Anberry," he replied ; " 'tis a great name, my mamma says, and for the sake of my father's relations I must be careful not to disgrace it, though they never owned me, nor noticed me."

At the name of Anberry, the lady had sunk agi-tated on the window-seat. " Come into the room, my dear," said she. Hamden obeyed, and was instantly folded in her arms, while her tears bedewed his face, as she tenderly saluted him.

It was lady Anne Auberry, the eldest sister of Ham-den's father. Struck by the innocent reproach his natural and spirited replies had given, not only to her-self, but all the family, for their wilful neglect of so

U   promising

promifing a branch of it, fhe made inquiries concerning the fituation of his mother, ordered her carriage,
took the child home, and from that moment adopted
him as her own fon.   At that period fhe was verging
upon forty, was ftill unmarried, and remained fo at
the time Hamden, returned from a tour he had been
making on the continent, was introduced to our heroine.

Lady Anne had fpared no coft in completing his
education.   She never forgot the premife he had innocently extorted from her at the moment fhe firft
converfed with him, and before he was fixteen purchafed for him an enfigncy in a regiment upon the
home eftablifhment.   He was now only twenty-two,
but what cannot intereft and money procure ?   Hamden Auberry, without once having been in actual fervice, was advanced to the rank of Major.

When lady Anne thus lavifhly poured upon her
nephew every advantage which wealth could beftow,
fhe in her mind purpofed making him her heir ; indeed, fhe looked upon him as the heir of the family.
Her eldeft brother's children were all puny beings,
and her fecond brother had never married.   She
therefore looked forward with the hope of one day
feeing Hamden one of the firft men in the kingdom.
One of the preliminaries fhe had fettled for his ad-
vancement was a marriage with fome woman of fplendid rank and fortune.   Perhaps lady Anne was not
quite fo anxious about beauty, grace, good fenfe, and
good humour, as Hamden himfelf thought was abfolutely neceffary ; for fhe had pointed out three feveral
women of quality, who, fhe affured him, would be
happy to receive his devoirs, and whofe alliance would
do him infinite honour.   But unfortunately one was
upwards of forty years old, another had a hump on
her back, coarfe, unmeaning features, and a difpofition that was the very counterpart of her form ; and
the third, though formed by the tendereft care of
young love, yet fo vacant, fo totally devoid of mental endowments,

And when the beauteous idiot fpoke,
Forth from her coral lips fuch nonfenfe broke,

That Hamden, though an enthufiaft in his admiration of female beauty, could fcarcely command patience fufficient to liften with an appearance of common civility.

His heart had remained untouched, and it was for
our heroine alone to call its tender fentiments into action. The artlefs, unaffected manner of Rachel, afforded him the moft delicate pleafure, whilft beholding and converfing with her; for it was fo apparent
in every word, look, fmile of her's, that fhe was unconfcious of her own charms, that thofe charms became the more ftriking, the more fafcinating. About
half paft ten, he waited on Rachel to the door of her
uncle's manfion, and then returned to tell his mother
fhe was the only woman he had ever feen, who in the
leaft appeared to him in every particular what a woman ought to be.

Hezekiah had been married very early in life, but
his wife lived only a few years; and from the time
of her deceafe, his houfehold concerns had been fuper-
intended by a diftant relation of his mother's, whofe
tall, thin figure, and auftere vifage, attired in the clofe
mob black hood, and other plain habiliments ufually
worn by the fect, looked, as much as it is poffible to
conceive any thing to look, like formality perfonified.
Nor was her drefs and perfon more ftiff and forbidding than was her manners. Ignorant in the higheft
degree, fhe valued herfelf on that ignorance; fhe underftood nothing of polite literature; and whenever
fhe faw our heroine engaged in any book, whether of
inftruction or amufement it mattered not, by her they
were all termed vanity and vexation of fpirit. The
productions of the beft poets were called blafphemy.
Hiftory was of no ufe; for of what confequence was
it to her what was done in the world before fhe was
born? And works of fancy, however excellent in
their kind, were all a pack of nonfenfe, and ferved only to fill young people's heads with proclamations.
To

To be seen with a book on any day except Sunday, was highly againſt her creed. For in her opinion needle-work, ſpinning, and attending to the culinary concerns of the family, were ſufficient to occupy every hour of the day. Her pickles and preſerves were excellent in their kind, and for good ſubſtantial roaſt and boiled diſhes, with ſolid plumb-puddings, and large family mince-pies, Tabitha would not give place to any woman in England. Hezekiah thought, with all her oddities, ſhe had his intereſt ſincerely at heart, and therefore continued paſſive, and ſuffered Tabitha to rule the family as ſhe pleaſed. But the maidens of the houſehold unanimouſly declared, that ſhe ruled with a rod of iron.

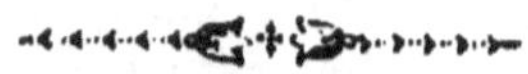

CHAP. VII.

Journey to London.

WHEN Hamden Auberry had ſeen Rachel to her uncle's door and rapped at it, politeneſs obliged him to wait till it was opened, which it was by Tabitha herſelf. She glanced her eye at the ſcarlet coat and the lace which decorated it, nor did ſhe entirely overlook the handſome form and face of him who wore it. But when, without noticing Tabitha, Hamden bowed to our heroine, and kiſſing her hand with an air of gallantry, wiſhed her a good night, ſhe became troubled in ſpirit that Rachel ſhould have ſubmitted to ſuch an abomination quietly.

With upright head, her long, ſcraggy neck ſtretching to its utmoſt extent, from a conſciouſneſs of her own purity, in ſilent ſolemnity Tabitha ſtalked into the parlour, where ſat Hezekiah almoſt dozing in his eaſy chair. She depoſited the candle on the table, and ſeated herſelf on his right hand. Rachel ſat down on the other ſide, and affectionately bending over the chair, aſked her uncle how he was.

" Why

"Why tired almoſt to death, thou mayeſt be ſure," ſaid Tabitha, not giving Hezekiah time to reply.

"Then it was a pity my uncle did not go to bed," ſaid Rachel innocently.

"Thou art both an unthinking and an unfeeling girl, Rachel Dudley, elſe wouldeſt thou know that anxiety for thy ſafety kept him up. But he has had ſo many of thoſe uneaſy hours ſince thou haſt been in his dwelling, that I can foreſee it will hurry him to his grave. Oh! Rachel! Rachel! thou art turned to vanity, to folly, to abomination. Thou art wilfully running into the ſnares of the wicked one. Thou doſt love to conſort with the children of diſobedience; thou delighteſt to behold their veſtments, ſhining with gold, and red in the blood of Jezebel."

"Bleſs me," ſaid Rachel, "what can you mean? Uncle, pray ſpeak to me. I hope I have not given you any cauſe for uneaſineſs. I ſent word that I ſhould ſup at Dr. Lenient's; had you ſent by the boy for me to come home, I ſhould have returned inſtantly."

Hezekiah had taken her hand, which in her earneſtneſs ſhe had laid on his knee, gave it a gentle preſſure, and was beginning to ſpeak; but Tabitha interrupted him, and he knew it would be in vain to attempt being heard, when ſhe was inclined to talk. So he relinquiſhed his intention, leaned back in his chair, ſhut his eyes, and inwardly wiſhed he could ſhut his ears alſo.

"Thou didſt ſend word, it is true," ſaid the perſecuting Tabitha, "but thou didſt not ſend word that a ſtranger would walk with thee; that thou wouldeſt lean on his arm, and ſuffer him to kiſs thy hand, in a manner not becoming a maiden who wiſheth to preſerve her reputation. And this ſtranger was clothed in ſcarlet and gold, and eats the bread that is purchaſed by murdering his fellow-creatures. Verily, I ſay, my ſpirit waxeth wroth when I think the daughter of Caſſiah Penn turneth from the worſhip of her father's houſe, and runneth after ſtrange gods, and delighteth to dwell in the tents of idolaters."

U 2

"I beg

"I beg your pardon," said Rachel tartly; "my father defpifed both formality and hypocrify."

"Oh thou offspring of a generation of vipers," cried Tabitha, "doft thou call our pure and undefiled faith hypocrify?"

"No! Heaven forbid I fhould," replied our heroine mildly; "it is only the uncharitable and infenfate wretch, who, having neither heart to conceive, nor underftanding to enjoy, the innocent pleafures with which a bountiful Creator has enriched the world, proudly arrogate to themfelves the right to judge and contemn their fellow-creatures; and furely it is the height of hypocrify to pretend to deferve the divine appellation of Chriftian, and yet harbour in the bofom envy, hatred and malice."

"Rachel! Rachel! child of folly, daughter of difobedience," exclaimed Tabitha vociferoufly, her meagre features flaming with rage, as though the fire within fhone through her fkinny cheeks and hollow eyes; "child of darknefs, hear me; thou art going blindfold into the pit; thou art walking barefoot over burning ploughfhares; but the foles of thy feet, like thine eternal foul, is callous and infenfible to the danger that furrounds thee. Had thy mother lived unto this day——"

"Oh! would to Heaven fhe had!" cried Rachel, her fpirits no longer able to fupport her againft the abfurd accufations of Tabitha. "Oh that fhe were alive at this moment; fhe would not fuffer her innocent child to be thus grofsly infulted."

Here fhe gave way to an involuntary gufh of tears; but fupprefling them as quick as fhe could, fhe kiffed her uncle with affection, "Good-night! God blefs you, my dear Sir," faid fhe; "the unhappy Rachel will not long be a trouble to you."

"God blefs you, my love," faid Hezekiah, "and grant us both patience according to the burthens it may pleafe him to lay upon us."

"Amen," faid Rachel fervently, darting an indignant look at Tabitha; then rifing and taking the candle from the table, fhe went towards the door; but
the

the natural philanthropy of her mind would not suffer her to part in enmity with any one.. She turned towards Tabitha. "Good-night," said she in a softened accent, "and Heaven forgive us both as we forgive each other." Tabitha was sullenly silent, and Rachel retired to her solitary apartment, wept a few moments, knelt, and commended herself to the protection of Heaven ; was composed and comforted by the action, retired to bed, and sunk into the arms of repose..

Sweet, heavenly sweet, are the slumbers of the innocent. Rachel's heart was uncontaminated ; envy, hatred, jealousy, were equal strangers to it.. Her sleep was undisturbed and refreshing ; her dreams the visitation of ministering angels..

When Rachel left the parlour, Tabitha began speaking to Hezekiah, but he arose from his seat. "My head aches," said he, "I can sit up no longer." Then taking his own candle, which stood ready on the table, he bade Tabby good-night and retired to his apartment..

"I will alter my will to-morrow," said Hezekiah, as he laid his head on the pillow; (for, some years previous to the death of Mr. Dudley, this will had been made highly in Tabitha's favour) "I will alter my will," said he, "it will not be right to leave my fair and good kinswoman Rachel, dependent on a person whose understanding is weak, and whose heart is contracted."

In the morning he arose with the same determination, and dispatched a person for the most eminent attorney of the neighbouring market town. He walked himself to Dr. Lenient's, wishing to consult with him, and to have him a witness to his new will. But unfortunately the attorney was gone to London on particular business, and Dr. Lenient had been called to Liverpool to visit a patient, who, having found benefit from his prescriptions whilst on a visit in the country, wished to have those prescriptions continued.

At dinner, Hezekiah ate less than usual, complained of an acute pain across his temples, and a coldness down the spine of his back.

"Why

"Why doſt thou not partake of that boiled foal?" said Tabitha; "the ſhrimp ſauce is good, I can aſſure thee, for I made it myſelf."

"I have no appetite for fiſh," he replied, puſhing the plate gently from him.

"Let me change your plate, dear uncle," ſaid Rachel, removing the one before him and ſetting one in its place on which ſhe had previouſly laid the wing of a chicken.

Hezekiah drew the plate towards him, cut a mouthful and raiſed it to his lips. But the effort was vain; his countenance changed; he ſunk back. It was a kind of paralytic affection. He ſtruggled to ſpeak, but could not articulate. By the order of Tabitha, he was put into a warm bed, and Dr. Lenient being juſt returned, attended on the firſt ſummons. He ordered the uſual applications, and waited to obſerve their effects. All the night he continued ſpeechleſs; but towards morning, by a violent exertion, he ſpoke, ſo as to be underſtood. Deſiring to be raiſed in the bed, he in faltering accents thus began:

"I called on you, my good friend, this morning, to aſk your advice and opinion."

"I wiſh I had been at home," ſaid the Doctor, "we might perhaps have prevented this ſevere attack."

"That is not my meaning," ſaid Hezekiah. "My time is come, and, ſkilful as you are, my good Doctor, I do not think you can ward off the ſtroke of death."

"I do not think I could," ſaid the Doctor gravely.

"Tabitha," ſaid the ſick man, reaching out his hand towards her, "I am much indebted to you for the unwearied attention you have for many years ſhewn me, and the care you have taken of my temporal intereſt. It has grieved me to ſee the little diſſentions which have of late taken place between you and my niece Rachel, who, though younger, livelier, more free from prejudice than yourſelf, is neverthelefs one of the beſt and moſt unoffending creatures in the world. Let me ſee you friends," continued he, taking Rachel's hand and joining it with Tabitha's.

Rachel

Rachel could not speak, Tabitha would not, and Hezekiah continued:

"You will find on the opening of my will, Dr. Lenient, that I have not forgot the services I have received from my ancient kinswoman; but I am sorry—I meant to alter—I wish her to give—" His voice again faultered—"to give her—" said he with extreme difficulty.

"Fifty or sixty guineas," cried Tabitha, interrupting him.

"No," exclaimed the dying man; then struggling violently, he at length articulated, "Give her half." They were his last words.   In a few moments he sunk again into insensibility, and before evening expired.

Now the good-hearted Doctor fully comprehended what Hezekiah meant when he said, "Give her half." But Tabitha wilfully misconstrued the expression; and when the will was read, which gave the house, land, cattle, plate, furniture, &c. to Tabitha Holdfast, in consideration of her more than sisterly kindness," Dr. Lenient intimating, that he expected she would make a fair and equitable division of the whole with Rachel, in compliance with what he understood to be the intention of the testator from his last words, she calmly replied:

"Friend Lenient, I am not accountable for what thou mayest have understood.   I am certain our dear departed brother Hezekiah—"   And here the handkerchief visited her eyes; but it returned

> Dry as the chaff, which, flitting in the wind,
> Too light to be deprefs'd by trifling showers,
> Defies the blast, and flutters o'er the heath;
> Or, like the downy plumage of the swan,
> White and unsullied.————

"I am certain," she continued, "he meant not the participation thou wouldest insinuate; for when (ever eager to interpret and prevent his wishes) I mentioned giving her fifty or sixty guineas, he said, "Give her half;" and by his dying words I shall most surely abide."

"He

"He meant to say," cried the Doctor vehemently, "that you should give her half of all he died possessed of."

"It may be to thy advantage, friend, (said she sneeringly) to have his last will so understood. The singular attentions of one of thy relatives to Rachel has not passed unnoticed; and I think thy family is remarkable for promoting its own interest at the expense of others."

It was a reproach too pointed to be misunderstood; but it sprung from a mind so debased, that it was beneath notice. The Doctor took his hat, and wished Tabitha a good night. Rachel arose to light him to the door.

"My good, dear girl," said he, "I would fain have procured from this woman a small independence for you; but it is in vain to flatter you with the idea. But this give me leave to say, Should you not hear from your brother, and your residence with dame Tabitha becomes painful, I have a home. My sister and myself both possess hearts, which I thank God are not yet quite petrified." Saying which, he shook her hand and left her.

Rachel soon perceived the full extent of her unhappy situation. The morning after the interment of her uncle, Tabitha paid her thirty guineas, and from that moment she found that she was looked upon as an intruder in the family.

Rachel was not of a spirit to brook the cold hauteur of Tabitha. Nor could she think of availing herself of the kind offer of Dr. Lenient. For, besides that she shrunk from the weight of obligation, she also felt there would be an impropriety in her seeking an asylum in the family of Hamden Auberry. She was not insensible to his merit, nor had she listened unmoved to the expressions of attachment that had sometimes accidentally escaped his lips. For Hamden knew he should have many obstacles to encounter, should he give way to a passion for a woman in the state of life in which fortune had placed Rachel. Lady Anne would never be be brought to approve of his allying himself to a perfon, who had neither rank or wealth to recommend her.

Rachel faw the ftruggle of his mind, and, attributing that to pride which was only the effect of caution, refolved never to intrude herfelf into a family which would look upon her connexion as degrading to its principal branch.

Having therefore formed a plan for her future conduct, Rachel took an affectionate leave of the worthy Doctor and his fifter, and a very cool one of Tabitha, and departed in the ftage-coach for London, refolving to confult and advife with her friend Jeffy Oliver, in regard to her executing the fcheme fhe had thought of for her fubfiftence till fhe fhould hear from Reuben.

Mrs. Auberry gave her a letter to a reputable family, with whom fhe propofed to board. Hamden was abfent at the time of Rachel's departure on a fifhing party, and on his return, his mother merely informed him that Mifs Dudley was gone to London; but wifhing to put a ftop to any further intimacy between them, fhe did not mention with whom fhe would refide, or how long her ftay might probably be in the metropolis; and as he was engaged to pafs the autumn with lady Anne in Scotland, he was not fo inquifitive as he might otherwife have been.

Rachel got fafe to the end of her journey without meeting with any adventure on the road. But unaccuftomed to travelling, fhe was greatly fatigued; and when fhe entered the bufy ftreets of London, the noife, confufion and hurry made her head giddy; the difagreeable effluvia too, which affailed her olfactory nerves as fhe alighted from the coach in a very clofe lane in the city, turned her extremely fick, and fhe would have fallen, had not a fpruce young man, who was waiting for another coach to arrive, caught her by the arm, and led her into the houfe, where a few drops and water revived her, and fhe began to inquire for a conveyance in which fhe might proceed to her lodgings. A hackney-coach was fent for, and while fhe waited for it, the young man re-entered the parlour where fhe

was

was sitting, introducing a middle-aged woman, dressed to the extremity of the fashion.

"Walk in and sit down, Miss La Varone," said he,
"I will order the negus immediately." Then turning to our heroine, he continued, "And how do you
find yourself now, ma'am?"

"Much better, Sir, I thank you," said Rachel.

"Have you been sick, ma'am?" said Miss La
Varone.

"I am not used to travelling, and was rather faint
when I first alighted; but it was only fatigue, and the
air of London is not quite so pure as that I have been
accustomed to from my infancy."

"Oh dear me! I don't wonder, ma'am, if you never were in London before, that it made you sick.
Then this lane is so close; and I protest it made me
as sick as could be. But pray, ma'am, to what part
of the town are you going? Perhaps one coach will
serve us both."

Rachel looked at the direction in her memorandum
book, and Miss La Varone exclaimed, "Well, as I'm
alive, we are both going to the same place. Mr.
Spriggins, this young lady is going to your aunt's."

Rachel knew but little of the world in general, and
less of London than almost any other place; yet there
was a something within her, a kind of native rectitude,
that told her not to be too easy in agreeing to the proposal of the strangers who said they would all go to Mrs.
Webster's together. Yet her politeness and good-nature was such, as would not suffer her to repulse them
rudely. Besides, there was something in the appearance of La Varone, however familiar her address had
been, that prepossessed her in her favour. She was a
small, delicate woman; her pale countenance, the
features of which were extremely regular, was ornamented by an animated pair of black eyes, and long,
dark eye-lashes. Her dress, it is true, was in Rachel's
opinion rather too gay; but she was totally unacquainted with the style of dress that might be fashiona-
ble in London, and therefore passed this circumstance
the more easily over.

Finding

Finding it impossible to separate herself from her new acquaintances, she contented herself with giving the hackney-coachman particular instructions where to carry her, and in less than half an hour found herself at Mrs. Webster's, in Dartmouth-street, Westminster. Mr. Spriggins, (who was shopman to a silk mercer in the vicinity of St. James's Park) boarded with his aunt, and Miss La Varone occupied the second floor of the house.

Rachel begged an early cup of tea, and then retired to the apartment prepared for her; where wearied nature was refreshed by several hours of profound sleep. But the fatigue which had accelerated her repose, gradually giving way to its effects, her slumbers became lighter, and about three o'clock, she became sensible of the (to her) unusual noises that surrounded her. The hollow voices of the watchmen, the rattling of coaches and carts, the riotous mirth of intemperate wretches of both sexes, who, under the black veil of night, prowled through the streets in search of prey; all together struck on the astonished ears of our heroine, who, not immediately recollecting where she was, sprang out of bed, exclaiming, " Heavens! what is the matter?" However, as Rachel was not troubled with weak nerves, and had in general great presence of mind, she presently grew collected, remembered she was in London, returned to her bed, and endeavoured to obtain another visit from the leaden-winged god. He listened, and was propitious to her entreaties, and at eight o'clock the following morning she continued still locked in his embraces.

C H A P.   VIII.

Visits—Curiosities.

THE scene of life into which Rachel had now entered was every way new to her. Her intentions in avoiding the family of Dr. Lenient on account

W   of

of young Auberry were laudable ; but her open and
ingenuous nature, fearlefs of guile, becaufe intending
none, was not competent to the tafk fhe had undertaken. Humane, generous, and credulous in the extreme, fhe felt that every human being had a claim
upon her affection ; and willingly allowing that claim
to others, fhe readily believed every profeffion of friendfhip made to herfelf.

. Mrs. Webfter was a woman of moderate underftanding, devoid of knowledge, and with a very
fmall fhare of curiofity, and being a widow with
three girls, the eldeft of which was but fixteen, fhe
had to work extremely . hard at her bufinefs, which
was that of a hoop-petticoat maker, to fupport her
family. From fuch a woman, Rachel had nothing
either to hope or apprehend. She enjoyed from the
effects of her care a very neat apartment, and regular
decent meals ; but as to any idea of a companion, it
was entirely out of the queftion. The daughters were
young, and their minds totally uninformed ; they
were of confequence unfit fociety for her. To whom
therefore could fhe look to enliven her folitude by
cheerful converfation ? Mifs La Varone had read a
great deal, though not in moft inftructive authors.
She had a confiderable degree of fuperficial knowledge, was chatty, good-humoured, and ftudious to render herfelf agreeable. She became the conftant companion of Rachel, and was unfortunately the moft improper companion fhe could have chofen.

Mifs La Varone was the daughter of a Swifs valet,
who, having faved a confiderable fum of money in the
fervice of a nobleman, and received a legacy at his
death, married the lady's maid, and opened a perfumery and toy-fhop, in which he fucceeded extremely
well ; efpecially when his daughter grew old enough
to attend the cuftomers, her pretty face and lively
manner acting as a talifman to draw young men of
fafhion thither.

But human happinefs is futile ! A fire broke out
in the neighbourhood, and their houfe was confumed
amongft a number of others, and as their property
was

was not infured, a few hours reduced them from a flate of competence to abfolute beggary. The old man received a hurt, in endeavouring to fave part of his ftock, which he did not long furvive. The mother again went to fervice, and procured employment for her daughter in the fame family. The eldeft fon of this family was pleafed with her; offered her a fettlement; and at the age of eighteen, La Varone quitted the protection of her mother, to accept that of a libertine. Her mother had perhaps a higher fenfe of virtue than perfons in her fituation are in general fuppofed to poffefs. She remonftrated, entreated, endeavoured by every poffible means to reclaim her; but finding all equally ineffectual, renounced her. And though fhe had, without murmuring, returned to her original way of life, and fubmitted patiently to the privation of thofe comforts fhe had many years enjoyed, and which had been the fruits of her own induftry, yet fhe could not meet fhame without repining. Her child's difhonour funk deep into her heart, and in a very fhort time put a period to her exiftence.

La Varone continued with her admirer till he married; fhe then removed from all her former connexions, into the houfe where our heroine was now become an inmate. She had been an eafy conqueft; her fettlement was confequently not large. However, fhe kept up a genteel appearance, and frequently received vifits from an elderly gentleman, a coufin, who was a member of parliament. She faw but little company befides; but fhe would expatiate for an hour on the charms of retirement; fo her living fo reclufe was not furprifing. Her favourite amufement was a play, and fometimes little excurfions in the country, where fhe would ftay four or five days at a time.

The day after Rachel's arrival in London was devoted to reft. Mifs La Varone was extremely attentive, invited her to take tea in her apartment, where Mr. Spriggins alfo attended, and the elder Mifs Webfter. Here they talked of the many curiofities to be feen in London. Weftminfter Abbey, St. Paul's Cathedral, the Monument, the Tower, the Palace; all

which

which Miss La Varone said they must positively visit, and the gentleman offered very politely to be their gallant.

Rachel was not devoid of curiosity. She had come up to the metropolis with the best resolutions in the world, and Mrs. Auberry, when she recommended her to Mrs. Webster's to board, thought she had rendered her young friend a very acceptable piece of service. But she never reflected, that twenty-five years make a most amazing difference in the manners and disposition of a person, especially if in that period they have suffered much affliction, and from narrow circumstances being unavoidably thrown into the society of people, whose educations having been circumscribed, are often the slaves of contracted, low ideas and illiberal prejudices; and it frequently happens, that those who are obliged to work incessantly for the support of their families, being wholly occupied in the hope of bettering their fortune, become inattentive to appearances, and overlook actions, which earlier in life would have struck them with horror. This was literally the case with Mrs. Webster. The Mrs. Webster whom Mrs. Auberry knew so many years since, and she to whose care she now recommended her young friend, were as opposite in person, manner, and way of thinking, as if it had not been the same, but two distinct people.

The second morning, Rachel took a hackney-coach, and drove to the house of Mr. Oliver, in the vicinity of St. James's. She was still in mourning; a grey tabby night-gown, with black cuffs and robins, a plain lawn cap, apron, handkerchief, and ruffles, was the dress in which she prepared to visit her friend Jessy. But a woman thus habited and in a hackney-coach was not likely to challenge much attention from the gay lackeys who waited in the hall of Mr. Oliver.

" Is Miss Oliver at home, friend?" said she to the footman who came to the door. A surly *No!* was all the answer she received, and the man was again shutting the door.

" Is

" Is she expected home soon ?" said she, putting her hand out to prevent it from closing.

" I know nothing about it," said the fellow.

Rachel had defcended from the carriage before the coachman had knocked for admittance, and was ftanding on the upper ftep of a flight of ftone ftairs which led up on each fide from the ftreet. Her figure had attracted the eyes of Archibald, who was at home at this time, and feated in a front parlour window, killing time with a political pamphlet. Hearing her voice at the door, and underftanding from the tone of the fervant's voice that he was not anfwering in a very civil manner, he opened the parlour door juft as she was turning to defcend the fteps.

" You were inquiring for Mifs Oliver, madam," faid he ; " she is at prefent out of town, but I expect to fee her to-morrow. Who shall I tell her did her the honour to call ?"

" My name is Dudley," faid Rachel.

" Dudley ! is it poffible ; the fifter of my friend Reuben ?"

" The fame !"

" How happy I am, Mifs Dudley !' Give me leave to wait on you to your place of refidence. I wish to afk after your brother ; I have alfo fome interefting intelligence to communicate to you concerning my fifter." He faid this as he handed her to the coach. Then calling for his hat, before Rachel could collect herfelf fufficiently to refufe or accept his propofal, he was feated in the carriage befide her, and inquired where he fhould order it to be driven.

" Perhaps, my dear Mifs," faid young Oliver as the coach drove off, " you may think it particular that I did not prefs you to enter my father's houfe. But to confefs a mortifying truth, neither Jeffy nor myfelf are allowed to take any more liberties there than we fhould be in the houfe of an entire ftranger. My poor father is ruled entirely by Mrs. Oliver, and his children have but a fecondary place in his affections."

" Pray make no apologies, Mr. Oliver," faid Rachel, having a little recovered from the flutter into

        which

which his apparently odd conduct had thrown her; "apologies are quite needlefs. I had no wifh to enter the houfe except my dear Jeffy had been an inmate of it. But you faid you had fome interefting intelligence."

"True, but before I enter on it, tell me, when did you hear from your brother?"

"I have not received the leaft intelligence from him fince he left England; and fometimes I fear——" Rachel's eyes filled; her bofom heaved.

"Oh do not fear," faid Oliver, refpectfully taking her hand: "Letters may mifcarry; you will no doubt hear foon. But apropos of Jeffy; has fhe not written to you lately? I underftood you correfponded."

"We did; but I have not received a letter from her for nearly two months paft."

"Poor Jeffy, fhe had nothing pleafant to employ her pen, and fhe always had an averfion to endeavouring to lighten her own forrows by impofing a recital of them on the attention of others."

He then proceeded to inform her, that his fifter had unfortunately (as it proved) been fingled out by a nobleman of elevated rank and fplendid fortune, as the perfon with whom he wifhed to fhare thofe advantages. He folicited her hand, was encouraged by both Mr. and Mrs. Oliver, but refolutely rejected by Jeffy herfelf.

"My father," continued he, "who (as I mentioned before) has no will but his wife's, has fent the poor girl into the country, debarring her of all fociety, and declaring fhe fhall ftay there till fhe accepts his Lordfhip; and I, who know her difpofition, think that fentence is tantamount to faying fhe fhall ftay there as long as fhe lives."

"She is right to perfevere in rejecting him," faid Rachel, "if fhe does not feel her heart fufficiently attached to him to incline her to fhare his pains and pleafures through life. For of all the miferies that can be endured by a human being, fure none can be fo fevere as being obliged to fubmit to the whims and caprices
prices

prices (for we all have them) of a perfon to whom we are perfectly indifferent."

Oliver gazed at her, as fhe thus, with unaffected freedom, delivered her fentiments on a fubject, which the generality of thofe young women with whom he was acquainted would have blufhed only to have heard mentioned. But Rachel was entirely free from affectation of every kind; fhe had no idea, but that a woman might fpeak on the fubjects of love and marriage, without fimpering, blufhing, and fifty other little foolifh prettineffes. Nor did fhe feel the leaft embarraffed in converfing with a perfon of the oppofite fex; for it had never entered her head, that every man who faw her muft fall in love with her, or that they could not pafs an hour in her company without entertaining her with praifes of her wit and beauty, and complaints of their own hopelefs paffion.

When the coach therefore ftopped, and Rachel afked him to walk in, he eagerly availed himfelf of the invitation; and after fitting with her till fhe was fummoned to dinner, left her, impreffed with fo high an opinion of her underftanding, that he thought her the moft fuperior woman he had ever known. She had promifed to entruft him with a letter to her friend Jeffy, and he was determined to call for it himfelf, that he might enjoy another half hour of her fociety. But in this he was difappointed; for immediately after dinner, Rachel wrote her letter, and leaving it with Mrs. Webfter in cafe it fhould be fent for before her return, fhe took one of the little girls with her, and walked to the houfe of Mr. Andrew Atkins, in Lincoln's-Inn, hoping to hear fome tidings of Reuben, and alfo to inquire how long it would be before fhe might expect to receive any money on account of the eftate in Lancafhire.

Being fhewn into a parlour, and having fent up her name, fhe was defired to wait till Mr. Atkins had dined, when he would wait on her immediately. In about an hour, he appeared, accompanied by the identical

Mr.

Mr. Allibi who had visited herself and brother in the country.

Rachel rose from her seat.

" Servant, Mifs," said Mr. Atkins, flightly bowing, and without afking her to resume her seat. " Pray what may be your commands with me?"

" I wifh to know whether you have had any intelligence from my brother since his departure from England."

" Intelligence? No indeed! I wonder you fhould think of my hearing from him; his going to America was a wild-goose scheme. What does he expect to get there?"

" He expects to take poffeffion of his father's eftate, which he purchased in Pennfylvania."

" Pfhaw! pfhaw! Dudley made no purchase there worth inquiring after. An uncultivated tract of land, with a paltry house upon it, which my very good friend and correspondent, Mr. Jacob Holmes, has informed me is entirely fallen down."

" Jacob Holmes, did you fay?" cried Rachel in breathless agitation. " Why that is the very man my father mentions in his letter to have left in charge of his eftate. He was brought up in my father's house. Can he advance such an untruth, when he muft be confcious—— ?"

" Come, come, Mifs Dudley, don't fpeak againft Mr. Holmes ; he is a very worthy, honeft man.. Your father lived in a very expenfive ftyle in Philadelphia, fpent a great deal of money, more a great deal than he ought. Even the trifling purchase he did make of land was not half paid for."

" Sir! Sir!" cried Rachel, waving her hand with dignity, " I muft not hear the memory of my father treated with disrefpect. You may have been taught to believe what you now affert ; or, perhaps, (darting an indignant look at him) your profeffion accuftoms you confidently to affert what you do not believe to be true. Be that as it may, I fee my brother and myfelf are two unprotected orphans." Here her cheeks affumed a pallid hue, her lips trembled, and fhe was un-

able

able to proceed; and though the unfeeling Atkins had kept her standing while he spoke to her, her agitation was now so great, that she was obliged to sit down, or she would have fallen.

"As I would wish to save you the unnecessary trouble of calling on me again, I have brought Mr. Allibi, who fortunately was dining with me, to give you any information you may require concerning the Lancashire business."

"I am sorry, my fair lady," said Allibi, "that it is not in my power to give you such information as you may perhaps expect; but so many unexpected demands have been made, that I hardly think the estate will ever be able to recover itself. I have here (drawing a memorandum book from his pocket) some few memorandums of the state of the affairs at present. Whenever you shall require it, Miss Dudley, I will lay a regular statement of the accounts before you, and submit the whole of our proceedings to your investigation."

Rachel felt that this seeming integrity was an insult to her understanding. Assuming, therefore, an appearance of fortitude that she was far from feeling, she exerted herself to rise from her seat.

"Good Mr. Allibi," said she, conveying as much acrimony into her looks and manner, as it was possible for her voice and features to express, "of what service will it be for me to examine or investigate those accounts? Did you, or your respectable client, Mr. Andrew Atkins, imagine me competent to the task, you would never have so readily offered it. But I am a woman—an orphan; young, inexperienced, unprotected; and even supposing I could discover errors, who is there to support my assertions? I am poor, and I can plainly perceive, you have inclination as well as reasons for keeping me so. Oh that my injured brother were but here!"

"You speak pointedly, Miss Dudley," said Atkins.

"I speak as I feel," replied Rachel.

"But you are too warm, my fair lady," said Allibi. "Pardon

"Pardon me," cried Rachel, "I do not think I am warm enough. Oh! that I could find words adequate to the indignation of my soul! Do not misunderstand me; for myself I am but little concerned. I have an innocent mind that can be humble when required, and hands that are not useless. But my brother is in a strange land; for him I feel a thousand fears. My father's memory has been traduced; on that subject, my feelings are too powerful for utterance. If my rash judgment wrongs you, gentlemen, Heaven pardon the error. For I leave you in the full persuasion, that on whichever side the wrong is, the great Redresser of injuries, the righteous Father of the oppressed, will impartially judge between us. By his sentence we must abide, and to him in humble confidence I submit my cause."

As she finished speaking, she hurried out of the house, to prevent their being witness to emotions which she was unable longer to suppress; and she found herself in the square opposite Newcastle-house, before she was sufficiently collected to remember to what part of the town she was going. Polly Webster, who had shewn her the way to Atkins's, had left her at the door, as she had some errands to execute for her mother in the Strand. Our heroine had imagined she should easily find her way home again; but when she found herself in a place with which she was wholly unacquainted, and endeavoured in vain to recover recollection sufficient to guide her to the right road, she began to be uneasy. She wished for a coach, but there was not one came near her but what was previously occupied. She walked straight forward through a narrow passage, which she imagined she had passed through before; it took her into High-Holborn. The throng of people, the multitude of carriages, and appearance of the shops, led her to think she was in the Strand; and turning to the right hand, she pursued her way, expecting every moment to reach Charing-Cross. But as she proceeded, she began to perceive the difference of the surrounding objects, and became seriously alarmed. A heavy shower appeared threatening in the air,

and

and even at Holborn-Bars, Rachel could not procure
a coach. The lightning had for fome time gleamed
in the horizon; the thunder which had rolled diftant-
ly now came nearer, and an univerfal war of elements
feemed approaching. Rachel looked round with increafing apprehenfion. The tempeft now burft forth
at once; wind, thunder, hail, and fheets of liquid fire,
rendered the fcene tremendous. To avoid the fury of
the ftorm, Rachel ran up an entry which led to a large
old-fafhioned manfion, and though not eafily terrified,
the late incidents had fo oppreffed her fpirits, that fhe
fat down on the fteps, and burft into an hyfterical flood
of tears.

"What is the matter, woman?" faid a man who
was coming from the houfe.

The brutal tone of this addrefs, the ferocious appearance of the fellow that uttered it, was an additional
caufe of terror. She rofe, endeavoured to fpeak, but
could not; and when fhe attempted to walk, her limbs
failed her, and fhe funk again upon the ftep.

"Why, miftrefs, you have taken a little too much
cordial to-day," faid the fame man; "but come, I'll
lead you down the paffage, and then you muft go on
as well as you can; for you can't ftay here."

Rachel, though overcome with terror, was perfectly
fenfible. She heard the remark made on her apparent
helpleffnefs, endeavoured to repel the violence of her
emotions, and exert that fortitude of which fhe was
poffeffed.

"I merely came here for fhelter from the ftorm,"
faid fhe; "and if I could procure a coach——"

"Well, miftrefs," faid a dirty, ragged boy, "if you
will give me a fhilling, I will call you one."

Rachel readily agreed to the propofal, and was putting her hand to her pocket, when there was a cry in
the crowd that was now gathered, that a pick-pocket
was amongft them. A young naval officer faid he
had loft his watch and purfe. 'Keep all in, keep all
in,' was the cry, and the throng rufhed up the paffage,
fo that Rachel found herfelf in an inftant furrounded by
a motley group of people, the chief part of which but

to have been obliged to speak to, would have filled her at once with terror and disgust. But what were her sensations, when, putting her hand again to her pocket, she found a strange purse hanging partly out, and felt a watch actually within it. Before she could speak, a woman seized her arm, and holding her hand so that she could not withdraw it, she cried that she had found the thief. Rachel's strength and spirits now at once forsook her ; she fetched a deep sigh, and fell senseless into the arms of the person who had been robbed.

"The poor creature is ill," said he ; "stand away, ruffians, and let her have air." Then carrying her to the entrance of the passage, he pushed back her hat, and untied her cloak. Her extreme youth, her beauty, the neatness of her apparel, all conspired to prepossess him in her favour.

"Had you not better send for a constable ?" said the wretch who had pretended to detect her.

"No," said the officer ; "I do not think she can be guilty ; or if she is, extreme necessity alone could have driven her to such an expedient. How are you, ma'am ?" seeing Rachel begin to revive.

She looked wildly round her, put her hand to her head as though endeavouring to recollect why or how she came there. At length the circumstances recurring to her memory, she looked stedfastly on the officer, and then on her accuser.

"You have been robbed, Sir," said she, "and your property found in my possession. How it came there, Heaven knows ; but as I stand in the sight of Him who rules the heavens, I do protest I am innocent."

The solemnity of the appeal, the conscious innocence of her heart, which beamed from her eyes and informed every feature of her face, rendered the truth of her assertion indisputable.

"I do believe you," said the officer ; "but even had I thought you guilty, what is the insignificant value of these trifles, when put in competition with the life of a fellow-creature, whom distress urges to actions from which the soul recoils."

The

The ſtorm was by this time much abated, and Rachel having ſent again to procure a coach, the officer ſaid he would not leave her till he delivered her in ſafety to her friends.   He was ſtanding at the entrance of the paſſage, holding the hand of our heroine, when a poſt chariot, that was driving haſtily through Holborn, being for a moment impeded by a number of carts and carriages, ſtopped directly oppoſite where they ſtood.   The glaſs was let down, and Rachel ſaw diſtinctly Hamden Auberry, ſeated beſide an elderly lady.   She alſo was certain, that he both ſaw and recognized her.   The blood for a moment forſook her cheeks, and then returned with impetuoſity, dying them of the deepeſt crimſon.   Scarcely was there time to exchange the glance of recognition, before the chariot moved forward again, and a hackney-coach drawing up to the door, ſhe ſtepped into it, and, accompanied by her protector, drove towards Dartmouth-ſtreet.

On their arrival at Mrs. Webſters, Rachel found the family in great conſternation at her long abſence (for Polly having returned without her, had been diſpatched again by her mother, who feared Rachel might loſe her way; and learning that ſhe had been gone ſome time from Atkins's, had returned as quick as ſhe could, in the hope of finding her ſafe at home).

Miſs La Varone welcomed her with tears of joy, and Mrs. Webſter ſaid ſhe was glad to ſee her ſafe. Courtney, (the name of the young officer) without particularly mentioning the circumſtances, ſaid ſhe had been diſagreeably ſituated, and he had been fortunate enough to be of ſervice to her.   But Rachel would explain the whole; her new friend, Miſs La Varone, ſympathized with her, trembled with terror, glowed with indignation, or melted with gratitude, as the recital proceeded; and in the end, ſaid ſo many obliging things to Lieutenant Courtney, that he began to think her more than agreeable; and overlooking the charms of our heroine, which had nothing but nature and ſimplicity to recommend them, he was powerfully

X   erfully

erfully attracted by the artful lures thrown out by La Varone.

The situation of Rachel, in regard to reputation, was now as dangerous as it was possible ; for Court-ney claimed the privilege of visiting her ; and Ar-chibald Oliver, when he returned from the country, and his sister, called to deliver the answer to the let-ter he had taken, and one visit led to another, till scarcely a day elapsed without his passing some hours in her company.

Rachel's intentions, when she first came to London, were to apprentice herself to some person who could instruct her in some laudable employment, whereby she might render herself independent. For in her opinion, the person who by the exertion of any talent, or the exercise of industry, could support themselves, was in every sense of the word as independ-ent as they who inherited wealth or titles from their ancestors. But these praiseworthy resolutions were from time to time put off, and her attention diverted to other objects, till she began to perceive the small sum of money she brought with her to London was very visibly diminished, and yet no plan put in execu-tion, by which it could be replenished. 'I must do something to-morrow,' said Rachel every night as she laid her head on her pillow. But to-morrow came, and La Varone had ever some new scheme of pleasure to propose. Juvenile indiscretion united with curi-osity, and a love of amusement, natural to youth, led her on from one day to another, till the last ten pound note was broken in upon.

Forbear, ye rigid, ye experienced matrons, to blame our heroine ; it is the particular blessing of youth to be enabled to enjoy the present moment, forgetful of the past, nor fearing the future. Then censure not those who eagerly gather the roses, unmindful of the briars that surround them, or who, delighted with their beauty and fragrance, forget, in the enjoyment of their sweets, the pain they suffered in gathering them.

Jessy Oliver had written to her, had endeavoured to advise and comfort her ; but Jessy stood in need of

advice

advice and comfort herfelf; and our heroine, though confcious that fhe was not acting exactly right, could not fummon refolution fufficient to combat inclination; but one party of pleafure fucceeded another, till fhe almoft loft the defire of employment, or the wifh for independence.

C H A P.   IX.

Variety—Courtfhip—Elopement—Letters.

WHEN Hamden Auberry firft faw Rachel at the entrance of the paffage in Holborn, he hardly could truft his fenfes; but on letting down the glafs and looking intently, he perceived it was no illufion, but in reality the woman whom he had thought the moft faultlefs, the moft perfect of her fex. His heart fhuddered; he dared not ftop the chariot in which was his aunt, or he would have immediately jumped out, and learnt from her own lips the reafon of her being in fuch a place; but before he could form any plaufible pretext for quitting the carriage, it moved forward again with rapidity, and looking out of the open window, he faw her go into the hackney-coach, accompanied by Courtney.

If he at firft had imagined Rachel had voluntarily deviated from the path of rectitude, a moment's ferious reflection made him reject the idea; and he began to be apprehenfive that her innocence and inexperience might have betrayed her into fociety and places, not altogether proper for a woman of character.

But how could he fatisfy himfelf? Or fhould fhe be furrounded with danger, how could he difcover her? how advife, or, if neceffity required, protect her? Had he known where to find her, he would have ventured even to entreat his aunt to take her under her protection; but he had not the leaft clue by which to trace her place of refidence. He thought of writing to his mother, for information; but lady Anne purpofed

poſed ſtaying in London but two days, and it was im‑
poſſible to obtain an anſwer in that time. However,‑
he did write, mentioning what he had ſeen, and requeſt‑
ing to be informed under whoſe protection Miſs Dud‑
ley was, hinting that he feared it was not what it
ought to be, or ſhe could never have been in the ſitu‑
ation in which he ſaw her.

On the day appointed, he accompanied his aunt into‑
Scotland ; where, ſituated on the fertile banks of the
Clyde, was an antique family manſion of lord Mont‑
morill, her elder brother. Whilſt there, he received a
letter from his mother, which ſlightly mentioned that our‑
heroine was well, and that the circumſtance he had ob‑
ſerved, proceeded from her ſtanding up to avoid a ſhower.

. She hurried over the ſubject as lightly as poſſible ;
for ſhe ſaw the growing paſſion of Hamden, and‑
knowing from experience the implacable tempers of
the family, wiſhed to diſcourage hopes which ſhe ſaw
he entertained, though againſt his own better reaſon.

Rachel herſelf was far from being eaſy when ſhe
thought of the incident, on the firſt night after ſeeing
Hamden ; (for ſhe ſeldom was allowed a moment for
thought, except in the hours devoted to reſt) ſhe felt
a pleaſure in reflecting he was in town. "I can ſee
him now," ſaid ſhe, "without incurring the illiberal
reproofs of Tabitha."

The heart of Rachel harboured not a wiſh or thought
but what might have been made public to the whole
world ; and while ſhe was conſcious of its rectitude, ſhe
felt proudly ſuperior to the little prejudices of vulgar
minds. She could not underſtand why ſhe might not
converſe with or entertain a friendſhip for perſons of
an oppoſite ſex, as well as with thoſe of her own. She
therefore indulged the hope, that Hamden would viſit
her during his ſtay in London ; but when day after
day paſſed on, and he did not appear, ſhe again thought
pride had prompted the neglect, and calling all her
own ſelf-conſequence to her aid, ſhe endeavoured to
think as little of him as he apparently thought of her.

Young Courtney, the officer who under ſuch fa‑
vourable circumſtances was introduced to the reader

in the preceding chapter, was the only son of his mother, and she was a widow.   He had two sisters also,
lovely, innocent and helpless ; their father had been a
veteran sailor, commander of a first-rate man of war,
in defending which from the enemy he lost his life.
The pension of a captain's widow at that period was
very precarious, and at the best but trifling, to maintain three women who had been accustomed to ease
and elegance.

Courtney gave them all the assistance in his power,
and had often thought he would never marry until
his sisters were settled in the world ; and then if he
could meet with a woman who could and would supply their place in attention to his mother.   But unfortunately, a few days acquaintance with Miss La
Varone, made him waver in his resolutions.   She
could assume any character she pleased.   She discovered
that her personal charms had attracted the inexperienced sailor.   She wished to marry, that she might with
impunity launch into extravagancies, which at present
the fear of a jail alone debarred her from.

La Varone, with a heart extremely depraved, possessed one virtue in an eminent degree.   She was what
the world in general calls extremely *prudent*, careful
to preserve appearances, and where her own personal
safety or interest was concerned, cautious not to incur
the smallest degree of danger.   By nature fond of
luxury, show, and expensive pleasures, she had the art
to *seem* frugal, retired, and studious.   She was sensible
that at thirty years old, the season for conquest was
past, and though she did not own to more than five
and twenty, and by particular attention to her complexion and dress, was not suspected to be more ; yet
she thought if she could secure a permanent establishment for herself before old age and neglect overtook
her, it would be the wisest step she could possibly take.

The name of Courtney was honourable, his person
handsome, his manners agreeable, and his family un-
exceptionable.   It was a conquest worth some pains.
La Varone artfully drew forth his sentiments in regard to the woman he might prefer for a wife, and

                                            appeared

appeared the very character his warm imagination and unadulterated heart had conceived as most charming. She spoke of his mother with respectful affection, of his sisters with all the fervour of enthusiastic friendship; but if he mentioned her visiting them previous to their marriage, she contrived to evade his solicitations; yet with such modesty, alleging such delicate motives for her refusal, that whilst it opposed his wishes increased his love.

Our heroine was equally with Courtney the dupe of La Varone, and rejoiced in the affection that subsisted between them; looking forward to their union, as a period that would at once insure their felicity, and secure to herself two sincere friends, in whose protection she should feel herself perfectly safe till the arrival of her brother.

During this interval of time, Rachel was frequently visited by Archibald Oliver. He had at first beheld her with admiration, listened to her with delight, and every ensuing interview had heightened those sensations to a degree which almost might be termed adoration. But Archibald possessed not a doit independent of his father, and that father he knew was, by his wife's extravagance, nearly ruined.

Though volatile in his temper, eccentric in his ideas, and violent in his passions, young Oliver was scrupulously honourable; and he would have deemed it the height of cruelty to engage the affections of a woman he could not with prudence marry, or to marry her when he could neither provide for her support, or for those helpless innocents of which he might become the father. And fearing to forfeit the highly valued privilege of visiting her, he confined his feelings within his own bosom. "She loves me now," he would say, like a brother; shall I then, by claiming more, lose even the affection I possess? No; I will adore her in silence, and pray that her felicity may be complete, though at the expense of my own."

One morning he entered the parlour (where La Varone and our heroine usually sat at work) and seating himself beside the latter, told her he came to make

her

her a partaker of his own uneafinefs. "Our dear
Jeffy," continued he, "has left her father's protection,
nor have we any idea whither the beloved fugitive is
fled.   Here is a note fhe left for me ; inclofed is a letter for you, Mifs Dudley.   The perfecutions the fweet
girl has lately undergone, I have concealed from you,
becaufe, as you could not alleviate them, I wifhed not
to make you participate.   But difguife muft now be
at an end.   This was to have been her wedding day ;
but early in the morning it was difcovered fhe was not
in her apartment.   The confufion this difcovery occafioned, reached me as I was preparing, with a defpond-
ing heart, to accompany the devoted victim to the altar ; and as I was rufhing out to inquire the caufe (for
my mind foreboded fomething fatal) the girl who ufually attended on Jeffy, came into my dreffing-room,
and in agitated filence put thefe papers into my hand,
retiring the inftant fhe delivered them.   I haftily tore
my letter open ; but it contained, as you will fee, nothing fatisfactory.   I learnt that a note had been delivered to my father, and wifhing equally to avoid him,
Mrs. Oliver, and the difappointed bridegroom, I took
a coach and drove directly here."   The letter to Archibald was as follows.

To ARCHIBALD OLIVER, *Efq.*

WHEN the altar is decorated, the priefts at hand,
and the knife is raifed, that will terminate exiftence,
who can blame the poor victim devoted to facrifice, if
it break the chain by which it is held, afferts the privilege of nature, and, bounding over the plain, fecures
at once both life and liberty ?   Brother, beloved brother, they have prepared the altar, but the deftined victim will efcape their fnares.

Deliver the inclofed to the friend of my foul, Rachel
Dudley ; if fhe contemn me, I will return a voluntary
facrifice.   For fo pure is her mind, fo unprejudiced
her opinions, foaring fo far above the common herd,
that I would abide by her decifion even in a caufe of
life and death.

Deareft

Dearest Archibald, though I am driven to the dreadful alternative of marrying the man I despise, or quitting the paternal roof, do not you forsake our father. I solicit, I conjure you, my brother, in the name of our sainted mother, forsake not our only remaining parent. I fear he will soon, very soon, stand in need of a comforter. I will be constant in my inquiries concerning his welfare, and whenever I find my presence necessary to his peace or comfort, I will appear. Any thing but truth I would have sacrificed for his sake. Could you see my heart at this moment, you would pity the anguish I feel in bidding you adieu, perhaps forever.   JESSY OLIVER.

Rachel wiped off the tear this letter had extorted, and proceeded to peruse the one addressed to herself.

To *Miss* DUDLEY.

WILL my dear friend pardon me that I intrude myself upon her, and by explaining my sorrows, make her a party in my concerns? I have suffered much persecution, dear Rachel, since we parted; and to avoid rushing at once into guilt and misery, I have taken a step for which the world will censure me. But what is the world to me? Had I voluntarily assumed the splendid shackles prepared for me, had I become a titled wretch, and promised faith and truth to one man, whilst every wish, every tender thought of my heart was devoted to another, would the approving smiles of that misjudging world, the adulation it is ever ready to pay to splendor and nobility, have compensated for the sacrifice I should have made of internal peace, of conscious integrity? No.—Admired, courted, envied, I should still have been miserable. The baseness of my conduct would be my daily reproach; I should have sought to banish reflection by dissipation, and who can tell where the career of guilt and folly might have stopped?

I have endured both stern commands and soft entreaties; I have been soothed and threatened alternately. That I might with more security follow the plan I had previously adopted for my future conduct, I pretended (Heaven pardon the deceit) to accept the husband my dissolute and ambitious mother-in-law had provided for me, and to-morrow morning I am expected to put on the Hymeneal yoke, and become a countess. But before the appointed hour arrives, I shall be far, far out of the reach of their tyranny. Let not my sweet friend, whose bosom is the sacred temple of purity, fear that I shall forget what is due to myself. That I am strongly attached to a worthy youth, I scruple not to confess; but he is a stranger to my passion, and in all human probability will ever remain so; for never will Jessy Oliver offer herself unsolicited to the acceptance of any man. My affections are pure as they are ardent; but the name of the object of them shall never pass my lips, or escape my pen. I fly from proffered wealth and grandeur, to obscurity; even from you, my dear Rachel, I will seclude myself. Were I happy or affluent, you should be my chosen companion, the partner of my heart. But I am the reverse, and will suffer alone. If you will condescend to receive and answer the letters of a fugitive, I have formed a plan by which we may regularly correspond; but do not flatter yourself that by that means you can trace me; nor do not, I entreat you, suffer my brother to know the means by which my letters are conveyed.

And now, my dearest Rachel, adieu! Fear not for me. I will never dishonour the name of my father, or forget the virtue of my sainted mother. Perhaps (my heart sinks at the idea, but perhaps) I shall never see you again. If so, may Heaven shower its choicest blessings on you, and inspire *me* with patience and fortitude to submit, without repining, to an affliction which would lacerate the heart of

JESSY OLIVER.

When Rachel had finished this letter, she imparted to Archibald as much of the contents as she thought necessary; but to all his entreaties of being permitted to peruse it she continued inexorable. She admired the resolution of Jessy, and had so good an opinion of

her

her heart and underftanding, that fhe felt confident of
her ftrict adherence to truth and rectitude.

In all their paft hours of friendly confidence; Mifs
Oliver had never fuffered a fyllable to efcape her lips
by which Rachel could guefs at her partiality to Reuben ; and at the time when they were moft together,
our heroine was too inexperienced to difcover the paffion of her friend by looks and geftures. Perhaps,
had fhe converfed much with Jeffy after her own acquaintance with Hamden Auberry, fhe might have
been more clear-fighted.

Soon after this circumftance, young Oliver, weary
of home, diffatisfied with himfelf, and more than ever
in love with Rachel, felt there was a neceffity for tear-
ing himfelf from her fociety. Befides, he hoped, in
travelling through the northern counties of England,
to be enabled to learn fome tidings of his fifter. A
diftant relation of his mother's refided in the beautiful
little town of Alnwick, in Northumberland ; thither
he repaired on a vifit. Its romantic fituation pleafed
him ; the fociety of feveral agreeable families in its
vicinity delighted him ; and if we add that a lovely
and interefting woman, whofe fortune was large and
independent, beheld him with affection, and fuffered
that affection to become manifeft, it is to be hoped the
fair reader will not blame him, if he lengthened his
ftay at Alnwick, and every day thought lefs and lefs
of Rachel.

After the marriage of Lieutenant Courtney with
Mifs La Varone, our heroine felt fomewhat difappointed that fhe had not been preffed to accompany
the new Mrs. Courtney into the country. The Lieutenant had, to be fure, folicited her company ; but the
bride did not, even by a fingle monofyllable, fecond
thofe folicitations ; fo Rachel faw them depart, fervently wifhed them hourly increafe of felicity, and
then fat down to reflect on her own fituation in London, without friends, without employment, and with
only eight guineas in her pocket.

" I have

"I have done wrong, (said she mentally) very wrong. I muft take more care, muft endeavour to be more prudent for the future."

As fhe ruminated on the paft, felt no fatisfaction in the prefent, and looked with fear and defpondency toward the future, fhe heard a confufion in the adjoining apartment, and the voice of Polly Webfter, who was her favourite, entreating a woman to have patience, who by her expreffions and manner feemed a total ftranger to that virtue. She opened the door, and learnt that Mrs. Webfter was indebted to this woman for tea, fugar, &c. (for fhe kept a chandler's fhop in the neighbourhood) nearly five pounds.

Now five pounds, to a perfon in abject circumftances, is a debt of as much confequence as five thoufand would be to one who keeps high company, a carriage, horfes, fervants, dreffes gay, and, as it is generally termed, lives in ftyle; nay, perhaps, ten times more. For the poor being, who for the abfolute neceffaries of life has incurred a fmall debt, may be dragged by a remorfelefs creditor to die in a prifon, unknown, unpitied; while he who, to indulge in luxury and fuperfluity, had deceived the expectations of honeft induftry, deprived the laborious mechanic of his due, or duped the unwary tradefman, is fuffered to proceed with impunity. Nay, even thofe who criminate his conduct, will flatter his vices, eat at his table, take him by the hand, and fmile in his face, whilft in their hearts they laugh at his abfurdity, pity his weaknefs, or condemn his depravity. Not but there are thofe, who, difcriminating between the embarraffments of neceffity, and thofe of wilful extravagance, pity the one and defpife and execrate the other. Yes, there are in this world hearts to commiferate misfortune, whilft they dictate to the tongue comfort, and to the hands relief to the fufferer. And thofe chofen, thofe fuperlatively happy few, muft furely be the favourites of Heaven. For the bleffing they delight to confer on others, will return a thoufand-fold into their own bofoms.

But I digrefs. To return to Mrs. Webfter: She could not pay the demand, and was threatened with

the

the law. Rachel had but eight guineas; but she could pay this demand and have three left. She stayed not to inquire what was prudent; she felt what would be humane. She followed the heavenly precept of " doing as she would be done by;" she paid the money.

The heart of Mrs. Webster dilated with gratitude; and the pain Rachel had endured from the departure and coldness of Mrs. Courtney, was forget in the transport of the present moment; so true is it, that real happiness must be the result of the knowledge and practice of virtue.

Mr. Spriggins, the nephew of Mrs. Webster, though awed by her superior sense and the dignity of her manner, was an ardent admirer of our heroine; but he had never yet breathed a word that could lead her to suspect his passion. La Varone, young Oliver, and Lieutenant Courtney, had contributed to impose silence on him, and keep him at a distance. But now they were gone, he could offer any civility to her without the fear of having his endeavours to please entirely frustrated, by officiousness or rivalry.

The second day after their departure, he came, and requested the Mifs Webfters and Rachel would accompany him to the play. He forefaw that the young ladies would not be permitted to go without Mifs Dudley, and also that her good-nature would not suffer her to decline his invitation, as by so doing she would deprive the juvenile party of a rational and (to them) rare amusement. His expectations were realized; and at an early hour they were all at the pit door of Drury-Lane Theatre. The performance was a tragedy and pantomime, both excellent in their kind.

Rachel, whose sensibility often usurped dominion over her rational faculties, banishing the milder reign of reason, was, during the tragedy, so entirely absorbed by the sufferings of the hero and heroine, that the splendid circle that surrounded her in the boxes was totally unnoticed. But between the play and entertainment, she looked round on the glittering throng; and in the stage-box, conversing with attentive earnestness with

an

an elegant and very young lady, she saw Hamden Auberry.

The lady laid her hand on his shoulder. Rachel discovered that her seat was uncomfortable. Hamden, as he conversed, twisted a curl of her luxuriant auburn tresses round his fingers.

"I declare I am out of patience," cried Rachel.

"At what, ma'am?" cried the officious Mr. Spriggins.

"At the players," said she; "they are so tedious."

"Yes, ma'am," replied Spriggins, "they are to be sure a long while."

At that moment Hamden had taken the hand of his fair companion and pressed it to his lips.

"I cannot endure it any longer," cried Rachel, "the pit is so crowded, and it is so hot." Rachel was not easily overcome; but her heart was more attached to Hamden Auberry than she was aware of. "It is so oppressive," repeated she, unwilling to acknowledge even to herself the cause of her uneasy sensations. "I must really quit the house," said she, gasping for breath. And then, before any effort could be made to get her through the crowd, a sudden mist came over her eyes, and she fainted.

The young Websters were frightened, and Spriggins was entirely occupied in supporting her, so that no method was taken to recover her. But an elderly gentleman, who sat near them, observed if they could lift her up, so that she might be above the crowd, it would accelerate her return to life. Accordingly, he humanely stepped up on the seat, and raised her in his arms. A smelling bottle was now applied, and some lavender rubbed on her temples.

The bustle this incident had occasioned in the pit, attracted the notice of the company in the boxes; and as the old gentleman raised the declining head of Rachel that she might receive the more benefit from the air of several fans, Auberry saw and knew her. Like lightning he sprang over the front of the box, and rushing through the company, was by the side of our heroine, when returning life began to animate her lips

Y

and

and cheeks; and when she opened her eyes, Auberry
was the first object that met them. The tender solicitude of his looks and manner, whilst he inquired into
the cause of her disorder, contributed to restore her
entirely; and having thanked the old gentleman for
his care, and made room for Auberry to sit between
herself and Polly Webster, as he held her hand, and
spoke to her of his mother, Dr. Lenient, and the rest
of their acquaintance in Lancashire, she entirely forgot both her indisposition and its cause.

Though the impulse of the moment had urged
Hamden Auberry, in direct opposition to every rule
of politeness or even propriety, to quit his company
and spring into the pit, when he beheld the lifeless
form of Rachel, yet when he now saw her perfectly
recovered, he remembered the necessity of immediately
returning to them, and apologizing for the abrupt-
ness of his conduct.

"I do not feel altogether satisfied, my charming
Miss Dudley," said he in a low voice, "that the society in which, perhaps, you are obliged to mix, is proper or congenial to your feelings. Who are these young
women, and the young man who attends them?"

"I am not indeed," said Rachel, "situated exactly
as I could wish; but I know not how to better myself."

"Where shall I call on you," said Hamden; "I
cannot now stay to say all I think. I must return to
my cousin, lady Lucy."

"Is that your cousin?" said Rachel, glancing her
eye upon the young lady in the box.

"Yes; I came to town by my aunt's desire merely
to accompany her; she is come upon a visit to a friend
of her mother's, and is going with her to make a short
tour on the continent."

"And do you accompany her?" said Rachel; but
she dared not raise her eyes to his face as she made
the interrogation; for she felt that her own was suffused with a blush.

"No; I shall only go with them as far as Dover.
But as we do not set forward till Saturday, I shall
hope

hope to pafs a few delightful hours in your fociety previous to my journey. At what time will you be at leifure to-morrow morning?"

"I am always at leifure to fee my friends," replied Rachel, with a fafcinating fmile.

Hamden's countenance expreffed his gratitude, and the pleafure her franknefs gave him, and preffing her hand, he wifhed her a good night, returned to the box, and a few moments afterwards, the whole party in which he was engaged left the theatre.

The remainder of the performance was entirely loft upon our heroine. Her perfon was prefent, and fhe faw the figures that paffed and repaffed before her; but her mind was totally abfent, and fhe might as well have gazed upon vacancy. She was diffatisfied with herfelf; fhe had difcovered that fhe was too much interefted in whatever concerned Hamden Auberry; fhe feared too that he had difcovered her weaknefs. Thefe reflections entirely employed her thoughts.

When the performance was ended, fhe mechanically followed her party out of the houfe. When freed from the hurry of coaches, chairs, orange-women, link-boys, and the crowd that had juft immerged from the play-houfe, fhe took hold of Polly's arm, and in filence purfued her walk home. When fhe entered the parlour fhe afked for a candle, and would have retired to her chamber; but Mrs. Webfter had prepared fome little delicacy for her fupper, and fhe had too much good-nature and politenefs to refufe fitting up to partake of it.

The curiofity of Spriggins and the two elder Webfters was excited by the behaviour of Hamden Auberry. They had talked it over as they walked home together, and all agreed that he was certainly a lover. The company he was with declared he was of a fuperior rank in life; but they had not been quite pleafed that our heroine had neglected to introduce them.

"He is a monftrous handfome man," faid Belle, the fecond daughter.

"He is well enough," faid the eldeft, "but he feems fo proud and felf-conceited."

"We'll

We'll joke Miss Rachel a little about him at supper time," said Spriggins.

" I wonder what made her faint," said Belle.

" Why lawk, Belle !" replied the sister, " you know she has always lived in the country, and so I suppose the lights, and the noise, and the heat——"

Just then they arrived at home, and in a few minutes they were all seated round the supper table.

" Miss Dudley has been very ill at the play, mamma," said Polly.

" Yes, indeed," cried the eldest, " she fainted quite away, and there was such a fine gentleman jumped out of the box and came to her, I believe he is an old acquaintance."

" I believe so too," said Belle, laughing ; " for he seemed monstrous anxious, and looked so happy when she began to recover."

" He is an old acquaintance," said Rachel, at once distressed and flattered by the manner in which his anxiety and assiduity was mentioned ; " it was Major Auberry, madam," addressing herself to Mrs. Webster ; " the son of our respected friend."

" Indeed ! Well, I have not seen him since he was an infant ; and besides, if he even remembered me, he is so much amongst the great folks, it would be beneath him to notice me, or any of my family, though his mother and I, when girls, were just like sisters."

" Yes, yes," cried Spriggins, whose self-consequence had been lowered by his being entirely overlooked by the Major ; " yes ! when folks get up in the world, they generally forget their poor friends."

" But I dare affirm Major Auberry is not one of those kind of people," said Rachel ; " he intends calling on me to-morrow, and I have no doubt but he will rejoice in being introduced to Mrs. Webster and her family."

" Well, we shall see !" cried Spriggins ; " but I am sure he is not overburthened with good manners, or he would have said good-night, or your servant, or some such like, to me, when he went away ; for though mayhap I am not so grand, nor so fine, nor so learned, I thinks I understands good-breeding as well as any
body.

body.   And for the matter of that, a man is but a man, and I don't fee why wearing a laced coat, or being called Sir, or My Lord, or Your Grace, makes one man a bit better than another."

Rachel found that it would be in vain to attempt defending Hamden againſt the complaints and prejudices of Spriggins, whoſe contracted mind and very ſmall portion of underſtanding, would not ſuffer him to comprehend thoſe nice diſtinctions which, allowing for the natural equality of man, ſtill preſerves that reſpect, that neceſſary ſubordination, due from inferiors to perſons of ſhining abilities, liberal education, and ſuperior underſtanding ; and the ignorant, ſelf-opinionated being who prates of equality, never once conceives the cauſe of the diſtinction, which education (more than any other cauſe) makes between man and man.   Perſons of large fortunes are enabled to enjoy the benefits of inſtruction in its moſt extended ſenſe ; and they who have cultivated their minds with care, whoſe taſtes and manners are highly poliſhed, feel as great a repugnance to the ſociety of the vulgar ignorant, in whom mean pride, obſtinacy and vanity in general, combine, as the pure and uncontaminated mind would feel in being forced into an intercourſe with the vicious.   But Rachel knew theſe arguments, if advanced, would have no effect on Spriggins ; ſhe therefore liſtened in ſilence to the end of his harangue, then wiſhing them all a good night, retired to her apartment.

⚜

C H A P.   X.

Matters of Conſequence.

THE next morning by ten o'clock, Hamden Aubrry was in Dartmouth-ſtreet.   He was introduced to Mrs. Webſter and her daughters ; to the former, as the friend of his mother, he was uncommonly reſpectful, and he ſpoke to the girls with ſuch freedom, politeneſs and affability, that when they went

Y 2

into

into the adjoining room, Belle declared he was a moft captivating man.

Polly faid fhe hoped, if he was going to marry dear Mifs Dudley, that he was as good as he was handfome. For if he was a king, he could not be too good for her.

"Marry," faid the eldeft, putting up her lip, "I dare fay he would be frightened to hear you fay fuch a thing. No! no! young men of his rank and fafhion don't often marry poor girls; if they did, I don't fee why fome folks might not ftand as good a chance as others." And fhe caft a fly glance at the looking-glafs, which hung directly oppofite to where fhe was fitting.

Hamden, in this interview with our heroine, felt his admiration increafe. Every circumftance that had taken place during her refidence in London, fhe recapitulated to him, with an ingenuous freedom that captivated his heart, whilft his reafon applauded the involuntary tribute of admiration and refpect, her manners and fentiments exacted.

When fhe had finifhed her artlefs recital, (which was drawn forth by his inquiries, not voluntarily obtruded on his attention) "You are, I fear, improperly, as well as uncomfortably fituated," faid he with energy.

. "I acknowledge it," replied Rachel, "but I muft bear it with patience; there is no remedy."

"What do you mean, my dear Mifs Dudley? You furely have friends."

"I dare fay I have, Sir, many friends; but I fhould be forry to trefpafs on their goodnefs."

"Is it poffible Mifs Dudley can imagine——" He was proceeding, but fhe ftopped him.

"Do not mifunderftand me, Major Auberry; I do not think meanly of my friends, but I am confcious of my own defects; I am too proud to live in a ftate of fervile dependence."

"Good heavens! what do you mean?"

"Nothing very extraordinary. My brother is abfent; my late dear father's agent, I greatly fear, is difhoneft;

honeft ; and perhaps I fhall find it neceffary to be induftrious, in order to continue in fome degree refpectable."

She faid this without embarraffment, and with a
cheerful fmile.   She felt no degradation in the idea of
exerting her talents to procure fupport.

Hamden was filent ; a certain fomething ftruck cold
upon his heart.   No wonder ; it was the cold, hard
drop that turns whatever it falls upon to ftone.   Poverty has a moft unaccountable petrifying quality ;
many a heart has it rendered impenetrable as adamant ;
many a bofom has it incafed in marble, or enveloped
in ice, fo firmly congealed, that only the fun of profperity, riding in full meridian, could foften or relax
it.   Hamden felt the cold chill run trembling through
every nerve ; but his heart defied its frigid power, and
glowed with more fervour.   He faid but little after
this explanation, and foon took his leave.

On his return to his lodgings, he thus inquired of
himfelf.   Do I love Rachel Dudley ?   Moft affuredly,
beyond all other women.   Does fhe return my paffion ?
That is a queftion yet to be determined.   If I might
judge from the intelligence of her eyes—But hope
may be prefumption.   Would I marry her ?   Yes, with
delight and tranfport, if fhe would accept me.   What ?
in defiance of my aunt's wifhes and injunctions ?

Here was a moment's paufe.   At length he proceeded in his queftions.   Would I be willing to relinquifh all hope of future affluence, honour, title, and
devote my life to obfcurity and Rachel Dudley ?   I
fear not.   I fhould repine at the advantages I had relinquifhed, and embitter her life by my own fruitlefs
regret.   Then is it honourable, by indirect attentions,
to lead her to fuppofe fhe has an exclufive preference
in my bofom, or to awaken expectations, which will
end only in difappointment ?   Certainly no.

After thus clofely interrogating his own heart, Hamden determined to avoid vifiting Rachel again ; but
on the morning following, he received a letter from his
mother ; it would be but kind to call and let Mifs Dudley
know her friend Dr. Lenient was well, and that Tabitha

Holdfast had taken to herself a help-mate of one of the faithful.

He accordingly went ; one visit produced another. Prudence on one side, and pride on the other, were for a while forgotten.   Hamden talked of love, and Rachel listened with complacency.

It was on a fine evening in the beginning of September, as wandering on the banks of the Thames, where a row of young willows drooped their pendent branches over the softly gliding stream, that Hamden (on whose arm Rachel reclined with the confidence of fraternal affection) spoke of the happy intercourse of congenial minds.

"Dear, charming Rachel !" said he, "it seems as though our souls were formed at the same moment, and partake of congenial particles."

"Our sentiments are certainly much alike in most things," said Rachel.

"And why not in every thing," cried Hamden eagerly.   "Why, my lovely friend, loving as we love each other, (for you do not deny though you hesitate to avow your affection) why do we not sanctify that affection by the most solemn vows ?"

"You have an aunt, Hamden Auberry," said Rachel with firmness, "and on her depends your future fortune.   She will not approve of the untitled, unportioned Rachel for your wife."

"Do not name her.   I will renounce her favour. I will henceforth live but for you."

"Hamden," said Rachel, and her features assumed a serene solemnity that was almost celestial, "Hamden, I have not expressed the feelings of my soul, because I was sensible of the impossibility of our ever being united with the consent of your aunt ; and know, though you were dearer to me than life itself, I will never intrude myself into a family, who would think themselves degraded by the alliance.   That I am an unconnected being, is certain ; no one has a right to say, Rachel, why dost thou so ?   But I have a heart that tells me when I err.   To the reproaches of this trusty, silent monitor, I will never subject myself; to

the

the contumely and censures of the world I am invulnerable; they too often misjudge and condemn the innocent unheard."

"Sweet, charming moralist, whither wouldst thou lead me?" said Hamden.

"To happiness, I hope," said Rachel smiling. "That I feel my heart glow with esteem to you," continued she, "is a truth I wish not to deny; but that esteem is pure; nor personal interest, nor hope of future aggrandizement, will ever bias me. You ask me for a wife; here is my hand; let us sanctify our loves in the face of Heaven. Enable me to satisfy my dear Reuben, when he returns, that I have not dishonoured the name of Dudley; and for the indiscriminating, curious, idle multitude, let them think as they may. Happy in your affection, their smile or their frown will be alike inconsequential."

The gratitude of Hamden was manifested in wild, enthusiastic expressions of everlasting love. But Hamden's pride still predominated, and he accepted the title of husband to an amiable woman, whose virtue and understanding would have done honour to a diadem; yet, fearing to forfeit the paltry distinctions of wealth and title, he suffered her to bear the ignominy of suspicion, and the bitterness of reproach, from those who neither comprehended or could estimate her merit.

They were married in St. John's Church, Westminster; and Rachel removed to a lodging provided for her by her husband in the neighbourhood of Mary-le-bone.

When Rachel proposed removing from Mrs. Webster's, she found no small difficulty in satisfying her inquiries respecting the cause of her removal. She had imprudently acquainted Mrs. Webster with the diminished state of her finances; when therefore on the morning of her marriage, which took place a little after eight o'clock; for Rachel, though she had now been some months in London, continued the health-giving custom of early rising, and frequently walked before breakfast, so that it was nothing extraordinary for her to be abroad so early; when, in consequence

of

of this union, she prepared to quit her lodging, and gave Mrs. Webster a bank bill for forty pounds, requesting her to get it changed, the old lady looked at her with a scrutinizing eye; and though not apt to make remarks, could not avoid speaking to our heroine in the following words:

"It is no business of mine, to be sure, Miss Dudley; but I am afraid you are going to do a very imprudent thing. To your family and connexions I am a total stranger; but for the sake of my friend, Mrs. Auberry, I could wish you had conducted yourself with more circumspection."

"In what, madam?" said Rachel indignantly, "have I transgressed the laws of prudence?"

"You have received the visits of several young men. Mr. Oliver, I concluded, was your lover for some time; but after visiting, taking you on parties of pleasure, and being as attentive as man could be, whisk he goes off into the country, and there's an end of the matter."

Rachel could not help smiling as she replied—"Mr. Oliver, I believe, madam, never thought of me in any other light than as a friend. I am so happy as to be esteemed by his sister, and for her sake he shewed me, whilst he stayed in town, more than common respect."

"Well, it may be so; but it had a very odd appearance though. Then came Mr. Courtney. I made quite certain that he would be the happy man, when, behold! instead of you, he marries Miss La Varone. To be certain, she was a clever sort of a body; but then one would have thought a young man would not be at a loss to choose between you and her."

"Well, you find he was not at a loss," answered Rachel rather petulantly.

"And now," continued Mrs. Webster, not noticing her reply, "now here has been Major Auberry, dancing attendance above a month past. I am afraid he means no good; he is, as one may say, one of the quality folks; and his aunt, lady Anne, would no more agree to his marrying a poor girl, than she would to his going to Jerusalem. What then does he design?
                                        Take

Take care, Mifs Dudley, do not let him make you his dupe. You are going from me ; for what purpofe, or into whofe protection, you have not thought proper to tell me ; however, that is neither here nor there. As I faid before, it is no bufinefs of mine. But when I think, that not a fortnight fince you fhewed me the contents of your purfe, which were very trifling, and declared it was all you poffeffed in the world, and that I now fee you in poffeffion of forty pounds, I cannot help thinking all is not as it fhould be."

"I thank you, madam, for your care and anxiety on my account," faid Rachel, who perceived, in Mrs. Webfter's manner, more of curiofity than real folicitude for her welfare, "but to quiet your apprehenfions, permit me to affure you, I fhall be careful never to offend againft virtue and morality. My conduct may incur cenfure, but fhall never be criminal. Whilft my dear brother is from England, I hold myfelf accountable to no one for my actions ; and whilft my own heart acquits me of any breach of my duties either moral or religious, I am perfectly indifferent as to what opinion the world in general may form concerning me."

Thus argued Rachel ; but her ideas were erroneous, and fhe found, when too late, it is not only neceffary to be virtuous, but to appear fo. Alas ! pity it is, but the femblance is often more refpected than the reality.

"I fuppofe we fhall fee you fometimes, Mifs Dudley ?" faid Mrs. Webfter with a fneer, as fhe took leave of her.

Rachel flightly anfwered in the affirmative, fhook hands with her and Belle, kiffed the affectionate little Polly (who ftood fobbing by the window) and put a guinea into her hand ; then ordering her trunk to be placed in a hackney-coach that waited at the door, fhe ftepped in, drew up the glafs, and a few moments conveyed her to her new lodgings, where her hufband was ready to receive her.

The attachment of our heroine to Major Auberry was pure as it was ardent. Accuftomed from infancy to confine her affections within a narrow circle, fhe would have felt no repugnance to seclude herself from all other society, could she have been certain by so doing to insure his eternal love and fidelity. She had asked leave of Hamden to inform Jessy Oliver, with whom she regularly corresponded, of the change in her circumstances; but he forbade her. She acquiesced in silence.

It had never entered her mind, that an unknown individual like herself, could excite the curiosity of her neighbours. She was the least inquisitive of any human being. "Of what consequence," she would often say, "is the business, pleasures or pursuits of others to me. I harbour no ill will towards any; and have I a right to scrutinize their actions? No."

Hamden Auberry, still the slave of pride, and fearing to forfeit the favour of lady Anne, suffered his wife to go by the assumed name of Dacres. Our heroine too was equally the slave of the same passion, but it was of a more laudable kind. He sacrificed the reputation of a virtuous woman, rather than relinquish the insignificant distinction wealth and power could give; and she nobly (though romantically) braved the censures of the world, to evince her thorough contempt of both.

⸺⸺⸺✦⸺⸺⸺

C H A P.   XI.

Across the Atlantic.

AS Variety is said to be the fascinating charm that intrances the senses, awakens attention, and, displaying her many-coloured wings in a thousand different lights, obscures from our view the scythe and glass of Time, and suffers him to pass unheeded by; at her shrine I kneel, her aid I invoke. Come, enchanting phantom, who, as thou passest momentarily, assumed some new, some charming form. Whether as pleasure, tripping lightly forward, thy temples wreathed with roses, and thy hands striking with sportive

ive

ive lay the dulcet lyre ; or whether, in the robe of forrow clad, with pale, cold cheek, and uplift, tearful
eye ; or cheerful induſtry, with placid ſmile, with boſom tranquil, and with moderate ſcrip, ſtored with
life's comforts, not its ſuperfluities ; or as meek patience, bowing with ſubmiſſion before the keen blaſt of
undeſerved calamity ; whatever ſhape thou doſt aſ-
ſume, to me thou art welcome. Haſten then, for
with thee ever comes the Muſe. Her veſtments white
claſped by a golden zone, her buſkined leg half bare,
her auburn treſſes floating in the wind ; her veil,
which part conceals her beauteous face, and part plays
loofely in the breeze, wrought with devices ſtrange
and rare ; Hiſtory, Poetry, Fiction and Truth,
blended ſo ſoft as to relieve each other ; ethereal
viſion, come ; I wait thee here. For many is the
painful hour thou haſt ſoothed ; many the heart-
ache thou haſt lightened. Wearineſs has fled at thy
approach, and the ſtill hour of night has been as cheerful as the full blaze of day.

' But, madam, if you pleaſe, we would prefer a little leſs of the figurative, and a little more plain matter
of fact.'

Pardon me, gentle reader. I forgot I was writing
the hiſtory of Reuben and Rachel, and was giving you
the hiſtory of my own feelings.

A poor ſubſtitute, you ſay. I acknowledge the
truth of the obſervation, and therefore return to my hero.

After a paſſage of thirty days, Reuben Dudley arrived ſafe in the Delaware, and on the thirty-ſecond
day after his departure from Liverpool, landed in the
city of Philadelphia. He had with him ſeveral letters of,
what is called recommendation from merchants in
Liverpool to their tranſ-atlantic correſpondents ; but
they contained nothing more than a general mention
of his family, and that his character and morals had
been hitherto unimpeached.

" I will not inquire out the gentlemen to whom
theſe letters are directed, till I have ſeen my good
friend Jacob Holmes," ſaid Reuben to himſelf, as he
walked up the main ſtreet. " He will, without doubt,

Z

accompany

accompany me, when I wish to visit them.   How glad
will he be to see me," continued he mentally.   "His
natural love to my sister and self, his gratitude to my
father——"

At the remembrance of his father, Reuben's heart
became full ; and when he seated himself in the tavern
to which he had been recommended, and began to reflect seriously upon where he was, and that it was more
than probable his father might have been in that very
house, in that very room, nay, he might have rested on
the identical chair he was now seated on, the fulness
of his heart overflowed at his eyes, and he indulged in
the effusion without restraint.

He had ordered some supper.   As the master of
the house came in with it, Reuben asked him if he had
ever known one Mr. Dudley, who had resided in Philadelphia between two and three years.

The landlord had, previous to the question being
asked, drawn a chair to the opposite side of the table
to that where our hero was seated, and when he heard
the interrogation, answered it by another.   ·

" I expect he is some relative of yours, by your being
so inquisitive about him."

" He was," said Reuben mournfully, " a very near
and dear relative."

" So I expect," replied the landlord.   " Pray where
is he now ?"

" In heaven," said Reuben, raising his eyes, whilst
every pulsation vibrated in exulting confidence of his
father's worth.

" You must not be too sure of that," said the landlord.

" Had you known him, Sir," said Reuben with a
firm and earnest manner, " you would have no more
doubt of his present happiness than I have."

" I did know him," replied the host.

" Then you knew one of the best men that ever lived."

" Yes, he was good in the worldly acceptation of
the word ; he did alms, told no lies, hated no one,
paid every man, yea, more than his due ; but all this
is

is vanity, filthy rags, unclean veſtments. He was not one of the choſen; he was in a loſt ſtate."

Here a diſpute enſued, in which Reuben evidently loſt ground with his antagoniſt; for Reuben argued with coolneſs, and took reaſon for his monitor; whereas his opponent was wild, enthuſiaſtic, and extremely ignorant. He had adopted ſome eccentric ideas in regard to religion, and he aſſerted that his opinions were right, " becauſe they were," and that all who did not think exactly as he did, were in the high road to deſtruction, for the ſame unanſwerable reaſon, " becauſe they were."

Before Reuben had finiſhed his ſupper, the landlord left him, to impart to his ſpouſe all he had learnt concerning the ſtranger. The curioſity of Jael was not ſatisfied with this intelligence of her helpmate's.

" Thou haſt learned nothing, Zekell," ſaid ſhe ; " I will go and queſtion the young man myſelf."

Jael entered the parlour.

" You are juſt arrived," ſaid ſhe, ſitting down in the place her huſband had juſt left.

" Yes, juſt landed."

" From England."

" Yes."

" What part ?"

" Liverpool."

" Liverpool ?"

" Yes."

" I expect you have got ſome kinsfolks in the city."

" Not that I know of."

" No friends, no acquaintances ?"

" Oh yes! Do you know Jacob Holmes?"

" Yes, to be ſure I do. Maſter has reaſon to know him; he is a dire hard man to deal with."

" What buſineſs does he follow ?"

" Buſineſs! Well, I expect you don't know much about him, to aſk that queſtion. Why Jacob Holmes is one of our grandeſt men, for all he be a Quaker. And then he married ſuch a grand woman ; why I expect ſhe had a matter of five hundred pounds to her fortin."

" Mr.

"Mr. Holmes is married then?"

"What, did not you know that? Well, I thought you were a boasting sort of fellow, pretending to know folks who you never saw'd."

"How long has he been married?" said Reuben.

"Why I expect it is about a year and a half ago."

"So long?"

"Yes, so long; and madam Holmes has got a sweet little baby, about three months old."

Reuben paused a moment, and then without reflection exclaimed, "Why he must have married immediately after my father's departure for England."

"And pray what may be your name?" said Jael, placing both her elbows on the table, and resting her chin on her hands, whilst her large blue glass eyes were fixed on the face of our hero with a most unmeaning stare.

"My name is Dudley," replied Reuben.

"So I expected," said she, and something like low cunning informed her broad and inexpressive features. "And so you are cum'd to look ater the fortin squire Dudley left?"

"Even so," replied Reuben, pushing from him the plate that contained his almost untasted supper. "How far from Philadelphia does the late Mr. Dudley's estate lay, and which is my nearest road to it?"

"Ah, young man!" said Jael, "I expect you be cum'd on a fool's errant. It matters not to you where it lies; he never paid for it; and cording to counts that we have heard, the squire owed a pretty deal before he cum'd from home."

Reuben started. "Of whom are you speaking?" said he.

"Of squire Dudley."

"What Dudley? what was his Christian name?"

"Name! name! I can't just now say; but I expect it was a bible name."

"Was it Reuben?" asked our hero eagerly.

"I do expect it was," said the woman, rising without the least emotion, and beginning to remove the supper from the table.

"Oh!

"Oh! my dear father!" exclaimed Reuben, and his respiration became so difficult that he was obliged to walk to the window and throw up the sash.

Jael replaced the dish upon the table, and with a look and manner to which no description can do justice, thus addressed him :—

"If squire Dudley was your father, I wonder how you got safe over sea. Nobody was surprised when they heard he was cast away and drownded; for he was as great a reprobate as ever lived."

"Reprobate!" repeated Reuben with vehemence, and his eyes flashed resentment, whilst his heart swelled almost to bursting.

"Yes, reprobate," repeated Jael, "and I expect you will find a pretty many folks in Philidelphy that will tell you as how here he comed over sea, and pretended to be a vast rich man."

"'Tis false!" cried Reuben; "I would stake my existence upon his probity. My father would have scorned to pretend to any thing more than he could make appear reality."

"But I say he did though," said Jael; "giving away his interest as a body may say, selling his goods at half-price, that, as he said, the poor might buy as well as the rich. Then if he saw a man that wanted, he never inquired whether he was a Christian or a Papish, but lent or gav'd him what he axed."

"And a just and beneficent God will reward him for it," said Reuben, raising his eyes fervently. "He is now, I trust, reaping the reward of his philanthropy."

"It mought a been all very well," continued Jael, not noticing the ejaculation of our hero, "had he only given away his own; but to deal so hardly as he did by that pious young man, Jacob Holmes—Oh! it was a wicked thing."

Reuben approached a few steps towards his hostess, and then stopped, fixed in curiosity and amazement; amazed at the malignity with which this ignorant woman endeavoured to asperse the memory of his father, (whilst every sentence till the last, must appear in the eye of pure religion and candour as his highest eulogium) and curious to know from what source this malignity proceeded; whilst Jael, leaning over the back of the chair from which she had arisen, her features still fixed and without expression, in the same monotonous tone of voice proceeded :—

"It is a serious thing, young man, a very serious thing, for one to be left gardeen to a wealthy child. Oh! it is a trying matter, a grand snare, laid by Satan, the mighty tempter, the great deceiver. Money is the root and spring of all evil; it is the bait the wicked one makes use of to draw the children of vanity astray, as he did thy father. Oh! it was an abomination for him to keep Jacob Holmes as he did, without even pocket money, whilst he was throwing away his interest by handfuls."

"I do not understand you," said Reuben; "Jacob Holmes was an orphan child, adopted, brought up and educated by the charity of my father."

"Ah! that was the story squire Dudley told, when he first comed here; but we knows better things now. It was the money of the good Jacob Holmes on which he was living; for I expect if it had been his own he would a been more careful of it. But thy father, young man, has wronged the orphan of his right, and made himself rich at the expense of the son of the widow, and the curses of the widow and the orphan will rest upon him and his children."

"So be it," cried Reuben; "I fear no judgment for my father's actions. Oh that I may be enabled to emulate his virtues, to tread his footsteps—But I feel I am to blame in listening to one, whose aim is to calumniate the memory of him who gave me being. What could he have done to deserve thy hatred, that even his sacred dust cannot rest in peace? Did he ever wrong thee or thy family?"

"No, not he; I expect he was the means of my getting a matter a twenty pounds or so, that I should a lost; but then, though it did me a kindness, it did not tell much to his credit, though (as master said) we got our money, and what matter was it to us who paid it?"

"True," cried Reuben, "that could be of but little confequence indeed; but pray tell me, how came my father to render you this fervice?"

"Why I expect it is fo long a ftory, you will be tired."

"Tell it as concifely as poffible," faid Reuben; "I will anfwer for my patience; and even fhould it be more lengthy than I expect, when a father's good deeds are the theme, what fon could be weary or feel his attention flag?"

Jael looked at him, with mouth and eyes extended. She comprehended nothing more than that he defired to hear how his father happened to pay her twenty pounds; fo, ftill leaning over the back of the chair, fhe began:—

"I expect it's a matter a three years agone, a woman comed over in a fhip from London, an fhe faid as how fhe comed ater her hufband. She was as pretty a body, I expect, as one mought fee in a hundred. Mafter and I was juft married, and got into this here houfe. So fhe comed an wanted to board with us, an fhe had a baby with her about fix months old. So fhe had plenty of money, an a golden watch, an a power of fine clothes; fo we let her have our beft room, an hired a girl to wait on her."

"Plenty of money, a gold watch, and fine clothes," faid Reuben mentally, and he turned from the felfifh narrator to hide his indignation and contempt.

"Well, ater a while," fhe continued, "we found as how the parfon fhe cum'd ater was not her hufband; he had kept her company, and I expect, promifed to marry her; but he would neither own her nor her child when he faw'd her here. So fhe did nothing but cry, and cry, and kifs her little girl; fhe was too proud to work, and fo, when her money was fpent, and her golden watch fold, fhe faid fhe wifhed to die."

"Poor, unfortunate girl," faid Reuben in a tone of commiferation, "how I pity her!"

"Pity

" Pity her indeed," faid Jael, " a creeter! When I
told her fhe mought get a good living by going out to
farvice, fhe faid fhe knew not how to labour for bread;
them was her very words, an fo fhe would not eat nor
drink, an ufed to go night ater night with her clothes
on, fitting on the floor, and refting her head on a chair
or the window-feat. She at laft grew fo weak, that
fhe was not able to walk; fo I went and axed her
what fhe meant by going on fo; for fhe know'd as
how fhe owed me above twelve pound; fo fhe only
anfwered me, ' fhe meant and wifhed to die, and at
once releafe me and herfelf.' But then fhe would
hug her baby, and cry, ' Poor little wretch! what
will become of you? It were better we both died together."

Reuben's eyes gliftened with the dew of fenfibility,
but he was filent.

" So at laft fhe fell into a confumption; I expect it
was all owing to her pride that was fo humbled and
mortified. So feeing as how fhe was like to become a
trouble to mafter, I told her how fhe muft go about
her bufinefs; for I wanted my room to let to fomebody elfe."

" Did you tell the poor dying creature fo?" faid
Reuben, in a tone expreffive at once of anger and commiferation; " did you tell her fo?"

" Yes, I did," faid Jael; " for you knows felf-pref-
ervation is the firft law in nature, and 'tis but right
one fhould chriften their own child firft. So madam
got up, and with her child in her hand crawled down
ftairs; and when fhe got into the kitchen, fhe fainted
away. So fquire Dudley was in the next room, and
he heard the buftle in the kitchen, and came out to
axe what was the matter; fo when I told him, he
threw me the money fhe owed me; but he called me
a very bad name. Then he got two men to carry the
fick body to his own lodging in an arm chair, an there
he had her tended and doctored; but that did no good,
for fhe died. An there he took the child, and had it
put out to nurfe, though every body faid he ought to
be

be afhamed of himfelf for doing any thing for fuch a fort of woman."

"Oh my father! my father!" exclaimed Reuben, "ought not thy fon to exult that thy character was fuch, that even the afperfions of thy enemies are thy higheft praife?——And where is the poor child?" addreffing himfelf to the woman.

"Dead; for ater the fquire went away, Jacob Holmes would not pay for its being nurfed; and who can blame him? There had been enough of his intereft wafted already."

"I tell thee, woman," faid Reuben, "Jacob Holmes never had any property whatever but what he enjoyed from the beneficence of my father."

"I expect that ftory won't do you much good here," faid Jael; "but howfoever, you axed about the child, an fo as I was faying, it went to the poor-houfe, and there it died."

As Jael finifhed this hiftory, fhe took the difh and plate from the table, and left the room, and Reuben fhortly after retired to bed, but not to reft. To find his father's memory traduced, to find Jacob Holmes in actual poffeffion of his eftate, and believed univerfally the lawful owner of it, was a fhock he had never dreamed of receiving, and knew not how to fupport.

As he had imagined he fhould, without the leaft difficulty, take immediate poffeffion of the effects his father had left in Holmes's care, and as he knew there muft be confiderable money in his hands, arifing from the fale of merchandize with which he had been entrufted, our hero had taken but a very fmall fum of money with him from England. Indeed his finances in general were in fo confined a ftate, that he could not command a fum of any confequence. It was therefore no fmall addition to his uneafy fenfations, that he was in a ftrange land, with very little money, and without a fingle friend. However, he determined the next morning to vifit Jacob Holmes; for, ftill unwilling to believe human nature could be guilty of fuch depravity, or that a man, adding difhonefty to ingratitude, would return the benevolence of the father by wronging the

fon,

son, he indulged a feeble hope, that his reception would be better than from what he had heard he had a right to expect.

After a restless and perturbated night, he arose with the earliest dawn, and having inquired for a horse, was preparing to visit Jacob, when, as he went to the door with the design of mounting, he saw the identical person he was going in search of just alighting. Spite of the intelligence he had received from Jael, Reuben's heart warmed with affection, when he beheld a person who had been so dear to his father, and who had borne himself and sister in his arms a thousand times. He darted forward, and took his hand. " Jacob," said he, in a tone of fraternal tenderness, " Jacob, how are you ?"

" Well, I thank thee, young man," replied Jacob, coldly withdrawing his hand, and stalking with upright formality into the house.

Though chilled by his frigid manner, Reuben felt his heart contract, yet he followed him into the parlour, and laying his hand upon his shoulder, cried, " Don't you know me, Jacob ?"

" No, really, young man, thou hast greatly the advantage of me ; I do not recollect ever to have seen thee before."

Nearly six years had elapsed since Jacob had left England, and a period of that length might naturally be supposed to make a material alteration in the person of a youth, whom it had transformed, as it past, from a cheerful, blooming boy, to the graceful, well-informed man. But still there was sufficient in his manner, voice and features, to inform Jacob Holmes, at one glance, who it was addressed him. But Jacob had found a short memory very useful on many occasions, and was determined to try its efficacy on this ; and therefore boldly asserted he had never, to his recollection, seen Reuben before.

" Look at me again, friend Jacob," said our hero, " you surely cannot totally forget the face of Reuben Dudley, the son of your friend, Mr. Dudley, of Lancashire."

" I do

"I do remember thee now," said Jacob; "but how is it, young man, that I see thee in the garb of the children of vanity? thy father wore it not."

Reuben was now struck by obferving the very formal and primitive appearance of Jacob. "I hope I am not the lefs pious," said Reuben with a fmile, "becaufe my coat is not cut in the fame fafhion as thine, or my hat quite fo large. I am come to inquire after my father's effects, and to releafe you from the trouble you have fo long had, of attending to concerns which may interfere with your own bufinefs and purfuits."

"Thou art welcome to Philadelphia, friend Reuben," said Jacob, affuming fome fmall degree of cordiality; "I fhall be ready to give an account of my ftewardfhip whenever thou fhalt demand it. In the mean time, go home with me, and fojourn till thou canft fuit thyfelf better. I am going acrofs the river on fome little matter of bufinefs; when I return, we will go together to my houfe."

"Ah!" said Reuben, after Jacob had left him, "I fear this man has a difhoneft heart; but I will not judge too haftily."

Towards evening, Jacob returned, and with our hero proceeded to the houfe of Mr. Dudley, which he now claimed as his own. It was fituated on the declivity of a hill, that, rifing gradually behind it, fheltered it from the wintry blafts, and whofe fides were covered with a variegated wood; the fpreading pine, the cedar, the wild walnut, the hiccory, the birch, the oak, were intermingled, and beautifully diverfified the foliage, whilft here and there the parfimon tree difplayed its tempting but deceitful fruit, which, like the frivolous pleafures of the world, are lovely to the eye when viewed at a diftance; but when tafted, difappoint the expectation, and its harfh acidity is rejected with difguft. Here too, in native beauty, bloomed the laureftinus, and here innumerable wild flowering fhrubs, gave richnefs and fafcination to the fcene, whilft the mild fouth-weft breeze wafted their delicious odours to the fenfes, refrefhing and invigorating nature.

ture. From the front of the manfion, the green banks floped gently to the margin of the Schuylkill, and difplayed the advantages of cultivation. Here were fields of ripened grain; here were paftures, where the fheep and cattle repofed in fafety, and feafted on luxuriant verdure. To a mind fo pure, fo every way formed to conceive and enjoy the beauties of nature as was that of our hero, the fcene was enchanting; he rode on, wrapt in contemplation and delight. At length perceiving the houfe, which juft peeped from between the furrounding trees, he afked, " Is that my father's houfe ?"

" That is my houfe," faid Jacob.

" And how far from hence is my father's place ?"

" This is the place he defigned to purchafe."

" Defigned ?"

" Yes, but he went away before he concluded the bargain, and I have fince made it mine."

They had now reached the houfe, entered a large gate and difmounted, when Jacob, with affected folemnity and humility, welcomed Reuben to his homely dwelling, and prefented him to his wife Dinah, a pretty Quaker, whofe heart was naturally good, but whofe underftanding was fcarcely above mediocrity, and had been cramped by prejudice, and whofe knowledge of the world extended not beyond her own immediate family concerns. She loved Jacob fincerely; he was in her eyes the firft of human beings; and when fhe prefented her hand to welcome Reuben, it was with an air of friendly cordiality; for he was the friend of her hufband fhe thought, and as fuch, claimed the firft place in her efteem, and was entitled to every mark of refpect and attention. She was more than commonly careful that her fupper fhould be good in its kind, and ferved with neatnefs. A chamber was prepared for him by her orders, and thither he retired at an early hour, to reflect on his own uncomfortable fituation, and lament the ingratitude and difhonefty of Jacob Holmes.

CHAP.

C H A P. XII.

THE next morning after breakfaſt, Reuben requeſted to ſee a ſtatement of his accounts, that
he might be a judge of what he ought to do ; but Jacob told him he expected his wife's father the enſuing
day, and as he had been confidentially entruſted with
the mutual concerns between Mr. Dudley and himſelf,
he thought he would be a proper perſon to be preſent
at the final adjuſtment of their accounts.

To this delay Reuben with reluctance conſented,
and the day paſſed on heavily enough ; for notwithſtanding the novelty, beauty and variety of the ſurrounding objects, his mind was too much occupied in
reflections on his own forlorn ſituation, and from
thence reverted to the inconveniencies and misfortunes
to which his beloved ſiſter might be ſubject, ſhould he
be detained from England, and by the fraud of Jacob
Holmes rendered incapable of remitting her any pecuniary aſſiſtance.

On the following morning, Jacob's father-in-law arrived, and he, with great formality bringing out a
heap of papers, began to read over to our hero long
accounts of money paid.

" And pray," ſaid Reuben, " where is the account
of the ſales of the merchandize from whence this money aroſe ? My father left very conſiderable property
in your hands, and I have every reaſon to imagine the
eſtate he purchaſed here was entirely paid for, as he
drew large ſums from his agent in England for that
purpoſe."

" Thou canſt not prove what thou doſt aſſert," ſaid
Jacob, with a look of malignant ſatisfaction ; " and I
believe thou wilt find it difficult to diſpoſſeſs me of an
eſtate, the title deeds of which are all made out in my
name ; and to prove my right thereto, I have the re-
ceipts given to me for various ſums of money, paid
by me at different times, till the whole was paid for."

A a

" But

"But tell me," said Reuben, "whose property was the money with which you made thefe payments? Was it not my father's."

Reuben fixed his penetrating eyes on the face of Jacob, as he made this interrogation, whofe eye fell beneath the fcrutinizing glance; he dared not meet the honeft look; his cheek turned pale, his lips trembled, and his tongue faltered, as ftooping, with a pretence of replacing fome papers in a box, but in reality to hide emotions he could not fupprefs, he replied, that the money was his own.

"Oh Jacob!" faid Reuben, "how canft thou affert fuch a falfehood? Does not thy heart fmite thee whilft thou art thus deliberately planning to rob the orphans of their juft due?" His heart fwelled; he could not proceed.

Friend Simcox, the father-in-law of Jacob, took upon him to anfwer:

"It was thy father, young man, who endeavoured to wrong the orphan of his juft due; it is thou haft occafion to blufh for his evil deeds. This worthy young man has improved the trifle of property Reuben Dudley left behind him, and all demands againft him difcharged, there remains a fum amounting to about fifty or fixty guineas, which Jacob is ready to pay whenever thou fhalt demand it; and I would advife thee to return home in the firft fhip that goes."

A converfation now enfued, which convinced our hero that he had little hope of ever obtaining his right; for was he even to apply to the law, money would be wanting to profecute his fuit, or to prove his right to the eftate, which was called Mount Pleafant. Mr. Dudley had with him, at the time he was loft, all the original papers neceffary to be produced, the duplicates of which were in the hands of Jacob. That all the papers were irrecoverably loft, Reuben had informed this unworthy fteward of by letter, immediately after the fatal cataftrophe.

There was another circumftance, which militated much againft him, and with which he was not informed till that hour. Mr. Dudley had ever placed an unbounded

bounded confidence in Jacob Holmes; he was a man of eafy difpofition, fond of agriculture, and fuch purfuits as might ultimately tend to benefit the country of which he was about to become an inhabitant, and to render his new purchafe at once beautiful and beneficial. He had therefore, after having furveyed the land, and had one converfation with the perfon of whom he was about to purchafe it, entrufted the whole management of the bufinefs to Jacob. The whole of the payment not having been made before he left Philadelphia, he had never had the deeds properly executed, and the news of his being drowned arriving before they were completed, Jacob conceived the idea of having them filled up in his own name. He had, from their firft arrival in Philadelphia, been artfully undermining the reputation of his benefactor, by reprefenting himfelf as a youth of fortune entrufted to his guardianfhip; and whenever he made a payment, he always gave the perfon to underftand that it was his own money that he was advancing to ferve his friend Dudley. This idea having been artfully propagated, and univerfally credited, and Mr. Dudley and himfelf being equally ftrangers in the place, Jacob found no difficulty in procuring the eftate to be fecured to himfelf. He found it much more difficult to filence the admonitions of his confcience. But the heart naturally ungrateful, by eafy gradations may be habituated to admit, and even approve, every other vice. Gratitude is the foundation and fource of all the moral virtues. For if we receive the many great and good gifts of our beneficent Creator without a grateful fenfibility, we no longer love him; and whom we do not love, we become indifferent, whether we obey or ferve.

Jacob ftifled the remonftrances of confcience; and even when he faw our hero, could he have done it without fear of the law, would fcarcely have hefitated to give him a quick paffport from this to a better world.

The accounts adjufted according to the plan Jacob had concerted, and which old friend Simcox never
fcrutinized,

scrutinized, because he wished not to be undeceived, the paltry sum of fifty-seven guineas was offered to our hero, for which he was requested to give a general acquittal of all demands whatever, on the person or property of Jacob Holmes.

When this money and this curious acquittal were presented to Reuben, the one for his acceptance, the other for his signature, his indignation arose beyond the bounds within which he had endeavoured to confine it.   He rose from his seat, pushing, with an indignant motion, the proffered money from him.

" Add not insult to injury," said he, " Jacob Holmes ; I would recapitulate who and what you are ; but there are several forcible reasons that oblige me to silence. And first—You, Jacob, are not answerable for the faults of those, whose memories the grave has consigned to eternal oblivion ; nor dare I speak of obligations ; for well I know he who conferred them, ever made it a rule to fix the seal of silence on his own good deeds, and the faults of his fellow-creatures.   As to taking the money you offer and signing this acquittal, they are alike repugnant to my feelings.   I have no demand on your property, Jacob ; I ask but for my own ; the property of my late dear father is mine and my sister's.   For myself, I value it not.   I am young, unencumbered, have hands to labour, or an arm to fight.   I cannot want bread.   But my sister, lovely, innocent, unacquainted with the world, must she be dependent ?   Must she court the smiles of that world ? Must she submit to the contumely of the haughty, the slights of the unfeeling, or the more humiliating pity of affected sensibility, and in return procure the scanty means of bare existence ?   No ! I cannot tamely give up her right, however I might relinquish my own. I do assert, Jacob Holmes, and you, friend Simcox, bear witness to the assertion, that this estate, this house, this land, the stock and all appertaining to it, is the joint property of myself and sister Rachel, inherited from our father, Reuben Dudley ; nor will I relinquish the claim whilst I have existence."

He

He took his hat, and walked towards the door; then turning, he added—

"Jacob, poor as thou haſt, by thy diſhoneſty, made me, I pity thee. Yes, Jacob Holmes, I pity thee. Thou haſt reduced me to poverty, and thyſelf to miſery."

Dinah, Jacob's wife, had overheard the converſation; not at firſt intentionally, but paſſing through the parlour that adjoined the room in which they were, and catching a word that awakened her curioſity, ſtopped. Curioſity, when once awakened, is hard to be repelled, at leaſt in women, ſay the oppoſite ſex. Whether we are more troubled with the impulſe than our fathers, brothers, or huſbands, I will not now diſpute; it is a certainty Dinah ſtopped to liſten to a converſation which had powerfully excited her's.

It has been remarked, that Dinah's underſtanding was not of the moſt brilliant kind; but ſhe poſſeſſed that plain, natural ſenſe which enabled her to have a full and clear perception of right and wrong. Her wiſhes were moderate, her wants few. She was equally a ſtranger to avarice, luxury and ambition. She liſtened to the accuſation of Reuben, and all that ſhe poſſeſſed of ſenſibility was awakened; not that ſhe feared to be deprived of part of the comforts and conveniencies ſhe at preſent enjoyed; but the man whom ſhe thought the firſt and beſt of all God's creatures, had been accuſed of fraud; if innocently, her indignation would fall on his accuſer; if juſtly, then Jacob Holmes was no longer the perfect being ſhe had ever believed him; and if guilty of diſhoneſty, Dinah felt ſhe could no longer reſpect him. Yet ſhe was unwilling to believe aught to his prejudice; ſhe therefore approached our hero as he left the apartment.

"Thou muſt not leave us in anger, Reuben Dudley," ſaid ſhe, laying her hand on his arm as he attempted to paſs her; "if Jacob has done thee wrong, I dare affirm it was not wilfully; and if thou canſt make it appear, he will make thee ample reſtitution."

"Do not detain me, madam," ſaid he, gently freeing himſelf from her hold; "I am in haſte to depart;

but I part not in difpleafure with you. God blefs you, and make you as happy as you are innocent." Then kiffing the child, which fhe held in her arms, he went haftily to the ftable, faddled his horfe, and without any oppofition, mounted and proceeded to Philadelphia.

Dinah entered the room where her father and hufband were fitting. " Good Jacob," faid fhe, " let not the young man leave us in anger. I do remember his father; I have heard him fpeak of thee with affection, as though thou hadft been his own child. I verily believe he did love thee, Jacob; for his fake, let me call back the young man."

" No," cried Jacob, with a ftern look, " ftay where you are (for fhe was about to quit the room); the youth has behaved unfeemly, refufes the money which I have tendered him, and lays claim to my whole eftate."

" And art thou fure, quite fure, Jacob Holmes," faid fhe, and her countenance expreffed fear and doubt, " art thou quite fure that he has no lawful claim upon thy property? In good truth, I thought he fpoke as though he were affured of his right."

" Dinah," faid Jacob, " thou art a good woman; thou doft underftand thy houfehold concerns; they are fufficient for the extent of thy capacity. I pray thee, Dinah, trouble not thyfelf with what is beyond thy comprehenfion. Thou art a ftranger to the world, totally unacquainted with the arts and deceptions with which it abounds."

" Verily thou fayeft right," fhe replied mildly, " but as I could not affert a falfehood without hefitating, nor claim what was the right of another, without blufhing, I judged by the firm voice and unembarraffed manner of the young man."

" If thou didft judge of him by thyfelf, Dinah," faid her father, " thou didft wrong."

" Perhaps fo, father; I am fimple, and uninftructed. But I hope I am not equally wrong in judging of my hufband's heart by my own; for I think, Jacob," continued fhe, and fhe laid her hand affectionately

ately

ately on his arm, " I think I would rather be poor and honeft, than rich at the coft of another ; wouldft not thou, Jacob ?"

Jacob could not reply, nor even lift his eyes to the face of his wife ; he rather unkindly fhook off the hand fhe had laid on his arm, and the child juft then beginning to cry, he bade her take away the noify boy, for it difturbed him. Dinah obeyed in filence, repaired to a diftant apartment, and as the infant drew from her bofom life's nourifhing fluid, fhe hung fondly over him and wept.

Our hero in the mean time returned to Philadelphia. His mind was haraffed, his fpirits depreffed ; he endeavoured to compofe himfelf, and to form fome plan for his future conduct ; but, inexperienced as he was, he wanted a friend to advife and direct him. " To-morrow," faid he, " I will deliver the letters I brought with me."

Reuben was elegant in his appearance, though perfectly plain in his drefs ; but there was an air of fuperiority, not pride or felf-confequence ; it was that native dignity of manner, which is ever infpired by confcious rectitude of heart and unimpeached integrity. His perfon was ftriking, and what would in general be termed handfome. It will naturally be fuppofed he was therefore received with politenefs, and would have prepoffeffed almoft every one in his favour, but that almoft all whom he converfed with were prejudiced perfons, who conceived that Jacob Holmes's intereft had been much injured by the extravagance and folly of his father.

From feveral to whom he delivered letters, (which letters were nothing more than a fimple annunciation of his name and family) he received invitations to their houfes ; but when his circumftances began to be fufpected, and indeed the opennefs of his difpofition led him rather to expofe than endeavour to conceal them ; when it was difcovered he wanted friends who would be farther ferviceable than merely giving him a dinner, or a bed for a few nights ; he found, by their diftant, frigid manner, that he was no longer welcome,

welcome, that he was thought an intruder. His independent spirit took fire; he no longer visited, he shut himself in his apartment, lived sparingly, and revolved a thousand different plans by which he hoped to immerge from obscurity, and rescue from oblivion the name of Dudley. He had applied to several professors of the law to give him advice and assistance for the recovery of his right; but his poverty was known to be certain, his claims were supposed very doubtful; no one would undertake the cause.

Can any situation be more distressing, than that of a young man, of brilliant understanding, aspiring genius, laudable ambition and uncorrupted heart, thus deprived of every means of improving his fortune, or exerting his talents, in such a manner as might at once be advantageous to himself and society in general? In a large and flourishing town, without a friend, without even an associate towards whom he felt the smallest degree of affection, how forlorn, how totally devoid of comfort were his days! A solitary individual, who looked on the surrounding multitude, whom business or pleasure had drawn together, and saw not one with whom the feelings of his soul could claim kindred, not one who conceived or commiserated his sufferings, or, should sickness overtake him, would feel interested for his recovery, or drop a tear of regret over his bier, should it please Heaven to put a period to his existence.

Depressed by his own situation, and tortured by reflections on what might possibly be the distresses of his sister, Reuben had not courage even to write to her. "Why should I torment her," he would say, "by an account of my ill success? Why write, when I have not one comfortable idea to transmit? No, I will suffer her to suppose I am no more; my silence will lead her to imagine I have paid the debt of nature. She will grieve, but time will soothe and lessen her affliction, which even at the first will not be half so poignant, as the knowledge of my existing in a state of obscurity, without money, without credit, without friends would occasion."

Jelly

Jeſſy Oliver too, would ſometimes intrude on his thoughts; but he endeavoured to baniſh hopes, which, ſpite of reaſon, would often ariſe. "She is loſt to me," he would ſay; "I ſhall never ſee her more, or ſhould I, will my ruined fortune entitle me to the hand of a woman of her rank? But Miſs Oliver is above valuing a man for the paltry diſtinctions of wealth. Then ought I not to repel, with the utmoſt force of honour, every ſelfiſh paſſion that would inſpire a wiſh to degrade her by a union with my humble deſtiny?"

Theſe were the hourly reflections of our hero. Night came, and he, cheerleſs, ſought the pillow of repoſe, courting oblivion in the arms of ſleep. But the ſomnific power was deaf to his ſolicitations; or if, perchance, he paid a tranſient viſit, ſealing his weary eyes for a few hours, Memory, ſtill wakeful, would repreſent paſt ſcenes, or fondly paint illuſive preſent joys.

Rachel and Jeſſy were the objects of his dreams. Sometimes he ſaw his ſiſter on the brink of a precipice, from the edge of which a horrid ſpectre ſtrove to precipitate her, when, as ſhe fell, Jeſſy appeared with arms extended to catch and ſave her from plunging into the dreadful abyſs that yawned beneath. Sometimes his fancy repreſented his ſiſter and Miſs Oliver embarked in a ſmall and ill-accommodated veſſel, on a tempeſtuous ocean; the ſky lowered, the winds howled, and glaring meteors ſhot along the horizon; the waves roſe tremendous, broke on the little barque, and ſhe diſappeared. Then in a moment he ſaw the fair form of Jeſſy leading his fainting ſiſter up the beach, when, as they ſtrove to avoid the encroaching tide, their feet would ſlip, and ſucceeding waves again immerſe them in the foaming flood; and then again an inſtantaneous change (for the viſions of ſleep are wild and unconnected) would repreſent thoſe dear objects of his fondeſt ſolicitude ſeated in an arbour of evergreens, twined round with myrtle flowers and roſes. He ſaw them, talked to them; ſweet ſmiling infants ſeemed to play around them. Archibald Oliver too was there, and a ſtranger of noble mien. But
ſuddenly

suddenly some new terror would arise; he started, awoke, and all the fascinating vision fled. Sleep thus agitated and disturbed afforded but little refreshment, and in a few weeks our hero was but the shadow of his former self.

About this period the natives, who had been driven back into the Allegany Mountains, and who had pitched their habitation, in different tribes, upon the furthermost banks of the Susquehannah, Allegany and Mohawk rivers, made frequent descents into the new settled parts of the country, plundering, burning and destroying with impunity every European settlement within their reach.

In consequence of the treachery and rapacity of these savages, it became necessary to send a military force to repel them, and guard the lives and properties of the inoffensive settlers; and Patrick Gordon, Esq. who at that time governed the colony, proposed raising a volunteer company for this service. Proper officers were accordingly appointed, and the company increased daily.

The noise this occasioned in the city awakened Reuben from his lethargy of despondency. The native spark of ambition, which had so long lain dormant, was fanned to a flame, and with the sanguine ardour ever inseparable from youth, vainly imagining to deserve was to insure preferment, he offered himself to the Governor, and was accepted.

His candour in speaking of himself and circumstances; his youth, his manners, his open, unembarrassed air, and intelligent, manly countenance, spoke volumes in his favour, and procured him the honourable appointment of standard bearer.

Early in the spring, they began their plan of operations, and marched towards the margin of the Susquehannah. During the spring and summer months, they had several rencounters with the Indians, and being in general victorious, they had driven and pursued them a farther distance into the country than they imagined, and the weather began to grow cold before they thought of returning. At length the officers
having

having unanimoufly agreed that it would be hazard-
ous, as well as of little ufe, to purfue their retreating
foe any farther, preparations were made for their gaining good quarters before the inclement feafon fhould
be too far advanced.   The main body had began their
march, and our hero, (who was now promoted to the
rank of lieutenant) with a fmall party, was left to follow the next morning with the baggage.

Amongft the party of which Reuben was fecond in
command, was an Irifh youth, who particularly attached himfelf to our hero.   O'Neil was ignorant, but honeft.   Like an unpolifhed diamond, his outward appearance was uncouth and rough ; but within was a jewel
of ineftimable price.   Simplicity, integrity and humanity were the characterifties of his foul.   This young
man was fo pointed in his attentions to our hero, that
it could not pafs unnoticed.   One day, when he had
been voluntarily performing fome little menial office,
Reuben thus addreffed him :

"By what good fortune, O'Neil, is it, that I am fo
particularly favoured with your kind offices ?"

"Arrah, my fwate mafter," faid O'Neil, "by no
great matter of good fortune, only that your Honour
happened to have a father."

"Did you know my father, O'Neil ?"

"Och ! and did you think I did not know him ?
Many is the time I havent ferved him, to be fure ; and
while Pat O'Neil lives, he will ferve any that wears
the name of Dudley, for his fake ; aye, by night or by
day, fair weather or foul, all's one for that.   And did
you think now I could ever forget how he paid the
money for that fwate crater, Madam Juliana, and how
he had her nurfed, and ——"

It now ftruck Reuben that he might, through
O'Neil, learn fome further intelligence concerning a
circumftance, which he had often thought of fince the
information he received from Jael, on the firft day of
his arrival ; for he naturally fuppofed that the Juliana
he talked of was the unfortunate woman, whofe forrows his father had alleviated.   He put feveral queftions to his humble friend, and gleaned from him a
tale

tale which cannot be better related than in his own simple language.

"It was in dear Ireland," said he, "about fifteen miles from Dublin's fwate city, that my honoured mafter had a houfe; I would tell you his name, but that I can't, becaufe, you fee, I promifed Madam Juliana never to breathe a fyllable of the matter. She was all the child he had; and he thought fhe was too good for the fun to fhine on, and fo fhe was; but fhe was not quite fo good neither, that is to fay, fhe might a done better than to liften to a fpallpeen of a lord that was an Englifhman, only that he was born in Dublin. So he faw her one day when fhe was riding out, and he fpoke to her, and rode home with her; and when my mafter faw who he was, he turned him out of the houfe, and never afked him into it; and I heard him tell Madam Juliana at fupper-time, that he was no bet-ter than he fhould be, an if he had faid not half fo good, he would have faid more in his favour than he deferved. I was a boy, pleafe your Honour, then, and half a guinea tempted me to take a letter and give it to her. Och! the remembrance of that makes my heart ache very often; for if I had not been fo eafily perfuaded, my good mafter and my fwate lady might a been alive and happy together now. So fhe did not mind what her father faid, but wrote to him, and met him; and one evening he brought a chaife and four horfes. It was after funfet, and the new moon gave but little light; fo fhe faid, "Patrick, will you walk with me as far as the Mill-Bridge?"

"Now it was October, and the wind was fharp. So fays I, ' It is cold, my lady,' fays I."

"A little or fo," faid fhe, and her voice feemed to tremble. "It is a little cold, Patrick, but here is fome-thing to keep you warm;" fo fhe put a crown piece into my hand. So we went out together, and as I opened the gate, fhe turned and looked up at the win-dows of her father's ftudy; for there was a big row of trees from the houfe to the gate, and his ftudy win-dows were right oppofite. So fhe looked at them,

and

and lifted up her hands and wrung them, and I heard her fob."

"You had better go back, Mifs," faid I; but fhe made me no anfwer, only walked very faft forward; and when I faw the lord and the chaife, my mind mifgave me, and I faid, "Och! Mifs July, what are you going to be after doing?"

"Do not be frightened, my good lad," faid fhe, "but go back and take this letter to my father."

"Go back?" faid I, "no! no! Pat O'Neil does no fuch thing; I could not bear to fee my poor old mafter die of the heart-break, or go crazy for your lofs."

"But you muft go back," faid the lord.

"But I won't," faid I; "I will follow my miftrefs to the end of the world, and farther too if needs muft."

"Och! your Honour, I cannot tell how I felt when I thought they were going away without me. He had lifted my poor lady in, who feemed almoft dying; fo I caught hold of her gown, and hung upon the ftep of the chaife, and fwore never to quit my hold till my hands were cut off."

"Let him go with us, poor fellow," faid my lady.

"He will betray us," faid the lord.

"No, I will not," faid I; "let me go with my miftrefs, and I will not fpeak a word to nobody; but I will protect her, fight for her, die for her."

"Get up behind," faid he.

"I fprung up in a giffey, and away we went. Well, that night we went aboard a packet, and failed away to England, and there a Roman Catholic prieft married them; but the falfe-hearted lord never meant the thing that was right all this while; for in a week or two he grew cool, and at laft told her he was no Catholic, and therefore not her hufband, and that to provide for her during her life, he had got her a hufband, and when fhe was married, fhe might go back to her father. So a captain ufed to come with him, and I don't know how they managed; but Madam Juliana was married to him, and I thought the next day fhe

would

would have gone diftracted. She tore her beautiful flaxen hair, and wrung her hands, and cried and fobbed. So then, in a little while her hufband went away over fea, and then after Madam lay in, fhe followed him, and when fhe came to Philadelphia, he would not own her, and fhe pined and pined, till at laft——"

Here the voice of poor O'Neil failed. His honeft heart burft forth at his eyes.

"Spare yourfelf, Patrick," faid Reuben, "for I think I know the reft."

"Not quite all, your Honour," faid Patrick; "for on the day before fhe died, your good father, Heaven blefs him for it, let me fee her. She was almoft gone, and fpoke fo low, I could fcarce hear her."

"Patrick," faid fhe, "I want to thank you for your fteady attachment to me. I would fain leave you fomething as a remembrance; but I have nothing left of any value."

"My dear, fwate, angel lady," faid I, "you will leave me the remembrance of your precious felf. I never! no, never! fhall forget you."

"I fent for you," faid fhe, "to tell you, Patrick, that, fhould you ever fee my father, he may know from you that I have been punifhed, juftly, I own, though very feverely, for my difobedience to the beft of parents. I leave my child an orphan, in a ftrange land; but my benefactor has promifed to take care of it. You, I know, will, to the utmoft of your power, protect it."

She fainted before fhe had finifhed; they took me out of the room, and I never faw her again. Och! your Honour, fhe is furely in heaven; for to die heart-broken, and in poverty, in a ftrange land, without any friends——Do you not think fhe is in heaven? do you not think her fins were pardoned?"

"We will hope fo," faid Reuben; "but difobedience to parents is certainly a deep offence againft the commandments of our Creator."

"But fhe was very penitent," faid O'Neil. Reuben was filent.

After this converfation, there feemed a kind of focial bond formed between Reuben and the young Irifh-
man;

man; the latter performing all the offices of a servant, the other practising all the kindness and benevolence of the best of masters. The autumn nights were cold; O'Neil would watch till he saw our hero in a slumber, then, adding his own blanket to the slight covering of Reuben's bed, he would wrap himself as well as he could in his great coat, and lie down on the ground beside him.

The baggage being placed in order ready for an early march, the soldiers and officers were retired to rest. O'Neil had, as usual, thrown his blanket over his master (as he delighted to call him) and the air being more than usually sharp, he found it impossible to sleep. He arose, and raking together the dying embers of a fire by which they had dressed their supper, began to re-kindle it. As he was thus employed, he thought he heard a rustling amongst the trees; and turning half round, perceived, by the faint light the fire cast around, the faces of two Indians peeping from behind a large tree. He gave a loud cry; the Indians uttered the war whoop; a scene of confusion and horror ensued, and in a few moments part of the little corps were slain, the rest wounded and made prisoners. Amongst the latter was our hero, and his faithful adherent, Patrick O'Neil.

CHAP. XIII.

Another Visit to savage Habitations.

THERE had, some little time previous to this event, been several of the Indian chiefs taken prisoners by the Europeans, and it was to this circumstance those, who were taken prisoners by the natives, owed the preservation of their lives, as the savages entertained hopes that by means of these they might procure the liberty of their captured brethren.

Their route lay across the country, and before they had reached their place of destination, a very heavy

fall

fall of fnow rendered the woods almoft impenetrable; but the Indians, inured from their infancy to cold, hunger, every fpecies of hardfhip, felt little or no inconvenience from the feverity of the feafon, whilft the Europeans funk under their accumulated fufferings; and of twelve who were taken prifoners, feven died by the way.

Reuben had been flightly wounded, and O'Neil had received a fcratch, as he called it, in endeavouring to preferve his mafter, from the tomahawk of an Indiar. But Reuben was by nature intrepid, and O'Neil was callous to every calamity that affected only himfelf. They mutually comforted and fupported each other, and were amongft the few who furvived at the end of their wearifome, pedeftrian journey.

The morning after their arrival at the Indian fettlement, the five furviving captives were prefented to the fachem, Wampoogohoon. His wigwam was larger and more commodious than thofe of his fubjects. It was well lined with fkins of various wild beafts, and on a kind of throne, covered with the fame materials, fat the fachem. At his left hand fat a woman, whofe complexion fpoke her of European defcent, and behind them ftood a young female, in appearance about feventeen years old. Her fkin was a fhade darker than that of the woman's; her eyes were of that kind of dark grey, which may almoft be termed blue, and yet, from the fhade of long black eyelafhes, may fometimes be miftaken for black. Their expreffion was at once foft and animated, and her dark auburn hair, which did not really curl, but hung in waves down her back and over her fhoulders, was ornamented with a few glafs beads, and a tuft of fcarlet feathers, fancifully arranged, and not entirely devoid of tafte. The reft of her drefs, though greatly fimilar to the other women, had a fomething of delicacy, in its formation and method of being put on, that was particularly pleafing to Europeans. Her figure was above the middle fize, yet not robuft enough to be thought mafculine, though every feature glowed with ruddy health, every limb difplayed the ftrength and firmnefs of her frame.

She

She ftood with her right hand leaning on the fachem's fhoulder, in her left fhe held an unbraced bow, and a quiver full of arrows was flung acrofs her back.

Wampoogohoon received the captives with a kind of fullen dignity. He fpoke to them in very bad Englifh, but they underftood fufficient to comprehend that he mean to detain them till the captured Indians were returned in fafety.

During the time he was fpeaking, Reuben looked attentively at the two women, who from their places, and the univerfal refpect paid them, he concluded were the wife and daughter of the chief. The penfivenefs manifeft in the countenance of the elder, the beauty and majefty of the younger, awakened in his bofom a wifh to be acquainted with their ftory; for he was certain they were of European extraction, though of what nation he could not determine, as they had neither of them fpoke.

At length, when the conference was ended, and the fachem waved his hand for them to depart, his wife arofe, and fpoke to him in the Mohawk tongue. Reuben perceived, from the foft tone of her voice and her earneft manner, that it was a fupplication. He anfwered, but not with the gentleft accent; fhe laid her hand on his arm, and repeated her requeft, in which fhe was joined by Eumea, his daughter. He looked irrefolute for a moment, then feeming to acquiefce in their demands, arofe from his feat, and taking his bow and arrows, was followed by his attendants out of the wigwam.

The two interefting females now came forward, and the eldeft, whofe name was Victoire, addreffed our hero in very tolerable French:

"Stranger, I am forry for your captivity, though my fituation amongft thefe Indians makes me appear your enemy. Yourfelf and companions are no doubt furprifed, to fee a perfon of my complexion fo intimately connected with one of theirs; my ftory may be told in a few words. My mother, a native of France, being of a proteftant family, and apprehending perfecution, emigrated to this new-found world,

in.

in company with her hufband, a man of ſtrict piety and principles. Their portion of worldly goods was not large ; they purchaſed a wild, uncultivated ſpot upon the borders of the Allegany, and by five years of indefatigable labour, rendered their little hut and ſurrounding garden, together with one field, tolerably comfortable ; but juſt when they began to taſte ſome ſmall degree of happineſs, which would ſcarcely have deſerved the name, but by being contraſted with the exceſs of hardſhip they had endured in clearing and rendering their little demeſne fit for cultivation ; then, at the moment when they hoped to reap the reward of their labours, a party of Mohawks came down upon them, rifled and deſtroyed their dwelling, murdered my father and two little brothers, and carried my wretched mother and myſelf, then only a year old, into captivity."

Victoire pauſed ; ſhe ſeemed affected ; a tear gliſtened in the expreſſive eyes of Eumea. At length the former proceeded :—

" My mother was a convincing proof of the exceſs of miſery the human mind can ſuffer ; ſhe ſurvived the loſs of a hufband tenderly beloved, and two children. I was her comfort, her ſtay, which held her to this world ; for my ſake ſhe bore captivity without murmuring, for my ſake ſhe wiſhed and ſtrove to preſerve her exiſtence ; ſhe lived till I was fourteen years old, and gave me every inſtruction which memory furniſhed, for ſhe had no aſſiſtance from books. She inſtilled into my young mind a knowledge and love of a ſupreme, benignant Being, and taught me to place my whole dependence on him, whoſe goodneſs was equal to his power.

" Wampoogchoon was the youngeſt ſon of the ſachem, who at that time governed this tribe ; he offered me his protection. My mother, in a dying ſtate, rather than leave me expoſed to inſult, adviſed me to accede to his propoſal, and I became his wife. His father and brothers are ſince dead, and you behold him a chief of the Mohawks. He is not unkind to me, and as the father of my children, I feel an affection

tion for him.   Eumea is the only furviving child I
have of fix ; for her fake, I wifh for fome intercourfe
with the Europeans, that her mind, which is not a barren foil, may receive the culture of education.   To
this end, I have requefted my hufband to permit you
to have a wigwam to yourfelves, where you may dwell
in quiet, till we hear of the fafety of thofe Indians who
have been detained by your party.   In return, I only
requeft you to exert your abilities to inftruct, in your
language, cuftoms, manners and religion, my child
Eumea."

Saying this, fhe prefented the Indian maid to Reuben, who affured Victoire he would do all in his power to return the obligation fhe had conferred.

He was then, with his companions, fhewn to a habitation that wore a trifling appearance of comfort ; in
it were three or four bear fkins, a quantity of clean
dry ftraw, fome dried fifh, venifon and maize, and
without was plenty of fuel.

Here our hero indulged himfelf in reflection ; and
often would his thoughts revert to his grandfather,
William Dudley, who was for many years in a fituation fomewhat fimilar.   But Reuben had feen too much
of favage men and manners to have a wifh to remain
amongft them, even though he might have been elevated to the higheft feat of dignity.

It was at once a comfort and amufement to Reuben, that he was obliged, for feveral hours every day,
to employ his mind, in order to cultivate that of his
pupil Eumea.   He contrived, by boiling the fhumak
berries, to make a liquid with which he could write on
white birch bark.   In this manner, he made an alphabet, which fhe prefently learnt ; and feeming to delight in attending to his inftructions, he experienced a
double fatisfaction in endeavouring to expand and inform her underftanding.   She was foon able to read
fhort fentences, which he compofed for her ; his hand
being generally employed, and his mind often totally
occupied in ftriving to recollect what might be of the
moft fervice to his lovely fcholar, he had little time for
reflection.

O'Neil

O'Neil laboured inceſſantly to keep their dwelling warm and tight; and ſometimes he went out with his gun, and brought home ſome kind of game, which ſerved to diverſify their ſcanty repaſts; and often Victoire would accompany her daughter to their wigwam, and on thoſe occaſions generally carried ſomething, which they thought a delicacy, ſuch as noa-cake, omanny, or ſuccataſh, viands compoſed of maize and dried beans; and thus wore away a very long and intenſely ſevere winter.   Reuben had been a priſoner above ſix months, and yet no news had arrived that could raiſe his hopes of ſpeedy liberation; and we muſt leave him amongſt theſe children of nature, and return to our heroine, whom we left married to Hamden Auberry, but living in the vicinity of Mary-lebone, under the aſſumed name of Dacres.

C H A P. XIV.

Scandal—Separation—Jealouſy.

IT has been already remarked, that Rachel had as little curioſity in her compoſition as any woman exiſting: ſhe was alſo by nature of a retired, quiet turn of mind, though eaſily led into ſcenes of diſſipation, in which, as ſhe generally mixed to gratify others, ſhe took but little ſatisfaction.   She therefore ſpent the chief of her time at home, either employed at her needle, or reading.   Hamden was fond of muſic; he had procured her a ſpinnet and a maſter.   She had a conſiderable taſte for drawing; Hamden was a proficient in the art; he directed and improved her judgment; pointed out proper ſubjects for the exerciſe of her genius, and with her book, her pencil, her needle, muſic, and ſome few domeſtic concerns, ſhe ſo ſweetly diverſified her time, that not one moment hung heavy on her hands.   Indeed, Rachel had, from her childhood, been taught that moſt uſeful, and to thoſe who practiſe it, that moſt pleaſant of all leſſons,

conſtant

conftant employment ; that it is better to be engaged in trifling purfuits (if innocent) than fuffer the mind to fink into inanity for want of exercife.

Hamden remained in London about a month or fix weeks after their marriage.   He then left her to return to his aunt, who was ftill in Scotland ; and at the time he bade his dear Rachel adieu, he purpofed returning to her within the fpace of two months.

After the departure of her hufband, our heroine continued the fame regular courfe of life.   But calumny, who has a hundred ears, a thoufand eyes, and ten thoufand tongues, not one of which is ever fuffered to flumber for an inftant, could not permit her to enjoy her favourite and inoffenfive employment unmolefted.

Though Rachel had imagined that the uniform tenor of her conduct was fuch, as might defy even the prying eyes of malice and envy, yet fhe felt there was fomething wrong in her appearance.   She went by an affumed name ; yet, confident that fhe was in reality the wife of Auberry, fhe alfo felt that though fhe had tranfgreffed the bounds of prudence, fhe had ftrictly adhered to the rules of virtue and morality ; and this internal affurance gave her great comfort. And when retiring for the night, fhe would reflect that her heart was in univerfal charity with all her fellow-creatures, that her purfuits were altogether harmlefs, and in fome degree laudable ; a fweet ferenity would diffufe itfelf through her bofom, and offering up her prayers for the fafety of her beloved Reuben, and her almoft adored hufband, fhe would fink into a flumber, as compofed and refrefhing as her own mind was pure and uncontaminated.

The heart that is itfelf a ftranger to guilt fufpects it not in another.   Such was the heart of Rachel ; without enthufiafm pious, without oftentation charitable, and innately virtuous, without an idea that there was any particular merit in being fo ; fince, without being infenfible to the inevitable mifery that muft and ever will follow the forfeiture of that ineftimable jewel, chaftity, fhe wondered how fo many headlefs women fell into an error fo repugnant to her own feelings.

As

As Major Auberry was certain he could not remain long with his wife, when he secured her a handsome and convenient place of residence, he was not forgetful of the pleasure that would naturally result from a companion of her own sex being under the same roof with her. In his search after lodgings or a ready furnished house, chance directed him to Mrs. Varnice, the widow of an attorney, whose pride would not suffer her to leave the house her husband had engaged but a short time before his death, and who would, to support that pride, (the real origin of which was meanness, not real dignity of soul) submit to any thing but labour.

At the time Major Auberry applied for the upper part of her house, she knew him, and that his name was not Dacres. "But he will pay me well," said she mentally; so she concealed her knowledge, and agreed to our heroine's becoming the mistress of the apartments.

When Rachel was first introduced to her, she observed her lovely, majestic form, and sweetly interesting countenance. Mrs. Varnice was short, rather too much *en bon point*, dark complexioned, and on the wrong-side of forty; but her eyes, which were of jetty hue, and whose brilliancy she endeavoured to increase by an artful tinge of rouge on her high cheek-bones, were animated and expressive, and she was not without hope that some future conquest might secure to her a second matrimonial establishment. To such a woman, the first appearance of our heroine was by no means prepossessing.

"She is certainly handsome (said she, on the day Rachel took possession of her new lodgings) she is handsome, I must own; but your pretty women have seldom much to recommend them besides their beauty." This remark was made to a poor relation, who was dependent on Mrs. Varnice for bread; an unfortunate being, who, from want of education, and extreme poverty, possessed a mind as abject as her circumstances.

Education, spirit of light, being of the first order, who in thy right-hand dost hold a magic mirror, displaying

playing to the aftonifhed fenfe of youth the wondrous,
fafcinating charms of nature ; who, ftill receding as
we purfue, yet ftill difplaying fomething ftrange and
charming, inviteft the admiring pupil ftill to follow ;
whofe left hand holds a tablet, on which is written all
that was learnt from thy inftructive mirror ; who as
thou paffeft, giving place to age, who hangs his head
and droops that thou canft charm no more, prefenteft
the tablets, whence fond memory gleans fomething to
cheer the laft cold eve of life, and being tranfmitted
to the rifing age, incite them to attend thy earlieft call,
follow thee through thy moft intricate labyrinths, that,
as thou doft afcend the hill of fame, holding before
them ftill the inftructive glafs, each rifing age may
take a higher ftep, till frail humanity ftands on thy
fummit :—Education, thou firft, beft gift that mortals
can receive ; thofe who know thee not, conceiving not
thy intrinfic value, flight thee, condemn thee, treat thee
with contempt ; but they who feel thy influence, benignant power, will revere thee, worfhip thee, and
court thy fmiles, humbly entreating that the rifing
age might fully comprehend and tafte thy beauties.

Rachel had received a good, though not a brilliant
education ; her mind was therefore free from prejudice.   Mrs. Varnice and her coufin Lettuce were totally uncultivated, and fuperftition and prejudice were
eafily admitted and encouraged.   The former of thefe
women, therefore, concluded our heroine to be a deluded victim to inexperience and affection.   She
thought the infatuation (as fhe called it) of Hamden
would not laft long, and wifely imagined, by paying
the moft marked attention to him, by giving up her
own opinion whenever it was in oppofition to his, and
in a hundred different forms, which fhe conceived to
be the height of complaifance, but which to Auberry
himfelf appeared to have partook more of abject fer-
vility, to fupplant her in his good opinion ; however, as he imagined her, in the main, a good-
natured, inoffenfive woman, he encouraged her advances to an intimacy with Rachel.   He knew the
purity of our heroine's mind, and native good fenfe
would

would prevent her receiving any ill impreſſions, or contracting any low ideas from converſing with a woman every way ſo infinitely her inferior, and at the ſame time thought her knowledge of the world might guard the inexperienced Rachel from impoſitions.

If the firſt fight of our heroine awakened in the boſom of Mrs. Varnice the malignant fiend envy, her manners and converſation aſſiſted to heighten it, and in leſs than a fortnight Mrs. Varnice pronounced her to be proud, conceited, fooliſh, in ſhort, every thing that was the direct oppoſite to her real diſpoſition. Yet ſhe concealed her opinion, and would take opportunities to admire her underſtanding, praiſe her ſhape, her complexion, even the tone of her voice. Rachel was not greedy of flattery; but where is the human being that can at all times turn a deaf ear to its adulating voice, or ſteel their hearts to its inſinuating qualities?

When Auberry left his wife to go to his aunt in Scotland, Mrs. Varnice had not an idea that he meant to return, and felt ſomewhat mortified that all her arts to attract his notice had proved ineffectual; but as ſhe found it would be to no uſe to repine, ſhe turned her thoughts to what advantage might be made of our heroine.

The parting between Major Auberry and his lady had been extremely painful on both ſides. Rachel's heart ſunk within her, and as the chaiſe drove from the door, her emotions became ſo violent, that Mrs. Varnice was obliged to lead her into her own parlour, and give her a glaſs of drops and water.

"Come, come, my dear Madam," ſaid ſhe, as Rachel endeavoured to ſuppreſs her tears, "you muſt not give way to this immoderate ſorrow; Mr. Dacres, I dare ſay, will ſoon come back again; I ſuppoſe he is not gone very far."

"Four hundred miles," ſaid Rachel, "appears to me an immenſe diſtance; and I know not how to account for it, but I feel ſuch an oppreſſion at my heart, it ſeems as though I had beheld him for the laſt time, and yet I know he will return as early as poſſible."

"O! to

"O! to be sure he will; he promised to come back soon, did not he?"

"He will come as soon as he can, I know; but the length of his stay does not depend entirely on himself. However, he has promised I should hear from him very often, and I shall count the moments with impatience till I can hope to receive a letter. I have been very troublesome to you, Madam," continued she, rising to quit the parlour; "pray pardon my childish behaviour; I will retire and endeavour to attain fortitude to bear this first (and I hope in Heaven it will be the last) separation."

Her eyes filled again as she spoke, and courtesying hastily, she repaired to her own apartment; and having disburthened her heart by giving a free course to her tears, she composed her spirits; and asserting that understanding which was ever ready at her call, she began to employ herself on a piece of embroidery, the pattern for which was drawn by Hamden; from that she went to her spinnet, and played as well as she could a trifling air which he had taught her. These employments amused and soothed her. She became composed, and determined, during this enforced and painful absence, to occupy herself in acquiring those accomplishments which she knew would be most agreeable to her husband. Every trace of the primitive puritan was now entirely abolished, except that she was extremely neat in her dress, and simple in her manners. She followed fashion as far as she thought it consistent with propriety, but no farther; and though strangers would pronounce her perfectly elegant at the first glance, were they to scrutinize the several articles that composed her apparel, they would be at a loss to say what particularly constituted that elegance. In short, Rachel was the kind of woman who gives title and fashion to every thing she wears, however plain its formation, however common the materials of which it is made.

The state of her mind after the departure of her husband was such, as precluded every idea of seeking society during the day. She attempted, but the at-

                    tempt

tempt was vain, to partake of a meal which the care of Lettuce had provided (for Lettuce had performed the office of attendant on the perfon of our heroine from the firft day of her refidence in the houfe of Mrs. Varnice) ; but towards evening fhe began to reflect, that the folicitude and attention of her hoftefs demanded fome return ; fhe therefore requefted fhe would come and take tea in her apartment.

It was now the middle of October, and the twilight at that period foon clofes ; it was fix o'clock, when the tea things were placed on the table ; a cheerful fire illumined the hearth, two wax candles lent their rays to enliven the fcene, the windows were clofed, the curtains let down, and perfect filence reigned in the apartments. The houfe was as retired as though twenty miles from London, and not a found interrupted the tranquillity of the furrounding fcene, fave now and then the rattle of a folitary carriage paffing to and from the environs of the city.

If there is a moment in which the human mind is more inclined to unbend, and place an unlimited confidence in thofe who profefs a friendfhip, it is, when fully comprehending the charms of folitude, we find that folitude may be enlivened by being participated by one who enters into all our feelings, and fmiles or weeps as the colour of our fate or expreffion of our fentiments excites the oppofite emotions. Such was the moment we have juft defcribed, nor was our heroine infenfible to its influence.

"I am glad to fee you fo much recovered," faid Mrs. Varnice, feating herfelf at the tea-table, and drawing the tea-board towards her, which Lettuce had juft brought in ; "fhall I fave you the trouble and make the tea?"

Rachel acknowledged her goodnefs, and acquiefced in the propofal.

"I fuppofe Mr. Dacres," faid fhe with a figh, "is now many miles diftant from me ; and fuppofe he writes at the firft poft town, when may I expect to hear from him?"

"That I cannot tell," faid the artful Mrs. Varnice, "unlefs I knew what road he took." "The

" 'The High North-road."

"Well, you may hear from him sooner, but I do not imagine he will write till he gets to York. He is a beautiful man," taking a miniature in her hand that hung by a ribbon round Rachel's neck, "a very handsome man indeed; and I think there is something in your countenances very much alike, very much indeed, juft about the eyes and the mouth; that pretty dimple, juft at the left corner. Well, you were certainly relations."

"No indeed, we were not, I never faw him till within eight months of our union."

"Indeed! Well, I could have fworn you had been coufins. Where were you married, in London?"

"In Weftminfter."

"In Weftminfter? what at the Abbey?"

"No."

"At St. James's Church?"

"No." ·

"Oh! you were married at St. Margaret's?"

· "No, I was not."

"Blefs me, then what church was it?"

"Pardon me, I am not at liberty to fay."

Mrs. Varnice fmiled. "Ah! I underftand now; it was a ftolen match?"

"Not entirely fo."

"What, I fuppofe your friends knew it?"

"I have no friends in England."

"None?"

"No, not one. I have a brother, a dear, refpectable, worthy brother; but he is in America."

"In America? Dear me; what all amongft the blacks and the wild Indians?"

Rachel could not fupprefs an inclination to fmile, whilft fhe anfwered, "No, Madam, amongft the European fettlers, who have, within the laft century, emigrated into the new world, which I underftand is a fertile continent extending from north to fouth, and conftituting one entire quarter of the habitable globe."

"And fo, your brother is gone over fea to thofe ftrange parts. And what could tempt him to leave dear little England?"   "To

"To inquire after property my father left there."

"Dear well, how odd! And fo your father died abroad."

"No, he was loft on his paffage home, even when in fight of his native fhores."

"Oh dear! how unfortunate! So you have no friends in London?"

"In London? No, nor in England, except my hufband."

"Dear me! Well, I hope he will prove a faithful, good hufband to you."

"I have no doubt of his faith or tendernefs."

"Oh dear no! I dare fay not; though men are ftrange, inconftant beings, will profefs much without meaning any thing, marry women under affumed names, and never care for them after a little while."

"There may have been fuch things," faid Rachel; "but for the honour of human nature, I could wifh not to believe them poffible till my fenfes convince me."

"Sweet innocent! I wifh you may never be convinced," faid Mrs. Varnice pointedly.

This exclamation awakened fomething in the bofom of Rachel, that could not rightly be termed either jealoufy or curiofity, but it was a mixture of both; and the artful Varnice led her on, till fhe had gleaned from Rachel (only that names were concealed) every circumftance relating to herfelf, her brother and her hufband.

After a day or two paft in that kind of uncomfortable, unconnected manner, which every perfon of fenfibility muft have experienced when feparated from the chofen friend of their hearts, Rachel began again to refume her ufual avocations. Her needle employed the earlieft hours of morning, after which fhe dreffed, and walked into the fields for air and exercife. Her dinner paft, fhe employed the intermediate hours between that and evening with a book, her pencil, or a leffon on her fpinnet; and the evenings were ufually paffed in reading to, converfing and working, or playing picquet with, Mrs. Varnice.

But

But during this period, it muſt not be imagined that ſhe was entirely forgotten by her quondam friends, the Webſters.   They had been indefatigable in their inquiries, till they found out her lodgings, and hearing that ſhe went by the name of Dacres, they were perſuaded that ſhe had forgot the reſpect due to herſelf, and become the miſtreſs of Hamden Auberry.

Mr. Spriggins, though at firſt mortified and diſappointed by her ſudden departure from his aunt's houſe, ſoon found conſolation, by transferring his devoirs to his eldeſt couſin, by whom they were very favourably received; and an old uncle having left him a decent houſe, ſhop and ſtock in trade, in a market town in Northumberland, he ſoon obtained the aſſent of Mrs. Webſter, and took her fair daughter, to ſhine forth in all the airs and finery of a London bride, and to ſet the faſhions for three months to come, to all the tradeſmen's wives and daughters in a little country town. His ſhop too, was newly painted and decorated in the London ſtyle, and Mr. Spriggins himſelf was ſo polite, ſo obliging, that he ſoon attracted a large number of cuſtomers.

Beginning the world thus, not only without embarraſſments, but with a ſmall ſum of ready money in hand, this young couple found, in a very ſhort time, that they were in a fair way to accumulate a fortune. The wife, though proud, vain, and fond of finery, was meanly parſimonious, and would ſtint her family in neceſſaries, in order to buy a finer gown, or give a more expenſive treat than her neighbours.   Belle Webſter was ſent for to be her companion, and ſet her cap at ſome of the ſmart young men, in hopes of an eſtabliſhment for life; while little Polly was left to aſſiſt and conſole her mother for the loſs of her two eldeſt daughters.

When Hamden Auberry reached his uncle's ſeat, he was received with ſuch affectionate tokens of joy by lady Anne, that he was almoſt tempted, in that moment of tenderneſs, to throw himſelf on her mercy, and confeſs his marriage.   Happy had it been, both for himſelf and our heroine, had he followed the impulſe;

pulfe; but he took time to confider, and that falfe
pride, which was his only foible, reprefented to him,
that he was fecure of the perfon and heart of Rachel,
bound to her by the moft irrevocable vows; he hazarded nothing, therefore, by longer concealment. But
to avow his engagements with a woman in refpect to
rank and fortune fo diametrically oppofite to what lady Anne defired, might forfeit her regard forever;
nay, this very pride flattered him that it was for the
fake of his wife he ftill wifhed to conceal their union,
and that the wealth and confequence in lady Anne's
power to beftow were only valued by him, as, by pof-
feffing them, he could elevate the woman of his choice
to a rank fhe was born to adorn. Alas! this was
falfe reafoning; it was in reality an unwillingnefs to
give up the refpect, the parade, the eafe and conveniencies, wealth is ever certain to infure.

Two days after his arrival in Scotland, the family
were furprifed by the fudden and unexpected appearance of lady Lucy. The tour to the continent had
been fhortened by an untoward incident, and fhe having, on her return, landed at Harwich, fhe proceeded
immediately north, without going to London. Lady
Anne was not difpleafed by the return of her niece;
fhe looked upon Hamden as the certain fucceffor to
the title and eftates of his late grandfather, but fhe
thought a union with lady Lucy might by no means
retard the completion of her wifhes, which were to fee
him at the head of her family.

It was the evening after the arrival of this lady,
that, fitting in a family way with only her aunt and coufin, and diverting them with her vivacity and innocent
prattle, when, turning fuddenly to Hamden, fhe cried,
" Ch! by the bye, Coz, how does your pretty Quaker
girl do?"

Hamden's face was but a trifle paler than his coat.
He hefitated, attempted to anfwer; but finding himfelf at a lofs for words, affected a laugh.

" You may laugh," cried fhe, " but I declare I
thought her very pretty."

" Who

"Who are you fpeaking of?" faid lady Anne, fixing her eyes on the glowing face of Hamden.

"Oh! he knows," continued the thoughtlefs girl. "and now I have the fcene full in my mind, I'll tell you, aunt. You muft know we went to the play.—"

"Nay, dear Lucy," faid Hamden, gaily catching her hand, "how can you remember fuch ridiculous trifles?"

"Your fervant, coufin Hamden; it was no trifle at the time. Now, aunt, I'll tell you how it was. Between the play and farce, I had obferved a very pretty, interefting Quaker, who fat in the pit looking very earneftly at Mr. Hamden. I fuppofe fhe had feen him before. Eh, coufin?—Well, dear aunt, the houfe was very full, and the pretty Quaker fainted; when behold ye, my gentleman here takes a leap over the front of the box, and rufhing through the crowd, flew to her affiftance. But if you had feen when fhe recovered——"

"A little moderation, if you pleafe, lady Lucy," cried Hamden, eagerly interrupting her; "you paint the fcene in fuch lively colours, that my aunt will fuppofe the bagatelle of confequence."

"And your manner, Hamden, does not contradict the fuppofition," faid lady Anne pointedly. "Pray who was this fainting damfel?"

"It was a Mifs Dudley," faid Hamden, in a hurried accent; "I was introduced to her when I laft vifited my mother."

"Indeed!" faid lady Anne, farcaftically.

"Yes, fhe was a great favourite of my mother's; but I underftand fhe is lately married to an old crony of mine, one Dacres. I am fure, aunt, you muft remember what friends Tom Dacres and I were when boys."

"And are you friends now?" faid Lucy with a half fmile and a fly glance at her aunt.

Lady Anne was ftruck with the evident embarraffment of Hamden; fhe therefore put an end to the converfation by rifing and defiring him to attend her to her clofet. Here a converfation enfued, which con-

vinced

vinced Auberry, that the moment his aunt should be assured of his having formed a family connexion with our heroine, would be the last of her favour.

"I must dissemble longer," said he.   Alas! dissimulation is seldom necessary, can never be laudable, and was in this case despicable.——But we will return to our heroine.

The first six weeks of her husband's absence she bore with tolerable patience; when a month more passed over, and no hope of his return, she murmured at the delay; but when, at last, week after week glided on, and Auberry did not appear, she began to despond.

Mrs Varnice was not surprised; it was what she had expected.   She by slow and almost imperceptible degrees endeavoured to undermine the principles of our heroine; but Rachel, though not quick at discerning evil (because almost a stranger to its baneful qualities) at last discovered her aim, and repulsed her with the scorn she merited.

But innocence is ever inadequate to oppose, with any degree of success, the united powers of envy and cunning.   In revenge for the contempt with which she had been treated, Mrs. Varnice suppressed the next letter with which Lettuce was entrusted to carry to the post, opened, read it, and committed it to the fire. By the tenor of this letter, she comprehended that Rachel fully believed herself the wife of Auberry; but this she knew before, and inwardly laughed at what she supposed to be the credulity of a fond, unsuspecting girl.

Having once began to interrupt the correspondence, she did not hesitate the next post-night to make Lettuce keep watch at the street door, and prevent the rap of the post-man, which would have immediately called our heroine down stairs.   The stratagem succeeded; she took the expected letter from the post-man's hand, paid the postage, and retired to her own apartment to read it.

It has often been said, that envy is its own punisher, and in this case the adage was completely verified; for when from this letter she discovered that Hamden really

ally was, and freely acknowledged himself, the hufband of our heroine, her heart overflowed with rancour, and fhe determined to hefitate at nothing which might be likely to poifon the happinefs of one fhe at once envied and hated.

One act of guilt leads but to the commiffion of another; it is in vain the human heart may think only this one little deviation, and I will ftop. As the bail precipitated from the fummit of a hill paufes not, but rufhes with amazing velocity till it reaches the very loweft part of the vale beneath, fo the human foul, giving way to temptation, finks from error into guilt, nor paufes till plunged in the loweft abyfs of depravity.

Another and another letter from Hamden was opened by Mrs. Varnice, whilft thofe from Rachel (whofe heart now began to throb with fear, doubt, and a thoufand anxieties, which none but thofe who are united to, and fuffering an early feparation from, the man of their choice can conceive) fuffered the fame fate. At length one arrived incloling a bank bill for a hundred pounds. At the fight of it, Mrs. Varnice turned pale; fear was the firft emotion of her bofom. But not even Lettuce was privy to the receipt of this letter. . Mrs. Varnice was not very economical; a hundred pounds would relieve her from fome few embarraffments. She looked at it, paufed for a moment, at length, committing the letter to the fire, fhe depofited the note in her pocket-book, and on the enfuing morning exchanged it at a filk mercer's where fhe purchafed a gown of rofe-coloured tabby.

This note would have been very acceptable to Rachel; for fhe began to be fenfible of the decreafe of her finances, and to experience the folicitude and pleafing cares of maternal tendernefs; and to prepare for the reception of a little ftranger, fhe had nearly exhaufted the whole of the money Hamden had given her at parting.

It cannot be fuppofed that the mind of Hamden was in a much eafier ftate than that of our heroine; but as he was now on a party of pleafure with his uncle, lady Anne and lady Lucy, making excurfions
from

from one part of Scotland to another, and ftaying but
a few days in each place, he reconciled himfelf to not
hearing from his wife, under the idea that her letters
might not follow him as he directed, and that he fhould
get them all together when he returned to Glafgow.
But when he returned, and found not a fingle letter
waiting for him, he felt the utmoft impatience, and
would have fet off immediately for London, but that
his aunt was attacked with an alarming fever, and to
leave her at fuch a period, would be the height of ingratitude. She lingered long, and even when pronounced out of danger, ftill hovered as it were on the
brink of the grave for many weeks, and at length,
change of climate was ordered as the only chance of
perfect reftoration.

Hamden, whofe mind was now tortured almoft beyond fufferance, finding that he fhould be obliged to
attend his aunt to Lifbon, whilft preparations were
making for the voyage, difpatched his confidential fervant to London, to make inquiries for and bear remit-
tances to our heroine. Though this man may juftly
be termed confidential, yet fo fearful had Hamden
been of having his marriage known, that even he was
not entrufted with the fecret, and Rachel was humil-
iated even in the eyes of her hufband's fervant. But
her manners were fuch as had ever fecured refpect from
James, and the honeft fellow, often when he thought
of her fituation, pitied her, and blamed his mafter.

Nearly feven months had now elapfed fince the marriage of our heroine, above five of which fhe had been
feparated from her hufband, and half of that period
had paffed in the continual diftrefs of alternate expectation and difappointment.

" I have been deceived," fhe would fay, whilft tears
of anguifh ftole down her cheeks ; " Hamden no longer loves, no longer thinks of me, and, forfaken of him,
who is there in this vaft univerfe, (for Heaven alone
can tell whether my dear brother is in exiftence) who
then is there that cares for the unhappy Rachel ? And
forlorn, forfaken, wretched as I am, I fhall give life to
a helplefs

a helpless innocent, whose father will perhaps blush to own him."

Rachel's days were joyless, and the tear of anguish fell nightly on her pillow. The rose no longer bloomed on her cheeks, nor did the animated beam of health and internal peace dance in her expressive eyes; pale, languid, heart-broken, she suffered in silence; for to whom could she complain?

Mrs. Varnice had exposed to her, her true character, and Rachel would not hold communication with a woman she despised. She nursed her grief in solitude. If she endeavoured to amuse the heavy hour, by her pencil or music, every flower she drew was moistened by her tears, and the chords of the instrument reverberated but the strains of melancholy.

It was a fine morning in the beginning of March, that, still considering it a duty to use every method to preserve health, (though life was no longer valuable) Rachel walked to the green park. It was an early hour; she did not fear being met by any one who knew her; there were but few by whom she would be recognized, and those few seldom visited the park except on a Sunday evening, to see and be seen. As with slow step she paced along the margin of Rosamond's Pond, she was startled by a voice which suddenly exclaimed, "Heavens and earth! Miss Dudley!" She raised her eyes, and beheld Archibald Oliver. A sudden emotion, something like shame, rushed upon her heart; she just articulated his name, extended her hand towards him, and, tottering to a seat that was near, she sunk on it almost fainting.

"Good God! my dear Miss Dudley, to what am I to attribute these emotions?"

"My name is Dacres, Sir," said Rachel; but her voice faltered, and the carnation visited her cheeks as she remembered her very apparent situation.

"You are married then?"

"Yes."

"May you be happy, happy as you deserve. But why thus alone? it is not surely proper. Where is Mr. Dacres?"

The

The former intimacy that had subsisted between Oliver and our heroine could alone have excused these abrupt interrogations; but Rachel had ever considered him as a brother, and new ties, new affections, had made him behold her now only in the endearing light of a sister.

"My husband is in Scotland," said Rachel, "whither he was called by business of consequence; but come (continued she, forcing a smile) if you are disengaged, walk home with me, and I will tell you all you wish to know, and in return be very inquisitive concerning your happiness."

Then, with that innocent freedom that gave a charm to all her actions, she passed her hand through his arm, and they pursued their way to her lodgings, engaged in such interesting chat, that they had reached the door before either imagined they were half way.

During their walk, Rachel told as much of her own story as could be done without infringing the vow she had voluntarily made to Auberry never to divulge his real name and family till authorized by him; and in return, she learnt that Oliver had experienced a very tolerable share of happiness in his matrimonial connexions, that his wife was then in town, and had just made him a father. Of Jessy he could give her no information, and since our heroine's marriage, that young lady had declined the correspondence of Rachel, alleging, as she no longer shared her confidence, she would not intrude her letters where she must suppose them unwelcome. This had at the time given Rachel much pain; but as Hamden would not allow her to explain her situation to her friend, she was forced to relinquish a correspondence so dear to her heart, and with it all intercourse with the only woman she had ever known whom she thought really deserved the name of friend.

Oliver could not on that morning set above half an hour with our heroine; but on the ensuing day he called, and drank tea with her. After this, scarce a day passed but he inquired after her health. He saw there was something of mystery enveloped her; he saw she was not happy; and though his knowledge of her heart, underftanding and principles made him reject the idea whenever it intruded itfelf, he fometimes almoft feared fhe had been imprudent.

To the afflicted heart, the voice of friendfhip is a foothing cordial. Rachel had not heard its adulating found for feveral months previous to her meeting with Oliver. She dreamt not of impropriety, and, unconfcious of evil, dreaded not cenfure. His vifits were always welcome, and the day paffed drearily in which fhe faw him not.

It has been already remarked, that the greateft and almoft only fault of our heroine was a too great opennefs of difpofition, in regard to her own circumftances or bufinefs; fhe never thought of conccalment, and nothing but the moft unbounded affection for Auberry could have prompted her to enter into engagements which would involve her conduct in apparent myftery, and oblige her to wear for a while the veil of conccalment. To Oliver, therefore, only concealing his real name and family, fhe was explicit in regard to her fears for the health and life of her hufband; fhe alfo, without hefitation, mentioned the embarraffed ftate of her finances. Oliver offered her money; but, though fhe fought confolation from the foothings of friendfhip, her fpirit rofe above pecuniary obligation. She was grateful for the offer, but firm in her refufal to avail herfelf of it.

On the evening when this explanation took place, Oliver had fupped with Rachel, and the hoarfe voice of the watchmen proclaiming half paft eleven o'clock, was the firft thing that reminded them it was time to break off their interefting converfation. They had talked of Reuben, of Jeffy, and the doubtful fate of thofe dear relatives had drawn tears from both their eyes.

"I muft leave you, Mrs. Dacres," faid he, rifing and taking his hat.

Rachel rang the bell; but no one anfwering, fhe took one of the candles from the table, and defcended the ftairs to light him out.

D d

"Good

"Good night, my dear Madam," said he; "do not come to the door, you will take cold."

"Good night, Mr. Oliver," said Rachel; and as he pulled the door after him, she turned the key, put the chain acrofs, and turned to re-afcend the ftairs, when, to her furprife, the parlour door opened, and Mrs. Varnice appeared.

"Blefs me," faid Rachel, "I thought you were all in bed."

"Oh! I dare fay you did, and hoped it too."

"Hoped, Madam! I neither hoped, nor cared; only I rang the bell for Lettuce to light Mr. Oliver out, and as fhe did not anfwer it——"

"I would not let her anfwer it; and let me tell you, Mrs. Dacres, (if that is your name) I think your conduct very unwarrantable; and if you muft have gentlemen vifiting you in your hufband's abfence, and ftaying till twelve or one o'clock, you muft get another lodging; for I will have no fuch goings on in my houfe. Mr. Dacres, (as you call him) if he is your hufband, will have no great reafon to be pleafed with your conduct; and if he is not, why, my houfe is a houfe of good repute, and the fooner you quit it the better."

Petrified with aftonifhment, Rachel could not anfwer for the fpace of a minute; at length, refentment conquering her fenfibility, fhe replied:

"Had I fuppofed you entertained fuch humiliating ideas of me, Madam, I would not fo long have remained an inmate in your habitation; but, painful as it is to me, I fhall be neceffitated to ftay fome little time longer till I can difcharge my account with you. I fhall not leave a houfe whilft I am indebted to the miftrefs of it."

"No, I'll take care of that," faid Mrs. Varnice, with a malicious grin; "I fhall hardly let you go in my debt when I can detain any valuable property to the amount. But I fhall fay no more to-night, to-morrow you muft look out for another place, and pay me how you can; for paid I will be, or you muft take the confequence, and fo good-night."

Rachel

Rachel would have said good-night, but the words stuck in her throat; she slightly inclined her head, and passing hastily up stairs, sunk almost fainting on the nearest seat. Lettuce, who had been tutored by Mrs. Varnice, followed her up, pretended to blame her cousin, and take the part of our heroine.

"I will not stay in the house," said Rachel, "but how to raise money to pay her."

"Dear! that would be no difficult matter," said Lettuce, "so many pretty trinkets as you have! These bracelets now——"

Rachel looked on them and sighed.

"I cannot part with them," said she, "they were the first present I received from my husband."

Well, but you have such a vast number of pretty things, your watch and your etwee!—"

This conversation let our heroine into a secret with which she was before entirely unacquainted—that she could raise a sum of money on these baubles without entirely parting with them; and she went to bed with a full determination to quit the mansion where she had been so much insulted, the ensuing morning. It may well be supposed she slept but little; short moments of forgetfulness, and those interrupted by horrid visions, were all she could obtain.

At the dawn she arose, and so earnestly did she set about a removal, that by twelve o'clock, she had paid the exorbitant demands of Mrs. Varnice, and was seated in her new lodgings; though to accomplish this point she had disposed of almost every thing of value she possessed, not excepting the bracelets, for which she had expressed so much regard.

Two days after this removal, James arrived, commissioned by his master to make inquiry after our heroine. The tale told by the arch-fiend, Mrs. Varnice, filled his honest heart with horror.

"Receive the visits of gentlemen, obliged to leave the lodgings in which his master had placed her, and go into others, on account of keeping bad hours, and other disorderly behaviour. Good Sirs," said James, I can hardly believe it; she was so good, so modest, so mild.   It made one's heart glad to look at her; and to hear her talk, would a made an old man young again. Body o' me! there must a been some witchcraft used to make her change so all of a sudden."

But to all James's inquiries of where she was removed to, they pleaded ignorance; and he being restricted in the time allowed him to make the journey, could not stay so long as he wished to make inquiries in the neighbourhood.   With a heavy heart, he set forward on his return to his master; but near Berwick, the carriage was overset in which he was travelling, and his right arm broken.

Hamden, agonized almost to distraction by his long absence, the cause of which he was not acquainted with, (as a fever and delirium, which immediately succeeded the accident, prevented James from taking any method to let his master know his situation) was obliged to embark with his aunt, without receiving the least intelligence of the fate of Rachel.

'She has forgotten me, she repents her union with me,' he would say, 'and seeks for an opportunity to break those engagements which I have hesitated to announce to the world.'

In these moments he would be ready to reveal all to his aunt; but the fear that Rachel no longer loved him, or perhaps was no longer worthy of his affection for her, always withheld him; and the voyage to Lisbon, though in itself extremely pleasant, seemed to the unhappy Hamden to teem only with vexation, and when landed, and the first bustle of seeking a lodging, &c. was over, he walked through the streets like a discontented shade; indeed, it was but the shadow of Hamden Auberry, for his better part was flown to the shores of Albion, where it hovered round the mansion in which he imagined still dwelt the object of his dearest affection.

CHAP.

Sorrows of the Heart.

IN the mean time, the afflictions of our heroine daily increased. Oliver had left London; she was without friends and without money, and to increase the sorrows of her heart, she became the mother of a fine boy about the middle of June. Before her confinement, she entrusted her hostess with the real state of her finances, and to retrench her expenses, had taken a room on the second story, where she suffered in silence all the miseries of disappointed love, added to the poignant sting of poverty. Once she wrote to Mrs. Auberry; had she addressed the letter to Dr. Lenient, she had done right. But Mrs. Auberry had received a letter from Mrs. Webster, which had prejudiced her against Rachel; she therefore did not mention to her brother that she had heard from her, and threw the letter into a draw, without deigning to give our distressed heroine the comfort of one line in answer.

During her confinement, she was told by the woman who attended her, that a very fine lady had taken the range of apartments on the first floor, which consisted of a dining-room, drawing-room, and bed-chamber; that she had taken them only for a few weeks, whilst her own house was finished and properly furnished. "She is a charming lady," said the talkative old woman, "and keeps her chariot, her own maid and footman."

All this intelligence appeared of so little consequence to our heroine, that she scarcely heard a syllable of the whole harangue; but the next day, as she was passing from the bed to the sofa at the other end of the room, she cast her eyes casually out of the window; an elegant chariot drew up to the door, and to her utter astonishment she saw Mrs. Courtney descend from it.

Lost in amazement, she sat down; that her eyes had not deceived her, she was certain. To what could

she

she attribute this sudden elevation of fortune? This was a riddle she had not power to unravel; but whatever was the cause, she rejoiced at the effect, and, forgetting the coldness she had experienced from La Varone immediately after her marriage with Lieutenant Courtney, conscious only of a pleasurable sensation, to find a person with whom she had formerly lived in habits of intimacy so near her, she wrote with a pencil on a slip of paper,

"Dear Mrs. Courtney, your friend Rachel is again an inmate of the mansion you inhabit, and flatters herself you will give her the pleasure of your company for half an hour."

This billet she sent by the nurse, and in a few moments Mrs. Courtney entered the apartment. The attendant withdrawn, and a few common-place inquiries past,

"You cannot think, my dear Madam," said our heroine, "what real pleasure it gives me to find Mr. Courtney's prospects so much amended, since your marriage."

"Yes, he is made a Captain; besides, a particular friend of mine, whom I had not seen for many years, has settled on me a very handsome income, which makes me quite independent."

"How fortunate!" said Rachel in the simplicity of her heart. "And where is Captain Courtney?"

"Gone to India."

"Is either of your sisters, or your mother-in-law in town with you?"

"Oh dear no."

"They are well, I hope?"

"Yes, quite well; that is, I believe so, for I have heard nothing to the contrary, but I have not seen them lately."

"No?"

"No, not for these three months past. But come, tell me, my demure friend, what changes have taken place in your fate since we parted."

With a look of mingled confusion and candour, in the simple language of truth did Rachel explain to

Mrs.

Mrs. Courtney every circumstance of her marriage and consequent uneasiness, still concealing the real name of her husband.

She spoke to a woman whose heart was impure, and who scrupled not to judge of others by herself. Besides, Mrs. Courtney had been to visit Mrs. Webster, and had learnt from her the manner of our heroine's departure from her house, and with whom it was supposed she resided. She laughed at the affliction Rachel appeared to experience from her husband's neglect, called her agony of heart ideal misery, told her the honey moon could not last forever, bid her keep up her spirits, and, promising to see her again in the evening, left her. Accordingly, in the evening she again visited her.

" I have been thinking, Mrs. Dacres," said she with a half smile, and looking sidelong from under her dark eyelashes, " that change of scene and air would be of service to you. I am going into Northumberland, to visit our old acquaintance, Mrs. Spriggins ; what say you to a jaunt ? You will travel at your ease with me in the chariot, Pelham will help take care of the child, and I dare say the journey will not be the less agreeable because it will take you near the borders of Scotland."

A tinge of carnation passed over the languid cheek of Rachel, as she said she should like such an excursion, but it was not in her power to take it.

" What, for want of money, I suppose ? Pshaw ! nonsense ! you cannot be wholly destitute ; a trifle will serve, and you surely wish to be nearer the Major than you are at present."

Rachel's heart beat quick, as she attempted to reply. Mrs. Courtney put her hand before her mouth,

" Come, don't deny it ; I have found out your secret, but I won't betray you. Perhaps, when you are within a day's journey, he may be able to visit you. London is at a vast distance from the banks of the Clyde."

There is nothing more difficult to a person of natural veracity than to be under the necessity of asserting
ing

ing a falfehood. Rachel felt the impoffibility of doing it, and remained filent. In fhort, her innocence,
her credulity, her ardent wifh to be near her hufband
prevailed, and fhe confented to accompany Mrs. Courtney into Northumberland. But, however liable to err
from the franknefs and candour of her temper, Rachel
had ftill that pride of foul which could not condefcend
to tell Mrs. Courtney that three guineas, and a few
clothes, conftituted the whole of her worldly poffeffions.
Part of thofe clothes, with fome very fine laces, were
difpofed of to pay the nurfe and other contingent expenfes; and with a mere trifle in her purfe, our heroine departed with her unworthy affociate from London.

Mrs. Courtney was deceived when fhe invited Rachel to take this journey with her; but it was the depravity of her own heart had deceived her, and before
fhe reached Northumberland, fhe difcovered that the
mind of our heroine was ftill uncontaminated, ftill
pure, and fhrunk from vice with difguft, turned from
immorality with abhorrence.

On their arrival at Mr. Spriggins's, Mrs. Courtney
was received with a profufion of compliments, whilft
Rachel was fcarcely noticed. She was fhown to an
upper apartment, and, weary as fhe was with the journey, fuffered to undrefs the child herfelf, and put him
to bed. She laid him on the pillow of repofe, and,
kneeling befide the bed, poured forth her afflicted foul
to her Maker. Her cheek refted on the fame pillow
with that of her infant, and her tears flowed without
reftraint. She felt that the pretended friendfhip of
Mrs. Courtney was only oftentation; fhe feared fhe
had more to fuffer than fhe fnould be able to fupport.
She prayed for refignation to the will of Heaven, and
her tears continued to flow, not from impatience, they
were the effufions of an afflicted fpirit.

After a few weeks refidence in the family of Mrs.
Spriggins, Rachel perceived that not even a fhadow of
refpect and attention towards herfelf remained in the
manners of the whole family. At meals, fhe was fuffered to take the loweft feat at the table, where fhe was
fometimes fo totally overlooked, as not to be helped

till

till every one elfe had begun their dinner ; and then
fhe was infulted by an affectation of friendly familiarity, fuch as, " Blefs me, Mrs. Dacres, I had forgot
you ; but why don't you fpeak ? you are at home you
know."

At thefe moments, Rachel's heart would fwell to
her eyes, and in ftruggling to fupprefs her tears, the
food fhe attempted to fwallow feemed almoft to choak
her.

Mrs. Courtney difagreed with and difcharged her
woman, and the next day requefted our heroine to rife
from her feat, and fetch her work from the other end
of the room. Had Rachel been independent, fhe
would without hefitation have complied with the requeft ; but Rachel was poor, and fhe felt the requeft
an infult.

" I am not qualified to fupply the place of your
fervant, Madam," faid fhe haughtily.

" Why I do not fuppofe you are," faid Mrs. Courtney, yawning indolently ; " but indeed, child, circum-
ftanced as you are, I do not know what you could do
better than endeavour to get a place ; though to
be fure your child is an objection."

The expreffive eyes of our heroine flafhed indignation, at the infolent manner and propofal of her often-
tatious friend ; but fhe difdained to anfwer. ' I am
not yet fallen quite fo low as that,' thought fhe, and
rofe to quit the apartment.

" I really am forry for you, child," continued Mrs.
Courtney, detaining her, " but painful as it is for a
perfon who is fo much interefted for your welfare as I
am to fpeak difagreeable truths, I really muft tell you,
that the haughty airs you give yourfelf are very un-
becoming ; you muft learn humility."

" I hope I fhall in time," faid Rachel indignantly,
" if I do not, I fhall profit but little by your endeavours."

" Come, come, you mifunderftand me ; if you do
not incline to do fomething for a livelihood, I really
think it would be advifeable for you to go on to Scotland to your hufband. I expect a friend of mine here

in a few days, with whom I am going to make a tour through the northern counties; if you choose to go with me in quality of a companion, and take the care of my clothes, assist me to dress and undress, I will pay you twenty guineas a year; but then you must leave your child here at nurse."

"No, Mrs. Courtney," said Rachel, "if I am obliged to eat the the bread of servitude, I will earn it of strangers, not of one who once thought herself honoured in being called the friend of Rachel Dudley. I will be the humble companion (or rather a slave on which ill humour may be lavished with impunity) to no one. I would gladly embrace your first proposal of seeking my husband, but you know I have not the means of prosecuting the journey, even by the cheapest conveyance."

"Heavens and earth!" replied Mrs. Courtney, with a look of well-affected surprise, "is it possible you can have come into this strange place without any money? And what do you mean to do, child?"

"To be no longer troublesome to you, Madam," said Rachel. "I thank you, Madam," continued she, "for the shelter your roof has so long afforded me," turning to Mrs. Spriggins, who had sat a silent and insensible spectatress of the scene, "but will no longer intrude; but this very night remove to a habitation better suited to my present humble condition."

She then hastily left the room. On the stairs she met Belle Webster.

"What is the matter, Mrs. Dacres?" said she; for the tears, which a laudable pride had restrained whilst she was in the presence of her insolent hostess and her companion, wounded sensibility forced in a torrent from her eyes the moment she had shut the door. "What is the matter?" said Belle.

"Nothing," replied our heroine, "only I have stayed here too long."

"Dear! I'm afraid sister has been vexing you; well, don't mind her, you know she never was very good natured."

"I do

"I do not mind either her or her affociate," faid Rachel; "but I wifh to releafe them from an unwelcome intruder, and fhall leave the houfe immediately. Do me the favour, Mifs Webfter, to requeft one of the fervants may take my trunk to the inn."

"Dearee me! I hope you are not in earneft?"

"In very earneft, I affure you."

"Well, now I'm quite forry."

"I thank you, Mifs Webiter. Will you afk the favour I requeft?"

"Oh! to be fure I will; but you won't go before tea?"

"Before another hour," faid Rachel firmly.

Belle was not overburthened with underftanding; fhe did not perfectly comprehend the delicacy of our heroine's feelings, nor did fhe give herfelf the trouble to think much about it; fo wifhing her health, fhe defcended the ftairs, and fent up a boy to take her trunk. It was between four and five o'clock in the afternoon, when Rachel, taking her dear boy in her arms, and followed by the lad with her parcels, left the houfe of Mr. Spriggins, and went to feek a lodging in a town, to almoft every inhabitant of which fhe was a perfect ftranger. She knew that the public inns afforded lodgings to travellers, and to one of the moft reputable of thefe fhe directed her fteps. Her purfe was but flenderly provided, but fhe augmented her little ftore by the fale of a gold locket, the laft thing of value which fhe poffeffed, and from which fhe took a lock of plaited hair; for it was the hair of Hamden Auberry, and to her a thoufand times more precious than the metal in which it had been enfhrined.

On the following morning, fhe inquired after a private lodging, and was recommended by the woman who kept the inn, to a mean apartment in one of the moft unfrequented ftreets in the town. To this humble afylum fhe retired, and felt a degree of melancholy pleafure that fhe could indulge her tears without reftraint.

It may occafion fome degree of furprife, that Spriggins, who had formerly been an admirer of our heroine,

ine, would suffer her to leave his house without either friends or money ; but the heart by nature contracted, and whose chief object has been self, is sensibly affected by an appearance of slight ; it can never either forget or forgive it ; and such a heart languidly moved in the bosom of Spriggins.

But those visitors, who had seen Rachel in the family, and now missed her, felt an awakened curiosity to know what was become of her.   To these interrogatories had the Mesdames Spriggins and Courtney simply answered, that she was gone home ; curiosity would have died, but they felt they had done wrong in driving her, poor and unprotected as she was, from their house ; and in palliation of so inhuman an action, threw aspersions on her character.   Not content with depriving her of the protection of their own roof, they prevented her obtaining that protection from any other, whose inmates were in the smallest degree respectable.

That the human heart is liable to error, and that on the eternal record our crimes and follies are enrolled, and will one day appear in dreadful judgment against us, is a solemn truth, which no person of common sense will attempt to deny ; yet we are led to hope, that the tear of unfeigned penitence will blot those offences out.   But the crime of slander is of so foul a die, its sable hue stains the sacred page, and only mercy infinite can purify it.   Oh thou Giver of life, guard, I beseech thee, my heart from ingratitude, and my lips from slander ; and for the rest, thy will be done.

During the period of these vicissitudes, Rachel had never omitted writing every week to her husband, only at the time when the birth of her son prevented her. These letters, written after she left the house of Mrs. Varnice, all lay at the place where he had desired them to be addressed ; and when James was sufficiently recovered to follow his master, he made them into a parcel, and took them with him.

But words are inadequate to describe the feelings of Hamden, when he by turns listened to the account
which

which James gave him, and read the pathetic letters of his wife; sometimes love, sometimes resentment predominated.   But when he read that he was a father, and that his once loved Rachel, in that season of sickness, was without the means to purchase the necessary accommodations and comforts to render the situation in some measure supportable, he determined to hazard every thing, own his marriage, and fly to her relief and comfort.

Hamden was ever impetuous; he resolved one moment, and the next put the resolve in execution.   Lady Anne heard him with more calmness than he had expected; but that apparent calm was deceitful; when he had finished, she upbraided him with his duplicity, imprecated misery on both himself and his wife, and with a determined air renounced him forever. In vain was every endeavour to soften her resentment, and Hamden embarked for England, without the smallest hope of being reinstated in her affection, or of ever being the better for her fortune.

Mortified pride, love and jealousy corroded in his bosom during his short voyage; and on his arrival in London, he repaired immediately to the house of Mrs. Varnice; for though Rachel had mentioned her removal, yet she had forgot to mention the name of the street to which she had removed; and though she was displeased with Mrs. Varnice, yet, as she did not know the extent of that woman's vileness, she spoke of her no farther than to say she had reason to think both Hamden and herself had been mistaken in her character.   This was not sufficient to deter Hamden from going to her house, especially as he conceived it the only probable means of finding Rachel.   But this visit did not serve to conciliate his affection, or awaken returning tenderness.   Mrs. Varnice told her own tale. Our poor heroine was represented as imprudent, if not guilty, in regard to Oliver; extravagant and thoughtless, in her expenses.

"Why indeed," said Aubeny, "I thought I left her sufficient to defray every expense till my return;

and

and when I found my stay protracted beyond my expectations, I forwarded her a hundred pounds."

"Well, who could have thought it?" said Mrs. Varnice; "before she left me, she, to my certain knowledge, raised money on her watch, rings, bracelets."

"Bracelets?" said Hamden.

"Oh yes! Lettuce pledged them for her."

"Cruel, unkind Rachel!"

"Dear! don't let it distress you so; I suppose her young friend Oliver helped her off with some of the money."

"Damn him!" said Hamden. "Oh! Rachel, Rachel, why have you used me thus? Oh! Mrs. Varnice, if you knew how I loved her, how I adored her! how at this moment her fascinating image twines around every chord, every fibre of my heart! you would wonder how she could be so ungrateful, so vile, so barbarous."

Alas! weak, credulous Auberry, had you instead of listening to this woman's infamous aspersions, treated them with scorn, and boldly asserted the innocence of your wife, and your full confidence in her truth and honour, her accuser, conscious of her own guilt and duplicity, would have retired intimidated within herself, and shrunk from a scrutiny, from whence she must have been assured her own falsehood would stand detected. But who will espouse the cause of an injured wife, when he who has solemnly sworn to protect her from all evil, listens with avidity to the voice that defames her, and joins with her worst enemies to precipitate her into the abyss of ignominy.

From the house of Mrs. Varnice, Hamden went to the lodging she had last occupied, and there, from a conversation with the woman of the house, learnt the route Rachel had taken, and with whom; but unfortunately, he also learnt that she had been visited almost daily by Oliver, during the period of his stay in London. Tortured almost to madness, he resolved to follow her, upbraid her with her perfidy and cruelty,

oblige

oblige her to relinqnifh the care of the child to him, and take an everlafting leave of her.

In the mean time, our heroine was drinking very deeply of the cup of affliction ; poverty was her conftant companion. The trifle fhe poffeffed, at the time fhe. left the houfe of Spriggins, was foon expended, and by degrees the remains of her wardrobe dwindled away, till two cotton gowns, with a change of linen, were the whole of her earthly poffeffions. She had inquired for work, but could get none. The dearth of amufement in a country-town makes every trifle, if wearing the appearance of novelty, become of confequence ; and what fpreads fafter than a tale of fcandal ? The circumftance of our heroine's coming from London to Mr. Spriggins, and quitting the houfe fo abruptly, had been talked over in almoft every family in the place, told a hundred different ways, and each narrator adding or altering fome circumftance, poor Rachel was looked upon, even by the woman of whom fhe rented her fmall apartment, as a fufpicious character ; and had fhe been inclined to partake the pleafures of fociety, fhe would have found the doors of almoft every clafs of people fhut againft her. But fhe had ftill the confolation of an innocent heart, and a firm faith and reliance on an omnifcient Deity, who would not fuffer her eventually to perifh. She fubmitted to her afflictions as to the wife difpenfations of his providence, and prayed daily for a more humble, more unrepining fpirit. She was entirely ignorant alfo, that any ftigma had been thrown on her reputation, and confcious of not deferving, fhe feared not the cenfures of a world, which, though fhe would not wilfully offend, fhe was but little folicitous to pleafe.

The neglect of Auberry funk the deepeft into her heart, when her thoughts reverted to the few happy weeks paft in his fociety immediately after their marriage. The tear of bitter remembrance would gufh from her eyes, and as fhe preffed her infant to her heart, it bled at every vein, that he, as well as herfelf, fhould be fo totally abandoned by his father.

It

It was one evening in Auguſt, when Rachel, having lulled her darling to ſleep, the twilight ſtill giving ſufficient light, took her tablets from her pocket, and, as ſhe leaned over a window ſhe had juſt opened to gaze at the ſerenity of an evening, that ſeemed to give pleaſure to the whole creation but her forlorn, unhappy ſelf, wrote with her pencil the following lines :

When the frame to the earth is bent low,
  By ſickneſs or ſorrow oppreſt ;
When the moments drag penſive and ſlow,
  And the heart it lies cold in the breaſt ;

When each ſocial comfort is fled,
  Nor friend nor companion is near ;
When reſt has forſaken the bed,
  And the pillow is ſtain'd with a tear :—

Ah ! then, what avails each gay ſcene
  Which Nature unfolds to our ſight ?
In vain Phebus riſes ſerene,
  Or Cynthia enlivens the night !

In vain is yon canopy ſpread
  Thus gorgeous, with ſapphire and gold,
When each ſenſe of pleaſure is fled,
  And each fond affection lies cold !

Haſte, Apathy, haſte thee, and bring,
  With poppies infuſed in the bowl,
A draught from the Lethean ſpring
  To ſteep in oblivion my ſoul.

Thy ſable ſtole paſs 'fore mine eyes,
  That when pale affliction I view,
No ſhades of paſt pleaſures may riſe
  To ſharpen her arrows anew.

But come, with thy ſenſe-numbing power,
  Aſſiſt me thoſe arrows to brave ;
Nor leave me till that happy hour,
  When I ſink to repoſe in the grave !

When ſhe had finiſhed, the full ſenſe of her own deplorable ſituation ruſhed upon her mind ; ſhe reſted her head upon her hand, and, unable to weep, a kind of ſtupor pervaded all her ſenſes ; and ſo entirely abſorbed forbed was she in her own agonizing reflections, that she was as perfectly lost to every surrounding object as if she had been no longer in existence. From this reverie she was aroused by the cry of her child, and in her haste to let down the window, she dropped her tablets. It was an awkward circumstance; for the window looked into a garden belonging to a genteel house that was in another street. It was therefore impossible to regain them that night; but she resolved to go early the ensuing morning to inquire for them; for they had formerly belonged to her mother, and were on that account highly valued by Rachel.

Accordingly, the next morning, as soon as she imagined she could gain admittance, she took her child in her arms, and walked round to the front of the house. The door was opened by a decent young woman, and Rachel was beginning to speak, when, turning her eyes toward a parlour, the door of which stood partly open, she saw Archibald Oliver, dressed in deep mourning, sitting at a breakfast table, and holding the identical tablets she came to inquire for, in his hand. She was surprised—she was silent.

"Did you wish to see my mistress, Ma'am?" said the young woman.

"Yes!" said Rachel, hardly conscious that she had answered at all.

There was something in the air and manner of our heroine, that, had she been clothed in the meanest apparel, would still have commanded respect. The young woman passed before her, and courtesying as she pushed open the parlour door, desired her to walk in, and she would call her mistress immediately. At the sound of approaching steps, Oliver raised his eyes.

"Good God! Mrs. Dacres!" exclaimed he.

Rachel was fluttered; she could not speak. A languid smile illumined her pallid countenance as she extended her hand towards him. But the expressive tear that burst from its glistening orbit, contradicted the appearance of tranquillity the smile was meant to convey.

E e 2:

"How

"How is it, Mr. Oliver," said she, when she could command her voice, "that I see you here?"

"A very unhappy circumstance brought me and still detains me here," he replied. Rachel glanced her eye over his sable dress. Jessy darted into her mind.

"Your sister!" said she eagerly.

"Is well," interrupted he, at once comprehending her fears, at least I have no reason to think to the contrary; but Mrs. Oliver is no more."

His voice faltered; Rachel was silent; she knew the folly and impertinence of common-place consolation. Oliver recovered himself, and having learnt from our heroine every occurrence that had taken place since he saw her in London, he in return informed her, that friendship for a very particular acquaintance of her's had brought him to that place—

"An acquaintance of mine?" said Rachel.

"Yes, Lieutenant Courtney."

"Courtney! You astonish me; I thought he was gone to India."

"He had an appointment of that kind, which was procured him by lord M——; but some discoveries which he made after he had even joined his ship, and had received sailing orders, compelled him to quit his appointment, throw up his commission, and follow his unprincipled wife to this place. Lord M. has a seat at Alnwick, which is only a short ride from hence, and Courtney having obtained sufficient testimony of her depravity and his own dishonour, came to me, and asked my advice in what manner he should proceed. See your wife, said I, and remonstrate with her. I will go with you. He seemed inclined to follow my advice, and we rode together toward this place. When we had proceeded a few miles, we saw a chariot and four driving furiously along; the liveries bespoke it the equipage of lord M. Courtney no sooner saw it, than, clapping spurs to his horse, he gallopped from me, and before I could get up with him, had stopped the carriage in which was Mrs. Courtney

ney and his Lordſhip. The irritated, impetuous huſband had dragged the ignoble peer from the carriage,
and, drawing a caſe of piſtols, preſented him one,
whilſt with the other he prepared to defend himſelf,
when one of the footmen ſtruck him acroſs the head
with the end of a whip, and he fell lifeleſs to the
ground.   Lord M. ſprang into his carriage again and
drove off, leaving me with my ſervant to take what
care we could of poor Courtney. We were nearer
this place than we were to Alnwick, and placing him
on the horſe before John, with great difficulty we got
him here. This houſe is kept by a woman who nurſ-
ed my wife; and as I thought he would be quieter
and better attended here than in a public inn, I had
him brought hither. The wound on his head is deep,
but the ſurgeon does not think him in ſo much danger from the effect of that as from the violent perturbation of his mind.

Rachel liſtened with aſtoniſhment to this detail, and
was ſo entirely abſorbed in reflection on the ſtrange
incidents Oliver related, that when the miſtreſs of the
houſe entered, and requeſted to know what her commands were, ſhe had totally forgotten the circumſtance that had brought her to the houſe. She heſi-
tated, bluſhed; at length, caſting her eyes on the
breakfaſt table, ſhe ſaw the object of her inquiry; but
the conſciouſneſs of her embarraſſed, awkward appearance, ſo increaſed her confuſion, that the inquiries ſhe
made for her tablets had more the appearance of ſub-
terfuge than truth. However, the maid having mentioned that Mr. Oliver had picked them up in the garden, they were delivered to our heroine, who, having
expreſſed a deſire to ſee Courtney, and promiſed to return in the afternoon for that purpoſe, took her leave.

Now, though Rachel did not know five perſons in
the neighbourhood where ſhe dwelt, even by ſight, yet
ſhe was herſelf known by every individual in it; and
her embarraſſed and heſitating manner, added to a
knowledge of the evil reports which were circulated
concerning her, led the woman where Oliver lodged,

to

to imagine she came to visit him, or Courtney, as she seemed so perfectly acquainted with both.

In the afternoon, Rachel determined to see Courtney. She had no idea that impropriety could be annexed to a visit which she conceived to be an act of duty ; and when she found him so extremely ill as to need the most constant and tender attention ; when she discovered that it was in her power to soothe his afflicted heart, and smooth the bed of pain, by an exertion of friendly assiduity ; forgetting every thing but that she had once been under obligations to him, she resolved herself to be his attendant till he should recover strength sufficient to enable him to return to his mother and sisters. Thus every morning she repaired to the chamber of the sick man, nursing him with the affection of a sister, and administering to him the consolation of a friend.

Mrs. Spriggins and her unprincipled guest were mean enough to employ their servants to inquire in the neighbourhood after our heroine, and be constant spies upon her actions. That she was often, nay, almost continually at the house where Oliver was, and where Courtney lay sick, they were assured of ; and though they knew that she constantly returned to her solitary apartment to her meals, which were scanty enough, and that she was always at home at an early hour in the evening, yet they failed not to attribute to motives the most degrading to the sex, a conduct which was the result of pure benevolence, and did honour to her heart, however it proved, that her head was not too much stored with worldly prudence and knowledge.

Things were exactly in this situation, when Hamden Auberry arrived in search of a woman, whom, one moment, he was ready to kneel and worship, and the next, to call down everlasting wrath upon her.

It may easily be imagined, that the story told by Mrs. Spriggins, Mrs. Courtney and family did not tend to soften his heart towards her ; so far from it, he poured forth a torrent of execrations, and vowed never to see her more. But when he had returned to his inn, and mused a few moments, he thought he
would

would fee her once more, u   her, and bid her an everlafting farewel; he had learnt in what quarter of the town fhe lodged, and at the dufk of the evening went to the houfe and inquired for her. She was not at home. At eight o'clock he called again; ftill fhe was not returned. Having obtained a direction to the houfe where he was told fhe fpent every day, and having affured himfelf that was the refidence of Oliver, he determined to keep watch before the door, and be himfelf an eye-witnefs of her leaving it, and at what hour. Long and wearifome was the night, and horrible were the feelings of Auberry. About twelve o'clock, he determined to leave her to her fate, and return with all fpeed to London; but before he had reached the inn, defire of revenge impelled him to return. 'I will tear her from the arms of Oliver,' faid he, 'and wreak my vengeance on both her and her paramour;' but then the memory of his child croffed his imagination, and with it the fond recollection of what the mother was when he firft knew her; a flood of tendernefs rufhed over his foul, and he wept like an infant.

In this diftracted manner did Auberry pafs the night, and the dawn of day found him fitting on the fteps of a door oppofite to the lodgings of Oliver. He rofe from the cold, damp feat, and with a heavy heart was giving a laft look at the houfe, when the door opened gently, and Rachel herfelf, with her child in her arms, came out.

Though during the whole night Hamden had fuppofed his wife was there, yet fomething like hope had fometimes led him to think he might have been deceived, and fhe might ftill be innocent; but this ocular proof was beyond all doubt. He reeled againft a poft, ftaggered and fell.

Rachel faw him; but, wrapped in a coarfe great coat which he had borrowed at the inn, with his hat flapped, it was impoffible, by the faint glimmer of the twilight, fhe fhould know him; fhe imagined it to be an inebriated perfon, juft endeavouring to return home; and fearful, fhould fhe be obferved by him at that early hour, that he might in fome refpect or other be

be rude to her, she quickened her steps, and before
Auberry was sufficiently recovered to speak or rise
from the ground, she was out of sight, and in a few
moments reached her own habitation. A little girl,
who was up on some particular occasion, let her in,
and she threw herself on the bed, in hopes to obtain
some repose, while Auberry returned to the inn, pen-
ned a hasty letter to her, which he left, with orders that
it should be sent by eight o'clock in the morning. He
then ordered a chaise and four, and proceeded with
all the rapidity of such a conveyance to London, seldom stopping even for refreshment, as though he
thought, by the velocity, of the movement, to leave
his cares behind, or lose the remembrance of them, by
attending to the various objects that passed in quick
succession before him.

In the mean time, Rachel had enjoyed about two
hours sleep, and felt herself greatly refreshed; for the
fatigue and anxiety of the night had exhausted both
her spirits and strength. She had attended as usual
the day before at the bedside of Courtney; towards
noon he had arisen, and was removed for the benefit
of the air into an adjoining apartment, and placed in
an easy chair near the window. The noise of horses
drew his attention towards the street. He looked out,
and saw his wife, accompanied by lord M. on horseback, attended by two servants in rich liveries. She
raised her eyes, saw the emaciated figure of her hufband, pointed him out to her dissolute companion,
and both burst into a loud laugh. Courtney was
unequal to the shock; he attempted to speak, but his
voice failed him; he gasped, groaned, and fell to the
floor. Alarming faintings succeeded each other, and
he was reduced to such a state of weakness, that the
medical gentleman who attended him imagined it almost impossible that he should live through the night.
Was it possible for Rachel in such a situation to leave
him? No! She had not been treated with sufficient
respect by the mistress of the house where she lodged,
to make her think it necessary to send any message to
her concerning her staying out, or her reasons for so
doing.   Towards

Towards morning, Courtney fell into a quiet fleep, and Oliver entreated Rachel to retire, and endeavour to take fome repofe. Acting from motives the moft pure and even commendable, without a thought or wifh in the fmalleft tittle derogatory to virtue, Rachel had no apprehenfion of incurring cenfure from any. How furprifed was fhe then, on awaking in the morning, to read the following note, which was brought to her by the little girl who had let her in.

" Mifstrefs Dakirs, ater the adventer of laft nite, you cant fuppos I will fuffer you to ftay any longer in my oufe, wich is a oneft oufe; and furdermore, I does not expect you to go without paying me every fardin of what you oes me. You muft go meditly, as I does not want women of your fort in my oufe no longer."

Rachel was really fo totally unconfcious of evil, that fhe was at a lofs to think what the woman meant by " the adventure of laft night ;" but going to her to inquire, was fo overwhelmed with abufe, that, weeping, trembling, almoft fainting, fhe retreated from the houfe leaving every thing behind her to fatisfy the rapacity of her inhuman landlady.

As fhe was going out of the door, fhe met the porter with her hufband's letter. She took it, broke the feal, and read that he had been there, that he had feen her, that he believed her loft to virtue, and that he abandoned her forever. Overcome by fenfations the moft agonizing, fhe fat down on the fteps of the door. The letter remained open in her hand ; her eyes were riveted to it, and only that fhe breathed, fhe might have been taken for a ftatue of fixed and mute defpair. How long fhe would have remained in this fituation is uncertain, or whether, finking into infenfibility, fhe would not have loft all confcioufnefs of her mifery, had not the woman with the diabolical malice of a fiend opened the door, and bade her begone from the ftep. Aroufed from her lethargy of grief, fhe arofe, folded her child to her bofom, and bowing her head in meek refignation, the forrows of her heart found vent at her eyes, and fhe obeyed in filence.

And

And what was there, in this moment of anguish, to support the sinking spirits of our afflicted heroine? Conscious innocence! And whilst humbled to the very dust, she could look up with hope and confidence to Him who is a rock of defence to the injured, a sure help to those who trust in him.

Wounded pride would have first impelled her to hide herself from Oliver, as she discovered, from the unconnected scrawl left by Auberry, that it was of him he was jealous, and had it been only for herself that she was interested, she would most likely have suffered every degree of misery before she would have asked relief of any one; but her child, the son of Auberry, the lawful heir to large possessions, for his sake she was resolved to stifle her feelings, and endeavour to convince his cruel father that he had injured her in the most unwarrantable manner.

She therefore went immediately to his lodgings, and calming her perturbed spirits as much as she possibly could, thus addressed him:—"Mr. Oliver, I am necessitated to request the loan of a few guineas, at the same time that I tell you it is more than probable I may never be able to repay you. Something has taken place this morning, which obliges me in future to forbear seeing you, or giving any farther attendance on our unfortunate friend."

"Good heavens!" said Oliver, struck with her pale countenance, swollen eyes and evident agitation; "what can be the matter? Wherever you are going, do not refuse me the satisfaction of knowing, that I may be able to assist, protect, comfort, be a brother to you."

"It is impossible," said she, "the world will not suffer it."

He comprehended the meaning of her words, and without reply tendered her his purse. She took five guineas from it, and then requesting to see Courtney, of whom she took a silent leave, she departed, leaving Oliver astonished and affected at her conduct. He mused a few moments, and then thinking, however rigid propriety might forbid her to visit the house he inhabited,

inhabited, or receive vifits from him, yet it did not forbid him following and difcovering her retreat, where he might fupply her with all the neceffaries and comforts of life. He fnatched his hat, and rufhed into the ftreet; but he was too late; Rachel was no longer in fight, nor could he difcover which way fhe had gone.

Our heroine walked to a poor cottage about a mile from the town, inhabited only by an old woman and her daughter. Here fhe agreed to board at a very low rate for a few days, and then fat down to write to her hufband. She endeavoured to explain circumftances that appeared fufpicious; but to think that Auberry fufpected her honour, gave her fuch inexpreffible anguifh, that fhe was frequently obliged to lay down her pen and weep. At length fhe finifhed, earneftly conjuring, if not for her own, yet for his child's fake, he would fend her fome relief, nor fuffer them to expire with want, or languifh out their lives in poverty and obfcurity.

This letter fhe directed to a coffee-houfe in London, which fhe knew he frequented, and requefting an anfwer to be directed to the poft-office at Newark, fhe left her infant in the charge of her old hoftefs, went herfelf and put her own letter in, inquiring at the fame time when fhe might expect an anfwer.

When fhe returned to her humble home, fatigue, anguifh of heart, and the violent emotions fhe had experienced during the day, had fo far overcome her, that fhe went to bed much indifpofed, and after a night of reftlefs agitation, fhe awoke from a fhort flumber fo ill, as to be unable to rife.

From that time, a period of three weeks was a total blank to Rachel. A fever, accompanied by a delirium, brought her to the verge of the grave; but the tendernefs of her good old hoftefs and her daughter, co-operating with a naturally good conftitution, and the attendance of a fkilful man of medicine, at length triumphed over the diforder, and fhe returned to life and a renewed fenfe of her forrows.

The firft thing fhe thought of was her expected letter. She difpatched the young cottager to New-

ark

ark to inquire for it; she returned empty handed; there was no letter there. Thus day after day passed on. The five guineas Rachel had borrowed of Oliver were totally expended during her illness, and no letter arriving from her husband, she was once more pennyless, but not totally friendless. The poor inhabitants of the cottage were *Christians*. Had she been stained with a thousand errors, they would not have thought it right to remember them when she was bowed to the earth by affliction. Their whole possessions were, the cottage, a small garden, a cow and two spinning wheels; but they dried the tear from her eyes by the voice of kindness, and told her she should be welcome to share their humble fare till returning health enabled her to join their labours for subsistence, if nothing better offered. During her illness, the old cottager had found Auberry's letter, and wishing to gain some intelligence concerning her family, had perused it.

"She may be guilty," said she, "but I have no right to judge her. She is sick and afflicted; it is therefore my duty to nurse and comfort her." She then returned the letter to the pocket from whence she took it, nor even after Rachel's recovery did she suffer her to imagine, by any word, look or hint, that she had seen it.

As soon as Rachel had gathered strength sufficient to enable her to attempt it, with slow and uneven steps she proceeded to Newark, determined to make inquiry herself concerning a letter; for she thought it impossible for Auberry to abandon her and his child to absolute want.

She went to the office, and was told no such letter was there. "Are you certain, Sir?" said she; "it must have been here some time, if it is here at all. Pray look amongst the letters that lay in the office; it is of more consequence to me than you can imagine. It is directed to Mrs. Dacres, to be left here till called for."

A young man hearing her repeat the name of Dacres, turned over a parcel of letters, and presented to

the

the trembling hands of our heroine the long-expected epiſtle from her huſband.

Rachel opened it ; a hundred pound bank note dropped from it ! She attempted to read it, but a miſt came over her eyes ; ſhe reeled, and would have fallen, but the young man caught her. He called for water, and an interior door opening, a young woman, very plainly habited, ruſhed out, ſupported and preſſed to her boſom the lifeleſs, inanimate form, calling on her to revive by the tender name of friend, her dear, unhappy Rachel. Life ſoon reviſited her lips and cheeks ; ſhe opened her eyes, and found her-ſelf in the arms of Jeſſy Oliver.

Leaning on the arm of this dear friend, and hardly daring to truſt her ſenſes left it ſhould prove an illu-ſion, Rachel retired into a ſmall, neat parlour, where ſhe ſoon regained ſufficient compoſure to peruſe her letter. It was ſhort, and the concluſion of it almoſt annihilated her. It was as follows.—

My adored Rachel,

THERE is ſuch an appearance of candour and ſincerity throughout your whole letter, that I cannot but believe you innocent ; prove yourſelf ſo, and on the receipt of this come immediately to London, and prepare to follow my fortunes to foreign climes. Our marriage is no longer a ſecret ; my aunt has diſcard-ed me. I have ſold my commiſſion, and in the deſ-pair I felt at your perfidy, have taken paſſage on board a veſſel bound for Philadelphia. If you love me as you ſay, and as I would fain think you do, you will not heſitate to leave England forever, ſince it is for my peace of mind that I ſhould do ſo. I cannot ſub-mit to live in it below the rank I have been accuſtom-ed to fill. If your affection leads you to be the com-panion of my voyage, the ſharer and ſoother of all my cares, I ſhall regret neither fortune nor country. If not, if ſome ſtronger attachment binds you to this ſpot, Oh Rachel ! I cannot bear the thought ; but ſhould it be ſo, why the farther we are divided the better.

"Incloſed

"Inclofed I imagine is a fum fufficient to difcharge any debts you may have contracted, and bring you to London. If you come, I fhall expect to fee you in ten days from the date of this letter. If not, farewel forever; we meet no more on this fide eternity, and I will ftrive if poffible to forget you.

HAMDEN AUBERRY."

Rachel referred to the date of the letter; it had been written near a month. "Then he is gone! left me forever! and thinks me the moft depraved of women," faid fhe; and her emotions became fo violent, that in her prefent debilitated ftate, Mifs Oliver feared fhe would have fallen into fits; at any rate, fhe thought it neceffary to take her home, and procuring a carriage, fhe herfelf accompanied her to her lowly habitation. By the way fhe talked her into fomething like compofure; fhe learnt every circumftance that had taken place fince their feparation.

Convinced of the purity of our heroine's heart, that her motives had been always right, though her conduct had been fometimes directly contrary to the rigid rules of prudence, fhe felt all her affection for her revive; and taking her hand when fhe had finifhed her detail, fhe cried, "Well, Mrs. Auberry, (as we fhall henceforth call Rachel) in return for the confidence you have repofed in me, I will tell you my ftory. It is a very fimple one, without one romantic or extraordinary incident.

"When I left London, I recollected an old fchool fellow I had at this place, of whofe fenfe and difcretion I had a very high opinion; to her I repaired, and through her means fettled the method of correfponding with you and Archibald, alfo the means of receiving a fmall yearly income, which I poffeffed independent of my father. I then threw afide the fine lady entirely, affumed the plain attire you fee me now wear, and with it a fimplicity of manners that might be likely not to betray my real rank in life. I then procured an apartment at a farm-houfe, that is fituated in a moft delightful though very folitary valley,

about

about three miles from hence. I purchafed a few books, with materials for needle-work, and diverfified my time with reading, working, and taking neceffary exercife. The productions of my needle, through my friend were fent to London and fold, increafing my little income in fuch a manner as to afford me all the comforts of life. I heard of my brother's marriage, and of his refidence fo near me. I longed to fee him ; but was too proud to think of throwing myfelf on the liberality of his wife, for I knew that Archibald himfelf was as poor as I was. I therefore continued my retirement and avocations. I have frequently thought of you, and from fome accounts which accidentally met my ears, was led fometimes to blame but oftener to pity you.

"But fhould I ever return to the gay world, my young affociates will, I have no doubt, be furprifed that I fhould have eloped from my father's houfe, changed my name, and fecluded myfelf above a year and a half in a cottage, yet never have met with a fingle adventure, or made one conqueft ; nay, if you will believe me, the impenetrable ruftics have entirely overlooked my beauty and accomplifhments ; and though I have appeared regularly every Sunday, when the weather permitted, at the parifh church, the Squire has not once noticed me, and I have remained entirely unmolefted.

"But I am weary of this dull famenefs of fcene, and you and I will now fet out together in fearch of adventures. This mad brained, harum-fcarum hufband of yours, though I think he little deferves fuch attention from us, yet we will e'en go after him. For if we fhould not find him, we may perhaps find fomebody elfe that will be glad to fee us."

Rachel comprehending that Jeffy meant Reuben, replied with additional penfivenefs, " Alas ! my dear girl, I have never heard from my brother fince he left England."

" So I underftand," faid Jeffy, ftill forcing a fmile, while her eyes were brimfull of tears ; " but I cannot reprefs a fond hope, which almoft amounts to a belief,

F f 2

that

that he is ftill in exiftence, and that we fhall one day meet again. As to Archibald, it will not be proper to let him know of our defign till it is too late for him to overtake and accompany us; for that would overthrow my whole plan of reconcilement between you and Auberry. And fhould the worft come to the worft, there is ftill my little annuity; we will live together, my dear Rachel, in humble, but contented independence. What our income will not procure, induftry fhall fupply. We will ftudy to fulfil the duties of our lowly ftation, and, enjoying the fweet confolation of an approving confcience, hold the trifling multitude, that is in general termed the *world*, in fo little eftimation, as neither to court its fmiles or fear its cenfures."

This was a plan too agreeable to the feelings of Rachel not to be immediately clofed with. This re-commencement of friendfhip, with a perfon fo dear to her heart as Jeffy Oliver, feemed to eafe her bofom of half its load. A very fhort time fufficed for the fettlement of every concern, either of Mifs Oliver or our heroine, and on the fecond morning after their meeting they were on their road to London. Rachel left ample teftimony with her aged hoftefs at the cottage, that whatever her other errors might have been, fhe was not guilty of the fin of ingratitude. Arrived in London, they made every inquiry after Auberry, and learnt that he had been departed above a fortnight, and it was univerfally believed to America.

It was late in the feafon for veffels to crofs the boifterous Atlantic ocean; the two fair friends could hear of none likely to fail to the port they wifhed, under a month or fix weeks. This appeared to the anxious and impatient Rachel an eternity; and being informed that a fhip would go from Liverpool in the courfe of ten days, they purfued their journey for that place, and arrived juft in time to fecure a paffage, as the veffel was to fail the following morning.

Reduced as our heroine was by illnefs, this long journey was almoft too much for her ftrength; but Jeffy Oliver had fine fpirits, and a conftitution which,

though

though not robuft, could fupport great fatigue without finking under it.   They alighted at the inn, and
refolved to indulge in a few hours reft before their embarkation, where we will leave them and make fome
little inquiry after Auberry.

When he had difpatched his letter with the money
to Rachel, he waited with the utmoft impatience the
arrival of the time in which he might expect her.   He
had in the firft hurry of jealoufy, rage and difappointment fold his commiflion, and taken a paffage on
board a fhip bound to Philadelphia, determined never
more to vifit his native country, where every bright
profpect of his youth had been untimely blafted.   The
reception of his wife's letter awakened all his tendernefs for her.   Rachel in want, depreffed, fick, broken-
hearted, was ever before his eyes.   'She may yet be
innocent,' cried he ; the very fuppofition feemed to
give him comfort ; 'yet the proofs of her depravity
were fo inconteftable——' here his heart glowed with
refentment ; 'I will at leaft fend her the means of
coming immediately to me.   If fhe comes, I will receive her with affection, if not, I will endeavour to forget that I ever knew her.'   In this frame of mind he
wrote the letter which conveyed the money to our heroine.

But when day after day paffed, and no tidings of
her neither by letter or any other means, he concluded fhe was totally abandoned, and in defpair of ever
knowing peace again, he embarked on his intended
voyage.   But tempeftuous weather enfuing, and the
brig in which he embarked being rather ancient,
fprung a leak, and they put into Liverpool to refit ;
where Auberry, giving way to the defpair that preyed upon his mind, funk into a ftate of inanity.   Both
mind and body became debilitated ; a hectic fever
flowly undermined his conftitution ; and when the veffel was ready to depart, he was too ill to make the
voyage, and fuffered her to go without him.   He
had gone to his mother immediately on his arrival in
Liverpool, where he explained to her all his caufe for
forrow, and felt every wound bleed afrefh as he peruf-

ed fome letters from Belle Webfter, which tended highly to criminate his wife. Doctor Lenient was abfent at the time of his arrival ; a fmall eftate had been left him in Ireland, and he had croffed the channel in order to take poffeffion and fettle fome very material bufinefs.

When Hamden had been with his mother about three weeks, the Doctor returned, furprifed to fee his nephew, and more furprifed at his very rueful appearance. He inquired what he had been doing to alter himfelf fo. "I have been ruining myfelf," faid Auberry.

"Odfo ! I hope not," replied the good-hearted Doctor. "What, have you been gambling ?"

"Yes, in the lottery of life, and have drawn a blank.. In fhort, my dear uncle, I have married a woman without either family or fortune, and am difcarded by my aunt ; but that I could have borne, had my wife been. faithful."

"Odds my life !" faid the Doctor, "matrimony feems no improver of happinefs ;. for this is the fecond tale of mifery I have heard to-day. What think you,. fifter ? juft as I landed from the packet, I faw two women ftanding on the fhore, ready to ftep into a boat that was waiting. One countenance I knew inftantly ; for though pale and greatly emaciated, there was ftill that character of fenfibility and virtue impreffed upon it for which I ufed to admire it.. It was our unfortunate young friend Rachel Dudley."

Hamden gafped for breath, but he fuffered the Doctor to proceed without interruption. "She had a fine boy in her arms," continued the Doctor, "apparently about four months old, and fpite of all we have heard,. I felt myfelf impelled to fpeak to her. Her companion was Mifs Oliver, whom we heard had eloped from her father's houfe, and who has not been heard of by her family for above a twelvemonth."

"Well, Sir," cried Auberry impatiently, "but what of Rachel."

"Why I'll tell you," faid the Doctor, taking off his wig and deliberately putting on his crimfon velvet «ap, and without noticing the emotions of Hamden ; "when I went up to her, and afked her how fhe did, fhe laid her hand on her bofom, and with a look I fhall never forget, anfwered, "Neither well nor happy, Doctor."

"I am forry, my poor girl," faid I, "for fome circumftances that I underftand have taken place, and knowing your extreme fenfibility, cannot be furprifed that they have injured both your health and peace of mind. But where are you going now ?"

"To America," faid fhe, "in purfuit of my hufband."

"You are married, then," faid I.

"Yes," fhe replied, and fixing her eyes on my face, "did you not know it ?"

"No, how fhould I ? I have been in Ireland thefe two months paft. Juft then the failors called to her to get into the boat. She tendered me her hand."

"God blefs you, my good Doctor," faid fhe. I fhook her hand, helped her in, and——"

"And fhe is really gone, then," cried Hamden frantickly.

The Doctor raifed his eyes ; the agitated countenance of his nephew alarmed him. "Yes, I believe fo," faid he in a doubtful tone ; "but why does it affect you thus ?"

"Why does it affect me ? Oh ! Sir, I am the hufband of Rachel ! It is me fhe is gone in purfuit of. I have deferted, abandoned, forfaken her ; I thought her depraved ; I was told——"

"Yes, and fo have I been told," faid the Doctor with vehemence, ftriking his hand on the elbow of his chair ; "but after beholding her meek, expreffive countenance, where candour and purity are ftamped on every feature ; after feeing her emaciated frame, and hearing her tremulous, plaintive accents, I would not believe the fmalleft tittle to her difadvantage, though millions joined to affirm it ! Young man, you have been hafty, and blinded by paffion ; have thrown away a pearl of ineftimable price."

Hamden's

Hamden's feelings were now too great for utterance. His mother foothed him ; but Dr. Lenient, who hated family pride, blamed the whole of his conduct ; and though before he went to bed he preferibed fomething to compofe the agitated fpirits of Auberry, yet when retired, his thoughts were wholly occupied by Rachel, wandering without a proper protector, in fearch of a man who had wantonly facrificed her happinefs and reputation on the altar of ambition and intereft.

CHAPTER LAST.

Where heaven-born Freedom holds her court
  Let me erect my humble fhed ;
Where all the arts with joy refort,
  And Science rears her laurell'd head.

WE left Reuben, in captivity, employing every leifure moment in expanding the mind and cultivating the talents of Eumea.   In this manner fix weary months paffed on, and ftill no hope of emancipation.   At the end of this period, tidings arrived that the Indian chiefs had been guilty of a breach of the European laws, and in confequence had fuffered death.   The fachem called a council of his elders and chieftains, and it was determined that Reuben and his unhappy companions fhould on the enfuing morning be bound to the ftake, and fuffer thofe inhuman tortures which none but favages could inflict, and none but favages fubmit to, without an endeavour to be avenged of thofe who inflict them.

Eumea was in the wigwam at the time this horrid fentence was paffed ; her heart funk ; there were but a few hours to intervene before it was to be put in execution.   In the dead of night, fhe entered the wigwam of our hero.

" Englifhmen," faid fhe, " awake, get up ; danger and death are at hand ; hafte, quit this place, flee into the woods that fkirt the mountains, and the God of
                                        the

the Chriftians go with you." In a few words fhe explained to them the neceffity of their immediate flight, and directing their fteps to a cavern in a hollow glen, fhe threw her arms round the neck of Reuben, bathed his cheek with her tears, preffed her cold trembling lips to his, and fobbing, Adieu! returned to her reftlefs bed to weep and pray for his fafety.

Innumerable were the hardfhips endured by Reuben and his companions, fkulking in caves, or deep woods, feeding on wild fruit, and even glad to make a meal of acorns; terrified by the ruftling of the leaves, or the fteps of wild though inoffenfive animals, natives of the uncultivated tracts through which they were obliged to pafs.

After three weeks wearifome journey, they at length arrived at a European fettlement; but fo reduced through famine and fatigue, that it feemed as though they were only arrived at a place of fafety that they might reft from all their cares in death. Even the ftrength and fpirits of O'Neil began to flag, and he bitterly regretted that he was no longer able to cheer, attend and comfort his dear mafter.

But what was the furprife of Reuben, when, the day after his arrival at this place, he faw Eumea enter the apartment where he was. He raifed himfelf from the bed on which he was reclining, and in a voice that expreffed at once furprife and pleafure, exclaimed, " Eumea here! what ftrange incident!" She ftopped him, took hold of his hand, and looking earneftly in his face—

" Is it ftrange that I fhould follow you; (faid fhe) were not you my inftructor, my more than father, my friend, and was it poffible Eumea could ftay behind you and live? Do not look angry; I know I have done wrong; for you taught me to love, refpect, and never forfake my father and mother. I tried to remember your precepts, I tried to obey your injunctions; but, alas! the filent night was witnefs to my anguifh, and the rifing fun could not dry the dew from my eyelids. If I flept, I faw you, liftened to you, and was happy. Fleeting joy! that but embittered

the

the moment of awaking! The flowers you had gathered for me the day before you left me, I bound upon my breaſt next my heart; I have worn them there ever ſince; they withered and dried, but every day I refreſh them with my tears. One morning, juſt as the day appeared, I aroſe, took my bow and arrows, and reſolved to follow you. My mother was ſtill aſleep; I looked at her, I knelt beſide her; but I dared not kiſs her leſt ſhe ſhould awake. I would have prayed, but you had told me that an undutiful child could never be a favourite of our heavenly Father; ſo I preſſed my hands on my heart, which throbbed ſo loud, it ſeemed to ſay, Oh! God of the Chriſtians, bleſs my mother! God knows every thought of the heart, and though I dared not pronounce his ſacred name with my lips, perhaps its ſilent petition may be read and anſwered."

Eumea pauſed; Reuben would have anſwered, but he was at a loſs what to ſay. O'Neil, weak and ill as he was, had moved towards her, and ſitting at her feet, leaning one hand on her knees, his head reſted on it, and his languid eyes were fixed on her face, as he liſtened to her with profound attention.

"It is my belief," ſaid he, "that God Almighty never turns away from the prayers of an innocent heart; and then to be ſure he knows all we want, when we can't ſpeak to aſk for even a morſel of bread. Oh! if we were only to have what we deſerved, we ſhould find but poor accommodations, in our journey through this world; but you ſee he was ſo good as to ſend people before us, to make every thing comfortable; and all he requires is, that we ſhall in return make things pleaſant and agreeable for them that come after us."

Reuben could not help ſmiling at O'Neil's morality. Eumea ſeemed loſt in thought, and ſcarcely to have attended to what he ſaid; but when ſhe found he was ſilent, ſhe again addreſſed our hero.

"So you ſee here I am; but what have I gained by following you? Nothing! for now all that I ſuffered before for your abſence, I now feel on account

of

of my mother.   But I will not return.   No; I could
not fupport my father's unkindnefs, and my mother's
reproaches, which would be the more painful becauſe
mingled with affection.   I will follow you, my dear
inftructor, I will be your handmaid, and love and
ferve you to the laft hour of my life."

"And fo will I," faid O'Neil, "and I'll weil ferve
you too, my beautiful Indian lady, every day and all
the day, and by night too, if fo be there be neceffity."

"And how did you know that you fhould find me
here ?" faid Reuben.

"I knew," fhe replied, "that this was the neareft
fettlement, and had I not found you here, I fhould
have travelled onward to Philadelphia; and had you
not been there, I fhould have thought you had died
by the way, and would have fought you in a better
world, the world of fpirits."

"You would not, I hope, Eumea, have dared to
rufh unbidden into eternity ?" faid Reuben.

"I fear I fhould," fhe replied; "for why fhould we
endure life, when the nights are paft in anguifh, and
every day is a day of forrow? When the wintry blafts
howl, when the fnow falls, and the froft binds up the lakes:
then, when confined to the wigwam, there is no comfort
within, but the tempeft of the paffions rages more furious
than the gale that bows the tall cedars, and fhakes to the
roots the ftately oak; why fhould we not fleep with
the infect or the reptile tribes, that pafs the dreary
feafon in infenfibility? And when the warm fouthern
breeze diffolves the ice, and bids the trees be green,
the bloffom come; when the blackbird whiftles mer-
rily, and the robin begins to drefs his plumes; if then
nor fragrant bloffom, nor cheerful bird, nor flower-
fpeckled field delight the fenfe, or foothe the tortured
foul, were it not better to feek repofe in other climes,
more fuited to our feelings? Or when the deer feeks
the deep woods, and pants though lying on the river's brink, when the fcorching fun dries the grafs and
parches up the ground, where is the harm if, plunging
in the wave, we quench the fever that confumes us,
or from our veins let out the blood, that rufhes with

G g

fuch

such fury through our frame, swelling the heart till it is near to bursting? Or even when the season of corn arrives; when clusters of wild grapes hang on the bending vines; when the berries, blackened by the sun, peep through the half-faded leaves; when the cool, soft breeze of evening, and the sweet air of the morning, affords refreshing slumbers to the eyelids, or unclofes them to pleasing prospects, that, being surveyed, makes the heart dance with joy—Ah! then, if the eyes are dimmed with tears and the heart oppressed with sorrow; is it a sin to seek that happy place where we can neither weep nor suffer more?"

"You have profited but little by my instructions, Eumea," said Reuben, "if you can argue thus."

"I will follow you, then," said she emphatically, "and endeavour to improve."

In about a fortnight, our hero and his companions were enough recovered to continue their journey. It was in vain he entreated Eumea to return to her mother, she persisted in following him. It was without effect that he represented to her, that in accompanying him she would be looked upon with disrespect by the European women; her resolution was taken and was not to be shaken.

The appearance of Reuben and his followers was miserable in the extreme when they entered Philadelphia; and what added to their misery was, that amongst them all they had not a single copper, nor any friends to whom they could apply for assistance. The forlorn group had crossed the Schuylkill, and with weary steps were approaching the city, when a venerable man of the society of Friends, riding out for exercise and air, surveyed them with an eye of compassion, and stopping his horse—"Friend," said he, addressing Reuben, "both thou and thy companions seem fatigued, and appear to have taken a long journey; from whence dost thou come?"

"From captivity," said Reuben.

"Yes," cried O'Neil, who, having recovered his usual spirits, pushed forward to speak for himself; "yes, we have been obliged to pay a pretty long visit
to

to the copper-coloured gentlefolks, and if we had not come away as we did, they would have fcalped us and roafted us, and then a pretty figure we fhould have cut! But this dear creature, who, though fhe is a little darkifh or fo, has a heart as beautiful as an angel: fo fhe told us what they were about going to do. Said fhe, Get up, my lads, and run away whilft you can; for to-morrow you will have no legs to run with. So away we came, and a fine trampoofe we have had. And now we have got here, I don't know that we are much better off; for if they had roafted us, we fhould not a lived to be ftarved to death; for a devil a penny have we got to buy bread."

"Neverthelefs," faid the benevolent friend, "thou fhalt not ftarve. I am not rich; but Heaven forbid that I fhould fuffer a fellow-creature to want while I have a morfel to give him, or a blanket to fpare to fhelter him from the inclemencies of the weather. I have a houfe on the banks of the Delaware, but a very fhort diftance from the city, and its doors were never fhut againft the unfortunate; come home with me, then, and bring the good Indian maiden with thee. It matters not to what nation, kindred or people they belong who are in affliction; I feel they are my brethren, and as fuch, I will gladly fhare my own comforts with them."

They heard with delight the genuine effufions of mercy and benevolence flow from the lips of the man of peace, and being directed by him, purfued their way to the habitation of hofpitality.

"A fmall manfion, built by frugality and furnifhed by fimplicity, fituated on the banks of the Delaware, and furrounded by a large and well-cultivated garden, was the dwelling of Stedfaft Trueman. Elizabeth his wife was not handfome, but there was fomething in her look, voice and manner, more charming than beauty. Her houfe, her children, herfelf, were pure emblems of neatnefs, innocence and induftry. She heard that fome poor guefts were arrived, directed to their friendly roof by her hufband, came into the kitchen to bid them welcome, and with her own hands

affifted

affifted to fet forth refrefhment. The children came round them, fome eagerly curious and inquifitive, and others timidly ftanding aloof, to obferve the ftrange drefs and appearance of the travellers.

In this afylum, Reuben and his companions foon recruited both health and fpirits. Their benevolent friend fupplied them with fome coarfe clothing, the joint product of his farm and his wife's induftry. In the courfe of converfation our hero mentioned his father's name.

"Dudley," faid friend Trueman; "I knew him well; a more worthy, honeft man never exifted. If thou art his fon, thou haft, I fear, been greatly wronged by the man Jacob Holmes. I have reafon to believe thy father was a man of ftrict integrity, and that he would not premeditatedly affert a falfehood. He did declare to me in confidence every particular of his paft life, and though he did not boaft of his good deeds, yet I gathered enough to believe that Jacob was the child of his bounty. But the man has fince fo boldly and folemnly contradicted that belief, that I dare not judge too rafhly; and Heaven forbid that I fhould condemn him; for, juft or unjuft, he is gone to give an account of his ftewardfhip before Him, who, requiring but humility, juftice and mercy from his fervants toward their fellow-creatures, will in no wife excufe thofe who flight his counfels, or break his commandments."

Reuben was furprifed. "Is Jacob Holmes then dead?" faid he.

"Verily he fleepeth with his fathers," faid Trueman. "He was greatly hurt about three months fince, by a fall from his horfe; the bruife was internal, brought on a fpitting of blood, which baffled all medical aid, and he went off fuddenly, when he fuppofed himfelf mending. Indeed, I was told he never believed himfelf in danger. More is the pity; the rod of affliction, that warns us of approaching diffolution, is a falutary and neceffary judgment, that as we bow under the correcting hand, we may implore that mercy which is never withheld from the penitent finner."

"And

" And who inherits his eftate ?" faid Reuben.

" His infant fon, who with his mother, ftill refides in the houfe."

" Mrs. Holmes is a worthy woman," faid Reuben, " and poffeffes an honeft fimplicity of heart extremely interefting. Oh bounteous Difpofer of events," continued he, and his foul expanded as he fpoke, " vifit not, I humbly befeech thee, the fins of the father upon the child; but may he live to be a comfort to his mother, a friend to the worthy, and thy faithful fervant to a good old age."

" Thy pious prayers, good young man," faid Trueman, " return tenfold on thy own head."

The unfortunate participators of Reuben's captivity being recruited, departed in fearch of employment; but himfelf, O'Neil and Eumea were detained in the habitation of friend Trueman, who wifhed to place our hero in fome reputable employ, meant to detain O'Neil in his own fervice, and thought the food and raiment neceffary to render the Indian maid comfortable, would never be miffed by his own family. The inquiries he fet on foot for employment for our hero made it univerfally known that he was returned to Philadelphia.

One morning, as he fat converfing with Trueman, he was furprifed by the entrance of Mrs. Holmes. She advanced to him with a firm but eager ftep, and prefenting her hand, " I am glad to fee thee, friend Reuben," faid fhe; " I did not hear of thy return till yefter even, or I fhould have come to vifit thee before."

Our hero cordially fhook her proffered hand, led her to a feat, and told her he was happy in an opportunity to renew their acquaintance.

" I expect thou doft know already that Jacob Holmes is gone home," faid fhe, her bofom heaving and her eyes fwimming in tears. Reuben bowed affent.

" Thou haft no right to regret his departure," continued fhe, " but he was the chofen friend of my heart, the father of my child, the fupport of his family; his lofs to me is irreparable." She paufed a moment. " I have, fince his departure," fhe continued, recovering her voice, " difcovered amongft fome old papers, which

                    I do

I do dope and believe he had never infpected, the at-
tefted copy of a will, and other accounts of confequence to thee.   Here they are; thou wilt find by
them that thou art the real poffeffor of Mount Pleafant.   I am fure I could not be happy to detain it
from the lawful owner, and I here relinquifh all claim
to it, and throw both myfelf and child upon your benevolence."   She then untied a handkerchief, and delivered the papers into the hands of Reuben, whofe
feelings on the occafion cannot eafily be defcribed.

Our hero, thus raifed almoft inftantaneoufly from
extreme poverty to a ftate of cafe, and indeed (what
in thofe days of moderation was termed) affluence,
made it his firft care to place Mrs. Holmes and her
fon in a comfortable habitation, and to fettle upon
them one third of all his father died poffeffed of.   He
placed Eumea with her, who affiduoufly endeavoured
to conform to the European drefs, cuftoms and manners; but fhe pined at being feparated from Reuben,
and if more than two days elapfed without her feeing
him, fhe would give way to the moft violent affliction.

Our hero had, previous to his campaign againft the
Indians, frequently written to his fifter; but thefe letters being directed to the care of Mr. Andrew Atkins,
were never forwarded to our heroine; indeed, after
the firft, he might have pleaded in excufe that he did
not know where to find her.

Reuben made every inquiry at the poft-office, and
of the mafters of veffels then arriving from England,.
for letters, but could hear of none addreffed to himfelf; and he meditated a voyage to his native place,
in order to bring his fifter over, and fometimes indulg-
ing the fond hope, that Jeffy Oliver might accompany
her.   But as he had much to fettle previous to taking fo long a voyage, he deferred it till the enfuing
fpring.

His friend, Stedfaft Trueman, had made a purchafe
of fome land fituated in New-Jerfey, near the mouth
of the Delaware; he thought it neceffary to vifit it
this autumn, and plan out the improvements he meant
fhould take place in the fpring.   He invited Reuben

to accompany him on this excursion, and he, wishing to see a little of that part of the country, assented. Their journey was extremely pleasant; but on the day preceding that they had settled for their return to Philadelphia, a cold storm, such as often precedes or accompanies the sun's autumnal passage across the equinox, commenced, and they resolved to tarry till its fury was abated. On the evening of the second day, it was increased to a tremendous degree, not blowing steadily, but in gusts, that threw the ocean into horrible convulsions, heaping up vast mountainous waves that seemed to threaten heaven, and leaving hollow chasms, in which the vessels (which they could plainly descry from the windows of the house they were in) seemed often to be lost, though in a moment after they appeared again on the summit of the highest wave.

Friend Trueman and our hero were greatly affected at the evident distress in which several small barks appeared; they stood anxiously watching them, till the curtain of night shut them from their view. The house they were in was situated at the entrance of Great Egg-Harbour; and as the storm abated in some trifling degree towards morning, Reuben and his friend arose with the earliest dawn, to see if any signs of wrecks were apparent, or if they could be of any service to the suffering mariners, who might, if luckily they escaped such a catastrophe, be in want of friends and assistance. They wrapped themselves in their great coats, and walked towards the sea, where they presently descried a ship dreadfully shattered, endeavouring to make the harbour. Her foremast and maintopmast were gone; some of her sails, torn in atoms, were fluttering in the wind, and the few she could expand were scarcely manageable.

Long they laboured, for some hours opposed both by wind and tide; at length the latter turned in her favour, and she fetched in, but not without making repeated signals of distress; and it was very evident, as she approached the shore, that she laboured heavily in the water, and all the spectators concluded she was in

danger

danger of finking. The fea ran fo high, no boat could, without imminent rifk, go to the affiftance of the wretched crew. At length a fifhing boat ventured off. The people on board had thrown out an anchor, but fhe dragged it, and the wind fetting acrofs the harbour, fhe was making ftern foremoft to the fhore. Juft as the boat reached her, fhe ftruck, and the cries of the affrighted failors and paffengers reached the ears of thofe who ftood on the fhore, waiting in fufpenfe and horror to behold the fate of fo fine a fhip and her unfortunate company. Several women were feen on the deck, and the fpectators feemed as though they could have given their own lives to preferve the lives of the fufferers.

When the boat reached the fhip, the people rufhed over the fides into her; the women were helped in, and in a few moments their fituation was as perilous from having overloaded the boat, as it had been before in the veffel. However, they put off, and made towards the fhore; the wind favoured them, and the fpectators exultingly cried, In five minutes they will be all fafe; but in a much lefs time, a fudden flaw took the fails; from the number of perfons on board, the fifhermen could not flack the fheets in time, and fhe overfet.

All the aim of thofe on fhore was now to fave, if poffible, the lives of fome, who, borne by the foaming furge, feemed almoft to reach the land, when the receding wave would dafh them back into the dread abyfs of waters. Spars faftened by ropes were thrown into the fea, while a number of men on fhore ftood ready to drag them to land, fhould any defpairing wretch feize them as the means of deliverance. Reuben was bufied in this humane endeavour, when he heard a fhout of exultation from a group of men employed in the fame manner at a little diftance. They waved alfo for more help. He therefore quitted his own party, which was more numerous, and ran to their affiftance, when he perceived that two women had been already fnatched from a watery grave; and

feveral

several men were, by the help of the spars, near the shore.

"Here," said the master of the house at which they lodged, "here, take this poor infant, and carry 't to the house, bid my dame make up a large fire in every room, and get all the beds ready. You must sleep on the floor to-night, Sir."

Reuben clasped the poor little dripping infant to his naked breast, wrapped his coat round it, and was delighted to find, by a faint moaning noise it made, that in all probability it would recover. He ran to the house, gave the child into the care of a kind-hearted Negro wench, and then returned to help the two women. One was entirely senseless, for she had dropped on the very moment she reached the shore; the other was unable to walk or speak, but yet could make signs that her senses were perfect. Reuben assisted to carry them in, gave them in charge to the women of the house, and then returned to the sea side; but soon perceiving nothing more was to be done, he came back to inquire after the little traveller.

"The women are both recovered," said a man, as he entered the house.

"I am glad of it," said Reuben; "might I be admitted to speak to them; they are no doubt English women, and will rejoice to find a countryman so near them, who is willing and ready to render them any service."

This message was carried to the ladies, and in a moment he was admitted. They were in separate beds in the same room. Reuben drew near that which was next the door; the person who occupied it raised herself partly, and exclaiming, "It is! it is my brother!" threw herself into his arms, which, sinking on the bed beside her, he had extended to receive her; for the moment he beheld her face, he recognized his sister, and the exclamation of 'Dear Reuben!' 'beloved Rachel!' mutually escaped their lips as they burst into a flood of tears.

And what were the feelings of Jessy Oliver at this moment? they were indescribable. She folded her hands

hands over her face, and the silent tears trickled through her fingers. Rachel recovered articulation first. "Reuben," said she, "there is a dear friend of both yours and mine; 'tis Jelly Oliver, who has been my friend, my supporter, my more than sister."

Reuben left his sister, and dropping on his knees by the bedside of Jelly, drew her hands from her face, and feeling more at that moment for her kindness to his sister, than from any other motive, pressed them to his heart, and cried, "May Heaven forever bless you." The ensuing scene may be conceived, but cannot be described. Reuben discovered, from the lamentations of his sister, that it was her infant he had brought to the house (she had dropped it at the moment of landing when her senses failed her, and imagined it drowned) and he had the exquisite pleasure of restoring it to her arms.

A few days reinstated their health and spirits, and our hero, with his friend Stedfast Trueman, escorted the happy Rachel and Jelly to Philadelphia. The former explained every circumstance of her marriage, and its subsequent consequences; and the latter when solicited to become mistress of Mount Pleasant, did not frown or threaten to be obdurate. They arrived at friend Trueman's house about midday, and after taking a slight refreshment, Reuben, with his sister and her charming friend, proceeded to Mount Pleasant. They were met at the gate by O'Neil.

"Och! my dare master," said he, "I'm mighty glad you are come back, for here has been a strange fort of a gentleman here, and for the matter of that he is here now, in our house, but he is sick; so as he seemed to love your honour, and talk kindly of my good lady your sister that I have heard your honour speak of, I put him into the best chamber, and sent for a doctor, and I hope your honour won't be angry, because you see I did as if I had been in your honour's place."

O'Neil would have gone on, had he not seen a chaise approach (for Reuben was on horseback). "And be these visitors?" said he.

"Yes,"

"Yes," replied our hero, "and the very fister you spoke of, and a charming lady, who I hope will soon become your miftrefs, O'Neil."

The honeft, affectionate O'Neil ftayed not to reply; he darted forward, and feemed as if he would have helped the horfe that drew the fifter of his beloved mafter. When the carriage ftopped, he waited not for ceremony; but as Jeffy ftood on the fide of the chaife ready to alight, he feized her in his arms, and bore her into the houfe; then running back, took the child from Rachel, (whom Reuben had helped out of the chaife) almoft devoured it with kiffes, and leaping, dancing and capering, cried, "Yes! yes! he will be happy after all, I knew he would, I was always fure he would. O that my dear Miftrefs Juliana was but alive now!"

Perhaps the reader has before this furmifed, that the ftrange, inquifitive, fick gentleman was no other than Hamden Auberry, who had embarked for Philadelphia immediately after his knowledge of our heroine's feeking him in that place; but the fhip in which he embarked being a faft failer, and fteering a different courfe to that purfued by the one in which was his wife, arrived fafe in the port of Philadelphia the very night before the commencement of the ftorm in which poor Rachel fuffered fo much, and fo nearly efcaped with life. His firft inquiries were for Reuben, and he was directed to Mount Pleafant; on his arrival there, he learnt that Rachel was not arrived, and that Reuben was abfent from home. Change of climate, the fatigues of a long voyage, and the anguifh of mind he had endured for fix months paft, had fo enervated his frame and fhook his conftitution, that when he attempted to remount the horfe that brought him, he turned fo faint as to be obliged to return to the houfe, where he grew fo much worfe, that O'Neil (as he had told his mafter) advifed him to go to bed, and fent for a doctor.

The meeting between our heroine and her hufband was all that real affection and fenfibility can imagine. Rachel wept, and regretted the pain fhe had unintentionally

tionally given him, whilft he implored her pardon for that falfe pride, which had firft expofed her to the fufpicions and infults of thofe who, envying her fuperior merit, rejoiced in an opportunity to level her with their own contaminated ideas.

About fix weeks after this happy meeting, Reuben received the hand of Jeffy Oliver. It was a day of feftivity. The gates of Mount Pleafant were thrown open, and every vifitor made welcome. To add to their mirth, a dance in the evening was to finifh the entertainment.

A focial meal, difpenfed with cheerfulnefs, and partaken with a true fpirit of hilarity, had been juft removed, when the parlour door haftily opened, and Eumea entered. Her hair hung loofe about her fhoulders; her eyes were wild, aud her voice broken. She rufhed toward Reuben and Jeffy, and taking a hand from each, joined them; then preffing them to her bofom, raifed her eyes to heaven—

"God of the Chriftians," faid fhe fervently, "make them forever happy. Wife of Reuben, thou art a happy woman, for thy hufband is a man of honour. He faw the weaknefs of a poor, unprotected Indian maid, he pitied her folly, but took no advantage of it."

Jeffy was affected by the fimple yet fervent addrefs. Reuben took the hand of Eumea, and would have made her fit down, but fhe refufed.

"No! no!" faid fhe, "Eumea will reft no more, know peace no more. I had raifed a deity of my own, built an altar in my bofom, and daily offered the facrifice of a fond, an affectionate heart; but the days are paft, I can worfhip no longer without a crime. Farewel," faid fhe, enthufiaftically clafping her hands, "do not quite forget the poor, poor Eumea!"

She then left the houfe, and Reuben fent a perfon to follow and fee that fhe came to no ill. She went home, but continued not long there; a young woman, who from her wild looks and incoherent language imagined her mind to be diforderd, endeavoured to detain her, but in vain. About the dufk of the evening fhe went out, and all inquiry for her was fruitlefs

till

till three days after, when as Reuben was giving fome orders to O'Neil, in that part of his ground that lay on the verge of the Schuylkill, they difcovered fomething floating on the water ; the garments befpoke it a woman.   Reuben's heart fhuddered ; they dragged it to the fhore ; it was the corpfe of poor Eumea. Reuben fighed, raifed his eyes to heaven, but was filent. Not fo O'Neil.   He fell on his knees befide the pale corfe, and his honeft heart burft in a torrent from his eyes.

"Och ! my flower of the foreft," faid he, "and art thou gone, and was it love that made thee leave us ? Beautiful, good, fweeteft cf favages—O ! thy poor O'Neil can pity thee.   And what fhall he do now thou haft clofed thine eyes ? Thou haft murdered thy fweet felf, and what is there now in the world that he cares for ?"

Reuben was ftruck with the fervency and humility that was at once exprefled by O'Neil; for it fpoke as plain as words could fpeak, 'I loved her, but I never dared to tell my love, left it fhould offend her.'

Our hero by degrees drew him from the contemplation of the melancholy object, and proper forms being gone through in regard to the body, it was buried in a field near the margin of the river.   O'Neil banked up the grave, twifted ofier twigs and fenced it round ; at the head he planted a weeping willow, and at the foot a wild rofe tree. Of a night when his labour was finifhed, he would vifit the fpot, fing old ditties, and weep whilft he fung ; and though he lived to good old age, O'Neil never knew another love.

After this period, our heroine for many years enjoyed an uninterrupted feries of felicity.   Auberry, entirely occupied by the cares of a mercantile life, into which he had fuccefsfully entered, and giving every leifure moment to the affifting of Rachel in the education of a beautiful rifing family, was entirely cured of jealoufy and ambition, and wondered he could have ever doubted the faith of his wife, cr have rifqued lofing fo vaft a treafure forever, rather than relinquifh the hope of being rich and great.

H h

Reuben

Reuben and Jessy were patterns of conjugal felicity, and that felicity was increased in the course of a few years, by the arrival of old Mr. Oliver, Archibald and Courtney.   The former had saved a ·trifle from the wreck of his fortune, which had been almost dissipated by a worthless woman.   Archibald brought with him an amiable bride in the person of Courtney's sister. The abandoned Mrs. Courtney had met the fate her vicious course of life merited, and died abroad, neglected by all her pretended lovers, a victim to disease, poverty and remorse.

It was in the seventh year of our hero and heroine's happy settlement in Philadelphia, that the latter was told one morning that a gentleman from England desired to see her.   She went into the parlour, and beheld, to her infinite surprise, Mr. Allibi.

"Mrs. Auberry, I presume," said he, bowing profoundly.   "I am happy, Madam, to be the first to wish you joy on a very great and unexpected accession of fortune.   Your husband's relation, lady Anne, is dead ; also her brother the Earl, and I may now salute you Countess of Montmorill.   Moreover," continued he, not giving her leave to speak, "I am to inform you, by order of Mr. Andrew Atkins, that yourself and brother, Mr. Reuben Dudley, being the only descendants of the lady Arrabella Ruthven, who married about the year 1644-5, with Edward Dudley, son of Henry Dudley, descendant of the unfortunate lady Jane Grey, and who relinquishing her title, embarked with him for America ; as I say, yourself and brother being the only legitimate descendants of that marriage, you are acknowledged joint heirs to the titles and immense estates of the house of Ruthven.   And I am commissioned by my very good friend, Mr. Andrew Atkins, to receive your orders in what manner he shall proceed in regard to said estates, and to inform you, your Lancashire estate is now, through his care, entirely free from incumbrances."

Rachel, overwhelmed by the rapidity with which Allibi related all this good news, and scarcely crediting what she heard, yet understanding sufficient, perfectly

fectly to comprehend the mean fineffe of Allibi and his dirty employer, in thus informing her of her acceffion of fortune, and making a merit of relinquifhing the Lancafhire eftate, in hopes of being made agent and fteward to thofe of much greater value, could fcarcely command her temper, whilft fhe interrogated him concerning the extraordinary intelligence he conveyed. However, being afcertained of the truth of his affertions, and received from him fome papers of confequence, with a long, fulfome, congratulatory letter from Mr. Andrew Atkins, fhe appointed him to call the enfuing morning, when her brother and hufband would be fure to meet him.

On the following morning, therefore, at a little paft eight o'clock, Mr. Allibi entered the breakfaft parlour, where he found Reuben, Rachel, Mr. Auberry and Mrs. Dudley affembled to breakfaft. After partaking a focial meal, and delivering and attefting to every neceffary paper, both in regard to their new acquifitions and the Lancafhire eftate, be was fomewhat aftonifhed to hear Reuben addrefs him in the following words:—

"You may think, Mr. Allibi, that by bringing us this intelligence you have greatly heightened our felicity; and in one refpect you have, as it extends our power of ferving our fellow-creatures. As to titles, both my brother Auberry and his wife Rachel, join with me to renounce them ; they are diftinctions nothing worth, and fhould by no means be introduced into a young country, where the only diftinction between man and man fhould be made by virtue, genius and education. Our fons are true-born Americans, and while they ftrive to make that title refpectable, we wifh them to poffefs no other. Let the titles then go, and fuch of the eftates as are annexed to them, to more diftant branches of our feveral families, or in cafe of default of heirs, let them fink into oblivion. Of the immenfe property of which we are become poffeffors, we fhall retain no more than will fet our fons forward in bufinefs, and give our daughters moderate portions;

the

the refidue fhall be equally divided amongft the indigent relatives of both families."

Allibi brightened at thefe words, thinking he fhould be conftituted agent in this bufinefs; but Reuben continued:—

"I am obliged to you for the trouble you have taken on my account, and hold myfelf your debtor for the expenfes of your voyage and other contingencies, which, whenever you pleafe, I fhall be ready to difcharge; and when you return, I will trouble you with a letter to Mr. Andrew Atkins, informing him he will be no farther troubled with my affairs, but will pleafe to fettle all accounts with Mr. Courtney, a gentleman who has kindly undertaken to go to England for that purpofe."

The poor, difappointed Allibi could fcarcely breathe at the conclufion of this fpeech; he fhuffled on his feat, attempted to recommend himfelf by reprobating the conduct of Atkins, but a look of marked contempt from Reuben filenced him; and, mortified beyond endurance, he rofe haftily and took his leave.

In a fhort time, Courtney embarked for England, fettled every thing according to the directions of Reuben and Auberry, made many an orphan glad, and many a difconfolate heart leap for joy. He liberated the poor debtor, afforded relief to deprefled merit, and wiped away the tear from the eye of fuffering virtue. The incenfe of gratitude afcended towards heaven, and was returned in bleffings on the heads of Reuben, Rachel, and their pofterity.

FINIS.

E R R A T A.

Vol. I. page 129, 14th. line from the bottom, for *wife* read *fifter*.
    page 170, 11th. line from the top, for *fifter* read *coufin*.

www.ingramcontent.com/pod-product-compliance
Lightning Source LLC
Chambersburg PA
CBHW051219120726
47905CB00004B/1185